FIREFLYS

MOSS NIGHTWING

Fireflys

The Glowstick Chronicles, Book 1

By Moss Nightwing

This is a work of fiction. Names, characters, places, and incidents either are the product of the author's imagination or are used fictitiously. Any resemblance to actual persons, living or dead, events, or locales is entirely coincidental.

Isbn 979-8-218-32711-8

First paperback edition June 2025

Editor: Norma Gambini

Cover Designer/ Formatter: Creative Shannonigans

Publisher: Queerly Beloved Services

BLURB

Simerra Just Wanted to Lay Low

So much for that . . .

The world went to shit seven years ago and Simerra has been trying to fit in ever since. Glows aren't easy to manage but everyone who survived the sickness has one, and everyone who didn't is either dead or was never sick to begin with. Simerra will do anything to protect her family and help them stay undetected by the government that hunts them, but when Nash crashes into her life after a scouting mission she's left to wonder who and what she's fighting for, and what she's willing to risk to win.

A New Adult book with YA and fanfic vibes.

For our littles: without them our sense of wonder would have faded
long ago.

CONTENTS

DISCLAIMERS

murder, gore, sexual harassment, guns, vomit, asphyxiation, ableism, abuse, corpses, the garbage government, blood, soldiers, funeral, mourning, grief, incarceration mentions, sensory overload/meltdown, kidnapping, racism, suicide mention, body fluids, torture, electroshock "therapy", near death experiences, indoctrination, coercion, sterilization mention, victim blaming, indoctrination, teacher abuse, whipping, needles, internalized ableism, beating mentions, brainwashing/ mind control, graphic depictions of violence, mass death, trauma

This is not a YA book. It is squarely New Adult due to the graphic details included for the systemic issues addressed within.

CHAPTER ONE

BAD PLANS MAKE GREAT STORIES

CW: MIND CONTROL, MURDER, gore

As the ones being hunted, we glow wielders stood the stillest and if discovered, we sprinted ahead of the rest. We wandered around on what felt like the millionth day of our journey. The irreparable structures that cropped up between the bright green foliage were more comforting than strangers ever could be. Our band of glow wielders were almost on top of the caregivers as they slowed to a near crawl. Mother raised her hand and the whole party stopped dead. Quite the accomplishment for a group with multiple families. Her stray curls danced around her head. I caught a glimpse of my brother Zane: all muscle, he stood coiled upon himself on a rock. His afro waved gently in the breeze, the only thing about him not locked in place. Nessa stood nearby. The hints of orange in her brown hair caught the sun, complementing her soft brown skin. Devin was on Zane's other side with Daisy atop his shoulders. Her hands wove in and out of Devin's locs as she held her seven-year-old self quiet despite the tension. Her braids hung still around her head. They were the only other set of actual siblings in the group. The lot of us were a mismatched quilt of family.

"There could be supplies in that town," Mother said.

"The sun is already past the high point," Mark protested.

"We need supplies."

Mother pushed forward again, and we followed. No one felt danger as she did, but that did not mean we were going to question it. Mark tried to aid her over a piece of debris, but she refused his hand. She was blind, not incapable. Her cane tapped against the offending piece of rock as she worked her way around it. The grass gave way to gnarled pricker branches. I was grateful for my jeans. Some weren't as lucky. Scraped legs flinched from the sharp thorns. An odd hum picked up, but it didn't sound like a market or voices, but machines? Mother signaled for us to hide. We booked it back through the prickers to the shelter of the wide tree trunks. Chests heaved and eyes bulged from stress and exertion. Nothing popped out from the distance or moved towards us from the broken road. The steady hum continued. Everyone was waiting, hoping for instructions as they vibrated in their efforts to stay still.

"Someone has to check it out," Devin said.

His clenched fists were the only indication of his true feelings. He was right. Someone needed to go, but I hoped it wasn't me. Who knew what was up there, and it was beyond loud if I could hear it from here.

"Simerra should go," Mark said.

Other adults nodded, clutching their own charges close. Could I really blame them? I wasn't nearly as valuable as their chosen kin; I'd rather one of them than Zane. I locked my joints in place to hide my worry. This was going to suck. *Powerful did not mean brave, people.* Mother's eyes flashed with rage.

"So quick to volunteer *others*."

"You say how powerful she is all the time."

Mother deflated, brow furrowing in worry as she glanced my way for a few fleeting moments. I tried my best to square my shoulders like she did when she led us.

"You can do it, can't you? You'll be fine," Mark tested.

I swallowed bile as it touched my tongue. *Don't let your voice shake. You can do this. You can be helpful.*

"Yes, I'll be fine," I repeated.

Everyone stared elsewhere: the trees and their scrapes held secrets in need of immediate study. At least there were no eye contact requirements right now.

"If she's going, I am too." Zane moved beside me.

"No."

I tapped my fingers together. Long to short. Short to Long. To hide my shock. Mother held her hand up to halt any questions. I bit back my complaints. *Maybe she had a better plan.*

"You're needed here. We can't have both of you off."

So much for that. This wasn't how I imagined dying but whatever. I could do this. If I was alone, I didn't need nearly as much control if I was attacked. See, there were positives.

"Well, we have Kate so I'm sure we'd—"

"Mom, we need him," Kate interjected before her mom could finish.

"I'll go," Devin offered.

He pushed Daisy gently towards their dad. Mark bounced her in his arms to distract her from our conversation.

"No, you should stay too," Mark argued.

"Her mother's right. We need Zane here, but that doesn't mean we should send Simerra alone. I'm going."

He flashed me a smile. I mirrored one back, relieved. Confusion contorted Mark's expression into a jumbled mess. What was with him and creating new complex faces for me to unravel?

"We should get moving if we plan to be back before dark."

Devin grabbed my gloved hand and led me away from the others. I followed, more than willing to let someone else be the leader of this excursion. When we were out of sight, he released my hand, maintaining a brisk pace. There was still a good mile or two before we reached the town. The trees here were younger and more densely packed. We wove between them, grateful for the cover.

"Are you worried?"

"I'm not sure."

"On the bright side, if it's bad, we don't have to wait to find out like they do."

"We still have to wait," I said.

We weren't at the source of the sound yet. What was he on about?

"Yeah, but we'll know first. How's your glow?"

"It's alright," I said.

"Can you use it if we run into trouble?"

"I hope so."

The trees gave way to grass and building chunks, forcing us to run from one to the next to stay hidden. The low hum was now a roar of machinery. The sound bounced back and forth, echoing off the foliage-covered structures. When that stopped working, we crawled on the ground. Devin's hands glowed slightly against the grass, but it was muffled. What a strange, misplaced shadow we must've appeared. An engine revved, and we both froze. He held a finger to his lips and I nodded. If we spoke, all the camouflage in the world would be useless. The machine continued on its path. I pointed to a group of bushes a little farther up before leading the way. A large blacktop filled with people came into view through the branches. They were playing tag, gossiping, and laughing. Soldiers lined the asphalt, eyes on their charges. A sharp bell rang out. The group fell quiet and moved as a unit back towards the building. There was no way. Those--- those were kids.

"Did you see the soldiers?"

"I wonder whose protection they're there for," I whispered back.

Devin scowled at the implication. A parade of trucks zipped past, but no more children emerged from the large brick building. Government logos covered the vehicles. What were all those kids doing at a government building in the middle of nowhere? This wasn't enough information to take back.

"The trucks come every two minutes. That's enough time to run up to the building. If you can help us blend in, we'll be fine," I assured him.

"Let's do it."

As a truck rounded a bend in the road, I sprinted towards the building. The smack of shoes on asphalt echoed back at me. I slammed into the building wall and collapsed in a heap as another truck rounded the corner. Devin's glow was the only thing between us and discovery. The shiny vehicle continued along its path as if nothing were wrong. At least that had gone smoothly.

We inched towards the corner of the building. Devin checked to see if the coast was clear. Tension rolled down through his body, but he kept looking. My curiosity bested me, and I popped my head around the corner.

A wave of nausea hit me. People stood in rows, chained at the wrists with hulking metal collars around their necks. One by one, they walked up and into a fire. They convulsed in silence as the flames licked at their bodies. Their skin blistered and blackened until they collapsed in the hungry blaze. The next person stepped in just moments later for the process to begin again. I scanned frantically for an explanation. Everyone here was around our age. Why weren't they using their glows?

There was a girl at the front about Kate's age, with three guards around her, and though she also had chains, she was dressed in regular clothes, not the blue outfit from the kids out front or the black outfit of the kids walking into the flames. Her blonde hair shone brightly in her glow. A mind control glow. Was it fear of the armed men that held them still and her glow that moved them forward? Was her glow so consuming that she could control every move of so many? And if it was, why wasn't she using it to help everyone escape? There were so many lives being lost. We had to do something. Devin's eyes were still glued to the blaze.

"It's a giant campfire."

My hair beat me in the face as I shook my head over and over. Everyone could die. I was as dangerous as those flames. I flapped, trying to focus. Why hadn't I brought my tangle? I needed a better stim. The familiar cold crept through me. I slammed my eyes shut, trying to calm the mounting panic.

"You have to. Simerra, they're dying."

My nerves spiked sharply again. *Focus, Simerra, before you hurt Devin.* I tapped my fingers against each other. Long to short. Short to long. Over and over, I ran through the familiar stim. I anchored myself in this quiet alternative the best I could.

"Are you ready to die if I do this wrong?"

"It's a couple of campfires."

"Well, you have to get us over there without being seen."

He faltered as fear crept over his features. And he had the nerve to tell me this would be simple when he was as worried as I was. Determination returned to his face. We'd need his optimism if we were going to have a shot at all. What were we thinking? I lightly tapped my glow and it vibrated beneath the touch, coiling over itself. Devin eyed me, curiosity alight in his eyes. I shrugged. Everyone's process was their own.

"Let's go."

Concentration scrunched his brow as we walked up the side of the building towards the fire. The smell of charcoal and beef filled my nose and I choked on the smoke. I clamped a hand over my mouth and nose to fight the urge to gag. We had people to save. Those outside the fire waited their turn like this was an old deli line. The skin on Devin's neck was pulled taut and his cheeks were flushed. We needed to move fast before his concentration broke.

"Hold your breath."

I plunged my gloved hand into the giant fire. My glow ripped through the blaze. Logs flew out of the pit still smoking and barely missing people's heads. The plain-clothes girl and the guards grasped at their throats while they gaped like fish. I wanted to stop the fire, not kill them. I shut my eyes and pulled my glow back, bundling it tightly the way Mother always encouraged. A deep shiver rolled from my heart to the tips of my extremities. My shaking knees gave way to the charred earth below. I vomited onto the warm ash as the world spun around me. Devin pulled me back to my feet.

"We have to go."

"But what about the rest of them?"

"I can't hold this much longer."

It was like fate hated us. As he spoke, the guards collected themselves. They stared over in our direction, not at where the fire had been but directly at us.

CHAPTER TWO

RECON

CW: DEATH, MURDER, GUNS, gore, sexual harassment

We leaned against each other for support. Our knees shook from the effort of having used our glows. I watched the guards, waiting for them to make the first move. Then, the people in their lines woke up to the world around them. Anger and fear mixed on faces and in their shouting. The guards shifted their focus off us and to the mob. I mean, I would have been pissed, too, if someone tried to kill me.

"Get them under control." The man jabbed the girl with his gun.

She fell to her knees. Her arms shook as she tried to stand once more. There was no way she could glow again so quickly after how much she had done. Even still, she tried, but her arms gave out and she collapsed back into a heap, crying.

"I told them we didn't need you."

He raised the barrel of his gun without hesitation and shot her twice in the chest. The glow wielders charged forward. All of them enraged. All of them glowing. Rocks flew through the air. Guards fired aimlessly into the crowd. People dropped to the earth spluttering and screaming, with blood pouring from bullet holes. It didn't take long for them to be overtaken. Their own screams echoed acrost the asphalt. An alarm blasted from the building. How the fuck were we going to get out of this mess?

I grabbed Devin's shirt and pulled him through the stack of corpses. The skin slopped off the bones beneath my feet. Someone's blood stained my shoe, but there was no time to stop. People poured out of the building, each of them armed to the teeth.

"Zigzag! It's the only way we'll make it," Devin shouted.

We ran in short diagonal lines to stay out of the scopes of our adversaries. Some shoved past me in a straight line. Targeted shots hit person after person. They crumpled to the ground. Those unlucky enough to have survived the shot wailed in agony. Tears blurred my vision. Would any of us survive today? *Keep moving. Keep running. You've got this. Ignore the burn in your muscles and don't stop.* I welcomed the crunch of leaves beneath my feet as we drew near the nature-reclaimed buildings. I tried to keep Devin in sight, but as we wove through the trees, I lost sight of him. If he were dead—no. I banished the thought from my brain with a shake. He had to be out here. The screaming brought me back to the reality of our situation. We were so fucked. I focused on my feet as I raced away from the massacre. Someone slammed me into a thick patch of prickers. I yelped and struggled against whoever it was but a hand covered my mouth. A shiver of fear raced up my spine. My glow uncoiled from my core of its own accord.

"Shut up or we're dead," Devin hissed.

I squashed down my glow frantically. Devin's muted glow lit his hands in soft light. If he could keep it up, we had a chance. I worked to calm my breathing before it got us caught. Boots crunched their way through the underbrush in organized groups of three. The first two passed us without hesitation, but a third stopped near our hiding spot.

"Did you see which way the targets went?"

"They were all running this way, towards the trees."

"And after they reached the trees?"

"I-I don't know."

"And that's why you'll never be promoted. Let's move. They couldn't have gotten far with their levels."

Before I could do more than spare Devin a glance, a new group hesitated near our thicket. What sort of shit luck was this?

"There was a girl who disappeared around here."

"They don't disappear, you idiot. They glow like fucking traffic lights. Tell me you know more than that?"

Did they always insult each other? It didn't seem like the type of thing that would build morale.

"I swear it disappeared right here."

"Then you can scout this area alone. Catch up when you're done."

The soldier's shaky hands clasped around his gun. He crept toward our hiding place. I crouched, ready to lunge out at him, my muscles coiled. If we were going down, this man was coming with me.

A loud scream ripped through the tension as someone dropped from the trees above. She wrenched the gun from his grasp and fired shot after shot into his chest. She threw the useless weapon down, moving her light-brown hair out of her eyes and all over to one side. Even as my heart thrummed from the danger, I found myself focused on her face. Her green eyes were filled with hard determination. It was entrancing.

"You can come out now." She looked into the bush at us. Well, shit.

"I know you're there. We don't have long before more of them show up."

We couldn't stay this close to a corpse anyway. I gestured to Devin that I would go first. He shook his head, but I ignored him. I watched her warily as I emerged. She waved exuberantly.

"That's better. I'm Nash. Short for Nashville. Good to meet ya. We should move."

With that, the strange girl spun around and ran into the thick of the forest. Devin looked after her, perplexed. I shrugged and followed. We didn't exactly have a plan. There was shouting up ahead, but Nash never flinched. We didn't run into any guards or soldiers or whatever they were, but the gunshots kept getting louder until it sounded like we should have been on top of them, but I didn't see anyone. Nash stopped, hand on hip.

"Cut it out, Echo."

Echo emerged from behind a tree. He was gangly with curly hair that barely covered his eyes, black clothes, and chains like the others.

"Where'd you find these two?" he asked.

"Oh, you know, hiding from the government in a bush. That one has a good ability on him. Don't know what she can do yet."

"Well, there's always a good ability with a shoddy one. No offense."

"You can't handle a weapon to save your life, and I wouldn't call that music festival a powerful anything," Nash shot back.

Devin seemed as confused as I was. Someone had to make a plan before we were found.

"I understand you have a thing going on, but if we don't move, they will find us," I urged.

Echo broke out laughing. Nash was quick to elbow him in the ribs, but it made no difference to him. Did I say something funny?

"Lead the way," Nash said, shooting Echo a pointed look.

"What's with her?" Echo asked when I didn't move.

Come on, think. What should we do? She saved our lives, but we didn't know them and Mark was sure to be pissed. Hurry up. Think of a solution.

"I think we should part ways," Devin advised.

No one had joined us in ages. Mother would be pissed. Mark would be pissed. This was a terrible idea. My head reeled.

"There are people out here trying to kill us and you aren't going to bring us with you? I saved your fucking lives. That guy had no idea where I was. I was safe. Echo was safe. We could have run on our own. Now, there's next to no light and you want to ditch us. How fucking dare you," Nash snarled.

Her breathing was erratic while she paced around. I was the cause of her unease and I hated it. Discomfort settled over my limbs like a heavy blanket. She was right.

"What are your glows?"

Maybe they weren't that dangerous. Maybe we could bring them back with us. They stared at me. Right, they called them something different. Abilities, was it?

"What are your abilities, and what do you know about that place?" I asked again.

"I can copy and create sounds. It's great for throwing people off my trail. Nash took really well to the weapons training in that shithole. She's great at it. If she saved your lives, I'm sure you saw all kinds of things. She knows all about guns and weapons and fighting moves. You have to see it."

I held up a hand. This wasn't the information I was looking for. This made her seem more dangerous to the group. I needed to know she wasn't as much of a threat as Zane or I were. We had to protect our families.

"What's her glow?"

"She's really helpful."

Devin raised an eyebrow. He wasn't buying it either. Was she really that powerful that he didn't want to tell us? So much for thinking we could bring her with us.

"She can jump high. And she can be ridiculously fast. Like, faster than any of us if she wants to be," Echo admitted.

"Guess you're not taking us then, are you?" she whispered.

Her shoulders slumped. It took everything I had not to vibrate. Their glows weren't that dangerous. As long as they didn't have weapons on them, I could swing this.

"Do you know what this place is?"

"It's a training facility of sorts. They take kids there. You walked in on recycling day." Nash shrugged, not an ounce of concern on her face. She must have been in shock.

The nausea was back. My shoes were soaked from the hot blood of those we couldn't save.

"When you don't take to the training well, your glow isn't helpful, you're too weak to keep up or too dangerous to keep, that's what happens," she finished in a whisper.

"Will you take us with you? Please?" Echo's eyes shone with tears.

Devin still looked conflicted, so I looked away. My mind was made up. I couldn't leave the girl who saved us to fend for herself. She'd be caught in a matter of days.

"You can come with us, but you'll have to tell us everything you know after we meet up with the others. Come on. It's getting dark."

I focused back on the path, ignoring Devin's confused gaze. It bored into me the rest of the way back and stung more than the brambles. Familiar cold filled me as I drew nearer to a shadowed figure ahead.

"Stop and tell me who you are," Zane ordered.

His hands glowed softly. I pointed my palms to the earth, but I couldn't stop the smile. We'd made it.

"It's us and two new friends. We found them in the town. They were about to be killed," I explained.

Nessa moved beside Zane. Her glow bathed everyone in a warm light. I stood tall. If I wasn't confident now, two people could be left without somewhere to go, and I wouldn't allow it. I had to be convincing. Zane was convincing. I could act like him for now. Nessa's light revealed Mark's rage and tense form. I flinched preemptively. I'd seen that look in his face before every "accident."

"Did you think before bringing them here? Where's Devin?"

"I'm right here, Dad. They saved our lives. I'm better than ever thanks to our new friends." He flashed Mark a brilliant smile.

Devin's hands were shoved deep into his pockets. The picture of ease. Mark held an arm open and Devin obliged, stepping into the embrace. The cool demeanor still clung to his frame, but it seemed harder won now.

"Simerra, where are your gloves?" Mark questioned.

"They were burned off by the fire I put out. They were burning people alive. We had to help them. Echo and Nash can tell us more about that place."

"So, you're gloveless, have been seen by whatever is going on out there, and you brought us more mouths to feed. Did you manage to grab supplies during your heroism?"

I bit my lip.

"I didn't think so."

"When the sickness took everyone's parents except Simerra and Zane's mother, you all took us in. We were wandering around and one by one, you found us, then we all found each other. If it wasn't for that, there would be no group. We would not have families. Daisy and

I wouldn't have you, Dad. You all showed us kindness. You saved us, and now we've chosen to help Echo and Nash like you taught us." Devin bit his lip, looking up at his caregiver imploringly.

"I taught you to be cautious." The anger had left Mark's voice and weariness took its place.

"I know you didn't mean to, but you also taught me this." Devin sheepishly leaned into Mark's side. His dad ruffled his locs and pulled him close.

"You've made your case. Echo, Nash, what are your glows capable of?" Mother asked.

"She can move faster and jump higher than your average person, and I can throw and mimic sounds. Nothing too exciting," Echo said.

Mom mulled it over. The group was quiet as we awaited Mother's decision.

"You can travel with us for now, but one mistake and you will be made to leave. Simerra, Zane, keep an eye on them. Do we need to move before we settle?"

"Yes," I said.

"Okay, does anyone have an objection?"

All was silent in the group. I didn't dare stim in case someone changed their mind. I nearly vibrated with how close to success we were.

"Then let's move. Nessa, you'll be with me tonight."

Her glow made its way through the group as Mother began traveling perpendicular from the compound.

Chapter Three

UNFETTERED POWER

CW: Death, guns, vomiting, death mentions, kidnapping mentions, gun shots, death, gore, asphyxiation

"Tough crowd." Some of the light had returned to Nash's eyes.

"We have a lot of people to protect." Zane folded his arms across his chest.

We waited for Nash and Echo to pass us before bringing up the rear. They were my responsibility now. Zane's eyes bored into the side of my head, but I didn't want to see any disappointment so I focused on my feet instead. He put a hand on my shoulder, but I shrugged it off. Concern riddled his features.

"What happened?" he asked.

"It was terrible. I've never seen anything like it." I stared off through the dark forest, hoping to replace the images flashing through my mind with something, anything.

"Are there others like you and me?" Hope clung to his voice.

"I don't think so."

They were dead. There was no part of me that wanted to be the one to tell him something so awful. I squeezed his shoulder, careful not to touch skin.

The sun was back before we made camp. I was unable to make out even the faintest light from the compound's towering structures. The adults clustered by the fire in the early dawn light after we were settled. I trudged over to the fire to see why they'd chosen to neglect the rest we all needed.

"You've said that three times. Is there a specific answer you *want*?" Nash snapped.

The caregivers weren't known for their gentle touches. It was cool to see someone stand up to them. The firelight danced alongside the fury in Nash's features as she stood between Echo and the pushy adults. The strain in her muscles, the soft curve of her stance as she stood defending the only person she had left was admirable.

"We have to be sure," Mother soothed.

"Sure of what? Did you miss Echo's chains? We weren't exactly 'in the know.'"

"When was the last time you were outside that place?"

"We were little. It was during the sickness. There were still families."

"What happened to your parents? Did they hand you over?"

"They thought the government could help us," Nash muttered.

I winced. Hadn't we all? All the commercials about the good of the government and the bright futures that awaited the "miracle children" who survived the sickness had filled every screen for months while the government quietly rounded up children. Sometimes, we still passed old billboards promising government aid to any surviving child.

"They trained us and here we are: fully trained," Nash said with a grand sweeping gesture.

"For what?"

"They were never clear about the particulars," Echo said.

"What do you know?" Kate's mom asked.

"I know Echo would *appreciate* being unchained."

Kate slipped forward, looking bored with the whole thing. Equipped with her handy pin, she undid the chains in a matter of moments. She set the heavy pieces on the ground before she ghosted back. It was times like this, I doubted she ever touched the ground.

"Thanks," Echo muttered.

"What can you tell us about the facility? Are there many more?"

"More than you can imagine."

"How could someone escape if captured?"

"If you're captured, it's already too late." Nash held up a hand, holding off the disgruntled adults as she stretched. "I can help you learn how to fight like them if you want."

"We only fight if we have to," Kate's mom asserted.

"You'll have to. How often do you train your abilities?"

"We use them to help around camp," I chimed in.

Shock settled into her creased brow. I should have kept my mouth shut.

"Yeah, that's not what I meant."

"Will they be looking for Simerra and Devin?"

"The two that brought us here? They might, but their focus will be keeping that place locked down. There are too many assets there."

I was taken aback by how callous she was. Was that something she'd been taught or how she'd always felt? Did I make the right call? A loud thwacking sound came from overhead. The trees whipped back and forth, creaking loudly with every bend.

"We have to move. We have to move now," Nash yelled.

"Why?" Kate's mother asked.

"Do you really want that thing to land while we're so close? We need to go." Nash booked it.

Everyone scrambled after her. I kept pace with Echo while Zane brought up the rear, guiding Mother. My lungs burned from the effort. The trees slowed, but we didn't. Nash guided us into a cave. Older glow wielders only entered once everyone else was safe and stood near the ivy concealing the cave mouth. Nessa glowed just enough for us to be able to see one another. Nash held a finger to her lips, but she didn't need to. Wide eyes and shaking frames could be seen all around. My heart thundered in my ears, making the crunch of leaves beneath soldiers' feet harder to hear. Devin's hands glowed softly. The deep black of his glow buried us in the shadows. Daisy gasped at the change. Well, shit.

"Over there," a soldier said from far closer than I would've liked.

My chest tightened. We were going to have to fight our way out of here. At least Zane knew what to do if I lost control. I tapped my fingers against my thumb. Long to short. Short to long Back and forth to keep my composure while the soldiers closed in. Nash winked and ran out into the sunlight.

"You're right. I am over here," she jeered.

She raced away, followed by gunshots and a stampede of footsteps. Devin peeked outside, leaving the rest of us to wait. I barely breathed, terrified we'd hear another shot or Devin's screams or the soldiers pounding feet, but silence stretched on.

"It's clear," Devin said.

Echo kept his eyes on the ground. Poor guy was probably terrified. Was Nash going to be okay out there? She said she was trained, but so were the soldiers.

"We need to move on," Mark suggested.

"We have to wait for her," I countered.

How dare he. She protected us even after they'd interrogated her, not that Mark had ever been one to display great character. And yeah, maybe it was bold to stand up to him, but he was clearly in the wrong.

"I know you want to help her, but we have to put our group first. If we die looking for her, then the sacrifice is in vain."

"She saved your asses," Echo accused.

I squared my shoulders. Mother was always telling me to act with my heart. Hopefully, she actually meant it.

"And I'm returning the favor."

I ran out into the morning sunlight. Zane could keep the others still. Progress was slow as I moved from tree to tree. It was the worst game of hide and seek. Given that I had no idea where anyone was or what the enemy even looked like, but Nash had run this way. A corpse decorated the forest floor neck bent at a sharp angle. Nausea wracked my body. At least I knew I was going the right way. A round of gunfire from straight ahead encouraged me onward. She had to be up here. I hummed softly to myself to calm my nerves. I would be useless if I shut down, so I had to avoid it until we were safe if possible. It'd be more intense later, but that was a necessary cost.

"You can't catch me and you know it."

More gunshots followed her pronouncement. Was she trying to get herself killed? What kind of strategy was this?

"Just give up."

I could see her high in a tree now. Most of the guns lay discarded, scattered among the weeds. Were the guns empty or useless with her being so high up? Even if they were out of bullets, what the fuck was I going to do? *Focus, Simerra.* I put my back against the scraggly bark of a tree and counted back from ten. I shook my hands in a desperate attempt to regulate. This was a terrible fucking plan, but there was no going back now.

"You'll have to come down eventually."

Now is your chance. You have to sound brave like her or no one will take you seriously.

"Hey, leave her alone," I shouted.

Their hands flew to their knives or guns depending on the goon. *That's it. Eyes on me. Pretend they aren't scary. They're just people. People that want to kill you, but that's fine. You're the scary one, remember? You have the scary glow.* I took off my glove in preparation.

"Run!"

"That's cute. All you low levels stick together. Max, you get her," he ordered.

The wind picked up again, and the boy I hadn't noticed moved to the front of the group. My hair whipped around my head, blocking chunks of my vision, but his remained still. My glow wove delicious cold around my extremities. My hair dropped back to the sides of my head. His smile faltered.

"You don't have to help them. They don't care about you."

He gestured towards the right, and I jerked to the side like I'd been hit with a wall. The sharp pain in my ribs tore at my focus. He charged forward, eyes full of rage, but slowed when he felt the difference in temperature near me. *You aren't the only one with fancy tricks,* I thought. He didn't hesitate for long. I dodged the knife but tripped on a log. I scrambled backwards as he advanced, slashing indiscriminately. Blood welled up from the cuts on my legs.

"Your glow is weak. Now you're going to die for it."

I was not *weak.* My glow swirled around my chest and through my palms. I pushed off the earth, leaving behind a wet patch as I stood tall. My glow coiled over itself as if waiting for permission, and I gave it. They clutched at their throats. I threw my arms open and they slammed into the surrounding trees. One fell silent as his head cracked open on impact. The others coughed and sputtered before they, too, lay silent. Nash's body careened to the earth.

Her limp body lay in a heap near the others. This wasn't supposed to happen. She wasn't supposed to get hurt. No, she had to be okay. I couldn't touch her. That would only make matters worse. I flapped my hands while tears clogged my vision. What was I supposed to do? There was no one else here. I scanned the greenery in search of a solution. I rocked back and forth. My breath came in gasps I couldn't control. What should I do? What should I do? What should I do? I stood up and ran towards the cave for a few frantic moments. They would never get here in time. I had to help her: right here and right now.

I ran back over to her body against the protestation of my wobbly legs. Her chest wasn't moving. She wasn't breathing. *Fuck. Okay, okay, CPR. What was that song again? They say you're supposed to do it to a song. Fuck it.* Touching only her shirt, I rolled her onto her back and set my palms in the center of her chest.

Okay, just have to keep the beat. I sat there rhythmically beating on her chest. She didn't even stir. I kept going. Tears streamed from my eyes, accompanied only by ragged sobs. She had to be okay. I didn't come out here to be the reason she died. My glow spread through my fingers. Unbidden, it sank into her chest, and then something wonderful happened. She breathed. She didn't shoot up or open her eyes but there was breath. I continued my rhythmic stimulation of her heart as my glow aided me. Her eyelashes fluttered and she gasped.

I took my hands off her chest and sat there, allowing her to take in her surroundings. I flapped, unable to contain my joy. She was here. She would make it. I lay down beside her. I was exhausted, but she was alive. The world was slightly off kilter, but it wasn't anything a little rest couldn't solve. The bird song slowly returned to the forest as we both recovered from the afternoon.

"What happened?"

"You fell from the tree." I kept my eyes skyward.

"Yeah, but why did I fall? Was that him?"

I shook my head, watching the white clouds pass by the treetops, so stark against the green.

"Was it you?"

"Yeah."

"You killed them."

"How are you feeling?" I asked.

"I'm sore but it's fine. I'm alive. We should get moving."

She leaned off to one side to nurse the injury. The fault line of each cut on my lower leg throbbed and every shift felt like I was shoving a knife into my side. I glanced around at the bodies.

"Should we move them?" I breathed.

Nash spared me a pitying glance. That wasn't a reaction I wanted.

"We should check them for supplies. You take the kid."

His face was blue with veins bulging down through his neck and frigid to the touch. I retched into the grass. So much for keeping down my breakfast. I tried to look, but acid burned its way up my throat in a desperate attempt to see the outside world. I stimmed to regulate. This time, I was successful. He had an ID on him and a bottle of aspirin. Good enough. I scrambled away.

"His name was Max." I held out the ID.

She snatched it from me and threw it towards the bodies.

"First time killing?"

I nodded. I rocked violently as the guilt rose to consume me. Nash set a tentative hand on my shoulder.

"Hey, look at me."

I kept my eyes firmly on the ground.

"Listen then. If you didn't kill them, they would have killed us or brought us back to that shithole I came from. You didn't have a choice, okay? Don't think of their names. They don't deserve the space in your mind."

I nodded. The name Max rolled over and over like a loose marble.

"I mean it. Killing is hard, and the first time is the worst. Let's get out of here before more show up."

• • • ● • ● • • •

Echo checked Nash over for injuries and worried the second he found a sore spot on her side and the bullet graze wound on her arm. Zane tried to check on me, but he felt a million miles away. He stuck by my side as we made our way through the deepest cover. We crossed the first river we found, making sure everyone got wet wading up it for half a mile before exiting on the other side. The cold from the river reached my bones even in the height of the midday sun. It didn't rouse me from my numbness but aided it. By the afternoon, Zane had a hand under one of my arms to support me. He only let go when we stopped for the night.

"Stay here. I'll help everyone with the tents."

It sounded like my head was full of bees and his words were one more jumbled thing left floating around in there. I nodded. The fluff around my brain shifted with the order. I sat there as the movements of the others washed over me, unable to be ignored but unable to be focused on either. Nash passed by.

"How are you?" I blurted out at her back.

She turned to see me huddled up on my stump.

"We're good. We're going to collect firewood." She gestured to Echo.

I nodded and allowed the numbness to swallow me back up. Zane guided me to the fire. I didn't eat that night. The bulging veins of the dead were emblazoned in my mind.

"Simerra, take first watch," Mother said.

Of course, tonight was the night she started asking for my help with things like that. Zane plopped himself down next to me. The orange flames danced in his brown eyes.

"Do you want me to stay up?"

"I can handle a watch. Night attacks are disadvantageous unless your glow is like Nessa's." The words were heavy on my tongue.

He held his palms down towards the earth in surrender.

"I'm not doubting you. I'll get some rest while you keep us safe, oh mighty watch woman." He bowed repeatedly as he backed towards his tent. I waved him off. He would give me shit over this even while worried. Mark strode past me.

"Put out the fire."

"There's no water."

He didn't respond. I looked back at the fire warily. I shut my eyes and focused inward. The cold rippled through my veins in pulsing waves. I plunged my hand into the fire. Cold air rushed around me. The main log cracked in half as the others pushed out of the pit. I waited, but no one screamed. I pulled my glove back on and settled into a looping watch path, but even with my best efforts, I was too tired to focus through the heavy darkness and my body's ache for rest. Better safe than sorry, but I couldn't walk forever. My legs shook with every step. I leaned against a tree. The rough bark was my last hope for remaining conscious. My heavy eyes focused on the darkness, but sleep didn't care about my plans.

. . • • • • • • • • ·

I awoke stiff and bug bitten but otherwise unharmed. I creaked my way to the morning fire in the hopes the smoke would scare any remaining bugs away. I was already itchy enough. Mother sat beside me. A small smile pulled at the corners of her lips. My shoulders slumped.

"How was your watch?"

"It was okay. I didn't see anything."

"Neither did I." She waved her hand in front of her face.

"I'm serious, Mother."

"You did well. I heard you put the fire out and with all of us so close."

I glowed in the moment. Not in the power kind of way, in the old way. Where everything in me was warm and normal.

"I want you to go with the others on the hunting trip. Keep an eye out for strange birds. Stay close to Zane."

"Yes, Mother," I said.

"Be careful," she advised.

It felt like she was looking through me. Her glow was odd like that. She always said it was like she could feel the level of danger of an object or event, but the particulars were as fuzzy as her vision. Strange or not, I would keep my eyes peeled for weird birds. Maybe being on edge the last few days would come in handy.

"I love you," I whispered.

She ruffled my hair. Her fingers brushed against my scalp with an awful scratching sensation that had my skin begging to be picked off. Tension consumed me, and my glow knotted and unknotted in my chest over and over again. The familiar cold spiked. *Not now. Why now? Come on. She barely touched me. I drew into myself tightly, trying to avoid hurting anyone. Just count to ten. Just focus. Just count. My hands flapped so fast, I could hear the wind moving through my fingers. Why did it have to make sound? I covered my ears, rocking. Just focus. Just count. Just count. Just count.*

When I was finally calm, I opened my eyes. Everyone jerked their heads away as if my gaze alone could hurt them. Embarrassment colored my cheeks, and only then did I notice the arms around me. Was it the pressure that brought me back? I craned my neck to see their owner. Of course it was Zane. No one else was bold enough. He smiled, not letting go. He had a new cut on his cheek. My eyes widened at the implication. I looked at my own gloved hands, searching for the tear. He squeezed even tighter for a second. I focused on his forehead.

"I'm so sorry."

"None of that. Focus on your breathing," he insisted.

His familiar cold soaked into me. I obliged and counted the seconds between each breath. He incrementally lessened the pressure to nothing.

"Let's see about these gloves." His voice was soft and kept the fear away.

The small tear was on the tip of one of the fingers. He pulled the familiar needle and thread out of his pocket, making quick work of the patch job.

"Sorry."

He gave my shoulder a quick squeeze. The thin fabric of my shirt created the necessary barrier. What had Mother been thinking? She was the one who insisted on all the rules in the first place. She was sitting nearby, listening to Zane and me. Another test. One I hadn't exactly passed. *There was always next time.* I heard it in her voice like an echo of past training days.

"It's time for me to hunt."

"Mother says I'm supposed to go with you." I scrambled after him.

"Then we better hurry or the others will leave us behind."

If I didn't look up, then the others' stares weren't real. Zane checked on me continuously on the way to the pond.

"I bet I can catch more than you!" Daisy crowed, all four of her bouncing in unison.

"That's just because there are more of you." Devin poked her in the side.

All four of her jumped to the right in sync. The Daisys stuck their tongues out, hands on hips.

"Watch it!" one of the adults objected as one of her copies landed in the way.

Her focus broke and they snapped back into her.

"That's not fair."

"I'm sure you can catch more fish than I can," I said.

She rewarded me with a huge smile and bounced all the way to the riverbank. The others set up the rods and settled in for the task. Daisy splashed a short distance away, enjoying the sun. Some used their glows to aid the process but in the end, this was a waiting game. You couldn't make a fish take the bait faster.

· · · · ● · ● · ● · · ·

By midday, we had caught enough fish to head back, and Mother was waiting for us. Without a word, she led the way out of camp.

"So Zane, I hear you caught the smallest fish," Devin teased.

"That's the only small thing about me. Want to see?"

He waggled his eyebrows, and the others roared with laughter. The lighthearted banter was back after the chaos of yesterday. I hummed softly while I counted steps. I didn't notice the bird swooping over-head, following our group.

Chapter Four
FIREFLIES

C I eased into the cool river water. It was wonderful on my swollen ankles. The bushes rustled behind me. Rock in hand, I stood on the slimy stones of the riverbed. Nash came into view with her palms turned towards the soil.

"What were you going to do with that?"

The rock splashed back into the water and my face flushed.

"At least your feet are shoulder width apart. It's not a terrible start."

"Start?"

"She speaks."

I kept my eyes trained on the opposite bank of the river. I wiggled my toes. The water moved between them and past me, downstream. I was going numb, but I didn't budge.

"Let's start over. What are you doing in the river? Unclean water isn't the greatest for cuts."

Like I didn't already know that. Regardless, I moved back a bit so only my ankles were submerged and tucked my chin over my knees.

The rushing water was the only sound between us. A few pieces of river grass swayed with the pull of the current. The stars emerged one by one. They were probably the only things unchanged from before. I could still make out some of the constellations I used to find with my father. Cygnus stood out prominently above us. It was always the easiest constellation for me to find. I searched the sky, finding Sagittarius and Scorpius next. Now, where was Aquilla?

"See something you like?"

Of course she would interrupt. I scowled at her. *Why couldn't she take the cue and go away?* Allistics loved indirect communication.

"I know I upset you. I'm sorry."

Was she saying that because she knew my mother was in charge, or did she really mean it?

"I wanted to check on you. It's been a wild couple of days. I'm not super sure how to do this. Um, so you like the stars?"

Did the words feel like rocks in her mouth like they did in mine sometimes?

"I used to search out constellations that matched my book."

I patted the rocky bank. Fully reclined, it was easier to see the stars, even if a few of them had yet to make their grand appearance.

Nash lay beside me; I moved away a bit to gain space but otherwise stayed put.

"Which ones are out right now? Is that the Big Dipper?" She pointed to a cluster of stars.

I flapped and giggled at the thought. Those stars looked nothing like that constellation.

"Hey, be nice." She blushed an adorable red so bright, I could make it out by the light of the moon.

"That's Cygnus. You're kind of pointing at his neck. Those are his wings about three fourths of the way down. You know, people aren't sure if Cygnus is Zeus in disguise or if he's the friend of the son of Apollo, the god of the sun. Apparently, the son fell in the water and Cygrus dove repeatedly, looking for him, so Zeus turned the boy into a swan and voilà, swan constellation," I finished with a flourish.

"Do you study that stuff?" Nash twirled a piece of hair around her finger in slow circles. Why did it feel like I could watch her do *anything* forever and not get bored.

"I used to, but now I admire them." I sighed.

"Well, you know a lot about it. Maybe you could, like, study it again," she suggested earnestly.

"If I could find a book on it maybe, but there aren't many libraries open anymore," I joked.

"There are at some of the training facilities. Maybe I'll steal a book for you." She smirked, casually looking back up at the sky.

"How can you joke about that when it hasn't even been a week?" I asked, shocked.

She mulled it over while I focused on the stars. I knew what it was like to be rushed when you needed time to compose yourself.

"I can either joke about it or let it hurt me. Echo's very serious about the whole thing, but that's not how I roll. How do you roll?" She propped herself up on one arm, looking at me.

We were almost touching again.

"Huh?"

Her closeness was distracting. Everyone else knew better and she should have too. I'd literally killed her a few days ago. How could she disregard her own safety so easily? Still, her eyes twinkled even in the darkness, and I found myself lingering over the curves of her features.

"How do you cope? Do you want to talk about the other day?"

"Oh, that." I shut my eyes.

It didn't make the questions disappear, but it made me feel better for a second, and then I saw their faces again. I shuddered. I scanned the stars for patterns. Anything to distract from reality.

"I don't know. I've never had anything to talk about before."

"I don't believe that. I'm sure some stuff bothered you."

"You must be mistaking me for Zane."

"If you decide you need to talk, I'm here."

We sat in mutual silence, both of us lost in our own contemplations for quite some time, until my back ached and my feet were numb.

***

"We're staying here for a few days, I think," Zane said.

"It'll be nice to have a break from all the walking."

"Especially with that leg," Zane finished for me.

I shrugged.

"Let's see it," Echo said, making a grabbing gesture towards my leg.

I propped it up for the group to see the oozing wounds.

"Those are nasty. Hang tight," Nash ordered.

She returned with a roll of gauze in one hand and a tube of antibiotic ointment in the other. There was no way Mother had cleared the use of medical supplies for something so new.

"Where did you get those?" I asked.

"I pulled it off the guys who chased us. Hold still, this is going to sting."

And sting it did. I'd love to say I took it like a champ, but I squirmed the whole time. I barely managed not to kick Nash even as she was wrapping it. The white gauze stood out against my dark skin. It was snug, but the cuts felt a little bit better.

"Thanks. How are your ribs?" I asked.

"I broke one, but it's fine. You?"

"Just bruised."

Everyone else was slowly making their way to bed. The looks the caregivers threw our way as they went past were far from unnoticed.

"I wonder how long they'll stare," Nash pondered.

"You'll get used to it," Zane said, not even bothering to look.

"Is it your abilities?" Nash pressed.

"Whatever it is, they find us curious. I tend to ignore them." Zane rolled his eyes, disinterested.

"Weird, should we head to bed too?" Nash asked.

"Depends, how tired do you want to be when we hunt tomorrow?" I stretched.

"I can't hunt," Nash whined.

"It's that or firewood collection. Pick your poison."

She kicked at the ground.

"Watch it!" Echo brushed dirt off his legs.

"You're fine."

"About as okay as you'll be hunting," he shot back.

"Now you're in for it."

His eyes widened as she stood up and lunged at him, knocking him clear off the rock. They thumped to the ground, laughing and wrestling and rolling back and forth in the dirt. What that must be like.

"Head to bed, you lot," Mother called over.

Nessa, Joey, and Kate were in a heap. Zane cuddled up to Devin, and Nash snuggled up to Echo. His arm wrapped around her. A pang of loneliness tore at me. Silent tears melted into my pillow. I rocked to soothe myself but it didn't help. I opted to walk around camp. It was peaceful, seeing camp by moonlight. Long shadows filled the gaps between tents, giving everything an otherworldly quality. I could see a figure a little way past the camp. I hung close to the tents, moving from shadow to shadow the way Devin had shown me.

Their breathing hung in the thick summer air. I snuck around the backside of a tent to get a better view from the other side. Mark hunched over something in his hand that I couldn't quite make out through the shadows. Strong wing beats carried it away. The bird's blue underwing was exposed during each powerful stroke. My breath caught in my chest. Mother's words clanged through my head. This was the last thing I needed. I stumbled backwards. Several sticks snapped underfoot. My glow pulsed along with my racing heartbeat. Well, shit. He lurched towards me. I willed my muscles to unlock but they wouldn't. He ripped me closer by the hair. I bit back a whimper.

"What are you doing out of bed?" he snarled.

Spit hit my face. I blinked rapidly, trying to locate the right words. I flapped, unable to find them.

"Of course you don't have a reason. Get to your tent," he ordered, shoving me in the right direction.

My legs crumpled and I landed face-first in the dirt. His cruel laughter filled my ears. My face flushed hot with embarrassment, my hands still flapping.

"And they think you're useful."

I flinched. I couldn't help but think of the man who had gunned down the girl who couldn't get her glow to work. I crawled towards my tent, unable to stand. I lay there, shaking with a head full of half formed thoughts until the sun rose.

• • • ● • ● • • •

"Morning." Zane yawned, rubbing his eyes.

I dipped my head in acknowledgment. He frowned, taking me in.

I cocked my head to the side, waiting for an explanation.

"Nightmare?" he asked.

What was he talking about? He pointed to my crotch, and I became painfully aware of the dampness between my legs. Damn it all. I turned away to try to hide it. I wasn't a kid anymore, but this kept happening if I got too scared.

"Hey, hey, it's okay. Let's get you to the river," Zane soothed.

Zane escorted me to the river and waited for me to clean off. I washed the soiled garment before redressing in the clothes he'd brought me.

"Almost ready?" Zane stared back towards camp.

I jumped into his line of sight with jazz hands.

"Well, I'm glad you're feeling better. Let's get some breakfast."

Mark slapped a portion onto my plate with a feral smile. Zane's eyes flashed with rage. He grabbed Mark's wrist as he was handed his portion.

"Thanks for breakfast today, Mark."

A thin layer of ice formed on Mark's wrist. He didn't flinch, but his eyes turned hard. He jerked his wrist away.

"No problem, kid."

Chapter Five

BRING A GLOW TO A KNIFE FIGHT

C W: ABUSE, TORTURE MENTION, murder mention

Daisy jumped into the river, splashing the rest of us with cool, clear water. It was a welcome reprieve from the summer heat that clung to my skin and clothes like a sticky hug. Devin jumped in and chased her downstream and away from our fishing lines. Echo cast his perfectly, but Nash looped herself into the line as she threw it. She yelped in pain from the center of the tangled mess.

"Hold still."

It was hooked under her shirt somewhere. I pushed it up, exposing her tanned back. I bit back a curse as I took in the crisscrossed whip marks that covered her. What had they done to her back there? A hook glimmered from her side. I removed it with a featherlight touch before pushing her shirt back down. I handed her the hook, smiling softly. If she wanted to talk, she would bring it up. She accepted it. Her guarded eyes searched my face for some sort of reaction, and I hoped I hadn't upset her. She'd been through enough. She cast her line poorly, but this time it made it into the river. The sunshine shimmered on the water. The hum of insects and bird song wafted amongst us on the breeze. I swatted more mosquitoes than I cared to think about, but at least we could swim to cool off as needed, and the mud from the bottom of the river made a great insect repellent.

"I think I caught one," Nash said.

"Pull it in," I encouraged.

She jerked on the line, and I had to cough to cover my laughter.

"Slowly. You don't want to scare it. The fish will let go if you do. Is it big?"

"I think so. It's heavy."

With painstaking care, she wound the line inch by inch. I saw the stick poke out of the water and tried my best to keep a straight face. She was so focused, she didn't notice until it was at her feet. The flush of her cheeks crept down her neck in record time. She looked up at me, mortified.

"It was heavy?" she reasoned.

I deserved an award for the blank face I pulled off even as everyone around us roared with laughter. I unhooked the stick and handed the line back to her.

"Now you know how to reel in a fish. I'm sure you'll get one next time."

I smiled as encouragingly as Mother did when she nurtured Zane's glow. She hesitantly recast.

When we wrapped up for the day, Daisy carried the coolers. They were overflowing for the first time in months. Most of us would eat well here out of the river alone. Maybe we could stay. I shoved the thought from my mind. We couldn't settle as long as the government was hunting us. I helped clean the fish and set them up to cook over the fire. We had it down to a science by now. It didn't even matter that we only had a few knives. We were still plenty fast. Nash's mouth scrunched up. So she could kill people without hesitation but didn't like fish guts? Would I ever understand her?

"When you're done, let's go for a walk." Nash pranced off towards Echo. Something about her was mesmerizing. The knife sliced into my finger.

• • • ● • ● • • • •

We wandered till the hum of camp disappeared behind us. Our footsteps on the soft earth blended with the melody of crickets and the soft sway of the trees in the night air. Nash straddled a fallen log covered in moss, watching me.

"Thanks for the help earlier." She swung her legs back and forth.

We had to leave camp so far behind for a thank you? I would never understand people.

"New skills are hard for everyone. You did great."

"I hooked my back like a fucking idiot, and you got an eye full of scar tissue."

"They were really hard on you at that compound."

She chewed on her lip.

I inspected the carpet of moss atop the log to give her time. I wanted her to feel safe with me more than anything in the world. Hopefully, this would help.

"It was no walk in the park, and I wasn't one of their best."

Her golden-brown hair framed her face. It was down from the ponytail I had grown used to seeing the last couple of days. It was longer than I'd thought. I rolled a piece of moss between my fingers. It had a damp, soft smoothness to it. The texture was perfect to stim with while Nash spoke.

"If you weren't in the training rooms, you weren't supposed to use them at all. Exercise was outside of the training rooms, but my ability was best suited for it. They acted like it made me hard-wired for chaos. When we were kids, they used to use me as an example, or a warning, for the others of what would happen if they broke the rules. They told us they were trying to help us or asked if we wanted to make our parents proud after hurting us. That place was awful." Her voice broke on the last word.

"It's okay to cry."

I had been told that so many times. Maybe it was what she needed to hear right now. I reached back in my memory to recall other things Zane had said to me over the years that might be helpful right now.

"No, it's not. Echo and I have to prove ourselves or you'll throw us out. We're fugitives. We aren't safe in or out of your group and here I am, *venting*. I could be training or proving how useful I am, but instead, I'm crying in front of a girl I just met."

"It's okay to break down. I have meltdowns and they're kind of similar. I stop talking like I did the other day or I'll scream and lose all awareness of my surroundings, and sometimes, I hurt myself. Emotional regulation is hard. It's even harder if you bottle it up. It always makes my meltdowns worse. It'll probably do something similar to your response. Crying could help you regulate."

"But how will I know when to stop?" Her voice wavered.

"When you feel better. I'll be here."

Loud sobs ripped from her chest, and her tears landed on me and the log in equal parts. I fiddled with my moss, allowing her to take the time she needed to feel and process after all she'd been through. I was in no rush, and she needed this. The sobs turned into a whimpering cry, then to silence. I peeked over, but silent tears streamed down her face so I looked back at my moss. I told her we would stay here until she was ready and we would.

She reached out and squeezed my shoulder when she was done. Deep tear tracks ran through the grime of the last few days, yet she seemed lighter. Some of her spark had returned.

"Thank you."

A bird changed branches above me. It cleaned its wing, revealing the blue coloring tucked beneath. Dread seeped into my bones as it flitted away.

"Nash, please tell me you saw that?"

"The branches?"

"There was a bird."

"There are loads of them out here. Maybe we should hunt them tomorrow."

"There was a specific bird."

"What did it look like?"

"It has blue on the bottom of its wings, and it's only ever one of them. Are they native to the area?"

"I don't think so. Have you told the others?"

"My mother told me to keep an eye out for any strange birds, and I've seen this one twice now, maybe three times, but I'm not sure."

"Let me know if you see it again, and I'll keep an eye out too."

"Thanks."

She waved it off. I wove through the scattered people near the fire and sat next to Zane, who passed me his plate without a word.

"See, that's kindness. Where's my food, Echo?" Nash questioned.

She settled down beside Echo and completed the circle.

"I figured you'd grab your own since you were gone forever, but if you're getting up anyway, can you grab me another piece?" Echo asked.

"No way," Nash said.

"I'll get you all more," Zane offered.

"What did you chat about?" Echo asked, brown eyes focusing on me.

"What a big doofus you are," Nash teased.

"You wound me. How can we continue to be friends with cruelty such as this between us?" Echo clutched at his chest.

"I'm sure you'll manage. Zane's back."

"Thank you." Echo bowed with a flourish before grabbing a piece of fish.

"Do you guys always walk so much, or is it because of us?" Echo asked around a mouthful.

"It's better not to stay still."

"Yeah, but from what I can see, you've never lost a member or had a run-in with the government. Why keep moving?"

"The new guy is right. We could just set up shop here. There's a river, plenty of trees for firewood, and we have the tents." Kate flipped her auburn hair, copper tones catching the sunlight as she chewed on her next idea.

A collective groan rang through the group. From what I remembered of her story, she was fairly well off before all this happened. Having to work so hard for even the clothes on her back was quite the lifestyle shock when she first got out of her house. She'd had to climb the gate in order to escape the bodies. Not that the experience had made her appreciate anything.

"What about winter, Kate? What then?" Zane shot back.

"Maybe not here, but a place like here farther south. Don't you want Daisy to get a real education?"

She turned her focus to Devin. He glanced over to where Daisy was playing then back at us.

"Of course I do, but you heard them. There are compounds in every state. I'd rather keep moving than risk her being caught," he argued, eyebrows pulling together in rage.

"It's not better than a stable home, and if you weren't so scared, you would see that. When was the last time Daisy had a week sleeping in the same place?"

"Leave my sister out of this." His voice was a forced calm.

The space around him darkened. Kate was either unaware or uncaring. With squared shoulders, she planted a hand on her hip.

"Your sister should be in this. Some of us are trying to look out for her."

"Look out for her? You only think of yourself."

"At least I'm thinking. Do you think she wants to run? Why don't we ask her?"

Devin's eyes were nearly black, and the darkness clung to him like sludge. It leeched out of him in long, snaking tendrils. Fuck. The stars disappeared from view. Kate's hand was at her sheath in an instant. Her knife reflected the dull orange light of the fire. Her eyes were trained on Devin.

"No fighting," Mother ordered.

"We aren't children, Sharon. I think we'll sort this out ourselves." Kate moved closer.

Zane and I shared a knowing look and got to work. Zane moved to Daisy's side, distracting her from the spat. I moved between Devin and Kate as Zane placed a hand on Devin's arm.

"What good will it do for you to fight each other? We're on the same team."

Uncertainty flickered through Kate's eyes as she readjusted her hand on the knife. I gave Devin a pleading look. He reined his glow in with a sigh and the firelight filled our campsite once more. I held out my hand for Kate's knife.

She waited until the blade was in my hand then pulled it back slightly before releasing it. I inhaled sharply as the metal bit into my skin. Joey stood to follow her, but Zane shook his head. She needed time to cool off alone. Daisy and Echo made their way over to our group, and the adults' conversation picked back up to a low hum. I stabbed the knife into the earth and pulled my sleeve down, wrapping it around my hand to stop the bleeding. Nash tapped my shoulder.

"Are you okay?"

"I'm fine."

"I saw what she did." Nash pulled at my sleeve.

"Careful! You almost got skin." I ripped my arm back.

"Why does that matter? You're hurt."

The temperature dropped as Zane approached. I gave him a pointed look. It had been close, but I was fine. I was in control.

"Have you stopped to consider that touching my gremlin of a sister could go very poorly for both of you?"

I stuck my tongue out at him, which he returned in kind. At least he could still joke.

"Like, how bad?"

"Like, I saw how tired she was the other day. You already know how bad. Do you really want to push your luck a second time?" He leaned in so only our little group of four could hear.

"I passed out. It's no big deal." She brushed it off.

Oh no. How was I supposed to explain that? We locked eyes and her own widened to the size of dinner plates. I guessed that was how.

"Fuck me. Did I die?"

I twisted the hem of my shirt around in my hands and looked to Zane for help.

"What the fuck do you mean you died?" Echo asked.

"Keep it down or everyone is going to want to know the specifics," Zane said.

"You died?" Echo asked.

"I mean. I guess I must have. I remember not being able to breathe, and then I woke up on the ground. But if I died, how did you bring me back?" Nash asked, perplexed.

"I did CPR. Well, mostly I did chest compressions." I rubbed the back of my neck, needing something to do with my hands.

"That wouldn't be enough," Echo pointed out.

Zane jabbed him in the side.

"Ow, there's no need for that," Echo mumbled.

"I'm fine, Zane. I kind of let my glow flow into you from my hands. You started breathing again after that," I explained sheepishly.

Her eyes were wide with wonder, so I rushed on.

"It's not like you were dead for a long time or anything. If the situation was even slightly different, I wouldn't have been able to help you at all. Somebody could have achieved the same effect with normal CPR."

"Thank you." Nash placed a hand on my sleeved arm and squeezed gently.

"Mind filling me in about your glow?" Echo asked.

"Cut it out," Nash hissed.

"It'll take your breath away." I smiled weakly.

Zane snorted. At least someone liked my answer.

"It's something with air, right?"

I nodded.

He nodded with a far-off look, as if filing it away in his head.

"Can I see your hand now?" Nash asked.

I unwrapped my injured palm, showing them the thin slice near my thumb and index finger.

"It'll be hard for that to heal. We should really wrap it."

"I can do it," Zane offered.

"He's really protective of you," Nash commented once Zane was on the far side of the fire.

"He's always been that way. Twins and all." I waved her off.

"No shit. Really?" Nash's eyes went wide.

"Can't you see the resemblance?" I asked.

"Now I can. I didn't realize twins didn't have to both be, like, fully the same," she explained.

Zane's face erupted in a huge Cheshire cat smile as he plopped back down beside me.

"Oh, we were, but I took care of that, didn't I?" Zane joked.

I cackled. The laughter lifted away my worry.

"I don't get it," Echo said.

"We were identical. But I'm a bit too boy for that now, wouldn't you say?" Zane asked.

"Cut it out. Laughing hurts!" I said between rounds of giggles.

Zane refocused on my injury. He glowed brightly, a layer of ice forming on his palm. I set my hand on his glacial palm. He used a frozen finger to rub the ointment in before he wrapped my hand in gauze. He shook the ice off his hand, smiling.

"We get better at that every time."

"You get better at that."

"You don't kill me, so I think it's a *team effort*."

I pushed against his chest and he fell back, feigning injury.

"You wound me, sister. This is how I die." He shut his eyes, going limp.

He lay there, unmoving in the dirt, so I threw pebbles at his face. He shook them out of his hair.

"I die and you throw rocks at me. That's a new level of rude."

"Go put the supplies away."

"Y'all are full of it," Nash commented.

"Full of good times!" Zane replied.

We all collected near the fire where Devin wove tales with the shadows. He was still upset, but at least he had something to focus his energy on. He was more elaborate than usual that night as he created giant images with minute details. He brought more than one dropped jaw to the group. As always, Daisy was his biggest fan.

Chapter Six

DANCING THROUGH LIFE

C

I made my way to the river, and I could feel someone behind me. I kept my pace, even as my heartbeat picked up. Why were they following me? What did they want? Maybe they were just going to get a drink too. If that was all, then why hadn't they said anything. I spun around, hands raised to defend myself, but it was Nash.

"You've got decent awareness. You'd make a great fighter." She meandered past me.

She cupped the running water in her hands, taking a long drink. What was she thinking? She could have gotten herself hurt again.

"You gonna have some?" she asked, stepping back from the water's edge.

She moved to the side of the narrow path, leaving just enough room for me. I brushed past her. My heart thrummed faster at the momentary contact. I knew she wasn't here to hurt me, so why was my heart acting like this? I rinsed my face, hoping to clear my head from the fuzzy warmth filling it.

Nash sat smack in the middle of the path. Seriously? I rolled my eyes all the way round in the most exaggerated loop I could manage and carefully stepped around her, nearly falling on my ass. She made no move to follow me so I looked back. Worry lines creased her forehead.

"Are you sure the adults can be trusted? How do you know them all? They don't look like any of you, except for your mom."

Ah, that. We did look like a ragtag group of misfits, and that wasn't far off from the truth. What was the easiest way to convey that in a reassuring manner?

"She's our actual mother. The others kind of found us, but they've helped us ever since."

"What about Mark? He means well?"

"He thinks I'm a threat to the others."

"I don't trust him."

She chucked a handful of pebbles into the stream. They pierced the surface with a thwack before disappearing. The bitter lie was still on my tongue, and I wasn't ready to tell another. A distraction was in order.

"Let's dance." I offered her a hand, but she didn't move.

"You're kidding, right?"

I gestured for her to stand up over and over until she eventually caved. I applauded as she rose to her feet.

"Now what?"

"Take your hair down." I undid my larger twist so the little braids could bounce around.

Her hair fell into her face in a thick, curly bunch. She looked up at me through her curls with a hand balanced on the curve of her hip. The last traces of the summer sun kissed her body, highlighting the strength of her muscles and the roundness of her belly where it peeked from the bottom of her shirt. I blinked a few times, looking for words. *Come on, Simerra, focus.*

"Now what?"

"Now we dance. Just make up a beat. Try it."

I smiled as confusion filled her face. I moved my hips side to side, swaying to an imaginary beat. I twirled around in an arc down the path towards her. My hands twisted through the air, making imaginary patterns. I pretended there was a drum counting out a rhythm for us as I spun around. Slowly, she joined me. We spun and twirled around, brushing past each other, nearly touching. I allowed my eyes to close as I swayed back and forth. Then, her hand was on my hip and electricity shot through me. Her hips moved with mine. My heart quickened as if I were still jumping around. I needed to play it cool. Nash was dancing with me!

"Is this okay?" she whispered.

The hair on the back of my neck rose. I had never felt like this before. I nodded and allowed her to guide my hips back and forth. We moved together. Nash's internal tempo swayed us gently. Before I could stop it, my shirt rode up, exposing my skin, and her pinky touched my bare side. I spun away. My eyes were wide with fear. I waited for her to gasp or give some other indication that we had just been in contact.

"Are you okay?" we both asked at the same time.

"I'm more than okay," Nash said.

"My side— You touched my side. You should be hurt," I explained.

I waited for her to agree and show me a ghastly injury. The smile dissolved from her face. That was more like what I'd expected. Now, where was she hurt so I could try to patch it?

"You didn't hurt me, Simerra. I'm okay. You didn't glow. Think about it. Wouldn't you be fatigued?"

She was right. I was a little tired from dancing, but nothing extra.

"I'm sorry I scared you, but I'm not hurt." She moved closer.

"You need to be more cautious."

She waited till she caught my eye and winked. What was that supposed to mean?

"Thank you for the dance. I do feel better. Should we head back to camp?" She offered a sleeve-covered hand and I took it. The hum of warmth that flooded my body was enticing and addicting. I could get used to this. We didn't break away until camp was in sight.

I walked over to the fire, still giddy, and plunged my hand into the flames. The fireflies blinked lazily in the dark. I moved to the edge of our tent circle, settling against a tree. I replayed the night's events over and over. It was exhilarating to feel her close to me. I wanted nothing more than to dance with her again. To hold her close and breathe in her warm, vanilla-tinted scent. Suffice it to say, the watch passed quickly.

• • • ● • ● • • •

We traveled the next day, only breaking when it came time for lunch. Nash carried Echo's pack again as he continued to struggle to keep up. It was strange to see someone so hopelessly out of shape. When we stopped for the night, I found myself walking away from the firelight into the darkness of the trees. I heard footsteps behind me and turned, spirits rising. The soft glow that lit the trees dismantled my hopes. It was Nessa.

"Looking for someone else?" she asked, smirking.

I shook my head rapidly. It wasn't what she was thinking at all. I wanted to talk with Nash, sure, but I hadn't been out here waiting for her or anything like that. That would be ridiculous.

"There's no need to deny it. Good luck with whoever it is." Nessa continued past me and into the trees.

I sank to the forest floor. I was being ridiculous, wasn't I? I rubbed my hand against my face. I wasn't quite ready to head back to the fire or to bed. Nessa glowed her way out of the forest off to my right, but I stayed put as full darkness returned. The moon was trapped behind the clouds. The only light was the soft flickering on and off of lightning bugs as they danced through the air.

"Beautiful, aren't they?" Nash said.

I turned to see her outline just out of reach.

"Yes," I agreed.

She crossed her legs and sank to the forest floor beside me. I worked to control my breathing even while my heart raced. Could she tell she had this effect on me? Could she also feel the thrum of electricity between us.

"I used to see them when we practiced tracking. It's been at least a year though."

She reached out and clapped her hands together. She showed me her empty palms.

"I guess it's better that way. I doubt they want to be caught. They are beautiful though," Nash mused.

"They're the only thing in nature I've seen glow like us."

"Yeah, the only thing that's free too." She laughed.

"We're free."

"We're hunted. Do you know how to fight?"

"It's not the sort of thing we focus on." I shrugged.

"What would you do if the government tried to grab you if you can't fight?"

"I would show them we aren't a threat."

"You mean like you've shown the other members of your group?" She cocked an eyebrow.

"That's different. I wasn't always this in control." I crossed my arms and went back to watching the fireflies.

"I never said they were right. I could teach you how to fight. If you wanted."

"I'm sure you have more pressing things to focus on," I stammered.

"You're worth focusing on. Let's start tomorrow night."

She squeezed my shoulder, her hand feather soft, and then she was gone. I set my own hand on the spot she'd touch, giddy at the memory. I would be seeing her tomorrow, and not just in the day's travels. What if I didn't take to the training? Would she tease me? *Please let me be good at this,* I begged the stars.

Chapter Seven

ROCKS HURT AND OTHER IMPORTANT TRAINING LESSONS

C W: CORPSE MENTIONS

I awoke to Mother standing at the entrance of our tent. She stared at the wall. The slight fogginess within her eyes was more visible in the morning light.

"Good, you're awake." She twirled her cane. The movement scattering mosquitos

"Sorry to keep you waiting." I scrambled to my feet.

"A walk will help you wake up. Lead the way." She gestured away from camp.

Using her cane to bump along the scattered roots littering the earth gave her the lay of the land. I ignored the songbirds overhead, not wanting to see Mark's pet. I had enough to worry about on the ground. I tapped my fingers together to help me regulate: long to short and short to long. I peeked back at Mother, wanting to be certain I was weaving a loud enough path for her to follow me. Each time, she was right behind me, an eyebrow perpetually cocked as if daring me to voice my concerns. We stopped in a quiet hollow. Each of us leaned against nearby trees.

"I needed to talk to you in private."

"We haven't done this in a while."

"Not since we last worked on your glow. I'm sorry it's been so long." She rubbed the place where her left pinky had been.

"I need you to start doing more night watches," Mother admitted.

I looked up from the leaf I had been fiddling with.

"I know they're boring, but I'm worried about what's following us," she admitted. "I can only perceive so much with my glow."

"You sense danger better than any of us," I asserted.

"I didn't ask you here because I pity myself. I know what I can do." She allowed her own glow to cast a glimmer on the surrounding trees.

"I saw a weird blue bird around camp and hanging around with Mark."

Mother stiffened.

"What was he doing?"

"It was in his hand, and when I got close, it took off. Maybe he has a glow too. Could that be the danger you feel?"

"It could be, but we can't act until we know more. You know I love you, Simerra. I need you to stay vigilant. Your glow could buy us valuable time if something does go wrong. I need your help to keep the others safe."

"What about Zane?"

"Your brother has never *killed* before."

My joints locked up, but I didn't dare breathe a word. Her cane rustled the leaves as she walked away. Blue-purple corpses filled my mind. The weight of my actions crumpled me to the forest floor. I dug my fingers into the soft earth, grasping for anything to ease the sadness. My other hand clamped over my mouth to dampen the sobs, but hot, wet tears wove new riverbeds of pain across my skin. I rocked back and forth to soothe myself as the tears continued to flow. Slowly, they gave way to silent rocking, and when they had dried, I wiped away the evidence of my pain. My throat was still tight when I returned to camp. At least now, I was useful for something. Even if it was just killing.

"Bad talk?" Zane asked, holding out my pack.

I shrugged.

"I'm here, okay. Whatever it is. We've got this."

Mother had said it was my responsibility alone. I couldn't tell him about it. I focused on the passing trees and tried not to have another meltdown. Zane frowned but turned to Devin and the others to chat.

We stopped early that day, having arrived back at a river, and not a moment too soon since everyone was starting to reek. Echo and Nash hardly needed any help at all during setup, leaving me free to wonder when Nash and I would meet. Should I wait until after dinner? Would we meet earlier because we had stopped earlier? I decided to wait until after dinner to walk back by the river. I didn't want to seem overly excited.

When dinner was over, I mumbled something to Zane about needing a drink and wandered over to the river. Nash wasn't there yet. I sat down and watched the water rush past, throwing bits of debris in.

A rock smacked into my back and I twisted around, looking for the culprit. Nash stood there holding another rock.

"You have to be ready for an attacker at any moment. They never used small objects on us, but for you, I think pebbles will work just fine. Find cover," she instructed, hurling another rock at me.

I scrambled to my feet and dove into the tall grass beside the river, not knowing where else to go. Another rock hit me in the side.

"Ow!" I protested.

"You have to find a better place than that."

A rock thunked down beside me. She was taking this way too seriously. I crawled to the edge of the river and hid behind a tree.

"That's better."

She made a show of dropping the rocks. I scowled. What was the point of all that?

"You always have to be able to find cover and fast. Even in the woods. I know it's an obvious lesson, but that doesn't make it any less important."

"What now?"

"Now we get into hand to hand. Let's see what we're working with. Make a fist and hit my palm."

She covered her hand with a scrap of cloth from her pocket. That wasn't a half bad idea. As long as I stayed focused on her palm and didn't miss and hit her fingers, we would be in the clear. I could do this. I pulled back and hit as hard as I could. Her hand barely moved from the impact.

"That's not bad. Now we just need to work on strength, and then we can really get into it."

***

We dipped our toes into the river; the cold water washed over my aching feet. It had been nice to be in contact with something, even if it was just to hit it. I felt accomplished.

"You aren't half bad."

"Don't lie. My hand is going to be bruised tomorrow from that time I forgot to pull back," I corrected.

The moonlight shimmered over our rippling reflections. It was easy to forget the world out here.

"No one becomes great overnight. You'll get there. Besides, you have your glow for when you get stuck."

I flinched.

"Was it something I said? I'm sorry."

"It's not your fault. My mother wants me to keep an extra eye out for danger." I swung my arm across my chest, holding myself together.

"Is it the bird thing?"

"Yes."

"When you see it again, I'll help you catch it." She held out a hand to help me up before pulling it back to rest on her neck. "Sorry."

I gestured for her to lead the way and smiled, not wanting her to think I was mad. I got a half smile in return before we wound our way back to camp. The moon cast long shadows over the grass. I pulled on Nash's sleeve, and I held a finger to my lips when she turned to look at me. *Please let it be Mother's watch.* A stocky figure stood by the far tents with their back to us, but I couldn't tell exactly who it was. Then a bird flew down, landing on the figure's outstretched arm. Every muscle in my body screamed for us to hurry up. I started rocking, unable to stop myself. I couldn't find the words to tell her who it was.

"I saw it too. Let's get to the tent," she breathed in my ear.

We slunk to the safety of the tent. The others were fast asleep. Nash propped herself up on an elbow.

"I thought none of the adults here had glows?"

"Mother does. It's how she keeps us safe."

"Is that why she—" She waved her hand in front of her face.

"That's rude."

Her hand dropped back to her lap.

"She can see shadows and vague outlines of things, just not great details. Don't ask her to read to you, but it's helped her. The second a shadow changes, she's aware of it. She doesn't get overwhelmed by the minute details because she can't see them. Her glow helps her perceive farther. It's the same out of focus quality, but she can tell if what's coming is dangerous. She helps us to respond accordingly." I clasped my hands together, having finished my spiel.

It had been years since someone had needed information about Mother's disability and glow. She used to look to me to inform those around us constantly.

"So Mark has a bird thing?"

"He's never told anyone, but Mother knows. She says we need more information before we do anything."

"That's bullshit. What if someone gets hurt?"

"Then we'll deal with it."

"We need to train you faster." She groaned.

My heart soared at the idea of more time around Nash. Not even the possibility of fighting Mark could dampen my spirits.

Chapter Eight

THE FUTURE

The next day, we hit a road so wide that the center was still intact. There were several lanes to this one. There must have been so many people to make this necessary. I remembered the old cars that used to whisk people around. Did the government still use this road?

"Now we're talking," one of the teens just ahead of me said, bouncing slightly. What was there to be excited about? The sun was twice as hot on the black tar than it was under the trees. An old sign lay in the center of the tarmac, claiming this was an interstate. It still had a lot of color, but a layer of grime and vines clung to it.

"Spooky." Nash tapped it with her toe.

"Spooky," Echo repeated in Nash's voice.

She grabbed a rock from the ground and chucked it at him. He pointed his palms at the earth but she hurled another.

"Don't make fun of me."

He pantomimed locking his lips and throwing away the key. She dropped her remaining artillery, satisfied. Our voices carried through the quiet group. Zane motioned for me to wait before he ran up to the front. I watched him quizzically until my eyes landed on a deer carcass. Zane raised his hand in a fist and we scattered towards the trees.

Mother whispered something to Zane. He left the cover of the trees for the road. I swallowed the rising acid in my throat. I ran out towards my brother. Nash fought with Echo from the tree line but it didn't matter.

"Of course you followed me," Zane teased.

"At least you're not alone. I'll keep watch."

I scanned for movement on the horizon. Flies buzzed around the carcass and a foul smell filled my nose. It squelched when he poked at the open wound. I nearly gagged. He wiped his hands on his pants.

"The blood around it is dry and there aren't any bite marks. Something hit it."

"I saw trucks at the compound."

"That means they're still using this road. See anyone?"

I shook my head.

"Let's go tell the boss."

We jogged back to Mother's side and relayed what we'd seen. Mark glared at me from over Mother's shoulder because *of course he did.*

"We'll stay by the side of the road." She raised her voice so everyone could hear her. "If anyone hears a vehicle, alert the group and hide."

Hushed whispers broke out as people wondered what we might encounter. Nash rushed over, wringing her hands together.

"What were you thinking?" she hissed.

"She was helping me," Zane defended.

"You didn't have to be out there. What if you'd been shot?"

"Then Zane would have needed my help because that would've meant there are people out there," I argued.

She threw her hands up. I caught Zane's eye. He shrugged, not knowing what to make of her either.

"She'll calm down. She's not used to others doing the dangerous bits while she has to hang back and wait," Echo whispered.

"It's about time someone looked out for her for a change," I said.

At an old gas station, we veered off onto a tiny street. Branches reached across from both sides, joining in the middle. Tall grass and flowers mixed in what were once front yards. Old cars sat abandoned in driveways covered in thick yellow pollen and dandelion tendrils. Had they run or waited in familiarity when the sickness ripped through? Mark directed us through every house on the road while the rest of the caregivers watched from the street. We found old medical supplies and some food, but most of it had long since expired.

"We need to hit a store," Kate commented after she picked her fifteenth lock that day.

Mark made us check the rest of the neighborhood before he agreed. We opened a few more houses en route but ultimately looked for a store that others hadn't cleaned out. A tall order, but there wasn't much else we could do.

"I'm getting a bad feeling about this," Nash said.

Her whole body was tense as we walked through the quiet neighborhood. Echo had a practiced calm about him. Was that for Nash or did he know something? Smoke coiled up around the trees ahead of us. The thick plumes filled the gaps between the leaves, darkening the bright sky.

"Sharon, what's going on up there?" Mark asked.

"I think we found the group that hit the deer."

"Is it safe to proceed?" he asked.

"I'm not sure."

"There's only one way to find out," Zane said.

"It would be unwise to split up. We don't know how many people are up there," I suggested.

"She's right." Nash cracked her knuckles.

"Yay." Echo spun his index finger in small circles.

The low hum of speakers started. Everyone froze. *No, not here. Not now.* I covered my ears in preparation for the blasting sound.

"These children are the future. Turn them in and save us all."

Horrified glances spread between everyone in the group. The glow wielders jumped to the outside. Kate pulled out her knife and so did Nash. The rest of us had hands raised and ready. A solitary shot rang out.

"We have to do something," I said.

"Don't break formation," Mark ordered. He opened his mouth to continue, but more screams cut him off.

"Then you're coming with us," I countered.

"She's right. Lead the way," Joey called from the back.

Zane and I matched each other step for step. I covered my mouth in horror. People clustered in doorways on the hill. The men below loaded up a small group of kids. They couldn't have been older than Daisy. A woman lay in the street. Her blood pooled out around her. The red mixed with the deep brown of the earth. I choked back the bile in my throat. Another woman knelt over the corpse. Her shoulders shook with the force of her tears. A soldier stood halfway between the woman and the spectators. His gun glinted in the midday light.

"I'll ask you again. Are there more? I'll knock down every door. We will find them."

"These children are the future. Turn them in and save us all," the speaker blared.

"Are they going to keep playing that?" Kate rubbed the back of her neck.

"There is nothing we can do. We should turn back now," Mark argued.

"We could end up directly in their path," I reasoned.

"We can help, right, Devin?" Daisy asked. Her eyes were as wide as dinner plates.

"You have my vote," Devin said.

"I don't like this. They have guns," Kate objected, pulling back into Joey's arms.

"We have you," Devin argued.

"Zane has to stay here to protect the group."

"I'm sorry, Mother. I'm going with the others," he asserted. "The kids and caregivers can stay up here where it's safe while we deal with the threat."

"These children are the future. Turn them in and save us all," the speaker screeched out once more.

We all shuddered.

"I'm destroying that thing." Kate pulled out a second knife.

I took a deep breath and walked into the valley. Zane was right behind me, and the others quickly followed. Time to kick some ass.

"I knew there were more of you. Where the fuck were you all hiding? Get in the truck and I won't shoot."

He twirled his gun lazily. How far would this man let us get before he figured it out? No one slowed down. We were halfway down the hill at this point. I couldn't stop the smile that slid across my lips. *You're in for it, my guy.* He trained his weapon on us. Cute idea.

"Hands up."

"Careful what you ask for," Zane called.

Zane froze the soldier's feet in place with the flick of his wrist. Three shots rang out one after the other. A shield jumped from his fingertips and the bullets buried themselves in the thick ice. We sprinted down the hill. Kate whipped past faster than I'd ever seen her. Her feet barely grazed the grass. She ripped the gun out of the soldier's hand and stabbed her blade into his arm. He cried out as blood spurted from the wound. The other soldiers opened fire on our group.

"Everyone, get down," I screamed.

Zane hit the earth and the others copied, covering their heads. I dug deep into my glow and shoved it with everything I had at the men by the truck. A curtain of air slammed into them. Their vehicle rocked from the force. They toppled over. Their guns shot skyward. I pulled my glow back towards my heart as fast as I could. It came happily, as if it had been given enough time to play that day.

"You're good!" I yelled.

My knees shook, but we were surging forward once more. Kate ripped their guns away, then she sat on the stack of them smugly. She kicked her feet lazily while she waited for us to deal with the rest. Even in a fight, Kate was still Kate.

"Who the fuck are you?" the leader asked.

"The future," Nash said, hitting him over the back of the head with his gun.

The remaining soldiers turned their palms towards the dirt in surrender. I waited for the onlookers to cheer, or clap, or do anything to show they were happy, but there was none of that. I looked up at them and they flinched.

"What should we do with them?" Kate asked.

"We have to kill them. If we don't, they'll report back and we'll have more of them on our tail," Nash stated.

"Just leave," a man said from the top of the hill.

He spit in our direction. His brow furrowed. Others nodded in agreement. Some shook their fists at us.

"Yeah, get out of here," a woman yelled.

"They're going to come back with more."

"No one asked you to do this."

"Monsters!"

"Freaks!"

Kate stomped over to me from her pile of guns.

"What the fuck kind of thanks is this?" Kate pointed her thumb towards the townsfolk.

"People are afraid of anything that's different," Echo lamented.

"It doesn't change that we either kill the soldiers or we have a bigger problem. These people are probably going to rat on us, and we have to take those kids with us," Nash rationalized.

"More mouths to feed. What were we thinking?" Joey buried his head in his hands.

"We were thinking this could have been us. I'm going to check on the kids."

I moved past the kneeling soldiers to the truck. Three kids cowered in the back corner. Their palms faced the earth and they wouldn't look at me. Two of them had rope marks on their wrists so deep, it must have been from months or years of mistreatment. They couldn't catch a break. No wonder these people weren't happy we helped. They hadn't wanted these kids to begin with. No better than a dog to chain in the yard. My glow coiled on itself, agitated. I took a deep breath. Now was a time for kindness, not revenge.

"I'm not here to hurt you. I'm like you."

I tapped against my glow. A soft light bloomed from my hands in the dark of the truck. A soft breeze tousled their hair. I reined it back in before I lost control. Their eyes lit up with relief and they hugged me. I kept my hands above my head where they couldn't hurt them.

"Be careful, okay? I can't actually touch you. My skin hurts people. Let's get out of this truck."

They clung to me as we walked out and back over to the others. They reminded me so strongly of all of us when we were little: lost, alone, and in need of guidance. Maybe we could be that guidance for them. It was worth a shot.

"They're so cute," Kate cooed.

"They're terrified. They won't let me go."

There was barely concealed worry in everyone's eyes. I focused on the little hands that clutched at my shirt, and I hummed to soothe all of us. Their grips relaxed. *Cool, so they like it too.* Nash jerked a gun up onto her shoulder. Her eyes were filled with determination. There had to be another way, a nonlethal way.

"Wait, okay?"

She nodded, shifting her weight to her other hip. I turned to Zane.

"Can you break the tires?"

He nodded slowly. *Step one planned. Look at that. Come on, Simerra. You need a plan. Any plan that doesn't involve death. Make it convincing or they'll ignore you.*

"You said the townsfolk are going to rat on us anyway. Why not just leave them tied up in the truck, unable to use it?" I asked.

"I can't be the only one sick of walking. Why don't we just take the truck and get out of here before backup shows up. We can leave this dump with the soldiers tied up. Those people probably won't move until we're gone," Kate said.

"That's not a terrible idea," Echo said.

"Thanks." Her face contorted into a half snarl.

"If we're keeping them alive, we need to act fast. They have a base to report back to and when they're late, scouts will be sent out. We need to search them for phones and get out of here." Nash marched off.

I ran a hand through my hair. When had life gotten so complicated?

"Joey, can you grab the others? She's right. We have to get out of here."

He turned towards the caregivers with a look of concentration. He turned back to me, blew on his knuckles, and wiped them on his shirt.

"Done. And I didn't have to walk over there. They'll be down in a second," he boasted.

One of the kids pulled on my sleeve. I peered down at the little one. My head cocked over the side. His eyes were wide with fear.

"Do we get to come?" he whispered.

"Of course you do. What are your names?"

"I'm James. That's Hannah and Kyle."

"It's nice to meet you. We're leaving very soon." I raised my voice so the approaching group could hear. "Daisy, can you keep an eye on them.?"

She pointed to herself, perplexed. I nodded. She puffed out her chest and rushed over to her new charges.

"My name's Daisy. I'm going to help you now." She held out her hand to the three children.

James took it cautiously. Daisy shook it, staying as professional as she knew how.

"Let's get you . . ." She looked to me for guidance.

"Into the truck," I coached.

"Into the truck. Follow me."

Daisy pumped her arms and led the way. She clambered right in and the others followed. The caregivers didn't seem nearly as convinced. Time for the hard work.

"You can't think this is a good idea?" Mark bemoaned.

"You can drive, right?" I asked, locking eyes.

I forced myself not to look away even as the unease of it set in. He nodded. Good.

"And you know where we're going?"

"Of course I do."

"Awesome, because we need to leave now if we don't want to get caught. You're our best bet."

He cursed under his breath. I fought to keep a straight face. That went better than expected. It still wasn't worth making eye contact. I'd have to find other ways to get under his skin next time. *Why am I planning on a next time?* Please let this be the end of the bullshit for awhile.

"Let's go. Simerra, you're in front with Mark, Devin, Zane and me," Mother ordered.

A lone man on the hill watched as we piled in. I kept an eye on the mirror. He grew smaller and smaller as we drove off, and then we took a turn and he was gone.

Chapter Nine

DEEP BREATHS

C W: DEATH

"Is anyone following us?" Mother asked.

"Not that I can see." I leaned back and forth to check the full scope of the mirror.

"This is a bad idea," Mark said.

I rolled my eyes. It was easy to talk big when the whole group wasn't watching, wasn't it, Mark?

"How far do we follow this road for?" I asked.

"We'll change course before dark."

"We may want to take a less direct path," Mother commented.

"I don't know that path as well. This is a lot of trouble for more strays," Mark muttered.

His knuckles were white as they clutched the steering wheel. *Okay, drama king. I didn't add fifty people. It was three small children in need of aid. Have some compassion.*

"How could you say something like that about kids? The fuck did you think about Daisy and me when you found us?" Devin interrogated.

Mark's eyes were fixed on the path ahead. The monotonous hum of the engine filled the cab. For how quiet this machine was, it was exceptionally fast, faster than I remembered any vehicle being. Greenery blurred past like a messy oil painting, each out of focus object blending into the next. Mark punched the gas harder, and we jerked forward from the force.

"There's something behind us," Mother warned.

The engine roared as he pushed us faster. In the rearview mirror, a small speck behind us glinted in the sun. I kept my eyes locked on it in the hopes of discerning anything substantial about it.

"How long has it been since we started driving?" I questioned.

"Long enough for them to reorganize. I told you about this being a bad idea?"

"That won't help us now. Focus on driving," Mother critiqued.

Devin, Zane, and I exchanged a look. Zane nodded and Devin gave me a thumbs-up. If this came to a fight, we were the most accessible and we were ready. It was in focus now. It was sleeker than the one we were in. We couldn't outrun this thing. Their engine revved, and they were practically alongside us. They waved their guns wildly in warning. Zane pulled Devin back against the seat.

"They have guns. Lean back," I filled Mother in as I rushed to follow my own instructions.

"Hang on tight." Mark rammed into the other vehicle. We were thrown into each other. My skin was touching the others'. I didn't breathe. I focused everything I had on not glowing, not hurting them. I squirmed back to my side of the seat, but the other vehicle rammed us back. This time, everyone slammed on top of me.

"It's okay, Simerra. Stay calm. You can do this," Zane said.

I locked my joints in place and held my glow in a death grip near my heart. One by one, they moved over. At least they were all still breathing. The military vehicle pulled ahead of us and stopped hard. Mark slammed on the brakes to avoid destroying our only chance at getting away. Soldiers poured out and surrounded our vehicle. They were armed to the teeth. This was bad. *Come on, Simerra. Think of something or you're all going to die. Oh wait. I mean, if death is a possibility anyway.* I jumped out into the sunlight. The soldiers smirked at me. A few even laughed. If I were them, one person wouldn't have looked intimidating to me either. Mother had said to protect the group from threats. These soldiers certainly counted. I adjusted so my feet were shoulder width apart like Nash had shown me. The most important thing right now was to breathe. I took my gloves off in preparation.

"Come on, little girl. There has to be someone older for us to talk to."

Their weapons dropped to point at the ground. My glow pulsed against me, listening. Nash had said the first time hurt the most. Here was to hoping she was right.

"Weren't you ever told not to underestimate a lady?"

The cold of my glow pulsed through and around me. The men dropped like flies. A few ripped open their shirts in a desperate plea for relief. The door to our truck slammed shut. Good, my family would be safer from me. One by one, the men went limp. Not so tough without oxygen, were they? One of them raised a gun with shaky hands. I pulled the air out of his very cells. He convulsed on the ground like a fish before the after claimed him. The air hung still with the weight of fresh death.

My glow snapped back to my core like a ripped rubber band. My knees gave way. The hot pavement bit into my palms, and blood jumped to the scrapes. Were they dead? I looked up through a curtain of braids to see them all still contorted upon themselves. Not a single one moved. I dropped my head back to the ground. We were safe.

Boots smacked against the ground. Nash came into view, her face lit by the sun behind her. She looked ethereal.

"What the fuck happened? Are you okay?" Nash's hand was featherlight against my back. I leaned into her touch, not caring who saw.

"Careful." Zane jumped out of the truck.

"Fuck your careful. She needs help," Nash spat.

Nash slung my arm around her shoulder and lifted me. Zane whistled. I raised my head. I wanted to tell them not to fight but I couldn't manage it.

"Don't push yourself." Her eyes softened as she looked over at me.

"You really shouldn't touch her."

"Fuck off. She's riding in the back with me."

"She rides up front," Mother called down to us.

Nash swore under her breath.

"It's fine," I mumbled.

"It's not fine. Let me at least help you there."

Nash and Zane worked together to lift me into the truck. I flopped back against the seat, grateful for the warm seat against my cool skin. I needed to learn to tone this down before it killed me.

"I'll see you when we stop for the night." Nash slid my gloves back on.

She squeezed my hand and electricity shot through me, not far off from how glowing made me feel. I tried to smile but only managed a grimace. She squeezed my hand one more time before she disappeared into the belly of the truck, then we were off. My body was still tingling from where Nash had held me. My head rocked back and forth against the window with the movements of the truck. Sometimes, there were old structures wrapped with climbing ivy. Hulls of history turned into luxury bird nests. The gaps in between were full of large trees and wildflowers scattered at the roadside unbothered by humans. The hum of the engine lulled me to sleep.

The late afternoon sunshine or Mark's sharp turn awoke me with a jolt. My muscles ached terribly, and my head throbbed. I stretched as much as the cab would allow, but it didn't do much.

"How do you feel?" Mother asked.

"I'm okay," I lied.

"How do you really feel?" Zane pressed when Mother turned away.

"I can move, but I wouldn't mind a weeklong nap either."

He smiled weakly. Did I look that bad or was it my corpse count? Relief at our safety coursed through me, and it was only marred by a fraction of the guilt I'd felt last time.

"You did a lot today," Devin commented.

"It was easy," I muttered.

"So, you aren't upset?" Zane asked.

I shook my head. Bad idea. It throbbed horribly in protest. How long was this going to last?

"I am, but it was easy. My glow—" I dropped off, unsure of how it would sound if I said it felt natural, and powerful, and like I wasn't hiding from myself. No, I couldn't say that to them.

"When you use it fully, you have to be careful. Just say the word and I'll help. I'll drop it for now."

He stared out the windshield as the sun sunk lower and lower in the sky. What kind of help could he give me? He had such a good grasp on his, and mine killed people. Mother's missing pinky flashed through my mind. Any practice needed to be done alone and away from people.

· · · ● · ● · ● · ·

"How are you?" Nash asked when we finally ditched the truck in the underbrush.

I shrugged.

"Where are we?" Daisy questioned.

"There's an old grocery supercenter about a mile from here. We're going to stay there tonight," Mother informed her.

Hopeful mutterings moved through the group. Nash stayed tight to my side. The mile was an eternity with my heavy limbs, but I tried my best to look okay each time Nash glanced my way. Nessa led our way into the store and through the isles, looking for food. Her bright glow illuminated the labels in the crevices of the deep shelves. We ate canned sausages and sweet corn. An air of calm settled over the group. Devin and Zane swapped stories with the others. Their shoulders brushed when they laughed or leaned in to hear better. Nash sat beside me.

"Whatcha thinkin about?" she asked.

"Nothing."

"Something's on your mind."

"I got to let my glow out unrestricted to keep us safe and I don't regret it. I felt free."

"Did you tell your brother that?"

"I told him it was easy," I mumbled.

"It's easy for me too. I was trained to kill efficiently. I barely get upset afterward anymore."

She took my hand in hers loosely and waited, but I didn't pull away. She would tell me if I hurt her, right? I ran my gloved fingers over her knuckles. I wanted nothing more than to live in this moment, close to her.

"Why aren't you scared of me?" I asked.

"You're normal. Nothing evil about it. Death is hard to deal with, but killing people is simple. You've done hard things for the right reasons, and we would all be dead if you hadn't acted."

She squeezed my hand gently before letting go. I missed the contact already.

"Want to pair up? We're supposed to share beds and all." I ducked my head to hide my blush.

"I was going to share with Echo."

"Maybe we can get one of the bigger ones and share?"

Nash laughed. Was I too eager?

"Let's get settled then. I think they're going to call 'lights out' soon."

I followed behind her on my tiptoes to a large bed. I wrapped myself in my sleeping bag so I wouldn't brush against her and carefully lay on my side. Knowing she was so close had my heart thrumming with excitement so despite my exhaustion, I was up for a long time before sleep managed to nab me.

CHAPTER TEN

ECHO

C^{W: ATTEMPTED MURDER}

During the day, I spent my time with the others: walking, hunting, mending, and trying to stay out of the way. And at night, I trained with Nash under a canopy of trees speckled by stars. This routine was comfortable after so many nights. I'd grown used to the ache in my muscles. I liked any opportunity to be close with her, even if she was punching at my weak points.

"You need to block and stay focused," she reminded me as she got in a hit on my side.

"Are you always this tough when you teach?"

"Only with those I care about."

I swung at her shoulder and she blocked it easily. *Oh, come on.* My arm swung through the empty space she'd already vacated. Wait, she cared about me? She kicked me in the back of the knees, and I toppled to the ground.

"Stay focused."

The night wore on and no matter what I tried, she dodged me at every turn. She dropped to the ground and swept my feet from underneath me. I landed with a hard thunk. That was going to bruise by morning. She helped me off the ground.

"Small improvements lead to big changes. Let's call it a night. You're working really hard."

"Thanks. I'm exhausted."

"I can tell." She laughed.

I wiped the sweat from my brow. Her breathing was even despite teaching me. Was I really that out of shape even with all the walking?

"Do you really care about me?"

I shouldn't have let hope worm its way in, but I cared about her so deeply, it made my bones ache. She unwrapped the T-shirts from her hands, carefully folding them and arranging them in the bag she had with her without looking up.

"I care about you too much."

How could you care about someone too much? Couldn't you stop and care about them less so it was the right amount? What did that even mean? *Focus, Simerra.* What mattered was that she cared about me and that made me vibrate with joy. If she was being honest, then so should I.

"I care about you too."

A flash of hope darted through her eyes. She moved closer. We were barely a foot apart. I longed to hold her hand and reassure her that I meant every word.

"If we were normal, I would have met you at school or when I was going to the mall or something."

"What would we be doing?"

The moonlight highlighted the flecks of gold and silver in her hair. The soft light exemplified how breathtaking she was. I worked to keep my breathing even. If I wanted to be this close, I had to be focused. How did she always get me so flustered?

"We would be holding hands." Her fingers brushed the back of my hand and I jerked it away.

"It's not safe."

"I held it before."

"That was different. I was exhausted."

"You said you're tired."

"My glow was tired last time," I corrected.

"What are you afraid of?" she whispered.

The gentle rise and fall of her chest brushed against mine. I longed to hold her even though I knew it would spell catastrophe for both of us.

"I don't want to hurt you."

"I know you can do this. Trust me."

She brushed the back of my hand, and this time I moved it into her searching fingertips. She interlaced our fingers, squeezing tightly. I waited for her to pull back or scream, but neither happened. A smile spread across my face. We were holding hands and I wasn't hurting her. Electricity raced up my arm and down through the rest of my body. For the first time in years, I felt warm.

"Are you worried?" I asked.

I wanted to stay like this with her, and that meant avoiding camp for a little while. There was nothing more I wanted than to listen to her talk and feel her close.

"What about?" she asked.

"Being followed."

"I'm worried about what will happen if they catch up to us, but I'm more worried about what happens to people like us if we don't fight. With you on our side, we've got a real chance."

"The caregivers will find somewhere we can settle safely. We have to be patient."

"I sure fucking hope so." She dropped my hand to move hers through her hair. "We should get back."

I shoved my hands into my pockets. I should have picked a better topic. Of course she was worried about the people following us. What had I been thinking? When we got to camp, she went into the tent, out of sight. Zane crashed down beside me, and I nearly jumped out of my skin.

"What was that about?" He poked me.

"Cut it out. We were training."

"Sure you were. What's going on between you two?"

"Nothing." I fiddled with my shirt.

"Spit it out. Let your twin bless you with wisdom." He placed his hand over his heart.

I shoved him over. I would be better off asking a tree for advice than him, but he did have a Devin so like, maybe he wasn't totally clueless. I searched for the right comforting phrase. Why could I never pull my words together in time? My shoulders slumped.

"How do you always know what to say?"

"I don't."

I narrowed my eyes.

"I wasn't finished. I never know if I'm saying the right thing, but when I'm talking to Devin, my goal is always to support him. If I'm not sure if I'm conveying it clearly, I always tell him, 'Hey, I'm here for you.' He knows that sometimes I'm going to mess up and say the wrong thing, but that's okay as long as we talk about it. Does that make sense?"

"It does. I need to go talk to Nash."

"You can do it." He gave me a double thumbs-up as I walked over to the tent.

"Simerra, you have a watch tonight."

"Yes, Mother."

Nash was curled up with her back turned to me. I knelt beside her.

"Nash."

I pulled at the topmost blanket. It fell to the ground in a heap. She was crying. I reached out before I caught myself. I pulled my hand back before I could hurt her. I tapped my fingers. Long to short. Short to long. I needed a clear head so I didn't mess up again.

"I'm sorry I hurt you. My topic choice was careless. You mean a lot to me. I was trying to keep the conversation going and I fucked up. I'm really sorry."

"You could say that again. My family gave me to soldiers like the ones looking for us. You think I can trust these adults to give two shits about the new girl?"

"I'm sorry. I know you're scared. I'm scared too. There are people actively chasing us, and the only idea I have is to follow the caregivers right now. It'll get us away from the soldiers and that's a start. I know I'm not good at this. Zane is much better with words and people, but I'm going to do everything I can to make sure you know I'm here for you and I'm going to keep you safe. If I mess up again, we can talk about it and I will fix it because I hate knowing I'm the reason you're crying. I'm here if you need to vent or if there's anything else I can do to help."

Her tears slowed. That was a good sign, right? She held out her hand, and I grabbed it. I slammed my glow as far down as possible. She needed me, and I was going to be there for her.

"Let's not talk about the future for now," she suggested.

"If that's what you want."

She nodded.

"Then that's what we'll do. I have watch tonight, but I'll be back right after."

"Be careful."

"Rest well."

I faced the way we'd come. If there was going to be trouble, it would be from that direction. I tried to focus on my watch, but my mind kept running back to our conversation. She was right. We'd been made to wander all this time without a real plan and I'd just gone along with it. What was the point? I yawned. My eyelids drooped no matter how hard I tried to stay awake.

An arm snaked its way around my throat. I ripped at it desperately. This had to be a dream. What were they doing? I opened my mouth to scream and warn the others, but a hand clamped over my mouth. I rammed my elbow into their side.

"Hold still, you little brat," Mark said.

Why the fuck was he trying to kill me? He'd been hostile, but this? I writhed in his grip. My glow coiled inside me, allowing oxygen to find a way into my closed off airway. There was still the problem that someone was trying to fucking kill me. I jerked forward, trying to flip Mark over my shoulder the way Nash had shown me, but instead we landed on our sides, still struggling. I kicked at the earth, searching for purchase so that I could use some kind of force.

"Mark, what's going on?" Mother asked him from somewhere behind us. His grip loosened as his focus waned. I took my chance.

"He's trying to kill me. Run," I screeched.

"Let my daughter go."

Her cane thwacked against his back over and over again. Mark recoiled, needing his arms to defend himself from her onslaught. The fresh night air found its way to my lungs. Mark wrapped his hands around Mother's throat and squeezed. She yelped and struggled against his stubborn grip.

"Let my mother go!"

I ripped my glove off and lunged, off balance and uncaring. My glow rose to meet my force. I wanted it to hurt. I wanted him to hurt. I punched him full across the face, allowing my glow to push itself into his very core. He clutched at his chest and fell to the ground. *Good.* That was where a dog like him belonged. He was not going to hurt either of us again. Someone grabbed my wrist.

"Don't touch her!" Zane warned.

If it wasn't him, then who was touching me? I spun and gave them the same treatment I had given Mark without a second thought. Echo convulsed on the ground. Fear played across his face. I took a step back. *No! Why hadn't he listened to Zane? I didn't want him to hurt. Shit, shit, shit.* I pulled my glow back as fast as I could. So what if Mark got up again. I needed to save Echo. How did I save Nash last time? Nash fell to her knees at his side, clutching his hand. When had she gotten here?

"What did you do to him? You're going to be okay, Echo. Just try to breathe." Panic colored her voice.

His eyes rolled back. The white of his eyes were on full display. I had a sinking feeling in the pit of my stomach.

"Somebody, help. Stop using your glow! Can't you see he's hurting?" she begged. Tears smattered her cheeks.

"I swear I'm not doing anything." I turned my palms towards the earth.

I wished I was doing something, then I could fix this, but my glow was tucked near my heart. All of this was after effects.

"You did this! Help him! Fix this!" she demanded.

Rage burned in her eyes. I recoiled. She'd never been this angry with me, and I'd never felt this powerless. I twisted my hands over top of each other. There was no good way to say this.

"I-I don't know what to do."

"He's dying. Save him. You saved me: now save him."

Large, broken sobs ripped their way out of her chest as she held his hand. His eyes had a faraway, glossy look to them. I didn't know how to tell her he was gone. She'd been gone when I'd brought her back too. I had to try. This was my fault. Please let my good intentions be enough to help him. I pushed my glow into his chest, but I couldn't feel a heartbeat even after I added compressions. His chest rose and fell with the entrance and exit of air but never with life. His hand lay against the muddy browns and greens of the ground without so much as a twitch. I kept at it. His chest rose and fell without response from his heart. The cold of Zane's worry seeped into me, but I didn't stop. I had to keep trying.

"An air bubble must have gotten into a major organ," Zane commented.

"I don't care what happened. She has to fix it." Nash's voice cracked over the words.

"She can't fix that kind of damage."

"I don't care!"

"Do you want her to die?" Zane roared back.

I worked to bring her friend back. This was the one person she trusted, and I couldn't take him away from her. So I kept going even as my vision began to blur and my own breathing hitched.

"I can't lose you both. Just stop. He's gone."

She flung herself into my lap, and I collapsed on top of her. We lay there, too tired to move, the three of us in a pile: Nash distraught, me exhausted, and Echo gone.

BURY YOUR DEAD

C

I awoke the next morning still in the same pile. Nash's breathing was slow and even. She was stretched out beside Echo and me. Echo. I took in the corpse beside me. The corpse I was responsible for. What had I done? People were going about their day. Some were eating, others tending the fire or the children, but it was quieter than normal. Was that for us? Was it because they were more scared of me than before? My heart sank further. Mark's body was a stone's throw away. I had to kill him. He would have killed me and my mother. Zane looked on from a few feet away. His face was a mixture of sadness and undeserved pity.

"I'm glad you're awake. The sun's going down."

My head jerked up. Was he serious? Had I really been unconscious that whole time?

"How's Nash?"

"She got up to get water then came right back. How are you? I thought we were going to lose you too."

"I feel like shit, but I'm physically okay." Mentally was a different story.

Nash sat up. Her eyes were red and her hair stuck out in odd bits. She walked away without a word.

"What's wrong with me?"

"It was an accident. Don't give me that. I mean it."

"He was her best friend, Zane. He was our friend." I put my head in my hands.

"What happened last night?"

"Mark tried to kill me."

"Of course the bastard did. Fuck him."

"I thought Echo was another attacker. It all happened so fast."

"He shouldn't have touched you. Everyone knows you can't do touch."

Did they? Nash and I had held hands right beforehand. Everyone was right to be scared of me.

"Echo deserves to be buried."

"We don't have time for that. You know we're being followed."

"This is worth it."

I walked away and grabbed Echo's clean clothes in the tent. Tears streamed down my face. No one in camp would look at me, but that didn't matter. It felt wrong to touch his corpse. Hadn't people used to pray or something when someone died? My father used to bow his head when he did that kind of thing. I bowed my head and smashed my eyes shut.

"I hope you find peace."

After a few minutes without any better words coming to mind, it was time to get him ready. He leaned against me while I worked his old shirt off. It was harder than it should have been, but it wasn't like his corpse could help me. I struggled to get his head and limbs through the appropriate holes of the new shirt, and the process was equally difficult for his lower half. Dirt was caked onto his exposed skin. Despite the dirt that was involved with burial, I wanted him to be presentable when Nash said her final goodbye.

Nash watched from nearby. I waited to see if she would say anything but was met with silence, so I continued on my way. A bucket full of river water balanced against my hip on the way back to Echo's side. The dirt and tear tracks on his face ran deep. He must have been so scared. A new wave of guilt crashed into me. This was the least I could do for him. In the half-light, it was easier to believe he was sleeping.

"He looks peaceful," Nash breathed.

I rested a shovel up against the tree in case she wanted to help. My muscles strained against the exercise, but I continued. Shovel after shovel of dirt was added to the pile from the widening hole. Once it was deep enough, I clambered out of the hole and into a crowd of people that wouldn't look at me.

"Can I get a hand?"

Devin stepped forward and together, we lowered Echo into the hole I'd made. He gave me a curt nod and returned to Zane's side. Their fingers interlaced.

"I'll miss you, you big idiot," Nash admitted softly to the body.

She shoveled the first pile of dirt onto his corpse. I picked up my own shovel and matched her pile for pile. The crowd remained through Nash's sobs. She sat beside the pile of earth like a living grave marker.

"He thought that you had to be watched over when you died in order to cross over fully," Nash said.

"Hey, Simerra," Devin called.

I froze. Was this when he was going to yell at me? I balanced the shovels on my shoulder and walked over.

"Can you help me bury Dad?"

Was this a test? I nodded slowly.

"Thanks. I don't want Daisy to see him above ground like that." He flashed me a picture-perfect smile. I couldn't wait till we were done moving dirt.

"I'm sorry for your loss," I consoled when we'd finished.

He waved me off. Was he too mad at me to accept my apology? He didn't look mad. Maybe he was in shock. This was a very sudden death.

"I'll go grab Daisy. Get ready," he warned.

There was no way to prepare for Daisy. She tried her hardest to hold it together, which only made it worse. Her bottom lip wiggled as she clutched Devin's hand. I wanted to apologize to her, but I didn't even know if she knew it was my fault so I bit my tongue.

"Goodbye, Dad." Her voice wavered.

"It's okay to cry. You loved him very much, and he looked after you. It's normal to be sad when you lose someone so special." I knelt before her.

"Are you s-sure?"

"Of course it is. I miss him too. Say good night," Devin encouraged.

"Goodnight forever, Dad." She waved at the grave the whole way back to camp. When everyone walked away I plopped down near where Nash kept watch. As the night continued, she told me stories about Echo. Her words memorialized him to the trees and our memories, giving him a new life of happy occasions he could exist in.

• • • • • • • • • •

The ache of the sleepless night weighed heavily on me as Nash and I returned to camp. Zane fell into step beside me. I gave him a weary smile. He tried to return it, but tension pulled at his jaw.

"Some people think these two deaths are proof that you're too unstable," Zane warned.

"He tried to kill me," I muttered, mortified.

"I know, but they don't care."

"That's bullshit. She's not dangerous," Nash argued.

"'We're all dangerous' is a better point. We all have powers we barely understand."

"What are they suggesting?"

"For you to be kicked out."

"They might as well kill her." Nash threw her hands up, disgust coating her features.

Zane's nostrils flared. Cold seeped out of him and filled the air with an icy chill.

"You think they didn't suggest that? I had to argue and plead for this to be an option," he hissed.

"I say we don't give them the chance," Nash countered, squaring her shoulders. "I say we leave."

"We'll never make it out there," Zane argued.

"We'll see about that. You can't be safe with people who want you dead," she reasoned.

"You think we can do this?" I asked.

"Think of it as an old-school rebellion. They treat y'all like trash and it's not right. This is just the biggest offense I've seen, and I'm sure other people our age will come with us if you encourage them too."

Nash took my hand in hers, and the familiar warmth spread through me. I would follow her almost anywhere.

"We should try to convince them now before the day's travel starts," I said.

We wove our way to where Mother usually stood to make announcements. My heart pounded against my chest. A few people stopped to see what was happening, but most continued with their tasks.

"You've got this," Nash encouraged.

I took a deep breath. If Mother could address the group, then so could I.

"I think it's my turn to speak," I said.

"What are you doing, Simerra?" Mother questioned.

"Many of you think the solution to another glow-related accident is my death. Is this the same fate you would assign any of us, or am I special?"

The glow wielders looked to their caretakers with shifting eyes. Disdain dripped from the condemning looks the caregivers threw my way. What, were they going to kill me? This was about their charges, my friends.

"You killed people," Kate's mom said, her talons digging into Kate's shoulder.

"You never trained me to use my glow safely, and I would argue you don't know how."

Nash squeezed my hand and Devin nodded along, but Zane looked like he was about to have a heart attack. The others seemed more unsure of their stance, but they were still listening. Their eyes darted between me and their caregivers. I could do this.

"You treat us like tools that can complete convenient tasks for you. We support each other more than you ever support us. Earlier this week, we showed that we can work together and keep each other safe," I reminded them.

"What would you have us do? Run headfirst into danger? What good does that do us?" Kate's mom asked.

"Not everything has to be about personal gain. Helping others has more merit than being selfish, and there are kids out there, like our new arrivals, who need support. The adults have shown us they're only in it for whatever keeps them safe. What does that say about why they took us in?" I tapped my fingers together. Long to short. Short to long. *Just gotta keep talking and avoid eye contact. I could do this.* I should have asked Nash to speak, but she was right. They wouldn't follow her. Not with her being so new. It was on me.

Fear flashed through a few adults' eyes as the twenty-somethings whispered to each other.

"You can't really believe her. She's just trying to save her own ass," Kate's mom reasoned.

"Why did you take me in, Mom?" Kate asked.

"I saw a child in need. You needed me as much as I needed you."

"What the fuck does that even mean?" Kate snarled, pulling away.

Her mom retreated behind the other caregivers.

"Are you afraid of me? Are you using me? Answer me!" Kate's voice rose as she spoke.

"Come to think of it, when was the last time our parents had to do recon or stand on the outside of the group?" Devin mused.

"We use the formations that keep us the safest," Mother said.

"Keeps who safest?" Joey asked.

"That's my point. They do whatever they want with us and we're supposed to follow along," I said.

"You're kids. What do you *expect*?"

"Shut up, Mom." Kate glowered.

"We could help people. We could make it so there is hope for people like us, a real home. No more running. No more hiding. No more deception. A real shot at figuring out how to use our glows. I'm leaving, and if what they're doing doesn't sit well with you, then you should come too."

Please don't let me sound like an idiot.

"I'm going," Zane said.

"Us to." Devin stepped forward, holding Daisy's hand.

A few others agreed, Kate among them, but everyone else remained silent. That was enough attention for one day. I jumped off my rock and flapped the anxiety away. This was a good day, but it was also a stressful one.

"Are you sure about this?" Tears made their way down Mother's bruised face and neck.

For a moment, I regretted my decision. She'd tried to protect us, but this group and her methods were no longer the safety net I thought them to be in childhood.

She shut her eyes and took a ragged breath. I hadn't realized how much this was going to hurt both of us. She was the only family I still had outside of Zane, but I still had to leave.

"We'll keep the newer children and get them to the town. Here's a map if you all change your mind. This place is supposed to be well protected and still safe. They may not have space for a large group, but it's worth a shot. I know I wasn't the best mother, but you're still my daughter." She wrapped me in a hug.

It was the first time she had hugged me since I'd brought the sickness home to our family. I had longed for contact all these years, but now it felt forced. When she released me, I busied myself with our now smaller group's packing needs. We were ready before the caregivers and didn't wait for them.

Daisy skipped ahead in triplicate, excited no one was stopping her. Zane tucked a flower behind Devin's ear, chatting about what we should hunt for dinner. Nessa kept an eye on Daisy so that she wouldn't wander off too far. Joey cracked jokes. And Kate was with us, bringing up the rear. Maybe our rebellious phase was bigger than those of kids from before, but the results were the same. For the first time in our lives, we were free. Well, as free as we could be in a country like ours.

Chapter Twelve

NASH

C"Where are we going?" Kate asked.

The others looked at me expectantly. Why was I the first one they looked to? Kate threw her head back and groaned.

"You don't even know," she lamented.

"I think the focus was more on the away part," Joey said, rubbing small circles on the back of her hand.

"We could go back to that store we hit and regroup. I know we didn't take everything, and there were beds there," Nash suggested.

"And if there are soldiers there waiting for us?" Zane pinched the bridge of his nose.

"Then we fight," I asserted.

Come on, Simerra. Sound like you know what you're talking about. Sound confident.

"It's the best plan we have. We can look for a map of the area there and figure out which direction to go next."

I walked through them and back towards the road. After a heavy pause, other pairs of feet moved to follow me. I smiled triumphantly and a slight bounce made its way into my step. It took most of the day to wind our way back towards the store. When we drew close, Devin grabbed ahold of Daisy and a hush fell over the group. I couldn't see anyone, but that didn't mean they weren't there. Everyone looked at me. I made one speech. How did that qualify me to lead our entire group for the rest of forever?

"Devin, you have the best chance of being undetected. Please check the store. If you find anything suspicious, come back and we'll deal with it together."

He gave a sloppy salute and headed off. This was too much authority for me. I fiddled with my hands the entire time he was gone. What if he got hurt? I shouldn't have sent him in alone. I could have gone with him. I could have gone alone. I was still worrying when he returned without a scratch.

"I don't think the soldiers realized we were here. Everything is how we left it."

"We should get inside quickly," I muttered.

I had been talking to myself, but here they were, agreeing with me. I was not used to this. I strode into the store and the others followed. They threw furtive glances over their shoulders to double-check for danger. Once the door was shut, everyone relaxed.

"Home, sweet home." Devin's arms spread wide.

I could feel their eyes on me once more.

"Home for now," I allowed.

Whooping and hollering echoed off the store walls. We had made our first camp. The others made their way to where we'd clustered the beds, and I scavenged the aisles for supplies. I passed over the old music players and phones that no longer worked for batteries and flashlights.

I wiped a mountain of dust off the items, dumping them into the small handbasket I had acquired on my way here. Nessa eyed the pile in disdain.

"Sometimes, you need a break. They're not you, but they work fine in a pinch."

She shrugged, turning back to her conversation. I looked around for Nash, but she wasn't with the others. There was a figure sitting on the farthest bed. Was that the one we'd slept on last time with Echo? I sat down opposite her quietly. The slight shaking of her shoulders was the only indication that something was wrong.

"Go away," she said through clenched teeth.

Shock froze me in my spot on the bed.

"Next time, I scream it."

I lurched to my feet and went back over to the others, dejected. A hush fell over the group.

"We should eat. Nessa, mind leading the way?" I offered weakly.

She obliged. We wound our way through the shelves, guided by her light. I could get used to this kind of hunting, even with all the spiders.

"Success!" Devin held two boxes of snack cakes over his head.

I set a can and a spoon over by the bed where Nash still sat. I left without awaiting a response. I wasn't who she needed right now. I was the only reason he wasn't here. Nessa was the last to go to bed. Exhausted as I was, I didn't lie down. If they were all going to look to me, then it was my job to take watch. I turned my flashlight to avoid attention and faced the doors. I turned on the light only to wake myself back up or to check on an odd sound. It was always a mouse scuttling across the floor. With the light returned the sound of footsteps. Nash's bed sat empty in the back corner. Whatever she was doing was none of my business. Maybe a walk would help her process everything. I stretched, but the hard floor was wearing on me. Devin tugged on my sleeve, and I nearly jumped out of my skin.

"I didn't mean to startle you. I'm up for the day. You should get some rest."

"Are you sure?"

"Yeah, you look like shit." He grinned.

Something clattered across the floor in the distance. Nash was more careful than that. I rose to my feet. The hair on the back of my neck rose as I did. The sound of distant footsteps continued. I looked around, spotting Daisy on a mattress only a few paces off.

"Get Daisy," I breathed. I crossed the room to Joey's bed as quietly as I could and set a hand on his shoulder. Joey jerked awake.

"What the fuck was that for?" he projected into my mind.

"Someone's here. Wake the others," I thought back.

His eyes went wide, but he did what I asked. They scrambled to surround Daisy, bleary-eyed and scared. Devin held a finger to his lips to answer Daisy's questioning gaze. She held her doll tight to her chest. Nash came up beside me, avoiding my gaze. At least I knew she wasn't out in the store, dealing with whomever this was alone. The footsteps grew closer, and they were all around us. How the fuck had I not heard them earlier? The temperature dropped as Zane reached for his glow.

"I wouldn't move if I were you," a soldier said.

Nash's joints locked up. Did she know him? More soldiers emerged with raised guns. How was it that we'd been away from the adults for a single day and I'd already gotten us all captured?

"Fuck you," Nash swore from the back of the group.

He clicked his tongue, looking her up and down. I stopped myself from blocking his view. For now, we had to hold still like he asked. We were too outnumbered.

"You look like shit," he criticized.

"I'm still the one that found a group of kids, ass hat," Nash shot back.

The man's face broke into a grin. Nash fell in with the others. Pain rippled through me. She said she was worried about my safety. She acted like she cared and I'd eaten it up. Angry tears spilled from my eyes. How could she do this to us?

"You did well. They didn't suspect a damn thing." He chuckled.

"We trusted you," Kate screeched.

"That's not my problem."

"Quiet, Nash. I don't need them riled up. That's for the training room. Now, where's that fool of yours hiding?"

"He died undercover."

"Shame. That little glow of his could have been useful. It's been a long time since we got a group all in one piece. The director's going to be happy tonight. I suggest you all do as I say."

Kate spat at him, a scowl contorting her features. She cried out as he lifted her off the ground by her hair. He threw her into Devin. Daisy wiped a tear from her face as they clambered to their feet.

"You're a bad man." Daisy stared down our captor.

"You don't know the half of it. Nash, with me." He bared his teeth in a feral smile. The man turned on his heel and disappeared into the shadows. Nash walked away and my heart went with her. They herded us towards the doors with threats and jabs from their rifles. Daisy tripped once and she was scooped into Devin's arms a moment later. He glared at anyone who looked her way until the truck door shut with a thud.

"And you want to help more people like that?" Kate asked.

"I never want anyone to go through this again," I whispered.

"Your little girlfriend doesn't seem to mind."

"She's not my girlfriend."

"If I'd known what kind of mess you'd drag me into, I would have stayed back at camp."

"You're not helping," Zane said.

"We're in the back of a truck. What do you think they're going to do when they figure out what our glows are?"

The memory of culling day swirled in my thoughts. The smell of charred flesh attacked my nose as if I were still there.

"Our best bet is to pretend we have weak glows and keep our heads down. I'm as shocked as you are." I fiddled with the hem of my shirt, in need of something to do with my hands.

"You're unbelievable." Kate kicked at the wall of the truck.

"We were eventually going to need to get to the compound to get people out anyway. Just think of it as a V.I.P. ride," I suggested.

"I don't want to be a V.I.P," Daisy lamented, clutching Devin's shirt.

"We're going to keep you safe. Stay close to one of us and we'll protect you, just like always," Devin said, hugging her tight.

She was too young for all this. We allowed silence to fill the truck, not wanting to worry Daisy any further. Soon enough, the truck started and we moved off to our new home.

Chapter Thirteen

BEHIND ENEMY LINES

C w: ABUSE, SEXUAL HARASSMENT, electroshock therapy

They filed us out of the truck and towards the facility Devin and I had broken Nash out of. Was she ever in danger that day, or was that a lie too? It wasn't like I could ask her. She was probably in her room, relaxing after a job well done. Was she ever honest with me about this place? A woman in short heels and a red dress smiled brightly at us as we filed in through the door. Her sandy-colored hair was stacked upon her head in a perfect bun, not a single hair out of place. Her brown eyes were hard even as she smiled at us.

"Good afternoon. It's so good to see more brave children to help the cause. Your country thanks you for all you are about to give. We know it won't be easy, but you can do it. Follow the rules and you'll be an asset to your nation in no time."

Her chipper tone wore on my ears. Would she always be like this?

"All personal items must be relinquished. We can't have you distracted by pesky reminders of the outside. Quickly please."

A hard edge entered her tone and the soldiers crept closer. We emptied our pockets. Small stones and other items clattered into a haphazard pile.

"Thank you. Now, remove your clothes."

She couldn't be serious. The others were equally confused. She gestured for us to hurry up. We had to play along for now. I was keenly aware of the onlooking soldiers as I removed my shirt. I swallowed back the bile that rose in my throat before I slid out of my pants. The others followed suit. We stood before her bare and shivering. This was probably one of the last places with AC and I hated it.

"That wasn't so hard, was it?"

She was met with silence, but she didn't seem to mind.

"On to the showers. Girls on the left and boys on the right. Choose wisely. That's how your rooms will be sorted." I locked eyes with Devin and nodded. As we walked to the showers, Daisy ran over to me. Zane hesitated in front of the guys' shower. I offered him a small smile. He returned it and disappeared. We could do this. Daisy clutched at my arm hard enough to leave marks. My glow was oddly quiet and I was grateful for it. She needed the reminder that I was here. The water was frigid, but that wasn't anything new for us. We returned to the main room shivering. The soldiers didn't try to hide their predatory gazes. I hide Daisy behind me. If they wanted to look, it would be at *me*, not a child.

"Good. Let's get you settled."

"What is this place?" Daisy peeked around my arm at her.

"Don't speak unless spoken to." She gestured to one of the soldiers who in turn reached for Daisy.

"Leave her alone," Devin yelled.

He raised the butt of his gun to smack her. I pulled her further behind me. No fucking way.

"Please, she's just a kid. Hit me," I offered.

"Bravery will get you nowhere fast," she sing-songed.

The man slammed the gun into my head.

"Again, Shane. She also spoke out."

I curled up on the ground and held my breath. The weapon cracked down on me again. My head slammed into the ground. My glow tried to jump to my defense, but I held it tighter than I had ever held it. If I lost it now, I would be dead and so would my friends. It fought against me but ultimately settled into an upset pulse in my chest. I stood on shaky legs. The world spun around me as I pulled Daisy close again.

"You're a dramatic little thing. Follow me." She spun around. The clack of her shoes echoed off the walls.

Zane locked eyes with me to check in. I shrugged slightly. Worry still burned in his eyes, but there was nothing I could say to comfort him here. Single file, we were guided through the building. It looked like the old schools we'd attended. Was that what this place started as? A shiver rattled my bones. How long would they leave us naked like this? She pivoted to face us.

"Two of you will have to share a bed. We weren't expecting to recover so many today. You four through the first door and you three through the second one."

Devin hesitated before he walked out of sight. Daisy pulled against me, but it was futile. Nessa and Kate followed behind us. The soft smack of feet on tile echoed around us. A lock clicked behind us. I let out a long sigh, but none of my tension went with it. Kate sat on the closest bed and lifted the blue cloth folded there. Weird, it was the same shade as the strange bird's underwing.

"Is this supposed to be clothes?" Her nose crinkled in disgust.

"It's better than freezing. Put it on." I brought Daisy to the end bed.

I picked up the clothes and my heart sank. There was only one set. I held it up to Daisy's small form. This could work.

"You get to wear a dress while we're here," I whispered conspiratorially.

"Really?" She giggled, bouncing up and down.

I smiled back. She raised her arms over her head, waiting for the clothing. The fabric settled down past her knees. I pinched the excess between her shoulders and wracked my brain for solutions. Aha! I shook my braids free of my ponytail and used my hair tie to restrain the extra fabric. Pleased with myself, I pulled on the remaining pants and sports bra. Good enough. Daisy watched for my reaction to see how upset she should be about everything. I bowed as low as I could manage, using the time to ensure my glow would not surface while I distracted her.

"May I have this dance?" I offered a hand.

Laughing, she took it, and I twirled her around the room. I ignored the looks from the other two. Right now, we needed to keep Daisy as calm as possible. My head throbbed with the movement, but she laughed too much for me to care. When her chest heaved from the exertion, I guided her back to the bed. She plopped down, humming to herself.

"Now that you're done with that, what do we do?" Kate asked.

"They're probably watching us." Nessa inspected her fingernails, not even bothering to gauge my reaction.

"I wonder if your girlfriend is enjoying the view," Kate snarked.

Worry lines creased my forehead. We were stuck in here together, and there wasn't a special "Nash knows me" treatment to my knowledge. But hey, maybe I'd missed that during the welcome banquet. But

I couldn't say that. No, I was supposed to find solutions and I hated it.

"That's uncalled for," I said coolly.

"Are you sure about that? You're the one who brought her to the group and then killed her best friend. Damn it. Why did we follow you?" Her hands morphed into claws before they settled into fists.

"We are stuck here until we find a way out. When you have something to help that cause, I'd love to hear it. Until then, I'd appreciate it if you didn't worry Daisy or hurl accusations."

"You better fix this." She stalked away to her bed and faced the far wall.

That could have gone better. Back on my bed, Daisy practiced addition and played while we waited. I stretched out on the edge to allow her enough space. I yawned, still quizzing Daisy. I drifted off to sleep before she answered my last addition problem.

"Wake up, Simerra," Daisy urged.

I blinked rapidly to adjust to the harsh lights overhead. How long had I been out?

"What is it?"

"I'm hungry."

"Okay, I'll get you some food."

Kate was sitting up with her knees pulled to her chest, and Nessa was sound asleep. Daisy looked at me as if I could glow the food out of the air. I couldn't let her down. I stood, drawing Kate's eye.

"Anything happen while I was out?"

Kate shook her head and retrained her focus on the door.

They had to know we were hungry. I stared into the camera above the door. If they were watching us, then we could ask them for things.

"Stay there, honey, okay?"

Daisy nodded.

"Excuse me."

No reply.

"We haven't eaten since before we were brought here. We're hungry." I shifted my weight back and forth between each leg.

Still no reply.

I rapped my knuckles against the door. An electrical current pulsed through my body. I cradled my now numb arm and bit back curses Daisy was too little to hear.

"What happened?" Kate was by my side in an instant.

"The door is electrified," I said through gritted teeth, still reeling from the pain.

"Please stay away from the door," a robotic voice instructed.

"We're hungry, you assholes." Kate flipped off the camera.

"Daisy is right there." I smacked her arm down.

Kate's eyes went wide and she looked back at Daisy. She was still standing where I'd asked her to with her arms crossed over her chest.

"I'm not a baby. I've heard swears before." She stomped her foot for emphasis. Her chin jutted out.

"We know you're not, but that doesn't mean Kate should act like that."

Kate didn't argue. Had the stars aligned? I hadn't realized she knew how to do that. Daisy's sigh drew my attention once more.

"I'm really hungry," Daisy said to her toes.

My heart ached for her. She walked over to us and I pulled her to me, squeezing tightly. "I'll get you food, little one. Give me a minute to figure this out." *Come on, Simerra. Think. Use that big leader brain of yours.* Daisy craned her neck to see the camera clearly.

"Can we please get some food?"

The lock clicked and four trays were brought into the room. Soldiers placed them on the ground and backed out of the room with hands on their weapons. There were three identical trays with a hamburger, some mashed potatoes, and some corn. The fourth one had a sandwich, chips, and some kind of colored gummy thing. Fruit snacks maybe? Did places still make those?

"What is this thing?" Daisy held up the hamburger.

"Take a bite. It's good." I laughed.

Her eyes sparkled with wonder as she devoured it and everything else on her tray. I bit into the sandwich. It wasn't half bad. Kind of like cafeteria food. This tray was probably meant for Daisy, but I wasn't going to tell her that. I shook Nessa gently. She blinked up at me, confused.

"Please was the magic word." I set her tray down.

She stared at it, unmoving. That was fair. Someone had to be cautious of the kidnapper's mystery food. It should have been me, but I was too hungry to care. What a shit leader I was shaping up to be.

"We've all eaten. Being hungry won't do you any good here."

She picked up the burger and took a bite. I left her to her meal.

"Do you think the guys figured it out yet?"

Kate locked eyes with me, nodding slightly. Huh, so she'd been able to tell Joey. At least his glow could maintain one continuous bond. The lights clicked off. Daisy squealed and ran into my arms.

"Lights out at 10 p.m," the voice stated.

"We'll see about that," Nessa said.

"Nessa, no!"

My warning came too late. Her soft glow filled the room. Ice flooded my veins. A soldier with a cattle prod marched in and rammed it into her leg. She screamed, curling into herself. The soldier left, and it was silent once more. Daisy shook. Her breathing was shallow and fast. I fluttered my hands around her, wishing to comfort her but unable to be in contact. My nerves were fried.

"It's going to be okay, Daisy. There's nothing scary in the dark," I lied.

"But Nessa—"

"I'm fine, Daisy," Nessa said in a strained voice.

"Why did they hurt you?" Daisy wailed.

"It's okay, Daisy. We're going to be okay. No one else use their glow. We should go to bed before we get in trouble for that too," I said.

Daisy sniffled and cried softly as she clambered into bed. If I wasn't such an out-of-control monster, I would have been able to hug her. To play with her hair to reassure her. Fucking something. But no. I wasn't strong enough to be safe. I tucked Daisy under the blankets before I lay on top of them and tried to sleep through Nessa's muffled sobs. I would have to check in with her in the morning.

• • • ● • ● ● • • •

When I woke up, Daisy was already eating. I checked for injuries. Finding none, I sank to the ground beside her.

"I was hungry, so I asked the camera again," she said between bites of cereal.

"That was very clever of you. Breakfast time," I called to the others.

They grumbled about it being too early but trudged over. I rolled my eyes.

"We used to get up earlier than this all the time," I reminded them.

"There weren't beds all the time," Kate argued, rubbing sleep out of her eyes.

Nessa gave two exaggerated nods in agreement.

"It's not like we missed anything." Nessa gestured to the locked door.

"How are you doing?" I gave her a pointed look.

"I'm okay. It's just sore." Her hand covered the spot on her leg.

Daisy skipped around the room, singing to herself. At least she was able to keep busy.

"What do you think that was all about?" Nessa breathed, her eyes trained on Daisy.

"We can't use our glows outside of their training rooms."

"Did your girlfriend tell you that?" Kate shot back with a glare.

"It was Echo actually," I lied.

Why was I still protecting her? She was the reason we were here. If anything, I should want to get her in trouble. No, that may be who she was, but it wasn't who I was.

"How do we tell Daisy that?" Kate asked.

"Daisy? I need you to promise me you won't use your glow," I called over to Daisy.

She opened her mouth to argue with me.

"Do you remember how Nessa got hurt?"

I saw Nessa flinch out of the corner of my eye. I felt bad bringing it up, but we needed to keep Daisy safe. Hopefully, she wouldn't be too mad at me, but I'd always appreciated direct communication and explanations, especially when I was younger.

She snapped her mouth shut and nodded.

"The people here aren't nice. They don't like it when we use our glows unless they tell us to. We have to do what they say right now. They're in charge," I explained.

She stared at me, puzzled, but after a moment, her features smoothed out and she nodded. She skipped off to play once more.

"I didn't mean we should tell her right away," Kate whispered.

"You asked how we were going to tell her, so I did it."

They exchanged a glance. My stomach sank. I'd done something weird and abnormal. I was just trying to help. Why did allistics have so many unspoken rules? I answered the question by taking care of the problem. Why was that worthy of a shared look I wasn't meant to be included in but was definitely meant to see?

"What's our next move?" Kate asked.

"We could ask to come out." Daisy skipped past.

"Do we have any other ideas?" Nessa rubbed her leg.

"We can't stay in here forever." I pushed myself to my feet and faced the door.

"Are we going to ask them?" Daisy twisted from side to side, full of energy.

"We are."

I squared my shoulders. Kate and Nessa rose reluctantly and blocked Daisy from view. I took a deep breath, exhaling through my mouth, and my fingers tapped against each other.

"Please may we come out?"

Chapter Fourteen

MIND YOUR MANNERS

"Of course it wouldn't be that easy," Kate scoffed.

"Wait a second," I urged.

The lock clicked, and the door slid open. Nash was standing there. A sharp pain tore at my chest. She really was against us. Was that a new bruise on her cheek? What had they done to her? Rage quickly replaced my sorrow.

"She's waiting for you," Nash said.

Disdain practically radiated off Kate. Nash turned her back and walked out of sight. Today was going to suck.

"Where's Nash going?" Daisy tried to peer around me again.

"Tell the others," I breathed to Kate as we passed through the doorway.

Our soft footsteps echoed through the near empty hall. The floors sparkled as if they were cleaned daily. Who had the time for things like that while the world imploded around them? Nash stood beside the woman from yesterday. Goose bumps prickled to life on my arms as she surveyed us. She was as well dressed as the other day, with the same perfect hair and pristine outfit. She even had nail polish. When was the last time I'd seen someone wearing nail polish?

"Aren't you a bright bunch? That's one of the fastest times to date. Good job." She made a note on her clipboard.

Nash shifted her weight back and forth. Her eyes were glued to the floor. It wasn't like her. Then again, I hadn't thought betrayal was like her either. I shook the thought from my head and waited for the woman to continue, remembering all too well my lesson from last time.

"I think it's time to start your training, don't you?"

We nodded. I cast my eyes to the floor. People in power usually liked that. It made you look more obedient or something like that. Mark always liked it at least, and she seemed like the kind of person Mark would have befriended.

"Perfect. What can you do?" she asked, pen poised.

Was it in our best interests to tell her? Did we have a choice? Nash had said strong glows were in danger here. Had she already given Zane and I away? Was it worth risking a lie in the hopes that stuck better than whatever she'd told them already. Half-baked plans swirled around in my brain. I tapped my fingers together on repeat to better focus. Long to short. Short to long.

"Come on. The government needs your cooperation to grow our beautiful nation." She drew out the words like a poorly timed poem. It scratched against my ears.

We looked between each other, trying to decide who should go first. The discomfort hung heavy in the air. Fuck it. If I went first, at least we could gauge her response. Hopefully, I wasn't as bad a liar as Zane said I was.

"I can put out fires," I said.

It wasn't a lie. If there was any part of Nash that cared about me, she would let the half-truth go. Her face was still blank, so the woman wasn't annoyed by my answer. Maybe I was in the clear.

"Lovely, dear. Who's next?"

"I can move faster than your average person," Kate offered.

"So you're like Nash here, perfect."

Kate clenched her hands into fists but didn't hurl any insults. I was sure I'd hear all about how pissed off she was later, but at least for now, she was safe.

"I can glow," Nessa said.

"Yes, you all do. What is your specialty?" She laughed.

"I give off light." A bright red crept over Nessa's face and neck.

The woman clicked her tongue, scribbling a long note.

"What about you, little one?"

A deep sense of discomfort filled me at her attempt at sweetness. It was as if a poison apple had been dunked in sugar. I squeezed Daisy's shoulder and nodded for her to answer. She gulped.

"I can turn into a bunch of me." Her legs trembled, and I wanted nothing more than to pull her behind me out of sight.

"That's fantastic! Time to get you all into your training rooms."

A huge smile blossomed across her face at our tense little group. A wave of nausea rolled over me. What kind of person enjoyed this?

"You can't all train in the same room. You can help your country the best by training your individual specific skills. Oh, look who's joining us!" She opened her arms as if to embrace whoever it was. The boys made their way over cautiously. Zane had three new bruises and the other two looked exhausted. Had they slept at all? Daisy tried to go over to Devin, but I grabbed onto her dress. She hung her head in defeat. Her soft cries moved through the space. Devin looked devastated he couldn't hug her but was resigned to our current reality. *She's okay. She's okay,* I thought as hard as I could even though he couldn't hear me. *I promise. I'm going to keep her safe.*

"You'll have to excuse me. The guards will take you to the right rooms. You have a big day ahead of you."

"You heard her. Move," a soldier ordered, gun raised.

Go where? Kate pulled on my sleeve. There was a man over to the right. I needed to get a grip. We walked in silence through the halls and up a grand staircase. The ornate details wrapped all the way up the hand railing and continued on the walls. What a fancy place to train the will out of people.

"One of you in each room. Don't make me say it again."

His gun pointed at my chest. Fear filled Daisy's wide eyes. I smiled encouragingly and moved towards the first door. I waited for her to enter her room then entered my own. The lights reflected off the sterile white walls. I shielded my eyes from the sensory ick of this terribly bright room. There wasn't a lot of furniture or things on the walls to lessen the effect of the refracted light. So much for fancy. One of two chairs was occupied by a man in a lab coat who stared with unconcealed hunger. His eyes were a muddled hazel, and he kept his black hair pulled back into a short ponytail. He wasn't particularly interesting to look at, but he must have thought I was with the way he stared. It was like he wanted to devour me without even the courtesy of knowing my name. I folded my arms over my chest to block his gaze and stared back at his eyebrows to mimic eye contact until he averted his gaze. Good. I was more than a thing to consume. He fiddled with his clipboard before looking up again.

"My name is Doctor McCarthy. I will be helping you unlock your full potential during your time in the program. Before we get started, there is a short visual for you to watch."

The door opened and a single soldier slid in. He stood rigid against the wall. So, they didn't trust me after all. Smart of them. Dr. McCarthy turned his back to mess with the TV. Was I not seen as a threat here, or did he have full trust in a single soldier? This place was an infuriating mess of contradictions.

"This'll just take a second. The damn thing was working the other day."

I mean, it was on. I could hear it even if the screen was entirely black, that high-pitched hum that other people never seemed to notice. He smacked it and the entire machine rattled on its little trolley. An image popped onto the screen. He pushed play, returning to his chair and pulling out a phone. How many times had he seen this? How many people had he walked through this place since it opened?

"Welcome, newcomer! I bet you have a lot of questions about your new home. Why are you here? Why does your government need your help? Why can't you play all the time maybe? Don't worry, all of your questions will be answered if you stay focused."

A man in a black suit popped onto the camera and waved. He had slicked back blond hair and a thick mustache, and he was way too cheery about all of this. I fiddled with the edge of my shirt while he babbled on.

"I'm the director. I oversee everything at these learning centers. We are very grateful you have arrived. Maybe your parents dropped you off when the government called. Maybe we picked you up and brought you here once we realized you were special. And you are special. Each and every one of you has special abilities that only you possess. Each one of you is completely unique. That makes you very special and very important to your government. You may have heard some people refer to these abilities as 'glows.' We like to categorize these as abilities to better nurture them."

A flower bloomed on the screen. Who made this thing? Unless they wanted it to look like an unhinged middle schooler's last-minute PowerPoint. Then they nailed it.

"You, too, can bloom here. Allow the doctors to help you grow. It is your duty to our fine nation. I know it's hard to believe, but there are some who wish to threaten your new home. The only way you can protect it is to lend the government your strength. The fear that the sickness brought is behind us, but now there is an even bigger threat: chaos. Chaos is what happens when people don't listen, child. Chaos is the enemy of free will and all of us."

Riot footage filled the screen. A building engulfed in flames finished out the clip. Definitely someone's extra credit project. There was no way they paid money for this. I focused on the smooth texture of my pants to stop myself from laughing.

"Your country needs you to be brave and steadfast in the face of chaos. The task you are charged with is not easy, but it is of the utmost importance. Do as everyone at the facility says and you will thrive here. The country's future depends on it. Thank you from the bottom of our hearts."

"Thank you" scrawled in bold filled the screen before it went black once more. Oh, thank fuck. There was no way I would've made it through much more of whatever that was.

"Yes, thank you for your bravery. The world is in chaos and we have to rectify it, don't we?" Dr. McCarthy asked.

I nodded slowly. Was this what he wanted?

"Good, now tell me about yourself." His pen was poised over his clipboard. That wasn't nerve-wracking. *Come on, Simerra, play the game.*

"I was with a few of my friends when we were picked up."

"It was hard to find food out there, wasn't it?" he pressed.

"No, it was okay. We—I mean, yeah, it was really hard," I corrected, noticing his furrowed brow.

The creases smoothed out, and I allowed my muscles to relax. I was not built for this.

"How many of you were there? Remember, honesty is very important."

"It was the seven of us and Nash."

"What happened to Echo?"

Did I lie or tell the truth? Nash hadn't given up what my glow was, so maybe she lied about how Echo died too, right? I mean, it was an accident. The circumstances were a bit dubious, but this place didn't deal in "kind ofs."

"He died in a random accident."

"That's what Nash told us. It's good to know you're being honest with me. Now, what can you do? Be as specific as possible."

I'd never been so happy that emoting took extra energy than I was in this moment. I carefully held my body in the same position while I internally breathed a sigh of relief. Only one big lie to go.

"I can snuff out fire if I put my hand into it."

"What about people? Can you affect them?"

He had me there. If I lied about this and then came in contact with someone during my time here, they'd know in an instant. All the little half-truths would be for nothing and we'd have a harder time escaping. I hated word games.

I nodded, biting my lip.

"How?" He gestured for me to continue. Excitement lit his eyes and he smiled. It was more creepy than encouraging, but that may have been intentional. *I could always touch you, but I'm not sure you'd enjoy the demonstration.* I allowed myself a small smile before I answered out loud.

"They die. It's like I put out their fire." That covered it. Now they wouldn't be surprised if someone dropped dead around me.

His eyes widened as he scribbled frantically. I searched for something to catch my interest while I waited for him to finish writing. The soldier stared at me with a hand on his weapon. Someone was eager to work. My stomach rolled at the thought.

"How often are people harmed if you come in contact with them?"

"I don't come in contact with people."

"That's very bright of you, an excellent choice, but when you do come in contact with people, what happens?" He flipped his chair around and hung off the back to stare at me.

"Sometimes, they get hurt."

"Hmm, can you control it?"

"Yes, I have to touch the thing to use my glow."

Relief flashed through his eyes. Great, we were on the right path. *Don't worry, mister doctor man. I'm no threat.*

"You're a low level. If you work hard, you'll be as useful as Nash. I know you may be angry with her now, but she brought you here so you can help and be helped. It's what's best for you. It's almost time for lunch. Follow the nice guard down to the lunchroom and try to get to know some of the other low levels."

"What about the high levels?"

"They're dangerous. Between you and me, most of them don't make it long around here. Since you're a low level, your time here will be full of learning and growth."

I smiled to hide my fear and tapped my fingers against each other. Long to short. Short to long. Was I capable of keeping a lie running the whole time we were here? The doctor gestured towards the door. I moved with forced ease after the soldier into the hallways. None of my friends emerged from their rooms. Were they still being questioned? If they were screaming, would I be able to hear it?

"Let's go."

I trudged after the guard. The only sound in the hall was our feet, mine bare and his booted, and they echoed off the vaulted ceiling. Elegant portraits and scenery pieces hung in golden frames. Each was accompanied by a little placard like a stuffy museum. Was that where they'd gotten the pictures from? This place was like something out of a book. I nearly bumped into my soldier when he stopped midstride. He pulled a giant door open and the sound from inside should have crashed over me. There were rows and rows of tables filled with people all in the same blue outfits, but it was silent aside from the tinkling of cutlery and the softest hum of voices.

"Have fun."

There was a table in the far corner with some open seats. Time to get to know my peers.

Chapter Fifteen

FOR THE GOOD OF OUR COUNTRY

CW: ABUSE, ABLEISM, SENSORY overload/meltdown, death mentions

I set my tray on the table and dug in. Hopefully, if I stayed quiet for a minute, they would get used to me. All conversation at the table stopped as they looked me over.

"Do you have a death wish?" a girl asked.

"I'm eating like everyone else." I kept my gaze on my pasta.

"Did you even do your test yet?" A hand popped up between me and my pasta, snapping rapidly.

"You mean the questions they ask when you watch the video?" I stumbled over my words. I hated when this happened. I wasn't scared; I was overstimulated. Two very different experiences, not that allistics ever believed me.

Laughter rippled through the group. Why were misunderstandings always seen as amusing?

"No. I mean the first time you use your abilities in the training rooms. Fucking low level." She scoffed. She clutched a cane tightly with her right hand. It matched our blue clothing perfectly.

I opened my mouth to reply.

"Don't bother, new girl. Go sit with the others." She shooed me off lazily.

"I'll sit here, thanks." I turned back to my food.

"What did I say?" She fiddled with her tight curls. Her eyes shone with annoyance.

"I know what you said, but I also know you can't glow right now, even if you want to. Not unless you want to get in trouble. So why don't we all eat our lunch and try to survive?"

"She's got you there." A different girl chuckled, winking at me. "My name's Trishauna or Trish for short. She/her please and thanks."

She stretched out a fist, which I bumped lightly. The leather of her fingerless gloves was so soft. Her blonde locs made it halfway down her back, and she had warm brown eyes. Was I in the clear?

"They may be watching now, but they won't always be," the first girl muttered.

"You better knock it off, Rachel," Trish said.

"What are you going to do: wheel me to death?"

"You know damn well it hurts when I run over your foot." Trish rolled her wheelchair back and forth for show.

"Not as much as if I crack you on the knee with this cane." Rachel twirled a curl between her fingers, giggling.

Rachel's cane was different from Mother's: shorter with a curved handle and a bulky tip for balance. Sitting down, she was a head taller than Trish and I. Her orange curls danced around her round face in a short bob, accentuating her green eyes. She was as beautiful as she was mean.

"There really is a food security issue out there, huh? What's it like?" Trish asked as I popped the last bite of bread into my mouth.

"We had to scavenge and hunt, but we were free."

Their eyes went wide. Was that too honest? Right, they all thought it was chaos and anarchy. These people didn't have a clue.

"I told you she was stupid."

"Rachel, cut the shit. When was the last time any of us got to talk to people from the outside?" Trish chided.

"Fine. Any other bold claims to make?" Rachel asked.

The table sat in quiet anticipation. I cocked my head to the side. What exactly would she consider an outlandish claim? I needed to watch what I said. I literally just got here.

"Why did you sit here? You have to know," Rachel questioned.

"I needed a seat. There's really nothing else to it."

"What she's getting at is, we're the high levels." Trish readjusted her fingerless gloves.

"I'm so scared."

"I like you," Rachel said.

People dumped their trays one table at a time. I raised an eyebrow at Trish. She held up a gloved finger. When all the other tables were gone, Trish wheeled herself away from the table with me close behind.

"You should go over with the others when we get outside," she advised.

"Why?"

"Look, as much as I'd like to think we aren't dangerous, we are. I don't want you to get hurt. Go make friends."

"I want to be your friend."

"I don't need any pity friends. Now go before I run you over."

I put my palms face down. She shooed me away. There were kids Daisy's age and younger and a bunch that looked like they, too, were in their twenties. Many stood and chatted. A few ran laps, kicked around a ball, or did something equally athletic. Then, I spotted a group of kids playing hopscotch. One of them looked like Daisy. I made a beeline for them, cutting through conversations and games alike.

"One, two three, four, five, six!" Daisy crowed as she hopped the pattern.

"Good job."

"Are you going to play with me?" She jumped up and down in anticipation.

I allowed Daisy to direct the rest of our outside time. She taught me the rules to each new game, and the longer we were out there, the more relaxed she was.

· · · ● · ● · ● · · ·

"It's time for your physical. Strip down and we'll get started," Dr. McCarthy explained back in his room.

Great, this'll be fun. I undressed and tried not to shake. I held my head high under his gaze. He pressed his cool stethoscope to my back.

"Breath in, good. Breath out, perfect. Do you have any injuries? If so, what are they?" He circled me like a vulture.

"My head hurts from yesterday, and there are some gashes on my leg from my time outside."

"Were you insolent when you first arrived?"

He jabbed at the cut on my scalp and I winced. Why would saying it hurt read as an invitation to poke at it? I took a deep breath to steady myself. I had to play the long game here. There could be no snarky remarks or quick rebuttals if I wanted us to have a chance.

"I spoke out of turn."

"You're smarter than that. Get dressed then go through that door. We're going to put out a few fires."

He held the second door open. It led to a larger room with stacks of wood in it. He pressed a button and each pile ignited.

"Go on."

If I started with the closest fires, hopefully I'd have enough control to keep him from feeling my glow. We needed that edge, and I needed the low-level classification. This had to work. My glow danced against my touch. I smiled as it snaked its way down my arm and plunged my hand into the fire. It went out with a hiss. Dr. McCarthy clapped in the background. At the next one, a few pieces of wood splintered off, but they were too small for him to see. I had to be more careful. I took measured steps to help my focus. My glow coiled tighter down my arm instead of listening. *Please don't make a show of this.* Sticks scattered across the room. I bit back a swear. In through my nose and out through my mouth. In through my nose and out through my mouth. I could do this.

"The last fire, Simerra."

My lip curled as my glow twisted in anger. Did he want to die? I sat cross-legged with my eyes shut. My glow hummed around me, extending past my arm to coil around my shoulders. *Here we go.* The log beneath my hand shattered into pieces. The chalky taste of burnt wood clogged my mouth and nose. My legs shook and my walk was less than perfect, but I managed to make it back to my chair. I fell into it, thankful for the support.

"Don't be so dramatic. That was a starter exercise."

That settled it. I was screwed.

"That's all the time we have for today. Get up."

He really thought I could walk right away after all of those fires? I blinked at him, unmoving.

"Why don't we give her some encouragement?"

The soldier's gun cracked across the back of my skull. My shoulders shifted with my head as it snapped to the left. Dots danced across my vision. I rocked back and forth. The movement comforted me through the confusion. He was speaking again, but I couldn't understand him. I kept rocking. My glow coiled around my heart, agitated. I rocked faster. I had to keep it inside. Everything hurt. Why did everything have to hurt? Even rocking hurt. Tears ran down my face.

The doctor tried to say something again but it was pointless. It was probably something about calming down. That wasn't likely to happen. I heard more than felt the next crack against my skull. Zane and Daisy popped into my mind. If I didn't calm down, there was a chance I'd never see them again. I hummed loudly, plastering my hands over my ears even as the stars danced before my eyes, even as they hit me again. I hummed the same tune over and over, adding different notes. Little pieces of control that I craved.

"I think she's self-soothing," the soldier commented.

"I don't give a shit what she's doing. This isn't part of the program. She's as defective as those high-level idiots we keep around. Hit her again."

I hummed louder in preparation. I moved with it to mitigate the pain. It helped some. I was able to open my eyes, but the world spun violently.

"There we are. Stop that noise at once. You were not told to speak, and now you're late for your next session."

I stopped humming, but the rocking picked back up a bit.

"At least you're quiet now. Come on."

I rocked forwards, pulling myself out of my seat, but I fell to my knees almost immediately. I scrambled to my feet, pulling my hands close as I rocked. The world was just too big right now, but I had to try. I stumbled a few times, but I managed to follow him. I rocked hinging at my waist, the repetitive motion comforting in the confusion of this place.

"It might please you to know some of your friends are in this session as well."

I looked up at him wide-eyed.

"I thought that might get your attention. If you throw a fit like that again, I'll leave you in the training room until you get a handle on yourself. Now get in there."

I ducked my head meekly. Once the door shut, I rocked faster. Why was I always so out of control? My throat tightened once more. I couldn't think about that right now. Breath, just breath. Someone stopped as they caught sight of me.

"Simerra!"

It was Zane. There couldn't have been more perfect timing.

"What happened?" he whispered.

"I lost control." I kicked at the squeaky floor. That was a terrible noise.

"Are you bleeding? What happened?" Rage flashed through his eyes.

"I couldn't calm down. I tried and it didn't work." I wrung my hands and fiddled with my fingers.

"It's not your fault. How badly does that hurt?"

"Like my head is splitting open."

He'd used that phrase to talk about a bad headache before and this was definitely like a bad headache.

"They'll probably leave a med kit in your room. Apparently, they refuse to help doctor wounds caused by 'insubordination.'"

"I couldn't stop," I cried.

"I know. It's not your fault. This place is strict. It's not your fault. Have you seen any of the others?" he soothed.

"Only Daisy."

I tripped over my own feet, but Zane caught me before I slammed into the floor. His eyes narrowed. Just great.

"You used your glow."

"They wanted to see me put out fires. What did you tell them about yours?" I asked.

"That I can make it really cold. They weren't impressed." He grinned sheepishly.

I giggled.

"Was it your glow that got away from you or sensory overload?"

"Overload," I muttered.

"Did you try humming?"

Did he think I was clueless? I'd been autistic my whole life. Maybe, just maybe, I knew to try humming.

"Did you see the blood?" I snarked.

"Fuck, I'm sorry. Is there anything I can do?" He ran a hand over the top of his fro. It looked a bit flat. How long till they gave us personal care items?

"You're doing it."

"Have you seen anyone?"

"Joey's in here somewhere. I caught a glimpse of Kate. She was giving them shit up on the third floor. I'm trying to get a decent map of this place for when we try to get out of here," he confided, eyeing the stoic soldiers lining the walls.

We had to. This was no place for Daisy to grow up. This was no place for anyone to grow up. Speaking of which.

"Have you seen Nash?" I worked to keep my tone even.

"The only Nash I know handed over my friends to the government, and I know you're not asking about her," Zane remarked, his eyes stormy and his shoulders hunched.

"I know what she did, but the things she told me make me wonder where she is."

"As long as she's far from us, I don't care. It's one thing to hand over my friends, but you and Daisy—"

Now wait just a fucking second. He didn't really just—

"Am I not adult enough to handle being here?" I asked, astounded.

"No, there are better environments for you to be in," he asserted.

"What the fuck is that supposed to mean?" I bit out. My hands clenched and unclenched from fists at my sides. I shook with the force of my rage.

"They already hurt you for being different." His hand hovered over my sore head.

"Me being different never bothered you before this."

"It doesn't bother me. I'm worried for you. The people here don't understand someone like you."

I crossed my arms over my chest and huffed to myself. How fucking dare he. He didn't speak until they called for us to disperse. It didn't bother me in the slightest.

"I'm sorry. I didn't mean it."

"You kinda did," I choked out.

"Are you going to stay mad?"

I shrugged. Was that really all he cared about? He compared me to a child.

"I promise when we get out of here, I'll make it up to you. We can dance or go fishing or catch fireflies or star gaze. Whichever you want."

It was an awkward walk to the meal room. We sat on the end of a table, far from others. Was that for our protection or there's? Nash never hid me from interactions I might handle poorly. Then again, Echo had never taken me seriously and that earned him a hand-dug grave.

Chapter Sixteen

DAISY

"It's not pretty, but it'll heal." Kate sat back and admired her hard work on my head wound.

"Thanks. I couldn't do it without you. How was your day?"

"Long and full of bullshit." She leaned back on the bed and placed her hands behind her head.

"Did you see that video?" Nessa asked.

"That was the most ridiculous part. Everyone here believes it too. Joey says it was the same for him," Kate said.

"How long before we believe it too?" Nessa replatted her long hair. There was a soft concentration in the slight crease in her brow. The tightness in her strong jaw was new, but the day had been intense.

"Longer than I'm willing to stay here. How was your training?" I asked.

"Awful. They don't like that I get tired so they kept saying, 'What a wonderful area to strive for improvement.'" Kate threw herself back onto her bed, bouncing slightly on the thin mattress.

"Mine put me in a dark maze and said, 'Navigate it.' There were things hiding in there like a corner full of spiders or pointy sticks. It was creepy, and I failed because I can't navigate for crap. She said my aptitude would increase through dedication to my country. Who does that?" Nessa griped.

"We did say the adults didn't train us to use our powers."

"No, you said that. Give me the adults back over this any day. I'll do all the watches they want. At least we were outside," Kate muttered.

"Same. I miss the sky," Nessa added.

"Even the bugs?" I asked.

"I will take on an army of mosquitoes to see the night sky. Bring 'em on," Kate joked.

"Everyone, remember this moment when we're all tired and covered in bug bites."

"Oh, I'll destroy them all. Remember, I'm fighting them." Kate laughed.

"I'll hold you to that."

Daisy yawned, stretching her arms high over her head.

"Does someone need sleep?" I asked.

She pouted. Her bottom lip jutted out and her eyes even watered.

"You've gotten better at that, but I'm not Devin and it won't work."

Her eyes watered even more. Shit. Did I ever think before I spoke, or was I the queen of putting my foot into my mouth?

"When do I get to see Devin again?"

"Soon. They're making sure we get settled first. You'll see him. I promise."

A single tear fell from her eye and rolled down to her chin. I hugged her carefully. We would get through this together. I pulled back and offered her a weary smile.

"We all love you so much, Daisy. Let's get you to bed."

• • • ● • ● • ● • • •

"Wake up. The door's open." Kate shook my bed.

I jumped up and the world spun around me. Not my brightest moment. I looked back at the bed to see it empty. There was no Daisy. Fuck. Fuck. Fuck. This was bad. This was really bad. Every cell in me screamed with panic.

"Tell Joey."

"Are you sure? Devin's going to freak," Kate warned.

"Do it," I ordered.

"What's going on?" Nessa stumbled out of bed.

"Devin's a wreck and begged us to find her," Kate breathed.

You have to focus or you're no help at all. I tapped my fingers on my thumb, long to short and short to long, over and over again.

"Can we leave the room please?" I asked the camera.

There was no visible change, but the door was still open.

"At least it won't zap us on the way out. Come on," I urged.

We rushed out of the room, looking for any sign of her. This place was huge. Where were we supposed to start? The panic was really setting in. I could feel it coil through my body and my glow. What if we couldn't find her?

"Should we split up?" Kate asked.

"We don't know this place well enough for that," I dismissed.

"Looking for something?" Nash asked.

I spun around to see Nash and Daisy hand in hand. Daisy waved enthusiastically.

"We went on an adventure!" Daisy held up a drawing.

"That's great. Can you come show it to me?" I coaxed.

Nash held on to her hand. Really? She was going to hold Daisy over our heads? My glow circled near my heart, agitated. I took a deep breath to try to settle it back down.

"What do you want, Nash?"

"To talk. The rest of you can have the day off. I already cleared it."

"You've got to be fucking kidding me," Kate muttered.

"You let Daisy out of your sight. It's a gross oversight on your part. I did you a favor. Just one conversation."

"Fine."

Daisy skipped over the tile, holding up her artwork proudly.

"She has so many colors. She let me keep some." She held up a fistful of markers.

"It's super pretty. Can you draw me a picture back in our room?"

She nodded ecstatically. Kate took her hand and guided her away. Nash and I stood in the hallway. I wished she were less beautiful to me after what she'd done, but apparently actions didn't affect how her eyes sparkled and her hair shone. *So much for being over her.*

"Aren't you going to say something?" she asked.

"No."

"Please come with me."

She led me to a small room filled with cleaning supplies. She gestured for me to sit beside her. The cleaning products were so strong, my head was already spinning, but I obliged.

"You took me to a closet?"

"There aren't any cameras in here."

"What do you want?" I asked, eyes narrowed.

"I want to know how everyone is doing. I know the first day can be hard here. You get used to it though. The schedule and all that." She waved it off like it was something mundane.

"We're being held captive because you handed us over, and now you want to know how we're doing?" I memorized the cleaners' names to keep from screaming.

She smiled up at me slyly.

I dragged my hand down my face. She had to be kidding. We couldn't be close anymore. She had to know that was coming when she did this. Why would any of us want to associate with her?

"It's not that strange when you think about it." She scooched closer.

I leaned back. My head brushed against a musty mop, but it was a small price to pay. Did she think before she opened her mouth, or did she say whatever popped into her head? I needed to know for scientific purposes.

"Yes, it is. We're here because of you. In the place you told me was awful."

"I know it looks bad, but we're both still right here." She held out her hand.

I choked back tears. *Pull it together, Simerra. This girl didn't deserve your tears, pretty as she is.*

"That's not how this works, Nash." I squeezed my eyes shut, unable to watch her reaction.

"Why can't it work like that? We're all safe."

"We're separated and being controlled. The very thing we fought to avoid."

"Everyone needed training. Look at what happened to Echo."

Bile rose in my throat. Was I the reason she'd handed us over? Had my inability to control myself sentenced my family to rot here?

"It was an accident," I breathed.

"I know. There is chaos out there. The only way to combat it is here," she explained passionately.

"This place is a prison."

"It's our only chance. I see that now. Echo's death was chaos. There was no reason for it. It didn't have to happen. If we were here—"

"They would have killed me in a fire like the one I saw the day I met you."

She shook her head, pressing her hands against her ears.

"I was defending myself from Mark. My life was in danger," I reminded her.

"It was chaos. It's what happens when you aren't under the care of the government."

She stared into the distance with frantic eyes. What had they done to her? Where was the courage she always exuded?

"You think there's no chaos here?" I asked softly.

"They can keep everyone safe."

Was everything she'd told me a lie? My head and heart ached at the implications. I couldn't think about that while she sat beside me. This was all too much. One more layer of fucked up to this nightmarish imprisonment.

"Why did you take Daisy?"

"I missed her. I missed you."

I had whiplash. Was she upset or not? Was she betraying me or my friend? Did she even know?

"Do what they say and the chaos can't get you anymore. Then no one gets hurt," she warned. "You should get back or you'll miss lunch."

She tumbled out the door and walked away without so much as a glance. I stood there in the hallway, more confused than before we'd chatted. Was that supposed to clear things up? I needed more information.

The room came into view, and they were all in the hall. Devin held Daisy tightly with Zane beside them. Joey and Kate stood close with

Nessa nearby. Everything looked right, except the soldiers loitering at the back. Zane noticed me first and waved.

"Now that we're all here, let's go. Follow me."

Zane bumped me. There was concern all over his face. I shrugged. Even if we could speak, I wouldn't have had the words to describe the conversation I had. He frowned but dropped it. The soldiers held the door open and we all shuffled in, hungry and excited to be together. I led us to the emptiest table I could find. It happened to be Trish's again.

"Hey, Trish."

The others settled around me. She looked over our group. She seemed more curious than frustrated, and that was a win in my book.

"You brought more low levels with you."

Zane snorted. I kicked him under the table. If he ruined my hard work this soon, I'd kick his ass.

"Where'd you find all of them?"

"These are my friends. We came in together."

Her eyebrows nearly disappeared into her hairline. She leaned her head onto a gloved fist. Oh great.

"Imagine that. Who's the high level? There's always one."

"No one," I said hurriedly before the others could give us away.

"How did you survive out there without a high level?"

"We got lucky," I lied.

I ate a bit of bread. It was still warm and fluffy. I would never get used to having food like this around. Everything was fresh, and seasoned, and warm, and it never ran out. This, I would miss.

"It's good you got here when you did. Follow the rules and the chaos can't get to you," Trish warned.

I froze for a second but forced myself to keep eating. What was with everyone and this chaos crap? I didn't have much time to ponder it as my personal doctor strolled towards us. His eyes were glued to me. Wasn't today our day off?

"I didn't think we had any training today." I cocked my head to the side, trying to appear innocent.

"The others don't." He scowled.

I closed my eyes, allowing his words to sink in. What a great day off.

"You did not finish your tasks yesterday. As such, you must return to the training room and complete your activities before finishing your rest day with the others. It's only fair that you finish your work, don't you think?" He tapped his foot, waiting for my response.

I nodded, keeping an eye on the approaching soldier. So quick to bring in the big guns. I hadn't even resisted. I should've known what to expect. I wasn't a baby before the world fell to "chaos." Some things never changed.

"Good girl. Follow me."

I smiled with as much confidence as I could muster before I rushed off to keep up with Dr. McCarthy. *Let's get this over with.*

CHAPTER SEVENTEEN

RACHEL

CW: ABUSE, SUICIDE MENTION, corpse, gore, torture, body fluids, torture, electroshock "therapy"

I clung to the wall on my way down the hall. They were really big on exhausting us here. Was that to keep us weak? Did it help them maintain control? I filed that thought away for later contemplation. The click of heels against the hard floors echoed around me. *Please don't be looking for me. Please leave me alone.* The sound grew louder until it matched my stride completely. I looked up to Karen. My heart sank. I stopped, and she followed suit, smiling. Did she have to bare her teeth like that when she did it? And why did they all have clipboards? I felt like a zoo exhibit.

"Hello, Simerra. It's lovely to run into you. How has your stay been so far?" she asked, clipboard posed as always.

"It's been great. I'm learning so much." I smiled meekly.

"Ah, and how are your friends doing?" she asked.

"They're doing well too. We're all adjusting."

"That's wonderful. How about you come with me? I've heard you haven't exactly been agreeable lately."

Fear flickered through my eyes. I tried not to change my posture, but a knowing look entered her eyes. Awesome. Great. Could I just do a kick flip off the roof instead?

"I knew you'd understand. I have an appointment I'd like you to watch."

She picked up a brisk pace. How did she manage in those shoes? I followed behind her rose-gold-clad form as fast as I could, but she remained strides ahead of me. We stopped by an unmarked door in the basement. I gasped for air against the wall.

"Stay close. The high levels are rather volatile. We wouldn't want you getting hurt." She held a cloth to her face.

The door swung open and a deep stench of decay filled the air. We moved through the dimly lit room to a large window.

"I apologize for the smell, dear. It's hard to find adequate cleaners that live long enough to get the job done." She gestured to a corpse I hadn't noticed off to the left.

A wave of nausea nearly robbed me of the little composure I had. His face was distorted as if he'd died screaming. His flesh was broken and oozing. She watched my reaction approvingly. I tapped my right hand against my leg, needing some sort of repetitive motion while everything in me screamed to run or fight.

"Your first body is always difficult, but you've seen bodies before, haven't you, Simerra? You've caused some."

I nodded, swallowing back the urge to vomit here and now. How many of my corpses did she know about?

"Excellent. Look out there."

On the other side of the glass, a huddled form in the corner was barely visible. Two soldiers stood on the far side of the room. She reached forward and pressed the button beside the microphone.

"Proceed."

The curled-up form shrank back more than I thought was possible. The soldiers pulled rods out of their belts. Electricity buzzed over the material. They took turns prodding at the person until they stood. I let out a muffled gasp. It was Rachel.

"You've met her before, haven't you?"

I nodded.

"You have to be careful around the high levels. Sometimes, they regress out of nowhere. This one was making great progress until she failed her evaluation."

"Did she kill that man?" I pointed to the fly ridden corpse.

Her head rocked back at the force for her laughter. Glad someone was enjoying themselves. I hated this woman more by the second.

"Oh no, dear. That's from this cell's last occupant. We haven't gotten around to cleaning it up yet." She winked. "She did attack her guard, but she should make a full recovery. Don't worry about her. All involved parties are handsomely compensated for inconveniences."

Then where was my inconvenience fee for being hit over the head? Okay, that was a bit dark even given the current situation, but seriously, what planet was she from? Dad was right. Hate and evil flourished off hardship.

"Let me out of here!" Rachel screeched.

She ran at the glass and bashed her hands against it. A soldier shocked her in the back and she collapsed to the dirty cement. Horror spilled across my features. When would this end? Could I help her? What was the point in showing me this?

"Don't worry, she can't see us."

"Please stop hurting her," I choked out.

"A lovely effort, dear, but that's not how this works. We take rule violations very seriously, and you don't have a strong enough glow to go around making demands."

I bit the inside of my cheek till it bled. I might have to sit back and watch, but I couldn't handle the idea of walking away from any of them. When we left, I was taking as many people as I could with me. I flattened my affect, fully resolved.

"How long will she be here?" I asked.

"Until she learns her place. Probably about a week. We must keep the chaos from getting inside these walls. If we can't, we've already lost, and the government doesn't like losing. I'm sure you understand. It's a dangerous world as you've experienced firsthand."

The only danger you should be worrying about is me. I bit my tongue. She spun away from Rachel's screams; her dress fanned out around her in an elegant swish.

"Let's get you back to your room."

When the door clicked shut, Rachel's screams were silenced.

"You have to love good soundproofing."

She flashed her pearly teeth. I was left in as much of a whirlwind as her dress, which swirled around her with every stride. When we reached the main floor, she faced me again.

"I'm sure we'll be running into each other more over the course of your stay. Have a good evening, Simerra."

"What's your name?" I called after her.

She tensed for a moment, but she did not turn back. Her heels clicked against the floor in defiance. The sound faded out as she turned the corner. I hated it here. I took deep breaths and flapped to collect myself during the rest of the walk to my room.

Everyone was there. Nash really had gotten us the whole day off. What kinds of things had she done to get that sort of privilege? Could I do those kinds of things? Rachel's screams rang in my ears. Zane approached me slowly, palms towards the earth.

"I know that look. How were the tests?" he asked.

"They were the easy part."

I crumpled with a thud. The cool tiles grounded me in the room. It was easier to talk if I stayed present. Zane searched for injuries.

"I saw a lot today."

Daisy was asleep in Devin's lap. He gave me a thumbs-up. At least she wouldn't hear any of this.

"The table we sat at is for high levels and one of them was missing today. I watched them hurt her."

"I thought you were training," Zane commented.

"I was lucky enough to do both." I snorted.

"Why would they show you that?" Zane asked.

"To show me what happens if we fuck up maybe? I don't know. Ten out of ten, I don't want to see it again, but I have a feeling I will. Remember that woman who greeted us when we first got here? She's the one who took me there."

"Some people say if you see her, it's always bad news. Like you messed up and there's no turning back. You may have gotten lucky," Devin said.

"I'm not sure lucky is the word I would use."

"I'm not saying this is the best thing that could have happened, but it could have been worse. Kids have disappeared after talking to her. Sometimes permanently."

"The fires," I muttered.

"Exactly. There are a lot of pieces at play here, and we need to learn the game before we start making moves," Devin advised.

"Astute observation, but last I checked, it was Simerra that was in charge," Kate said.

"No, it's okay. He's right. We're going to have to work together in order to survive. See what you can find out without getting in trouble. Tomorrow, I can only guess we go back to not really seeing each other.

Say good night and head to bed. Training here is intense, and we have to be ready."

"I really don't like this," Zane said.

"Neither do I, but I'll probably get to see you again soon. There's that enrichment thing we have together. We have to hang in there till then. We'll be okay."

He placed a hand on my head. I was surely too tired to hurt him, right? I held my arms open, waiting for permission. He followed suit and we hugged. He was careful not to touch too much skin, but it was nice to have the contact.

"Hang in there."

"I will."

"Please may we exit the room?" Joey asked the camera.

The door opened with a click then shut right after they passed the threshold.

"What now?" Nessa asked.

"Now, I crawl to my bed and we go to sleep. I wasn't kidding. The training will only get more intense from here. We have to play their game until we find a flaw."

"And then?

"And then we destroy them," I mouthed with my back to the camera.

COLLECTING NAMES

An alarm blared overhead. The sound cut into my brain, causing a full body cringe. Daisy covered her head with a pillow. I hummed in an attempt to drown it out. This was too much input. No one moved as we waited for instructions, but they never came. Daisy sat up and the sound died instantly. I kept my hands over my ears for a few more seconds as I adjusted to the silence. My brain slowly processed thought again.

"What the fuck was that for?" Kate yelled at the camera.

Nessa placed a hand on Kate's shoulder in an effort to calm her. Kate shoved it off. So it was going to be that kind of morning.

"Can we please know what's going on?" Nessa asked.

"Time for your schedules to begin. Rise and attend breakfast." The door slid open.

"Are you coming? They said breakfast." Daisy jumped up and down.

"Let's go then, little one," I said.

She skipped down the hall. Her shirt-dress swished as her arms swung back and forth over the material. Other kids trailed in, some in groups while others came in alone. Several of the loners were recognizable from the high-level table. We chatted softly about nothing important, ever cognizant of the soldiers. The rich smell of cinnamon and blueberry wafted up to me from my muffin. If possible, I would have crammed the entire thing in my mouth at once, but I settled for a giant bite. Trish played with her food as she stared off. A soldier stood too close to the table for me to fill her in. Was this a test?

· · · ● · ● · ● · · ·

"Good morning. Let's go straight to the training room."

There weren't any fires waiting for me. He waved me forward from the far side of the glass. *Okay, doc, I'll bite.* The ground beside me burst into flames. I yelped. My glow jumped from its place coiled round my heart and spread through me. I allowed it to rush from my hand. The fire went out with a hiss. A new fire popped up right away. It flickered before I stopped myself. I needed to touch these things. They were getting the bare minimum from me, not a show, not extra knowledge about my glow. Only the bare minimum. I stomped down on the fire, but a third fire was quick to replace it. It was a very repetitive session. Small burns peppered my skin, cleansed only by my sweat.

"Excellent job today. Come sit," he said over a speaker.

I tapped my fingers on each other to refocus as I walked towards him. I counted every step. I needed all the tricks I could think of to ensure my glow was wrapped tightly back where it belonged. It used to leave me alone when I was tired. But now, the extra use made it stronger, like a new muscle. One that didn't really care to listen all the time. The soldier's hand clenched around his weapon. What did they tell the soldiers about us? Patriotic music scratched out of the old TV's speakers, and the director popped back on the screen. Did he ever stop smiling?

"Job well done. You've earned it. If you're watching this, then you are advancing with our training program on or ahead of schedule. We know it's not easy and you'd rather be playing, but you're part of something very important here. We're happy you're taking this as seriously as we are. I know you're wondering what this means for you. Well, keep this up and there are special privileges for participants like you. How does extra time outside sound? Time to be social and make friends? Maybe some art supplies? These things can all be yours if you keep working hard. Thank you from the very bottom of my heart."

The doctor studied my features. Was there a certain way I should look after that video? Was I doing it wrong? Was I going to get in trouble for not responding? I clenched my teeth. Talking was never the answer here. He smiled and walked to the door. I passed.

"It's time for lunch. Our guard friend will take you."

The soldier's boots clacked against the floor in perfect rhythm. What was this guy's story? I followed him down the empty hallway.

"Do you ever talk?" I whispered, hoping the softer volume would be met with less vitriol.

"No."

I squinted. He was fucking with me, right? He spoke in order to reply to me. Was that supposed to magically not count?

"You just did."

He spun to face me. His eyes widened with fear. Now I'd done it.

"Shut up before we both get in trouble," he hissed, nostrils flaring.

"There's no one here to yell at us," I reminded in a whisper.

He huffed but didn't argue. We continued in silence to the lunch-room. He held the door open, and the soft hum of voices washed over us. It couldn't hurt to try again, could it? I took a step into the room.

"What's your name?"

"Cal," he breathed back.

I kept my stride even as I continued over to the food table. Cal, huh? I could work with that.

$$\cdot\ \cdot\ \bullet\ \bullet\ \cdot\ \bullet\ \cdot\ \bullet\ \bullet\ \cdot\ \cdot$$

I caught up to Trish on the blacktop. She held a hand to her eyes to guard against the sun. I shifted so she was in my shadow.

"I need to talk to you."

"Figured as much, but shouldn't you get out there and find your friends?"

I shrugged. Daisy was likely playing with her new friends. Besides, this was important. If I wanted to get the high levels out, they needed to trust me.

"I figured we could do laps?"

"Oh no, I get enough of that in enrichment. Let's enjoy the sun near a loud bunch." Trish made a sad attempt at a smile that I returned, unsure of how else to respond. We stopped near a group of kids playing a rambunctious game of two truths and a lie. I leaned in and pretended to fix her hair.

"I know where Rachel is."

"Is she okay?" Her knuckles turned white on the push rings of her chair.

"She failed an assessment."

Trish hung her head. Tears slid from her eyes through the curtain of her locs while she collected herself. I played with her hair to avoid attention and soothe her. She relaxed slightly under my touch.

"Is she still alive?" she mumbled with tears still in her throat.

"Yes."

"Then she'll be back. She's one of their best. She's never failed before." She shook while she cried but otherwise, she was silent.

I pretended to point out people or things we could be talking about as she recovered. The soldiers didn't seem to notice I was full of shit. Sometimes, this place made it too easy. She took a deep breath and fixed her face.

"How do you know what's happening? Usually, they tell high levels and only enough to put us on edge."

"A well-dressed lady caught me in the hall. She tried to scare me."

"The dirty blonde in heels all the time, right? That bitch told me if my glow was so strong, it should be able to take me out of this chair. She's always nasty. I've never met someone who hates chaos as much as her. Damn it, Rachel. What were you thinking?"

"She's going to be okay. Maybe the woman was wrong."

"Karen? She's never wrong." Trish's voice faltered.

"Are you sure?"

A puzzled look crossed over Trish's face as she thought it over.

"Let's get inside. Everyone in," a soldier ordered.

There were groans from all around, but we moved towards the doors all the same. There were more of us than soldiers. Obviously, they had guns, but why did no one ever try to escape or protest? Were they all brainwashed? I kept pace with Trish. She had enough to think about; we both did. I had a new name.

I followed the others in and smiled at my doctor. It was easy to fake joy with progress being made. "Are you ready? Of course you are. In you go." He gestured to the larger training room.

I made my way with tentative steps. I didn't want to rush towards anything too dangerous. The ground beneath my feet caught fire. My glow surged, called by the pain in my feet and legs. It went out with a hiss.

"Faster this time."

Fire jumped up under my feet, and the heat tore at my flesh and clothes hungrily. My glow quelled the flames immediately. I wouldn't be able to walk if we kept up this pace. I stepped to the right in the hopes of avoiding the fire patch for a second or two. The ground ignited directly below me once more and I screamed, outraged by the pain. My glow pulsed out from me and for a moment, the flames were gone, but they popped up again. I glowed again, but the second I stopped, the flames popped back up stronger. Was this some sort of joke?

"See if you can stand in the fire without being burned."

"Please stop."

There was no reprieve. If he didn't knock it off, I wouldn't be so careful to avoid his oxygen needs.

"You can do it."

The next fire rose like a wave from both sides and crashed over me. I collapsed to the floor in agony. The flames licked up my body greedily. My screams echoed off the walls, but the flames persisted. Each flap of my hands only caused more burns, but I had no other way to cope with the pain. He was going to let me die here. My glow rose unbidden and curled around me, pulsing lightly over my entire form, and a deep cold set into my bones. I traced my finger over a flame. The warmth was undetectable. Those were flames. They persisted for seconds or minutes until Dr. McCarthy was satisfied and turned them off.

"Excellent job. Let's do that a few more times."

I clenched my fists so I wouldn't curse him out. I urged my glow forth again, embracing the cold. *Careful how much you teach me.*

Chapter Nineteen

GET IT TOGETHER

CW: INDOCTRINATION, DEATH MENTIONS

A large oak door riddled with minute details of a cityscape below the government's crest was before me. On the other side was a meeting I wasn't allowed to opt out of. I tried. I'd been awarded new clothes but conveniently, the good doctor had been out of shirts. I tapped my fingers together. Long to short. Short to long. The familiar stim held me together. *Here we go.*

Heads jerked towards me. There were people from the high-level table, strangers, soldiers, and Karen. My skin itched from the attention.

"You're all here for being bright, fast learners. You're also getting older. Bad thoughts and questions are normal. We welcome you to take this time to talk to us. Let us ease your minds. Let us guide you. We are here to be your stewards away from chaos and towards greatness."

People shifted around in their seats. Trish played with the rims of her chair. Others avoided eye contact. Karen's hands jumped up to her hips.

"This won't do. I know at least one of you must have something that's bothering you."

Her fingers taped against her side as she stared us down. Was there a right answer here? Were we here for doing something wrong? A pimple-covered guy raised a shaking hand. *You sure that's a good idea, bud?*

"Yes, Frank? How can we help you?"

"I wonder what it's like outside sometimes." His body shook as much as his voice.

"We've told you what it's like: there's chaos."

"I wonder how my family's doing. I miss them."

I cringed internally. Frank was going to land himself in the basement if he didn't take the hint. Karen had a way of warning you with how rigid she got. I'd been studying her every time we crossed paths, which was a ridiculously high number of times in the last month or so.

"Your family had fallen victim to the chaos before we found you. You know that. Don't you, Frank? Is there anything else?"

Frank didn't look up. He couldn't see the contempt thinly veiled behind her sugar-sweet tone. Karen focused exclusively on Frank.

"I want to go home."

Everyone froze. Rage flashed across Karen's face. She nodded to a soldier, and he was restrained.

"I didn't mean it. It's not for real. I swear. Please, I'm sorry. I promise. I'm sorry!" Tears and snot ran down his face and neck in thick globs.

"Quiet now. We are going to help you. We'll do everything we can to get the chaos out of you. This is a good thing. You'll be feeling more like yourself in no time," Karen soothed.

They dragged a screaming Frank from the room. Everyone seemed smaller now. They all huddled atop themselves as if to ward off Karen. She flattened out the bottom of her dress. Only careful words could save me now. *Please let this work.* I raised my hand.

"What's your question, dear?" She leaned forward like a viper queueing up to strike.

"I'm scared I won't be good enough to help get rid of the chaos outside."

A few others nodded. Karen's eyes softened. Success.

"We have a training program for each of you. It's specifically catered to help you gain control of yourselves and defeat chaos. You are in good hands. If you work hard and do as you're told, you will excel here."

I couldn't shake Frank's face from my mind even after Karen had sent us on our way. Part of me was happy it hadn't been me. Part of me was guilty for feeling that way. Zane was drenched in sweat and his breathing was labored. I raised an eyebrow, but he just shrugged. Someone was taking this exercise thing too seriously. The burns on my lower legs rubbed against each other. I didn't limp. I didn't need Zane worrying more than he already was.

"Why were you late?"

"I had a meeting to see if the chaos was getting to me." I rolled my eyes.

"Well, has it?" Zane asked.

My brow furrowed.

"I'm joking."

I smacked him on the shoulder.

"Don't take it so seriously."

"Zane."

"If we take it too literally, it'll drive us mad."

I huffed and pointed to myself. *Come on, Zane. Piece it together.*

"Not that there's anything wrong with interpreting things literally. There's a lot of shit happening here. We can't let it get to us."

"They dragged someone out of the room for being homesick. We have to learn from them to outsmart them. We can't do that if we don't take them at their word."

"You don't think they'd actually kill us, right? They're going to talk to that kid they pulled out, not hurt him."

Words tumbled around in my brain as I searched for the right sentence to get through to him. He had to see that this place was filled with monsters hiding behind regulations.

"They torture people for not agreeing here. I've seen them kill people. Don't think for a second you're safe because you have a glow."

"What am I supposed to think? When was the last time you had three meals a day? Or a roof over your head? Or saw a doctor? This place is weird, but they're taking care of us."

I stared at the wall of the gym so he couldn't see my shock and anger. I swore, sometimes I regretted having a twin. This place wasn't good for us. Sure, they were okay about some things, but they were cruel and controlling too. And yet somehow, here was my brother, playing into their hands.

"So were the caregivers, but we left them make our own decisions. You can't do that here. Are you telling me you haven't gotten hurt for doing something wrong? What do you think they would say if they knew you were a high level?" I hissed.

"They said they were excited to see one with so much control. They'd never seen one without a condition before." His chest puffed out.

My jaw dropped, and unease made a home in my stomach.

"What were you thinking?" I asked in horror. I tapped patterns on my leg, trying not to scream at him.

"They aren't afraid of me. Aren't you sick of people being afraid of you?" He sounded so broken.

I wanted to comfort him so badly. Of course I was sick of people being afraid, but this was too steep a price. I couldn't pay for my discomfort with other people's murders.

"Those people they murdered were high levels and those deemed useless. You willingly put yourself into one of those categories. What happens when they decide you're too dangerous? When they ask you to kill?"

Uncertainty tore at his expression and his shoulders slumped. Good. He needed to remember those things. His feet dragged on the squeaky floor. Our brisk walk morphed into a crawl. I gingerly placed a hand on his covered shoulder and squeezed.

"I don't want to lose you to this place. Do what you must to stay alive, but don't for a second think these people actually care about you. The next time you think we're safe here, think about how they shocked Nessa for glowing when Daisy was scared of the dark, or how Devin is banged up, or how we have no control over our schedules."

"We can gain some control if we do as we're told," he muttered.

"Please be careful. I can't lose you too."

"You won't."

I swallowed against the tightness in my throat, unable to reply. The soldiers ordered us to our next meetings, and I was saved from having to.

Cal guided me to the next room. There were rows of chairs all facing a board. I sat in the closest one and awaited further instruction. The others chatted away, but I didn't have it in me to make friends.

"That's my seat." A girl's hand smacked down against the desk.

The others fell silent. Of all the days, today was the one someone wanted to fight me? I didn't have the patience for this.

"I didn't see your name on it." I kept my eyes on the blackboard.

"Move now and there won't be any problems," she threatened.

You have got to be kidding me. It's a fucking chair. I stood and glared at her forehead. It was close enough to her eyes, she wouldn't notice the difference. I waited a moment for dramatic effect before I leaned in so that I was a hair's breadth from her ear.

"That seems like a great way to end up on the list for recycling day."

She pulled back. Fear flickered in her eyes as it warred with her agitation. I raised an eyebrow, waiting for her decision. She shoulder-checked me but moved on to another seat. So they were aware of what went on here. Interesting.

"Today, we will be focused on the environments to the north and the specific challenges they present when combating chaos. There will be a quiz next week."

It was a dull few hours, but not dull enough to warrant seeing Nash at mealtime. I was on my way to my usual table when she popped up beside me. She linked her arm through mine and steered me to the end of a table. She ate as if nothing had changed. Occasionally, she smiled between bites. I couldn't raise my fork until I knew what she wanted. I hated how much I missed her.

"It's good to see you."

That was what she thought was important enough to pop up for? A frown splayed across her face.

"Aren't you happy to see me?"

"I'm not sure that's the right word for how I feel. What are you doing here?"

"I have a schedule to keep too. This is the last dinner slot of the night. It so happens we're both in it today."

"There's no way we just ended up at the same dinner. Not after what you did."

"Are you still upset about me bringing you to safety? You would have died out there."

"At least I would have been free," I shot back.

"No!"

Heads turned and a soldier ordered us to quiet down. Nash ducked her head as if she'd been struck. I wouldn't put it past Karen to hurt government favorites. Those scars on her back came from somewhere. I poked at my potatoes.

"Let's talk about something else," I offered.

"How's your training going?"

"It's okay. How's yours? I know you had a hard time with only using your glow in the training rooms."

I reached out, but she recoiled before I could touch her hand. I slid my hand into my lap. I deserved that.

"That was just a story I told you. This place is great." Her smile halted somewhere between her lips and her nose. The usual crinkle it had when she was actually happy wasn't there.

"If everything is so great, then you must not have any new injuries."

She faltered for a moment before she rolled her eyes.

"I still have lessons to learn. They wouldn't hurt me, or you, if not to help drive us forward." Her voice cracked over the last word. I ignored the jab.

"How are you doing with Echo's death?" I pushed.

"I miss him," she whispered.

There were tears in her eyes. She dropped her head so that her hair fell into her face. I reached out again and brushed my fingertips along the back of her hand. She moved it closer so I could continue. I couldn't imagine how sad she must be. Did she have anyone to talk to?

"I'm sure he misses you too."

I chewed on my lip, searching for more words, finding none. I stroked the back of her hand for the remainder of dinner. When we were ordered back to our rooms, I gave her hand a gentle squeeze before I rose with the others. *Hang in there, Nash.*

There was a first-aid kit waiting for me. I rolled up my pants to expose the charred flesh. The smell was horrendous. I rubbed salve into the wounds, biting back screams. The syringe at the bottom of the kit was labeled antibiotics.

"Mind stabbing me with this?"

Kate and Nessa eyed the syringe. So much for help. I smiled at Daisy who watched me, slack-jawed.

"And how was your day?"

"I practiced multiplication and learned a new song. Do you wanna hear it?"

She straightened up and sang for us. It was all government worship. I bit my tongue. One wrong word and they might take her away from us. I applauded when she was done and she bowed, giggling.

"You've had a big day. Why don't you head to bed?"

She groaned but clambered into bed nonetheless. When her breathing evened out to a slow pace, we gathered on Nessa's bed.

"We have a slight problem," I warned.

I filled them in on everything. Kate tapped her leg to keep herself quiet even as agitation worked its way through her tense form.

"So she's changing her schedule to see you after everything she's done?" Kate fumed.

"Looks like it."

"You have to avoid her. She could put us in more danger than she already has."

"I think we can learn something from her."

"I'm sure she's great at teaching betrayal."

"We're losing Zane. He *told* them he's a high level. Nash may be the only one that knows this place well enough to help us understand him. Maybe we can save them both," I offered weakly. I knew how it sounded, but the words were out of my mouth before I could stop them. Was it silly to hope? Yes. But was I doing it anyway? Of course.

"You still care about her," Nessa said.

"I'm sorry that I have feelings, but I won't put us at risk over them. If I can save her, great. If it'll get us killed, I won't."

"Swear," Kate ordered.

"Really, Kate?"

"Swear on Zane that you won't put us in danger over your girlfriend again."

"She's not my girlfriend. Fine, I swear on Zane that I won't put you in danger over Nash. Are you happy?"

"No, but I figured that's why we're leaving," Kate sing-songed.

Chapter Twenty

OVERSTIMULATED

CW: MELTDOWN, ABLEISM

I removed myself from the bed limb by limb to not wake Daisy. The burns on my ankles ripped against their scabs as I contorted around her. I ground my teeth together, entirely focused on the feeling as they rubbed back and forth. The others were still fast asleep from the previous day's excitement. I matched my breathing to the gentle rise and fall of Kate's chest as I moved through some basic stretches. My muscles protested the movements. Every piece of me coiled with stress, yet I continued and slowly, they began to unbunch. My shoulders dropped, allowing my neck to move with a lightness it hadn't possessed in a while. I continued until the overhead alarm went off.

The sound was different today. The pitch had changed and not for the better. It sliced through my brain mercilessly. My hands clamped over my ears, but it didn't make a difference. All I heard, all I saw, was the alarm. It was so bright. When it stopped, I stayed in place to gather myself. *Focus on your heartbeat. Come on. Just like Zane taught you. Focus.* My hands moved from my ears to flap around my head and I rocked softly. *In, two, three, four, out, two, three, four. In, two, three, four, out, two, three, four.* Their eyes burned into me, but I was no more able to stop than they could stop breathing. I flapped my hands harder. My glow uncoiled from around my heart. *No, no, no.* I needed to have control. I needed to focus. *Don't hurt your friends. In, two, three, four, out, two, three, four.*

"What was that for?" Kate grumbled.

"I think it was because of how long it took to wake us up." Nessa moved around the room, straightening up.

"We're going to have to leave the room soon. You have to get up." Kate knelt beside where I rocked.

"You know she can't just get up."

"What do you want me to do? She can't stay here like this." Kate ran a hand through her auburn hair.

I cringed. Why did they have to be so loud? My glow wound around my heart, pulsing offbeat. *Come on. Focus. Stand up. Come on.* I jerked to my feet. My knees shook beneath me, but I was up. I continued to flap, my eyes trained on the floor.

"That's it. Let's go to breakfast," Kate encouraged.

"Can she do that? Do you see her right now?" Nessa whispered.

It sounded like she was talking in my ear. It was as loud as Kate's nervous steps and Daisy's humming. How was anyone supposed to focus around here? I pulled my arms close. My hands became loose fists, and I shook them in front of my chest.

"May we please eat in our room so our friend can calm down?" Nessa called to the speaker.

There was no reply.

"So much for that." She sighed.

"That means you have to pull it together. We have to leave the room. It's dangerous for you to be out of control," Kate urged.

Fuck. She was right. She was right. She was right. I needed to get better control of myself. I needed to do better, to be better. I felt something cool press into my hand. I looked up to see Daisy standing on tiptoes as she pressed the stim into my shaking palm. She smiled at me before taking a few steps back. It was a tangle toy like the ones I used to have. I let out a soft coo as I twisted it around my hand. The soft clicks and the sheen of the plastic drew me out of my own head. The pressure was still there, but I could kind of focus now.

"Where did you get that, Daisy?" Kate asked with practiced calm.

"It was a gift from Nash."

The other two exchanged knowing glances. I refocused on the tangle in my hand, twisting it over itself. I moved towards the door, still focused on the stim.

"Daisy, did Nash say anything else?" Kate asked.

"They have to stay in the room," Daisy grumbled.

Fear jolted through me. I needed this. It had to come with me. How was I supposed to stay calm? A lump rose in my throat and tears splashed a path down my cheeks. Dejectedly, I placed the tangle in Nessa's outstretched hand. I scrubbed away the tears. They had gotten me into trouble last time. I tapped each of my fingers against my thumb. Long to short. Short to long. It wasn't the same, but it was something. I lurched out of the room and down the hall. The others hung back several paces. They were right to worry. Echo's corpse flashed before my eyes, followed directly by Daisy's father's. I blinked rapidly to remove the images. We were nearly at the cafeteria before they faded. My fingers tapped on each other over and over again. This was my quietest stim, and with any luck, no one would notice.

When I went to grab a seat, the others did not follow me. My insides knotted around themselves. I ducked my head lower and found an empty table. Maybe seeing someone sitting so far removed from the others would encourage them to keep their distance. I poked at the potatoes and tore the pancakes into little pieces. A tray smacked down on the table beside me. I recoiled from the sound as my hands raised before me. I could feel my glow awake and ready.

"No need to be on the defensive," Trish teased.

Her own palms pointed down towards the floor. I returned to pattern tapping against the smooth table. My glow settled back against my core.

"Hey, you good? You seem off today?"

I scowled into my tray.

"Maybe that was the wrong word choice, but something is obviously going on."

"Disagreement."

The word clawed my throat on the way out. *Please let it be enough.* I didn't want to speak again. The other high levels settled in around us. Rachel was not among them. I could still hear her screams.

"What's the long face about? Aren't you all excited? We're getting a visitor next month." A high level waggled his eyebrows.

I cocked my head to the side.

"You know they'll probably cancel it like they did the last four visits." Trish waved it off.

I put my hand under the table so I could shake it. Mother always said a hidden stim was best. What an odd time for her to be right.

"Who's coming?" I asked flatly. One meltdown and it was like I forgot everything I had learned about etiquette. I berated myself while I awaited a response.

"Wow, your doctor is slacking. It's just the biggest person to grace our lives. The director."

Oh, him. Was he as insufferable in person as he was in those videos?

"She doesn't seem very impressed." One of the guys snorted.

I tried to rearrange my features. They continued to stare. *Come on, emote already.*

"Cool." I gave a thumbs-up and my lips twitched towards a smile.

"You are having a shit day, aren't you?" Trish laughed.

A scowl creased my forehead, and I chewed the inside of my cheek.

"You are in a mood. That's for sure," a girl down at the end called.

I put my folded arms on the table and buried my head. I could not win today. I was so tired. So, so tired.

"Lay off her. I think I know what's up," a new voice said.

He tapped my shoulder lightly. I recoiled, not wanting to hurt anyone. That was bare skin. I took in all six feet of his form. His kind brown eyes peeked through his long hair. He had a strong jaw with soft features. The others spoke, but I couldn't understand them. I stayed coiled upon myself, not wanting to hurt this hulking being before me.

"I'm not here to hurt you. Here," he whispered.

He passed me a small, sparkly container. I grabbed it. The sparkles swirled around in liquid. A smile spread across my face as I moved the object closer then farther away as I watched the sparkles catch in the light. It was wonderful.

"That's what I thought. This one's got trouble focusing. They need a sensory break."

I mean, he was only half wrong, but I wasn't going to correct him if it meant I got to stim. I played with the sparkly water for the remainder of breakfast. When it was time to part ways for the day, I went to hand it back to him, but he waved me off.

"I can always make another one. High-level privileges." He rolled his eyes. "They aren't what they're cracked up to be. You probably picked the smarter path of the two of us."

He winked. I gaped at him. A sly smile hung on his lips. He waved one last time before he turned and jogged back to the other high levels.

I forced my feet to carry me onward. Was he saying he knew I was a high level? Or that he knew I was autistic? Or was he searching for answers the same way I was? The cool plastic of the shiny stim helped me. I glanced back, and I was met with his smile as he raised a finger to his lips. I spun back around, heat rising to my face. My glow unsettled from around my heart and rushed through my limbs. The cold vibrated through me. I took a deep breath and focused on the steady rise and fall of my chest. There would be plenty of time to panic during training. My doctor came into view, and I hurried to his side.

My feet dragged against the hard tile. I kept my eyes on the patterns below my feet and the plastic jar in my pocket. He opened the door and smoke wafted around me. I hazarded a glance out the window and into the training room. It looked like a hurricane had passed through. There were broken branches thrown about and bits of cloth scattered.

"Did someone else use this room before us?" I asked.

He continued scrawling notes. His outfit was crisp as always. His green tie was the only break from the monochrome of his pants and lab coat.

"Do you have other students?"

"Do you think you are the only one that needs saving from the chaos?" he asked, pen poised above the page.

Had I said the wrong thing? My glow spiked before recoiling. It wove round my heart like a snake. Was it alive? I put a hand to my chest, unsure of how to take that idea. Dr. McCarthy awaited my response. Damn it, what was I supposed to do now? What was the question again? Right, other students.

"It looks like a lot of destruction out there. I hope they're okay."

I looked as close to his eyes as I could. My brain buzzed unpleasantly. He didn't seem convinced. What now? I twirled a piece of hair between my fingers the way Kate did when she was in trouble and dropped the eye contact. The doctor sighed.

"It's noble of you to worry about the other students after only being here for a short time. Your compassion is impressive. I'll be sure to note that in your file." Dr. McCarthy reached out to pat my head, and I took a step back reflexively.

"Excellent job. It's good to see you taking the necessary precautions. You are thriving here."

I nodded, unsure if my voice could hold through much more conversation. Staying focused was a losing battle, but I still tried.

"This is unorthodox, but you seem exhausted and you're doing very well. You may spend your morning session resting."

My eyebrows knitted together. Wasn't the whole point of this place to train? To get strong and then go out and conquer "chaos"?

"Lie down if you'd like. Unless you'd rather train today?" He raised an eyebrow.

"Thank you."

I shuffled over to the corner away from my soldier. I felt marginally better. It was still Cal and not someone new. I curled towards the wall. I shut my eyes and allowed the pulse of my glow to lull me to sleep.

Chapter Twenty-One

Admittance of Power

"Wake up."

"Wha—" I fumbled over the word, my head full of fuzz.

"If you don't get up, you are going to be late."

Cal placed a hand on my shoulder and shook me. I jumped to my feet as my glow unwound from my heart and raced to the spot the hand had been moments before. I held my hands out, palms up and ready to hurt whoever it was. My mind raced back to training days with Mother.

"You need to focus." Mother's cane rested on her chest and she held a rock in each hand. To my left, teenage me shook, hands raised.

I clenched my hands into fists. I remembered this day.

"I can't do this. You know I can't." She hung her head.

"Look up, Simerra. You have a duty to this family," Mother insisted.

Teenage me cried out when a rock smacked her in the forehead. I winced.

"Mother, please," she cried.

"You have been babied long enough. You need to master this. Come on. Your brother is worlds ahead of you. Get your hands up."

A sob broke free from my chest. Mother picked up a rock the size of my head. I winced in preparation, but it wasn't enough. I felt the rock collide with her leg and screamed as she did against the pain.

I heard someone gasp for breath, but it didn't sound like Mother. I blinked rapidly. A shadowy figure flashed in and out of sight. I squinted. Who was that?

"Simerra!"

I rubbed my eyes, urging the figure to come into focus. My heartbeat was in my ears. The person in the room coughed and spluttered. I shook my head and focused on the figure again. Cal was on the floor, gasping for air. What was wrong with him? The pieces clicked together. I ripped my glow back inwards. The familiar cool settled over me. The glow slithered up my arms and back around my heart. The doctor wasn't in the room. Of all the times to disappear. When had he left? Why had he left?

"What the fuck was that?"

"I'm so sorry."

I rubbed the back of my neck. What was the right way to say? Sorry I almost killed you, but also please don't tell anyone what you just experienced? Yeah, no clue.

"I didn't mean to hurt you. I thou— You touched my shoulder. Sorry."

He leaned back against the wall, still panting. I fidgeted in place, waiting for the verdict. How fast would he run to tell someone?

"You are lucky there are no cameras in here," he finally mustered.

"I don't touch people for a reason."

He laughed. His eyes softened and for a second, he looked around my age. The lines on his forehead spread flat. New ones formed around his eyes with his laughter.

"I can see why. That's an intense ability you have there."

I opened my mouth to argue but thought better of it. I'd nearly killed him. My glow pulsed particularly hard at that. Did I want to kill him? The thought had my stomach in knots. Should I apologize again? What was the social protocol for almost killing someone?

"I'm sorry."

"I'm fine, so we're good. How did you keep this from them? Put out fires, my ass. It was like you ripped the air out of me."

"It's vital that no one finds out. It would put my friends at risk." It would put Nash at risk. "Please."

"I'm not going to tell anyone." He smiled sheepishly. "This is the most fun I've had since I got here."

"What do you mean?"

"You don't miss anything, do you?" He chuckled.

"Oh, ya know, just every other normal social cue. It's no big deal."

"You're funny. I like it. To answer your question: I'm what happens when you pass the program. Let's get you to your next session or they'll have both of our heads."

I might as well have trained with how tired I was. Cal opened the door and gestured for me to walk through it. So we were back to not talking? I followed him back down the hall. With each step, I weighed my options. I could still kill him and blame it on my glow, say he touched me and it was an accident, but he was as close as I was going to get to having an inside guy. Nash's face flashed through my mind. Yeah, he was the closest. Besides, the idea of killing him didn't sit right with me. I was going to have to trust him. He could prove useful if I put more thought into it.

I stepped into the same room as the other day. Of course the girl I pissed off was already there. I picked the seat behind her. She swiveled to look at me, a triumphant grin on her face. I couldn't help but roll my eyes. She was every bit as annoying as I thought she was. Her smile faltered for a moment.

"Not so big and tough today, are we?"

A man in a suit walked in and cleared the white board of the old lesson and readied his green marker on the smudged surface. His handwriting was neat and uniform across the board despite how fast he scrawled out notes.

"The teacher's here."

She spun around in her seat. Finally, some peace. I felt Cal's eyes on me, and it was oddly comforting. Unlike the predatory eyes of older soldiers I'd caught gawking. Were they all once like us? Stuck in these seats, learning bullshit about chaos? If they all passed the program, then they all believed it or they convinced Karen and the others they did. A soldier on the other side of the room stared at me with unconcealed hunger. A shiver raced up my spine.

At lunch, the rude girl fell into step behind me. I smirked. Halfway there, I heard her steps falter. That was right. The big bad high levels sat over here. I had to give her credit for not giving up. Everyone glared at her.

"Go sit with your own," Trish hissed at her.

"She's sitting with you."

"She's with us. You couldn't hang if you wanted to, so turn yourself around and go be average somewhere else." Trish waved her off.

The girl's face turned bright red before she scuttled away. I dug into my lunch.

"You gonna tell us what that was all about?" Trish asked.

"She's from my strategy class. I took her seat the other day." I shrugged.

"You low levels fight over everything, no offense," Trish said.

"None taken. I've mostly been ignoring her."

"Good. The last thing you need is trouble. You'll find plenty by sitting with us," Trish asserted.

I snorted at the idea before coughing overtook me. Food did not belong in my lungs, but here we were, in this ugly checkerboard cafeteria while my food tried to do the government's job.

"I think trouble finds me no matter where I go." I stared at the bite of pasta on my fork. "I might as well have fun along the way."

Perhaps I came across cocky, but it was better than coming across scared. Trish looked at me with an emotion I didn't recognize. I tried to run her expression against others I'd seen in the past, but I couldn't nail it down. I'd have to ask Zane later. If I got to see Zane later. My throat tightened at the thought. I peered down the table, trying to spot the boy from earlier.

"He'll be here soon," Trish informed me.

She fiddled with the zipper on her bag before putting it back on the handles of her wheelchair. Her chair was overflowing with little, multicolor pouches and other bits and bobs.

"Medical supplies," she said.

Was I really being so obvious? If only the nap had afforded me a bit more energy, then I could mask better before I pissed someone off. Love myself as I may, I was not ready to face the fallout of an angry allistic so soon after a meltdown. I was lucky I got to rest at all today. It was quite the reward for my hard work. Why was I celebrating performing tricks for people who kidnapped me? I squirmed in my chair. So this was how they gained our obedience. Small acts of kindness in a sea of cruelty. Life jackets only the most desperate would accept. What had they done to make Zane this desperate, to make Nash? A tray clattered against the tabletop, taking me out of my thoughts and back to the lunchroom. To my left sat the guy from earlier. He met my eyes with his own. I looked to the side of him, but the brief eye contact already stung my brain. Why did people have to place value on eye contact? Focus obliterating, painful, old-fashioned—I was getting away from myself. He was still looking. I kept my eyes to the left of his.

"I thought so." He took another bite of food.

My eyebrows knitted together. Had I done something?

"Your secret's safe with me."

It clicked together, and I couldn't help but laugh. It bubbled up from my core and tumbled from my lips. My glow vibrated softly with it. My right hand flapped. So that was why he'd let me borrow the stim jar.

"You think I'm hiding being autistic?" I asked, still flapping.

That took the cake for the most outrageous thing I'd heard while here, and I had seen the welcome video.

"Aren't you?"

"I stopped caring about who knows I'm autistic a long time ago. I interact with the world differently than most, but that doesn't make me lesser."

"Huh, I wouldn't broadcast it if I were you. The adults will think they mislabeled you as a low level. I'm only telling you to keep you safe. I'm Jack by the way."

"I'm Simerra, and I can keep myself safe."

I couldn't tell if he was being nice or if there was another meaning to his words, but Zane had taught me long ago not to trust everyone who claimed to be trying to help. Zane was the only one I could trust to talk plainly and honestly to me.

"I'm not saying you can't, but being a high level isn't great. They don't trust us like they do you guys. They have good reason to be cautious, as we are more dangerous. We aren't allowed to move around without being watched, even after we graduate. The closest we'll get is going on missions, and even then, we'll have handlers. So do yourself a favor and avoid all of this crap." Jack's shoulders slumped as he talked.

"At least we're away from the chaos." The last word felt wrong in my mouth, but I said it anyway.

It was his turn to laugh at me. A deep, belly laugh that sounded like it should have shaken the table.

"Quiet," a soldier said.

Was he another program success story? We all ducked our heads. The volume of the table dropped back to a low hum to match the rest of the room.

"You're a funny one. I don't have you figured out yet but give it time. I look forward to learning more about you," he informed me.

"We'll have plenty of time while we're here." The lie slid from my lips before I'd even thought about it.

All those lessons with Zane had paid off after all. Was it right to lie to him? Should I tell him? Was it safe to fill him in? Before I decided, he turned back to his plate. I would leave it alone for now. I listened to the conversation as it bubbled around me, pulled the jar from my pocket, and shook it. The glitter swirled around in the liquid. I watched it race round and settle before I shook it again and again. I kept my flapping hands under the table where the soldiers and attendants couldn't see.

"Hey, everyone's leaving. It's time to dump your tray," Trish said, breaking through to me.

"Right, sorry," I apologized, rubbing the back of my neck.

I forgot how into it I got with stims sometimes. I felt worlds better. I'd have to remember this little jar for next time I was overwhelmed. It was mesmerizing.

"Come on then." Trish set her tray on her lap and wheeled it over to the trash.

I peeked around for Jack, but he was already gone. I hurried to catch up to Trish as we made our way outside. She led the way over to a group of boisterous kids.

"I heard you and Jack talking. I wasn't trying to listen, but you were sitting next to me. He's not usually the helpful type. He's more of a quiet observer."

"I seem to have that effect on people. Or are you telling me you're normally welcoming to low levels, Trish?"

"I'm not convinced you are a low level. You're shy like one, but there's something about you."

I was once again thankful for my flat affect. It seemed like a skill she would benefit from. There was fear and worry on her face. Poor neurotypicals, they really did wear their emotions on their sleeves. Maybe I could trust her. Nash's betrayal stood in my memory like a warning bell. I pushed it off. We couldn't get out of here alone. We'd need allies, and strong glows were the best place to start. Besides, if there was any group that needed out, it was the most heavily watched and punished. *Please don't let me be wrong.*

"I'm not a low level," I breathed.

Trish put her hands on her hips and waited for me to continue. *Here goes nothing.*

"I have a powerful glow. It isn't safe to tell the doctors that. I need them to think I'm less of a threat," I explained.

Trish crossed her arms, still not speaking. The words cascaded from my mouth.

"I can't stay here, Trish. I know what it's like on the outside, and it's rough and hard work but there's freedom. You've been taught that there's chaos out there, but all I see here is pain and dysfunction. We're treated like things, not people. What they're doing to Rachel—"

"Leave her out of this," Trish said coldly.

She needed to understand. I had one shot at this before she went to the soldiers about me. I had to make this count.

"If we were outside of this place, she wouldn't be hurt for having different ideas or failing a test. We would have a chance."

"And what about when the government comes to round us up again, huh? Or when Rachel needs a break from walking because of her immune disorder? Or when my wheelchair gets stuck on a cracked road?" Her voice wavered even at a whisper.

I took in Trish's chair. The wheels were larger than the chairs I was used to seeing from before, and the backrest ended midback. It was sportier than the bulky hospital ones I was used to.

"Have you considered an electric chair?" I asked.

"Have you considered there's like no electricity out there? And where would you get that kind of chair?"

"We could modify yours," I suggested.

"How."

I refrained from rolling my eyes. These were valid questions, but I needed to know who was coming to know who to accommodate.

"I don't have the details worked out yet. That's why we're still here. If we could get someone to mod your chair and find a high level with moderate control over electricity, we could power it and you could leave this shitscape. If enough of us work together, they'll have a hard time stopping us. We will find a way to accommodate Rachel while we travel or take breaks if and when she needs it."

"Medications, proper diets . . . you're talking about a serious production if you plan on taking high levels with you. Haven't you heard we all have something going on?"

"We are just as deserving of a good life as anyone else. How much support you need shouldn't affect that," I asserted, "I'm sick of being backed into staying places for the benefit of others. We deserve the same autonomy and I'm willing to fight for it; so are my friends. Don't you want to see the world for yourself? Don't you want to protect your friends? Don't you want to see them thrive?"

"You make it sound so simple."

"I'm not saying it'll be easy. It'll be one of the hardest things you've ever done, but that does not make it any less worth doing. I respect you. I want to offer you the chance to get out of here too."

"If you pull this off, they'll never stop looking for you. You'll never be free of them as long as the government stands."

I grinned. Now she was getting it.

"You're definitely a high level. I'm in."

Chapter Twenty-Two

DR. MCCARTHY

C W: SEXUAL ASSAULT, COERCION, vomit, sexual harassment

The next few weeks passed in a blur of training and planning. I spent the evenings chatting with Kate and Nessa, piecing together what this building looked like with little updates from Kate on how the boys were doing peppered throughout. We made copies of Mother's map for everyone. Glimpses of each other throughout the day were fleeting at best. This place was designed to keep glow wielders from talking, but I didn't let it slow me down. We each focused on a different piece of our escape. I was charged with gathering intel.

Suddenly, not being able to block anyone out was a respected gift, not just an overstimulating curse. Sure, I was exhausted from listening to all the conversations around me, but listening for key words eased the burden the more I worked at it. It was kind of funny. Everyone was so determined to appear unaffected by the "chaos" of outside, but those same people were dissatisfied.

They wanted a change. They were bored with the classes they were in. They wondered what it was like outside. They wanted more free time. They wanted less harsh training. They wanted their autonomy back. The scale on which they were discontent made me nervous. Would we be able to provide for a group that large? Nessa was worried, but Kate, well, she was Kate. I smiled, remembering how giddy Kate was at the idea of turning this place on its head.

We were all excited to leave with two key exceptions. Joey said the last time it was mentioned while Zane was still awake, he'd waved them off, claiming it wasn't safe outside. Devin and Joey now waited for him to fall asleep to plan. In our room, we had Daisy. She sang songs about the government and would talk for hours about the things she learned and how much fun she had each day.

Thankfully, she was always first to fall asleep so we could focus on the plan, but I was worried. Would the two of them refuse to leave? At least with Daisy, we had Devin. She asked for him almost daily. Surely, she would come with us, even if it was only to stay with her brother. We could work on the rest of it later. At least we didn't have to worry about them hurting her. Well, not anymore than they hurt the other well-behaved kids.

There was still the issue of Nash. After seeing what this place had done to two of our own, I couldn't understand how the others didn't empathize with Nash. She was as much a victim as the rest of us. This place was insidious. They figured out what you wanted and held it out of reach. Their praise was earned when worked to exhaustion. Too tired to think. Too tired to rebel. And if not, well there was always recycling day. It had been three weeks since the last one. No doubt there would be another soon, and I still hadn't seen Rachel. Trish wouldn't survive losing her friend. You could see it in her hunched shoulders. She'd stopped talking. Instead, she opted to poke at her food. If I wanted to help Trish, I was going to have to help Rachel, which was why I was in this predicament to begin with.

I kept my palms towards the earth. My head bowed in submission. Goose bumps broke out over my bare arms and torso. I did my best to hold still as Dr. McCarty continued his inspection. Out of the corner of my eye, I saw him appraising my body. My stomach churned fiercely. His foot tapped against the tile. I focused on the rhythm as I held still. I could play this game.

"Go get Karen," Dr. McCarthy ordered Cal.

I heard the door swish open before it clattered shut once more. His hand brushed against my shoulder and I stiffened. Was this why he'd sent Cal away? He picked up a strand of my hair and inhaled deeply. I shut my eyes. My hands knotted into fists. I would not feel bad when we tore this place apart. It would be the justice they deserved.

"In another life." Dr. McCarthy sighed. He dropped my hair and moved back to his seat on the other side of the room. "You sure do behave well for someone making ridiculous requests."

Did he want me to reply? I could still feel his eyes combing over every inch of me. *Think about fishing with Nash, or stories by the fire, or literally anything else.* The door opened once more and in swept Karen.

"This one wants to help a girl named Rachel." Dr. McCarthy turned back to his clipboard.

Now he knew how to keep his eyes to himself? Gross old man.

"Do you? You know Rachel is in isolation due to her weakness in the face of chaos. Why should I remove her from it before she has been fully rehabilitated?" A sickly sweet smile played on her lips.

What did I have to offer? I wasn't even sure I'd get this far honestly. *Come on, Simerra. There has to be something.*

"Why don't you and your doctor work out a plan on how you can earn the privilege of helping Rachel? Cal, with me. There's a disturbance on the second floor you can assist with."

Cal went stiff. That wasn't a good sign.

"Don't worry. It shouldn't take too long. Alert me after their plan is made, and I'll have Rachel returned to her normal schedule. Doctor." She gave Dr. McCarthy a curt nod.

Cal hesitated, anguish tearing at his features, and then he, too, was gone. The door clicked shut and I was once more alone with Dr. McCarthy. My heart raced. I was unsure of what caused Cal's concern but sure I would find out soon. I chewed my words to ensure their careful delivery.

"What sort of plan are you thinking?" I asked.

He eyed me hungrily. I took a step back. What kind of deal had I agreed to?

******** You can skip down from here if you don't want to read the above cw. It's fade to black****

"I think we both know. Undress."

This was bad. This was really bad. *Come on, say something. Anything.*

"I'm not— This isn't— I just want to help Rachel," I choked out.

"It's very admirable of you."

Deep breaths. Deep breaths. I was going to get through this, but only if I stayed calm. His eyes devoured me. The urge to vomit was growing from the pit of my stomach. I closed my eyes as if it would protect against the onslaught. It took mere moments for him to close the distance between us. My hands flapped. I tried to still them, but it was flap or scream and I had to endure this. He chuckled. His hot breath tickled my ear. Everything in me said to fight or run yet neither were options for me. I held my ground as he consumed me. A dullness spread over my body. His touch seemed distant. I welcomed the dullness with open arms. Anything to get away from this. Anything to forget.

******* The aftermath is below**** cw meltdown

I came back to myself as Dr. McCarthy straightened his clothes. He caught me looking at him and smiled sheepishly, as if he'd been caught with his hand in the cookie jar.

"You can't blame me. You're quite a specimen. You have a bright future here."

I scooted myself into the corner of the room. He clucked his tongue, wiggling a finger back and forth.

"Get dressed. Cal will be here to collect you soon. Great plan by the way."

With a wink, he vanished out the door. I crumbled and pulled my legs up to my chest. I ached down to my core. How had this happened? I surveyed my skin, taking in the bruises that blossomed purple and deep blue. Bite marks covered my torso. Why hadn't my glow killed him? Another wave of nausea crashed into me. This one took me under. I wretched to the side then tucked my knees back under my chin. My throat burned from the acid. I swallowed, trying to clear it, but I vomited again. I scooched away from what remained of my breakfast.

I rocked back and forth, humming loudly. Why had this happened? My glow was supposed to keep me safe. I couldn't even do that. A scream ripped its way out of my throat. My hands smacked against my head over and over. The pressure gave me something to focus on. I screamed again, my fists slammed against the ground, the walls, me. I hit and tore at everything within reach, but mostly it was my own skin. My throat was hoarse. I didn't care. Nothing mattered. I was gross, worthless. I clawed at my bruised arms; the pain was the only thing I could focus on. Tears soaked my face and ran down my neck. I was a mess. Everything was a mess. I was a giant, gross mess that couldn't even keep myself safe.

"What's the point in having you if you can't protect me?" I screamed.

My glow vibrated against my chest, rubbing softly back and forth. I clawed at it, trying to rip it out. Pathetic, useless, worthless, talentless. Why was this happening to me? Why? Why? Why?

"Hey, hey, please don't hurt yourself. I'm so sorry I had to leave. If they knew I cared, I'd be reassigned." Cal sat beside me.

I uncurled enough to see his face. It was filled with rage despite his calm tone. I flinched, waiting for the next terrible thing to happen. I rocked back and forth, the repetition helping me. My fists flailed to their own pattern. His hands fluttered near me but didn't make contact.

"I'm sorry. I'm not going to hurt you. I swear. It's me. It's Cal. You knocked me on my ass the other day, remember?"

I did remember, but I couldn't stop. This was the only way I could process the world right now. I wanted to tell him I understood, but words were too hard. I wailed louder, frustrated and angry at my inability to communicate with him.

"I'm going to help you. I'm going to grab your clothes, okay?"

I watched through tear-filled eyes as he crossed the room to where my clothes lay scattered. He picked each item up carefully, walked over, and set them before me. I kept rocking.

"We have to get you out of here. You need to get dressed."

There shouldn't have been a need for me to get dressed again. I sobbed harder.

"I'm sorry. I— How can I help? Can you talk?"

I shrugged, unsure.

"Okay, that's a start. Where's Dr. McCarthy?"

I pressed my hands over my ears, not wanting to hear his name. Fuck him. Fuck that man. That monster. How could he do this to another person? I screamed, unable to control how I was feeling. My fists beat at my skull as I tried to process what was done to me. To his credit, Cal did not try to stop me or tell me I was overreacting. He sat there, listening to me scream, trying to block my fists with his own hands but never restraining me. When the screaming stopped, he smiled at me, tears in his own eyes.

"What can I do?"

"Don't. Know."

I chewed on my nails and around the edges of my fingers as I worked to ground myself.

He held out my clothes.

I pulled them back on, noticing the bite marks on my upper thighs. Bruises smattered my skin from where his teeth had been. I vomited again, all bile. I had already expelled everything else from my stomach. I wiped my chin on the back of my hand and took a deep breath in an attempt to steady myself. Tears remade pathways down my face like I was a waterfall before I finished the breath. So much for pulling myself together. I was a mess. A giant, gross mess.

"Allow me to help you," Cal pleaded.

He held out his hand. I took it, ready to try anything. My glow rushed towards the point of contact, but I forced it back. I needed this, and the glow that couldn't even keep me safe was not going to get in my way. A false calm lapped at the edge of my consciousness. Cal's hand glowed softly. So this was his ability. I let it fill me with a false ease. My tears slowed to a drip. My next deep breath was much more productive.

"That's it. Deep breaths. I don't know if this is comforting or not, but he's never done this before."

"Then why me?" I spat out.

My free hand clawed at my side once more. The false calm was the only thing keeping me from another round of screaming.

"I'm hoping it means it won't happen again," Cal explained.

Again? This could happen again? I mean, of course it could. I wasn't dead. I wasn't actually in pieces, even if it felt that way. Once the bruises healed, I would be the same exact person I was before. Still following all the shitty rules in this terrible place. Still able to be hurt like anyone else. Wait. There had been a reason for all this. I grabbed Cal by the sleeve of his shirt.

"Rachel," I demanded.

"She's safe. I saw Karen take her out of isolation and point her at the lunchroom. She's safe thanks to you."

I released him and leaned back against my heels. My ankles shook with the weight of all that had transpired. Small blessings. Trish would take care of her. She'd be back to herself eventually. Would I be? I shook it from my mind. My body screamed against me, but I pushed myself to my feet. The world spun; I caught myself against the wall. I squared my shoulders and straightened up.

"Let's go."

"Can you walk?" Cal asked.

I shoved off the wall and took a few shaky steps. There was a burning between my legs I wasn't ready to think about. I gritted my teeth and nodded. I could do this.

"Okay, I'll get the door."

I shuffled forward. Smaller steps didn't agitate everything as much. When I made it out into the hall, I leaned against the wall. I didn't care what piece of fancy art I leaned against. If they didn't want it leaned on, then maybe they shouldn't have let me get hurt. By the time we'd made it down the hallway, my chest heaved from the exertion.

"We have to keep moving. Someone's coming."

Cal placed a hand on my elbow. I plastered myself against the wall. Tears rushed to my eyes as if they'd never left. He drew his hand away as if I'd burned him. I didn't mean for that to happen. I barely understood my reactions, so he had no hope of deciphering them. How was he supposed to get me anywhere? The click of boots set my heart into overdrive. We were both screwed if someone saw me like this. Cal put himself between me and whoever was coming. They stopped to the far side of Cal. I shrank behind him, hoping to disappear.

"What are you doing here? Let me pass. I know her."

I knew that voice. I looked up to see Nash trying to get past Cal. She gasped, getting a good look at my face. I could feel the self-inflicted bruise on my eye from when I lost control of myself.

"Did he hurt you? What happened? You aren't supposed to hurt students without cause," Nash spat at Cal.

"Not him," I breathed.

Nash stopped struggling to better hear me.

"What happened?"

The low hum of conversation filtered towards us from the far end of the hall. Were more people coming? What would they think of our little group?

"Do you trust me?" Nash asked. Her green eyes held no judgment as she waited for my response.

I could still get lost in those eyes, and as much as I knew I shouldn't, of course I trusted her. I trusted her with everything I was.

"Yes."

She put my arm around her shoulders, and she steered us up a flight of stairs and down a different hallway. It was full of smaller versions of the room I stayed in. I wrestled with my glow. I was not going to hurt her. Sweat beaded on my forehead from the effort. It was a good thing she was helping. I was in no position to support myself and control my glow. I wasn't that good. I let her guide me into a room and over to the bed. I backed up until I felt the cool wall against my shoulder blades. Cal rubbed a hand against the back of his neck, perplexed. Nash didn't even spare him a glance.

"Are you okay? What happened?" She sat before me.

The concern in her eyes felt so real. I ached for this to be reality. I was probably still back in the other room, still being hurt. I surveyed this space. There were clothes thrown in the vicinity of an overflowing hamper. The ground was littered with weights of all sizes. Pictures filled the walls. Postcards from places she'd likely been while off combating "chaos." She also had a desk. There was a notebook open on it. A drawing of the night sky filled the page. I could even make out one of the constellations. I had shown her that one. A small piece of me rejoiced.

I glanced out the window. It was odd to be so close and so far from the open air. They really had designed this place to suck your soul out. Cal stood with his arms crossed by the door. The hard look on his face softened when he noticed my gaze. So he didn't like Nash. Did he know who she was, or was he worried because he didn't?

"She had a run-in with a doctor," he supplied.

Nash looked over at him. Agitation burned in her eyes.

"And you did what? Look at her."

I pulled at her sleeve, cutting her tirade short. Her eyes were stunning as always, even as they shone with worry.

"It's not Cal's fault. Karen made him go," I muttered to my knees.

"I'll lay off you, I guess. Shouldn't you go patrol or something? She's safe here."

"I'm her guard specifically. You know that."

Were they waiting for me to be more indoctrinated before I would be allowed to roam the school unsupervised? Speaking of indoctrination, Nash seemed really worried. She knew she was the reason I was here, right? I wouldn't have been here to be hurt if it wasn't for her.

"They'll let her stay with me. They usually allow for recovery time so as not to hinder training anyway."

"You know they aren't going to count this as an event that needs recovery time. It's not like she got hurt training."

"We aren't acquainted. I'm Nash."

His hand went to his belt. Was he reaching for his gun all because she said her name? What information was I missing this time?

"As I was saying, they'll let her out of training for a while if she's with me. Feel free to stand guard at the door if you have to, but I won't have you in my room."

Cal looked past her to where I sat.

I nodded.

Cal left the room without another word.

"What happened?"

The false calm from Cal was gone now. I could feel my stomach turning again. My face must have given it away since Nash passed me the trash can. I heaved into it. What a pretty sight I was.

"You heard what he said."

"That's barely an answer."

My throat felt tight, and tears rose unbidden to my eyes. They streamed down my cheeks and blurred my vision. Was this an answer? Did this count? Why couldn't I get a handle on myself? I grabbed the small stim jar from my pocket and shook it. The glitter swirled round and round, but it wasn't helping. Things like this always worked when

I was overstimulated. Why wasn't it helping with this? Did I not deserve it? Sobs racked my body.

"Oh, Simerra."

Nash set a blanket over my shoulders and hugged me. I gave myself over to the crushing despair contained in my body. I cried for what had been done to me. I cried for the pain of my injuries. I cried for being trapped in this place. I cried for Zane being brainwashed. I cried for all Rachel had endured. I cried for the Nash I thought I knew. I cried for the confusion of her being nice now. I cried for all of it, and she didn't stop me.

We sat in the pit of my emotions. My sobs were the only sound, and the changing shadows were the only indication that time was still passing. I hardly felt real. Nash didn't lie and say it was alright or try to get me to talk again. She sat there in the storm with me. When my tears slowed, she rose and grabbed me a water bottle. I gulped it down. My throat was scratchy from my bouts of screaming earlier. I felt more in control than I had in the observation room, but I still felt disgusting.

There was a knock at the door. Nash squeezed my shoulders gently before removing herself from the bed. I missed her touch already. I looked on forlornly as I waited for her to return. The door shut softly, and then she was back. There was an overflowing tray of food in her hands. I eyed it hungrily.

"Do you mind if we eat on the floor?"

I shrugged.

"Thanks. Grab whatever you'd like."

I grabbed a piece of pizza off the stack. Nash grabbed a yogurt. She smiled. It was the prettiest smile I'd ever seen. I focused on my food, not trusting the words that could come out of my mouth. She didn't press me. We made our way through the mountain of food. I felt infinitesimally better when we cleared the tray.

She offered me her hand.

I hesitated.

"You won't hurt me."

A small bit of warmth entered my heart. I took her hand and stood beside her.

"How about a shower?"

I opened my mouth to protest, but she leveled me with a look. I shrugged, smiling.

"That's what I thought."

She knocked on the door before opening it. Cal was on a cot, book in his hand. He really took his job seriously.

"I'm going to take her two doors down to shower."

He nodded, returning to his book. Did people still publish books, or was it from before? Nash guided me into a tiled room and under some hot water. It stung my injuries at first, but it was wonderful once I'd adjusted. She set a caddy with soap down on the far side of the curtain and pushed it under to me.

"Don't forget to take those clothes off." I could hear the laughter in her voice.

My face flushed redder than it already was from the heat of the shower. She was right. I kicked off the pants and underwear, flung off the bra, and kicked it all out to her. She gathered it all and walked off. My nerves started to rise, but I tried to focus on the hot water. My muscles sang from the soothing effects. Fully soaked, I examined the contents of the cart. She had shampoo and conditioner and a separate body soap? She even had hair and scalp treatment supplies. She really must be someone special. The few other times I'd showered here, the water had been lukewarm and I'd had a single bar of soap for all of us to share and our soldiers watched. There was never a curtain. Maybe I should behave enough to land me in a spot like this. What was wrong with me? All this likely came at a cost. It might have even been a direct result of her selling me out. I pushed the thought away. For a little while, I wanted to forget all the bad. I inhaled the scent of shampoo and hummed softly to myself. My hair became soft again under the bubbles.

When I was done, I turned the water off, and Nash passed me a towel through the curtain. Once dry, I wrapped the towel around myself and emerged from the shower.

"She lives!" Nash proclaimed.

I winced at the echoing sound.

"She lives," she repeated in a stage whisper with jazz hands.

I almost smiled.

"I'll take it," she said with a wink.

She offered me her hand and I took it. My glow was alert, but it stayed around my heart. Back in her room, she took care of my injuries as softly as she would have cared for her own. Once they were wrapped, she helped detangle my mess of hair. With leave-in treatments and delicate fingers, she helped rearrange it into the natural fro I'd swapped to after taking out my old style a few weeks ago. She made me brush my teeth and put on deodorant. "All the essentials," as she called them. She passed me shorts and a T-shirt so I didn't have to live in a towel in the same green as her own clothes.

"I'll get your stuff washed and see if we can't find you a shirt to keep permanently."

I sucked in a deep breath and dropped the towel. There were bite marks all down my torso and along my inner thighs. They looked how my jaw felt. I pulled the clothes on mechanically. At least the outfit hid half of them, and it was more covered than I'd been in weeks. A tired numbness spread throughout my body. It was a welcome reprieve from the pain and embarrassment.

"I'll take the floor." She gestured to the sleeping bag next to the bed.

I bit my lip. This was her room. She deserved to sleep in her own bed.

"I'll be fine. Get some rest."

If she was sure . . . I clambered into her bed and snuggled beneath the comforters. I was more tired than I thought. Not even the chaos of the day could keep me up. It was moments before I was asleep.

CHAPTER TWENTY-THREE

GREATER UNDERSTANDING

CW: ASSAULT AFTERMATH

C

I woke up slowly the next morning. This bed was worlds softer than mine had ever been, like lying on a cloud. I pulled the pillow closer to my face and inhaled deeply. It smelled so comforting, like home. I waded through the fog in my mind, trying to name the smell. I rolled over, pulling the blankets up towards my chin. They were heavier than the little blanket I had with Daisy. Had they finally relented and given us more supplies? A thought wiggled past the haze of sleep, something dark. A terrible truth. I shoved it away, opting for the comfort of my sleep-fogged brain. It was so warm and so safe in this moment surrounded by that smell.

As the haze faded, a scratching sound like pen on paper filled the air. When did we get paper? I opened my eyes to see the picture-laden walls and it all flooded back: Nash taking care of me, Cal getting me out of there, the doctor, all of it. I pulled at fistfuls of hair to ground. To feel something other than the bone-deep ick that worked its way back through me. Tears soaked my arm. I wished desperately to go back to dreaming. I took a jagged breath of air. Nash's smell filled my nose. Right, I was in her bed. A chair creaked and then there was a body wrapped around my own.

"It's going to be okay. I'm here."

My glow purred, happy she was near. Could glows feel on their own? Right now, I wanted to know other things, like why me? What had I done to deserve this? Would Nash even want to take care of me if she knew what happened? I cried harder at the thought. Nash held me close. The smell of her shampoo swirled around me. Every once in a while, she would murmur a soft nothing of encouragement or a reminder that she was there. Slowly, it devolved from sobs to tears to soft whimpering sounds. I peeked at her through my blanket burrito. Her hair swayed back and forth. Oh, we were rocking. How long had I been doing that? Nash didn't seem to mind, so I didn't try to stop. The movement allowed me to focus on not sounding so pathetic.

"How are you feeling?" Nash asked.

"I'm okay."

I coughed to clear my scratchy throat. *Come on, sound like a person.* Who knew how long I was going to have with her before things went back to normal.

"Do you want to go get food?" she offered.

I nodded.

She pulled away, and I bit back a whimper. The closeness was the only thread holding me together. Nash handed me my blue clothes. I unwrapped myself from the blankets and pulled them back on. Once dressed, I glanced down at my bare torso. Was this why it had happened? No, I'd dressed like this from the moment we got here. My clothing wasn't to blame.

"Sorry, they told me they're still out of shirts. The shipment should be here soonish."

That wasn't it at all. I slung my arm across my chest, holding my opposite shoulder. I felt like I could hold myself together more this way. Like maybe all the broken pieces would stay vaguely human shaped as long as I held them in place.

"Ready to go?"

I nodded.

"No words today?"

I shrugged.

"No problem. Let's go."

She offered her hand and I took it. My glow still purred as it rumbled around my heart. She guided me down the hall to a room much smaller than the lunchroom I was used to. It was set up similarly with a buffet line at the front, but there were no soldiers hanging around except Cal. People glared and at first, I thought it was me, but the looks lasted after I passed them.

"They aren't used to having guards during their mealtime," Nash explained.

Made sense. You worked your butt off to not need supervision and then there was a soldier interrupting your meal? I'd be annoyed too. What had the other people in this room done to earn such privileges? I mulled it over as I grabbed two burgers off the middle stack and a brownie. They really pulled out all the stops if you behaved. Nash guided me over to an empty corner table away from the others.

"Don't worry about the looks."

Most were unashamed and didn't even look away when I stared back. I took a bite of my burger. Let them look. What did it matter?

"Wait here," Nash said.

She walked off to the food line and reached in a big white box. She fiddled around with a few things, and then she skipped back and set down two bowls. I waited for her to explain, perplexed.

"It's ice cream," she said.

Say no more. I dug in. It was colder than I remembered, but it tasted the same. Nash giggled into her own bowl. I raised an eyebrow. She shook her head at me and gestured for me to slow down.

"Don't forget to breathe. If you eat that too fast, you'll get brain freeze."

I rolled my eyes, then the tingling coldness filled my palate and my head.

"Now that's an attractive face. It helps if you put your thumb on the roof of your mouth."

I took her advice and immediately began to feel a bit better.

"Maybe now you'll slow down."

I shrugged.

I was practically finished anyway. Where had they gotten this? I mean, it stood to reason that not everywhere had fully shut down, but I'd always thought it was like a few farms scattered around the country making essentials, not ice cream. Then again, we had almost completely avoided the remnants of society, so maybe I didn't have the best idea of what was out there. Did that mean this facility contained the best of what was left? I fucking hoped not. Nash set our dishes on the cart, and we made our way back to her room. Cal was close behind us all the while.

"You can go get food. We won't leave the room until you get back," Nash assured him.

He nodded curtly.

The click of his boots bounced around the mostly bare hall. Only a few smaller paintings decorated the walls. *Hurry back, Cal.* With a sigh, I entered Nash's room. It looked the same as when we left it. Fairy lights twinkled above her bed. Thick books were littered on the floor. They were all opened to different places. Her notebook lay open on the desk. A glowing woman stood emboldened on the page. Her hands were raised with palms pointing towards the viewer. Her hair whipped around her face and the trees swayed. Intense focus shone from the expertly crafted furrowed brow. I walked over to inspect the picture, my hand tracing the lines of her silhouette.

"That's a pretty rough sketch," Nash said.

"It's beautiful."

She smiled, her whole face lightening.

I reciprocated.

It was so nice to be able to communicate like this. I forgot how much I enjoyed it.

I flapped my hands before I realized what I was doing. I shoved them behind my back. I wasn't supposed to do that around people here.

Her smile faltered.

"It's okay. You're happy. I'm happy too. Like this, right?"

She flapped one of her own hands. Was she mimicking my movements?

I squealed softly.

She nodded, still flapping.

I flapped back slowly, not sure if she was serious.

She grinned again. Her whole face lit up. She looked her age instead of battle hardened. There was an unmistakable sparkle in her eyes.

I flapped, giggling happily. I rocked heel to toe and toe to heel on my feet with little bounces on the toe end.

She echoed me, still smiling. Still flapping.

I tensed every muscle in my body to the point of shaking and giggled before I released them from the stiff hold. I flapped bigger and allowed myself to occupy space. Nash did the same, backing up slightly so we would not bump into each other. I hadn't felt this free in so long. We continued on like that, both of us moving our bodies. The carefree joy I felt built by the moment. Years of tension melted away, creating space for my authentic self. Mark said no one would ever love me like this. The longer Nash bounced and flapped with me, the less I believed it. So what if this communication was nonverbal? She cared no matter how I communicated. The rest of the world ceased to exist. All that mattered was Nash and me and our flapping hands.

We spent the evening in comfortable silence. The old cell phone in the corner played songs I didn't recognize, most of them without words. Nash sketched in her notebook while I colored an old sketch of hers. Every so often, we would swap pieces to admire what the other had accomplished. She passed me the picture I'd seen the first night again. It was beautiful. A girl surrounded by fireflies was standing tall and strong and smiling. My work was amateur in comparison, but she complimented me anyway. When it came time for dinner, she held out her hand and I took it. Cal's eyes bored into my back. I knew how this looked. I tried to shake the guilt during dinner to no avail. The door clicked shut with a somber finality.

"I feel it too, and I know we have to talk. I'm not trying to get out of it, but it's getting late. Let me take care of your injuries, and then you should get some sleep. We can discuss everything in the morning. I'll answer your questions to the best of my ability. You can take the bed with all the blankets," Nash said, avoiding my gaze.

The bed was super soft, and I wasn't in a big hurry to get back to business as usual. Walking hurt, so I couldn't imagine trying to train, and the thought of seeing Dr. McCarthy again—acid rose in my throat. I gestured for the trash. Nash passed it to me, not missing a beat. I heaved and spluttered into the bucket. Only when my stomach was empty did the nausea pass. I wiped my mouth on the napkin Nash handed me.

"I really think you should rest another day. You aren't feeling your best. Trying to train right now wouldn't be beneficial," Nash argued.

Don't cry. Don't cry, I begged myself. I swallowed the knot in my throat. My eyes were heavy, two brown pools swathed in sadness. Nash picked up our art supplies then made her way to the door.

"Let her friends know she's injured and receiving treatment."

"Stay put till I get back," Cal warned.

"We're going to bed, I think. And don't worry. I'll call it in tomorrow."

Cal muttered something else in reply but Nash waved him off, shutting the door. She left only the fairy lights to twinkle in the darkness. Pretty little sparkles of hope. They cast an ethereal glow over everything, including Nash. She looked like a goddess. I forced myself to look away. I nestled down in the covers and breathed in Nash's comforting scent, drifting closer and closer to unconsciousness.

"Are you awake?"

My half-asleep brain tried to piece together a response, but my head was too fuzzy with exhaustion.

"I didn't think so. The girl in the picture, the one you got excited about, that's you, Simerra. I know you can't see it right now, but that you is in there: strong, in charge of your glow, and happy. I know you're strong enough to get through this. I'm going to do everything I can to help you. If that means I let the chaos in, so be it. Screw what Mom would say. Screw what any of them would say. I can't lose you. I care for you more than I care for myself." She stopped her proclamation to take a jagged breath. Was she crying? I wanted to get up and hug her, hold her tight and tell her I felt the same. I cared too. Tiredness had me frozen in place. Her words faded with my consciousness into blurry obscurity where they were promptly forgotten.

CHAPTER TWENTY-FOUR

BEAUTIFUL DISASTER

CW: ASSAULT AFTERMATH, STERILIZATION mention, victim blaming, indoctrination

The next week passed like a dream. Nash took care of me, showing me around this floor where others like her lived. Apparently, being like Nash afforded a lot of freedom. More freedom than I'd ever had in my life. Did those few days after we left the adults really count as freedom, or did you have to make it at least a week before claiming that title?

When we weren't out roaming, we were making art in her room, dancing, watching the birds from her window, or crying. I spent more time that week crying than I wished for anyone to know. Nash knew I was hurting, yet she never questioned me about it. She would sit with me and sing softly or hold me until I was able to stop. She never pressured me to tell her why I was sad, even when she cared for my wounds. It was why I didn't press her, not that morning or any morning since. We had yet to have a serious talk about what us spending time together meant or how she was able to get me out of everything.

Why did this place trust her so much? Come to think of it, why did they trust everyone on this floor? I was the only one with a guard on this floor. They didn't need soldiers here. Were they program graduates? It would make sense. Nash was as brainwashed if not more so than Cal, displayed by the way she talked about this program. She'd said something about a mission when we were all picked up. Fuck me. Nash was a fucking soldier. Just my luck.

I set my pencil down as I wrapped my head around the implications. It should have come sooner given Cal was wearing a similar deep green. I felt like an idiot. What was I supposed to do now? I pressed my hands into my face and dragged them down. The pressure helped me to focus on my current plight. We had to talk about this. I'd put it off for too long already and I couldn't in good conscience continue, even if words were still hard. It had been a week since I'd used a full sentence. It was the longest I'd ever been gifted silence. I chewed my lip, unsure of how to begin this conversation. I must have taken too long since Nash looked up, puzzled.

"We have to talk."

"Yeah, we do. Your line work is getting a lot better! See, I told you practice makes perfect," Nash deflected.

"We can't keep putting it off."

"We could for like a day or two more. Hasn't it been great pretending it's like it was before?" She fiddled with the marker in her hand.

"But it's not like it was before. We're stuck inside a government run shit show."

"You can't really think that. We've been having fun, right?"

"We've been playing pretend while one floor down, people are being beaten for talking, or training until they pass out, or who knows what else."

"This place is designed to keep people safe. Its very existence is proof that chaos can be conquered. That the youth of today have a promising tomorrow. Once the chaos out there is eradicated, this will all have been worth it."

"Do you even hear yourself? The only chaos I've seen is here. Look around."

"No, there's chaos out there. That's why Echo died. It's why we attacked government officials. It's all the chaos out there. Those people were full of it," she extrapolated.

"Then what about the woman who begged them to leave her children alone? Government officials killed her."

"The chaos had gotten to her."

I had to get through to her or I was going to lose her. The thought of being unsuccessful made my heart ache.

"Echo was an accident. Those happen, Nash. Sometimes, our glows are too big and too strong, and sometimes people get hurt because of it. We were kids when we got these abilities or gifts or whatever you want to call them."

"The chaos got him," she rebuffed, only half hearing.

"I was being attacked when he grabbed me. He was trying to help, but I thought he was someone else. My glow hurt him. He's dead because of me, Nash, not the chaos, not anything else. You have to know that," I contested.

"The chaos—"

"You have to come to terms with this, Nash. Echo is buried out there and it is my fault."

She put her hands over her ears and screamed. Cal slammed the door open, gun out. I stood between the two of them, hand raised. He raised an eyebrow, questioning the scene before him. Nash's scream melted into gut-wrenching despair. Cal's face softened and his gun returned to his belt. He backed out of the room, shutting the door. I lowered my hand and watched as Nash sobbed. Her whole body slouched from her pain. I wanted to wrap myself around her like she had me this past week, but I had no right to comfort her. I was the source of her pain. I bit back my own tears as I sat as her guardian, remembering all the nights she had sat with me through mine.

"I'm so sorry, Nash. If I could go back and change it, I would. I never meant to take him from you. I was scared, and I was careless, and now he's gone." My voice broke over the words like a poorly tuned instrument.

I set a hand on her shoulder and squeezed gently. She threw herself into my arms. I pulled her in tight and didn't let go. Her fingers knotted up in the fabric of my shirt.

"I'm here. I'm not going anywhere," I murmured.

We sat like that as the sun finished its path through the sky and gave way to the moon. It illuminated her weeping form. Anytime I thought she was done, she would mumble his name and repeat the cycle. I ran my fingers through her hair to soothe her.

Her breaths were the ragged in and out of someone who knew they should breathe deeply but couldn't remember how. I deepened my own breathing to help. Bit by bit, she matched mine, then she went limp in my arms. Rest finally claimed her. I continued to play with her hair as she slept, too scared to move her. I looked down at the sleeping angel in my arms. Her face was a mess, with hair plastered to her cheek with dried tears.

A few hours later, she stirred. She mumbled to herself, rubbing sleep out of her eyes. She peeked up at me through a curtain of hair. Her green eyes were heavy with pain.

"You know, Echo was doing better in his training than I was when we first met. He had a room up here. Mine was still on the lower level. Any skill he worked on, he had in spades. I always did the risky stuff. He was more of an asset to this place than I'll ever be. He was dedicated to fighting the chaos." She smiled. "He used to say, 'The only thing worse than chaos is someone that doesn't try.' He gave everything one hundred and ten percent, even making people laugh. He thought laughter would help us in our fight. The higher-ups never really agreed with him, but he was so good, they let him have it. He loved trying out jokes on new recruits."

"I guess I only ever knew part of him."

She nodded, her cheeks puffed out. I poked at one. She blew air at my face. I crinkled my nose.

"What, don't like my morning breath?"

"It's not the grossest thing, I suppose."

"You'll regret that." She smiled, but it never reached her eyes.

I shrugged and waited for her to direct the conversation.

"I miss him. More than I thought possible. It makes me wish we'd never left to fight chaos. Ridiculous, right?"

"You wanted to protect your friend. There's nothing shameful about that."

She twisted around in my lap to see my face clearer.

"You really believe that? We're the generation the sickness cursed. We have to make up for it by fighting the chaos it sowed throughout the world."

She sounded like a pamphlet. Did this place do pamphlets? I could see it now. Send your kids here, folks. They're the future! This institution is not liable for injuries or fatalities incurred during the training process. Send your kids in today! I pushed the absurd idea to the side. *Focus, Simerra.*

"What happens when there are no more kids to be rounded up? When everyone is at a place like this? What happens next?"

"There will still be work to be done. They'll need training to manage their abilities, and those who've been overtaken by the chaos will have to face strict rehabilitation. There'll be clean up and—"

"And then what? When all that is done, is there a future in which we get to be free of this place?"

"That's not the point." She sighed.

"There has to be a part of this where we get to leave. Daisy's not a soldier. She'll never be one. She's a kid."

"A kid that needs structure."

"A kid that needs her brother. Who she barely gets to see."

Nash darted to her closet and started pulling things out. Scarves, knives, socks, old underwear, and books flew through the air. I pressed against the wall, trying to stay out of her way. She arose victorious, a thin book clasped in her hands. She poured over the pages while she flipped back and forth, and she chatted to herself about how "this paragraph was close" or that section "wasn't right."

"Here." She pointed to a section of text at the bottom of page 96.

"I can't read that from here," I said.

With a huff, she pulled the book back towards herself.

"Anyone over the age of twenty that has passed the program is eligible for distance learning and possible termination of contract. One must file proper paperwork and agree to mandatory sterilization, especially if of a higher level and in pursuit of this option. All applications will be thoroughly reviewed by the director and include a written component and an interview to ensure only those truly ready to battle chaos in all its forms are returned to the world."

"They're talking about wiping us out," I whispered.

This place was a living nightmare. I tapped my fingers against themselves. Long to short. Short to long. Nash's brow furrowed. She looked between her book and me eight times before she dropped it. She sat back on the bed, one leg tucked underneath her for support. What could she say to make any of that sound even remotely beneficial to anyone other than the government?

"It's a way out. We can work with that, right? Eventually, we could apply together," she continued in a small voice. "What choice do we have?"

"We could leave. We could work together and find a hole in their defenses and get all of us out of here. You, me, Daisy, Devin, Zane, Joey, Nessa, Kate, and anyone else we can get to come with us. We could get out of this place."

Nash's eyes bulged out of her head. She looked more cartoon than person. I waited as she processed. This was a conversation we needed to have. I had waited too long already.

"That is the absolute worst idea!"

"The only reason they found us last time was because you helped them. This time, we could be prepared. We could take supplies to get far enough away and from there, we can make what we need. If we work together, we'll stay safe. Don't you want Daisy to have the freedom you have?"

"She will one day. If she studies hard."

"She's practically a high level. You know how hard that would be for her. She'd miss Devin too much anyway."

"What does Zane think of your plan?"

All of my energy zapped itself from my body. Zane. My fool of a brother. I could practically hear him arguing with me, saying the same regurgitated crap as Nash. The two of them would get along great now. I scowled. This was not how I wanted them to sort out their differences.

"He's starting to believe the stories about chaos. He thinks it's great that we're getting training here."

"He's not wrong. Knowing how to use your ability lowers your risk."

"You know most of their tactics now. You could help us teach ourselves. Who knows better how hard or long to push someone with glow work than another person with a glow? We could end all the strict punishments. We could teach with kindness, and people would treat us with kindness in response."

"What you're talking about is chaos," Nash argued.

"What I'm talking about is a life free of government control," I said.

"They have our best interests at heart."

"They call anything out of their control chaos. I can't live like that," I snapped, turning away.

"I think I finally get it."

What was she going on about?

"It's starting to make sense why you're covered in marks. You don't listen to the doctors at all," she accused.

Twist the knife, would you? What the fuck, Nash? My glow leapt to my limbs with delicious, familiar cold. The pictures on the wall moved to a breeze that wasn't there. How dare she. Had she not realized the bite marks were, well, bite marks? I had cried for a week in her arms. I should've known. Angry tears splattered my face.

"How could you say something like that to me! Why act like you cared all week if you were going to throw it in my face at the first chance you got? Do you have any idea how used I feel? How dirty? I want to rip my own skin off where he touched me."

She watched me stand before her. My body shook as I spoke; my muscles all tensed and released randomly. My right hand flapped as I tried desperately to maintain a semblance of control. I could see each piece of what I'd said starting to click. About damn time.

"He took everything from me. Do you get it now? Do you need me to spell it out for you? I have nothing. I'm nothing," I choked out.

I leaned back and slowly put my hands where his greedy paws had touched my torso. I showed her how my hand could replicate the pattern on my neck. Her eyes widened with each display. I curled inward, hiding the marks from her stare. Now she knew my shame.

I wished I could say she fell to her knees or told me everything was going to be okay, but this wasn't a fairy tale. There was no magic moment where she took my hand and didn't let go. She gaped at me like a fish out of water, warring with what this place told her was true and the reality of it set before her.

"So what happens now, Nash? Are you going to turn me in?"

She was taken aback by my bold words, but I didn't have the patience to ask like an allistic. She was either with me or I was wasting my breath on someone who would betray me again. *Please let her be with me.* I didn't think I could take the pain if she wasn't. Not after this. But, if she was still in there under all the crap this place did to her, I was not going to leave her behind.

"I'm scared of this place and of that doctor. I cannot stay here and lead any kind of productive life. Do you remember the fireflies and dancing through the trees? We could have that again. We could be us again, but we have to get out."

"Like your friends would ever want me to come with you." She glowered.

"Like I'd let them stop me. Nash, I want you by my side. I want us to help people and get out of here together," I implored, searching her face for any sign there was hope.

"You don't mean that," she argued.

I laughed. I couldn't help it. Couldn't she see she was everything I wanted even when this place had her all mixed up?

She cocked her head to the side.

"I care about you. I care about you so much, it's hard to breathe. The thought of you not coming with us—" I swallowed the lump in my throat. "If you won't come with us, I don't know what I'll do."

"You'll stay," she pleaded, wide-eyed.

"No." My voice broke over the word. "I can't force everyone else to stay in this shit hole, not even for you. I'll keep going for them, but I don't want to. I want you to come with me. I want us to face this together. Everything is easier with you by my side. This week has been awful, and you helped me through it, not the doctors, not the learning facility, not Zane, you. And I want to help you mourn Echo fully because this place is not letting you."

"The chaos," she protested weakly.

"If this is chaos, then let us be a beautiful disaster."

I offered her my hand. *Don't leave me hanging, Nash.*

"If you were anyone else, I would have already reported you," she murmured.

"Yeah, but I'm special." I winked. A sly grin slid acrost my face.

She put her hand in mine. Her eyes were full of uncertainty. A bright smile spread all the way up to my eyes. I pulled her towards me, and she squeaked when we collided. We fell to the bed in a giggling mess. My glow nestled back by my heart, purring once more. I had never been so thankful in my life. Nash was coming with us. My heart soared with joy. From the look in her eyes, I thought hers was too.

Chapter Twenty-Five

UPDATES AND CHECK-INS

C W: ASSAULT AFTERMATH

That evening, Nash's hand hovered over the marks on my torso. Her face bunched up.

"How are you feeling?" she asked, not bothering to look up.

"I'm still here." I shrugged noncommittally.

She swatted at my side before leveling me with a stare. So much for getting out of it.

"I'm okay." I added a fake smile.

"You aren't," she deadpanned.

I exhaled in a huff. What did she want me to say? I searched for the right words to comfort her.

"I see what you're doing, and I want you to knock it off. Just because I'm a hot mess doesn't mean you can't be too. We're going to get through this together, right? That's like the whole point," Nash reminded me.

"Maybe."

"I *did* graduate top of my class," she bragged. Her chest puffed out as she postured. She was adorable.

"Oh, well, la-di-da. Aren't you special?" I ruffled her hair. She shook it to the side so she could see again. She ran her fingers through it, fixing all the wavy bits I had messed up with my antics. The sun was going down again.

"You could stay here longer." Hope filled her words.

I closed my eyes. I couldn't make a clear decision while looking at her. I had been away from the others for so long already, and we still had details to nail down for the plan to work.

"You know I need to go back. They're probably worried sick."

She groaned and threw herself back against the pillows.

"It's not forever. We're getting out of here," I reminded her. A small smile played on my lips.

"How will I know when it's time?" She fiddled with a strand of her hair.

"I'm thinking we'll do it when the special visitor is here."

"When security will be tripled?"

"Yup, when security is overworked and stretched too thin. It's all about perspective. When we leave, it'll be anything but quiet. Believe me, you'll know when it's time." I'd had a few ideas about flashy exits. There was no way to quietly take any large number of people out of here anyway. May as well leave with a bang.

Nash seemed convinced, which was good since I wasn't one hundred percent sure I was. I mean, I still had time to hammer out all the details, right? I could worry about this later. There was a far more immediate danger on the horizon. I had to tell Kate that Nash was coming. I walked to the door and gave Nash a final wave before walking out of her room and back into reality.

"Can you take me back to my room?" I asked.

"It's about dinner time. Why don't I take you there first?" Cal suggested softly.

I nodded. We passed the elevator, opting for the stairs instead. My muscles protested the stretch, but it was good for them. Cameras decorated the hallway as if to punctuate the danger we were in. Cal pushed the door open to the meal room and made a flourish for me to walk through. I took a deep breath to gather myself.

"Keep me updated," Cal breathed.

I stayed the course over to the food table, careful not to break stride. I surveyed the room. The low bubble of voices made my ears ring. I had not missed the clatter of silverware or the mass of bodies. Nash and I had missed a few meals in the last two days. It was time to play catch-up. It was a delicious problem to have. I took in the sea of faces. Nothing recognizable stood out, not even the high-level table. Maybe they had eaten during an earlier slot. I wove through people, trying to find a seat. Someone's waving arms grabbed my attention. I looked over to see Nessa flagging me down. I swallowed the nausea rising in my throat and made my way to her table. Devin, Joey, and Kate sat together. I tucked into my food.

"Are you going to make us beg? What happened?" Kate thumped her fist on the table.

I took a long drink from my glass. The cool juice was the only break I was going to get before filling them in.

"Nash found me when I was between courses. She wanted to spend time together." The lie slid too easily from my lips. I was getting too good at this.

"I knew it. That slimy bitch hurt you," Kate accused.

I gripped the table. My glow jerked around my chest cavity. I needed to stay calm.

"It wasn't her," I spat out between clenched teeth.

Kate's eyebrows disappeared into her hairline. The others worked to hide their shock. *Calm down, Simerra. You're overreacting. You need to be calm so you can convince them Nash is safe. You've got this. Breathe. Count how long you inhale and exhale. Breathe. In, two, three, four. Out, two, three, four.*

"It was my doctor," I admitted.

"What'd you do to piss him off?" Joey questioned.

I bit back the bile and flinch combo his words smacked me with. What had I done? Really? That was the question of choice? And people said I lacked tact and awareness? *For fuck's sake, Joey.*

"It has less to do with making him angry and more to do with making a deal." I played with my hair. It was something to focus on besides their faces, a brief and nerve-saving reprieve.

"Well, out with it. Don't leave us guessing," Kate pushed.

I knew the words I needed to say, but they were lodged in my throat. Tears escaped my eyes as I struggled to voice my pain. Silly tears from a silly girl who thought she could make a deal with those monsters masquerading as agents of peace.

"Woah, you don't have to tell us. Ease off her, Kate. You okay?" Devin asked.

I shook my head. Tears fell to the table. My voice refused to work. So much for holding it together.

"I wasn't trying to upset her."

"It's obvious she's upset about it. We have enough information. You said Nash found you? How did that go? Is she brainwashed?" Devin redirected.

I inhaled roughly. The knot in my throat barely moved, but I felt calmer. I repeated the process until I could see through the tears, the fuzzy outlines becoming people again. I could do this. I had to.

"She took care of me."

I searched for words that wouldn't give away how much time I'd spent lounging. Guilt set in. They'd been training, and I'd kicked it with the person who'd landed us here in the first place. There really wasn't any way around this. Well, shit.

"She wanted to spend time with me like we used to. It was almost like we were before we came here."

"You mean before she betrayed us? You told her to fuck right off, didn't you?" Kate interrogated.

"Not exactly. I told her our plan. Easy with the death glares. She's on our side. She's coming."

"Not on your life."

"Real mature, Kate," Devin said.

"We have to consider the bigger picture. Nash is a soldier. That means we might be able to get information on guard rotation and any security measures around this place we'll need to avoid to have any hope of escaping," I speculated.

"Anything else we should know about?" Joey asked.

"If there are people you trust to keep it quiet, tell them. We need to see how many are coming with us."

"You make it sound like you already have people in mind," Devin observed.

"I've told a few that I trust."

"You trusted Nash," Kate grumbled.

"And she has her head more than Zane does and he's still coming. As I was saying, I have told a few people who are in charge of larger groups. At least some of the high levels are coming with us."

"Are they like Zane?" Joey asked.

I tried to hide the hurt from my face. Were they like Zane? Were they more in control of themselves than I was? Were they normal? I checked his face. He seemed earnest enough. Was I reading way too much into this? He was allistic. They circle talked for ages given the right topic just to avoid hurting someone's feelings. No, this was too direct. It was an honest question.

"They've never hurt me if that's what you're asking. We need to find someone who can modify a battery for a few wheelchairs and someone that can control electricity to charge them. We also need to raid this place for supplies. I was thinking of asking a soldier or two for that."

"You seem to have thought this through." Nessa elbowed Kate in the ribs.

"I get it. It's a solid plan. I'll go along with it, but I don't have to like it," Kate griped.

"No one said you had to. This will only work if we're all on the same team. No one deserves to be trapped here. We need to help as many people as we can escape with this wave."

"What are you suggesting?" Joey asked.

"We're going to book it once we get out until we're safe and established, right?" Devin said.

"Oh, for sure, and once we're settled, we can come back."

"And rescue the others," Devin said, our shadows shifting slightly as he grinned.

"Exactly. No one left behind."

"Do you know how many soldiers will be after us if we do that?" Kate groaned, pinching the bridge of her nose.

"Could you live with the guilt if we didn't come back?" Devin leveled her with a look. "So we're in agreement then. Get the fuck out of here, get safe, make a plan, then come back and turn up. I can get behind it. It looks like dinner is over so perfect timing," Devin finished with a dramatic hand flourish.

They all groaned. So much for catching up. I hung back and Devin waited for me.

"You really should talk to someone about what happened," he whispered. Concern practically rolled off him.

"I'm fine."

"It doesn't have to be me, but you should talk to someone. You look tormented."

"Way to be blunt," I grumbled at my shoes.

"You prefer it that way." He shrugged.

His muscled arm brushed mine. I moved to the left, creating distance between us.

"Have a little faith. I can hold my breath longer than that," Devin teased.

"Let's not test that, okay?"

He dumped his tray and held his palms towards the ground in mock surrender. I pushed him playfully.

"You two, knock it off. Keep up with the others," a soldier ordered.

We laughed, picking up the pace. The lights clicked off as we headed towards the exit, the doorway our only source of light. We really had been dawdling. I scrunched my eyes against the bright lights when we entered the hall.

"This way," Devin said from my left.

I followed his voice the rest of the way to my room. It was simpler to rely on instead of the over saturated visual input I was getting. Everything was so much brighter and louder than it'd been at Nash's. When we reached the rooms, Devin disappeared into his with a final wave.

Kate and Nessa sat together. Daisy fiddled with both of the tangle toys. I'd almost forgotten about those. She squeaked loudly when she saw me. I held up my hands, and she stopped a hair's breadth away from me, vibrating with energy.

"I missed you so much. Did you miss me? Did you really go see Nash? Are you back for good? Did you have fun? What was it like? What did you do? Kate said you weren't coming back, but you're here so she was wrong. I'm so happy. You're so great. I really missed you!" She clasped her hands together and rocked on her heels.

"I missed you too, Daisy. Kate was worried, that's all. It's good to see you too. Are you enjoying having the bed to yourself?"

She shook her head. Her braids smacked her in the face from the force.

"Careful there, little one. You may change your answer after tonight. The bed is only meant for one person." I laughed, rocking back on my heels.

"I missed you. I'm glad you're back. Besides, I like sharing. It's more like before but without the chaos." Her face scrunched up. "Is it okay to miss before?"

"I'll tell you a secret. I miss before too," I whispered conspiratorially.

"We were like a big family."

"We're still family, Daisy. They can't take that away from us."

"You promise?" Her little eyes were so wide.

"I promise. Only talk to us and Devin about it okay?" I urged.

"You can count on me." She handed me one of the tangles before bouncing off.

"What if we aren't able to pull this off? I've yet to hear about anyone else trying something like this. If we fail . . ." Nessa twisted her hands into the hem of her shirt.

"Then we better not fail. We have two weeks to pull this plan together. That's more planning than we've ever put into anything. We

can do this, but we should get some rest. It's going to be a long two
weeks."

Chapter Twenty-Six

DO I HAVE A CHOICE?

C W: TRAUMA, ABUSE, TEACHER abuse, whipping, flashback mentions, blood

My hands shook through breakfast. I bounced my leg. I looked at the glitter jar. I even tried to hum a song. Nothing helped. The closer we drew to training, the worse it became. Did I have to go? We could break out of here right now and I wouldn't ever have to see my doctor again. It was all wishful thinking. I knew we had to wait for the "special guest" or we risked being underprepared and failing. With measured steps, I made my way down the hall where the doctors all stood waiting for us. I spotted Cal first. A trickle of relief found its way to me. If he was there, maybe this would go okay. My eyes fell on Dr. McCarthy, then the nausea hit me like. I forced my feet to carry me forward even as everything in me demanded I run. One step after the other, I walked to his side.

"Are you ready for today's lesson?" His eyes traveled over my torso, lingering on the marks.

"Yes, Dr. McCarthy." The words tasted like sandpaper, but hey, I still managed to say them.

"Good. This way."

I caught Cal's sympathetic smile, but I couldn't muster one in return. It was a miracle I wasn't vomiting. Anything beyond that was out of reach. I followed the doctor to our white room. I couldn't look away from the corner. My heart beat erratically. Dr. McCarthy offered me a seat and I took it. My hands gripped the edges of my chair. I needed something real to hold on to, to remind me of what reality was. I slipped in and out of my foggy memories. One second, I was listening to him explain today's tasks, and the next, I was thrown back to that moment in the corner. His eyes were on me all the while. I could do this. It was two weeks. Just two weeks.

"Let's get on with your training."

"Yes, doctor."

I rushed from the small room into the training arena. I inhaled the stale smoke and burnt wood. Those smells hadn't been there when I'd been hurt. This was a new day. I was safe. Okay, now I was ready. Time to focus. A fire jumped up to my right. My glow spiraled down my arm; the fire spluttered beneath my hand, not going out. Had they turned up the difficulty of all this again? I pushed against the fire, submerging my hand in the flames. This time, it fizzled out. I looked up at the viewing window, triumphant. Dr. McCarthy made a lazy circle with his index finger. I looked around to spot three more fires. I took pleasure in putting them out. Each one was practice for the day I would take his fire. I looked up at him when I finished. *Bring it on, asshole. One day soon, I will crush you.*

The force of my conviction scared me more than that room did. Was I so ready to kill again? Could I really touch another human with the hopes of eviscerating them from this world? I glanced up at his smug face. Rage and nausea wrecked my body. Yes, yes, I could. I ripped the oxygen from any fire set before me. My breathing became labored, but I continued. This was the most fires I'd ever been able to take out. I was tired, but I could stand. Hatred was a great motivator.

"I'm going to call it for today. We have something to do before you continue on with your schedule."

My glow pulsed along to my heartbeat. I felt safer with it so close to the surface of my skin. Any touch would be deadly. I stood with my feet shoulders width apart, hands on hips, chest heaving.

The doctor popped in a tape, and I watched the old TV come to life.

"Have you been making progress with your training? If you're seeing this, then there's a good chance you are and I want to congratulate you! This is a momentous occasion!" the director crackled out of the worn speakers.

You'd think they would buy a new TV or something with all the funding this place spent on hallway art.

"You kids are our greatest assets! When the sickness came, you showed your strength and grit, coming out victorious over the disease! Your diligent hard work can help us thrive over the chaos that encapsulates our society."

Images flashed across the scene: first, a burning hospital, then an abandoned store. Next, people were running and screaming. What were they running from? Was this what they thought it was like outside? A group of people spreading fire from building to building flashed across the screen, then it was back to the director's face.

"You see, you're vital to protecting our nation and the good cities that remain."

Images of a peaceful row of houses popped up. Birds chirped off screen. Someone walked a dog. People still had pets? On the screen, people waved to one another. They all looked so happy. The image faded away.

"I know that was shocking. You've never seen such a peaceful place. It's able to stay like that because only a chosen few are allowed to stay in these cities. In our efforts to maintain this order, we need young adults like you to step up and lead the charge against chaos. We need soldiers with the skill to do what must be done so that there can be peace. When you are ready to serve your great country, your doctor can play the next tape so that we can get you on the path to success. If today is not your day, you may revisit this decision at any time throughout your training. Please note that acceptance of this offer fast-tracks your training and gets you in the field three times sooner. Acceptance into the program is celebrated."

The director raised a glass of something. When had he gotten that?

"A toast to your successful future. For the good of the country!" He took a long drink from his glass as the screen faded to black.

"Are you ready to take the next steps?" Dr. McCarthy asked, tape in hand.

"I think I'll pass today, thank you."

So this is how they did it. Threw temptation straight in your face only to rip it away and force you to work for them for the rest of your life. Fuck this place.

"When you're ready, proceed to your next task." He waved me off.

Cal held the door open for me. Dr. McCarthy's chair creaked. I didn't know I could tense further, but I did. Every muscle locked in place. I waited for whatever clever phrase he was about to hurl in my direction, not that it mattered. There was nothing he could say to make me change my mind. I was not going to work for the government, not even for two weeks.

"It may interest you to know that your brother has already agreed."

My fingers tightened on the doorframe as I fought for composure. I pivoted on my heel. Dr. McCarthy's grin came into view. He was serious. Damn it, Zane. I was starting to regret having a twin. I plastered a smile on my face and clasped my hands tightly behind my back. So much for having a choice. I tapped the toe of my shoe against the floor. It was the only sound in the room as everyone waited for me to speak.

"I accept the offer. I want to protect our country from chaos." I forced as much "happy" into my voice as I could remember how to.

Mother would have been proud of how much affect I had.

"Excellent. Let's play the next tape, shall we?"

I swear, Zane, someone is going to have to protect you from me when I catch up with you. This is bullshit. I tapped my fingers against my thumb as I waited for the static-filled screen of lies.

"People need to rewind these things when they're done with them. What ever happened to common courtesy? I'll tell you, it's going the same way this TV is. Out with the old soon enough if I have anything to say about it."

The director popped back into view, sitting on a backwards stool. He broke into applause and Dr. McCarthy joined in.

"Congratulations! I am excited for you to continue on your journey at this fine establishment. You are pivotal in the pursuit of a world in which chaos cannot devour the next generation like it almost did yours. You stand at the precipice of greatness. With the help of your doctor, you will prepare for your evaluation meeting where you will meet yours truly. My next planned visit is______."

A long pause began. I looked to the doctor, confused. He riffled through his notes.

"The seventh of this month. A few short weeks away."

"Thanks, doctor."

Another pause began.

"Thank you, director, sir," Dr. McCarthy replied.

They both laughed. Was I in some sort of dystopian nightmare world? Never mind, those were places for quirky teens, not underwhelmed, overworked twenty-somethings. We could use an upbeat underdog right about now though. Too bad.

"I'm sure you're eager to hear what comes next? To start, you are upgrading to a better room! From now on, you'll be living in a double. If you keep at it, with hard work, you'll end up in a single. All that space for you and only you! Picture it. Now, for your responsibilities. You will move up to a strategy period with others like you. If you are a high level, we also will add a secondary class of private tutelage as we assess how you may best serve your country. Remember, if you are feeling any inclination towards chaos or hear anyone else whispering of chaos, you must do your duty and turn them in. Those who are diligent and aid their country will be handsomely rewarded. Those who fall victim to chaos will undergo reeducation. Everyone wins except chaos!"

"Good one, director!" Dr. McCarthy said.

"Thank you, doctor. Dear student, I wish you well as you continue your studies, and may you pass the final test like so many before you. I look forward to witnessing your mastery of the chaos that threatens us all. You are the future, and with you, we will protect our world."

The flag waved in slow motion across the screen before it faded to black. I swore this place was going to make me lose it. A room change? They had to be kidding me. At least now Daisy would have a bed. I'd have to find her during enrichment, or maybe I should let the others explain? I moved towards the door once more.

"Not so fast. Take these forms with you. I expect you to read them over by tomorrow."

I reached out, grasping the forms. He pulled them closer to himself, and I moved with them. What did he want?

"I want to wish you good luck on everything, Simerra. I'd hate to see my favorite fail."

I shuddered. His grin grew till it swallowed a third of his face. I ripped the papers out of his hand and stalked back across the room and out the door before he could say anything else. Cal led me to a room off the main hall. It was small but padded.

"It's soundproof in and out," he said.

"Are you sure?"

He nodded.

That was all I needed to know. I screamed at the top of my lungs. I screamed about this fucking program. I screamed about becoming a soldier. I screamed about Zane. I screamed about that doctor. I screamed about that stupid room. I screamed, and screamed, and screamed until I was out of air and my lungs ached from the exertion. My hands hurt. Come to think of it, my head hurt too. I blushed. Shame crept up my spine. Had Cal watched me beat myself up?

"It's nothing. Everyone struggles here. Come on, you have your level one course before lunch. Your favorite person's in there."

I squinted. Was he teasing me, or was Nash in my class suddenly? As we arrived at the room, I realized he meant the rude girl. Her ash-gray hair was stacked atop her head in a messy bun, her hazel eyes watching the door.

"Miss me?" I muttered as I sat behind her.

She pursed her lips but otherwise ignored me. I had to give it to her. She really was trying. What would Kate say to her?

"Look, I don't want you to hate me any more than the average person, but you make it way too easy to piss you off."

She turned around, smirking. Huh, maybe Kate's way was effective. I'd have to remember this for later conversations.

"I could say the same thing about you. I'm Karley." She offered her hand.

"I'm Simerra. Touch is a terrible idea."

She blinked rapidly and retracted her hand as if I'd stung her.

"Are you a high level?" she hissed.

Oh, great. Come on, Simerra, lie. You have enough people that know already. Lie for your friends' sake.

"I'm not a high level, but I am still getting a handle on my abilities. I'm trying to be considerate. Not everything is a plot to undo you," I explained.

"You obviously haven't been here long. Everyone is out for themselves. Last week, Sarah sold out another low level for a cupcake." She scowled.

"What happened to the low level?" I asked, leaning in.

"She was hauled off for reeducation. What else?" She shook her head, and a few loose hairs fell into her face.

"This place eats people alive for sport."

Her eyes sparked with interest as she leaned on the back of her chair. This was a good start. All those lessons on people skills needed to prove their worth or what was even the point? *To be normal.* Mother's voice rang in my ears. I rubbed them, hoping it would keep her out of my head. Thinking about her now wasn't beneficial.

"You seem weird," Karley observed. "I'm not saying it's a bad thing. You're weird for here, if that makes any sense. It's a good thing. It means they haven't broken you."

I rolled my eyes. Zane had told me what a crap compliment that was a long time ago. Did she think I was born yesterday? She tapped my desk and electricity danced from her fingertips. She snapped her hand back to her chest, watching me. Well, if we were going to show off and trust each other. I smiled and raised my own palm, putting a few pieces of paper on it. I held my other forefinger up, urging her to be patient. *Please don't let me down now.* I nudged my glow gently. It uncurled lazily down my arm. The pieces of paper lifted off my palm and swirled around in the air. Karley's face lit up. I pulled my hand back before anyone else could take notice.

"I knew it."

"That's a nifty ability you've got there," I said, fiddling with the paper on my desk.

"You like it? I'm the only one in my family to survive it. It used to be my brother's. Too bad for him, I'm a fast study," she quipped.

"Now may not be the time, but one day, you'll have to tell me. Someplace sunny." I smirked.

What would Mother say? How had she persuaded everyone to join up? I thought back to our solo days before the big group formed. Most of what I remembered was incomprehensible fear and running. So much running.

"Maybe I will. Let's chat tomorrow." She turned back towards the front as the lesson began.

"Let's talk about the relief stations along our sewer systems. Who can tell me what a relief station is?"

"They're the places where you can stock up on supplies. They are both above and below ground. They are the perfect rendezvous point if you have acquired a chaotic youth. They will be comforted by the presence of supplies, which leaves the perfect opening for collection," Karley answered.

Heat rushed to my face. Was that what the old store had been? Was that why she was so distant? Was it guilt? I pressed my eyes shut. My fingers drummed against the desk as I regained focus. There was no point dwelling on the past. We were good now.

"Miss Simerra, would you like to educate the class on the frequency of the relief stations in our area?"

What had Nash said? We were halfway between all the compounds in our area, right? So that would mean there was likely one between each of the compounds.

"They're halfway between every education center to ease personnel retrieval." I tripped over the words but at least they were out.

"Pay attention next time and perhaps you'll sound confident in your answer."

Laughter erupted around the room. My ears burned as I ducked my head. I didn't miss this part of school. I opted to tap my fingers against each other to draw less attention.

"As she said, these points ease retrieval. Imagine all the time saved. What is it? Yes, you?"

We all swiveled to see who had raised their hand. It was a girl in the back. Her raven hair draped around her face, tapering off at her shoulders. Her dark eyes seemed to welcome the stares.

"Isn't all that useless once you go too far west? The centers are farther apart."

"They are farther apart but the relief stations are equally spaced out." The instructor waved her off and turned back to the board. She raised her hand again, this time not waiting for permission to speak.

"Yeah, teach. I'm not getting it. It sounds like a load of shit if you ask me."

A few students giggled. Others gasped. Either way, we all waited with bated breath to see what the teacher would do. You could see the vein in his neck popping out as he puffed up his chest, enraged. He gestured for her to come up to the front of the class. The girl didn't move. *Please get up. It'll be worse if you don't.* Other kids snickered to themselves.

"Quiet, all of you. Get up here, you ungrateful brat," he bellowed.

Flecks of spittle flew from his mouth. He looked like an offended dog, all teeth gnashing and ready to attack. She sauntered up to the front of the class, pulling her shirt off on the way. Next, her bra hit the floor. I adverted my eyes. I doubted she wanted us staring. What was she thinking?

"I've warned you before. You'd think you'd have learned after last time."

I looked up in time to see a whip crack down against her back. I stifled a gasp with my hand. Was this what Nash had been talking about? He raised the whip before bringing it down once more. Her brown skin ripped open this time. She gripped the desk for dear life. Tears streamed down her face, yet no sound left her mouth. Again, the whip came down on her back. As he raised it, blood flecks splattered across our desks. I felt the warm liquid hit my face. The soldiers stood stoic around the room. I flinched as the whip cracked down on her again. She screamed. The sound pierced my ears.

"This will teach you to disrespect me in my own classroom, you vile scum. You don't deserve salvation from chaos, you pathetic punk." He punctuated each sentence with another strike of the whip. "Let this serve as a lesson to all of you. Pay attention to your lessons and mind your mouths, lest you end up like this one. Undeserving of your place in the center."

A sob broke from her chest. I couldn't sit here and do nothing. I released my white-knuckle grip on the desk and sprinted up the row of chairs. Whispers erupted from all around. I put my hands up between the injured girl and the teacher, bracing for impact.

Chapter Twenty-Seven

PROTECTING OTHERS

C W: ABUSE, WHIPPING, BLOOD/NEEDLES

"Get out of the way. I'll deal with you after," he growled. He took in my form with wandering eyes.

I didn't know I could feel disgust on this level. I lowered my hands but otherwise didn't move. If he wanted someone to hurt, he'd have to settle for me.

"I said move!" he roared.

The whip raised over his head, a final warning. I flinched but stayed, waiting. This girl couldn't take much more. What was I if I didn't stand up for her, for all of us? I planted my feet, the whip coming down as if in slow motion. If I used my glow, we were all screwed. At the last second, I spun, throwing my body on top of hers. The whip kissed my skin, hungry for blood. It stung like running through prickers. I could handle that. He brought it down again. I rolled my shoulders to shake off the pain. He hit me again and again. I maintained my position over the cowering girl. I would not be moved until they forced me away.

"You little shit. You're worse than the first one. Now class, tell me why Simerra is being punished."

"She interrupted your punishment of the chaotic one," someone supplemented.

"Correct, and now she will feel it. This is what happens when you venture towards chaos even in the pursuit of friends," he said to the class. He turned back to me and promised, "I will *break* you," before raising the whip again.

My knees shook violently with the force, but I remained silent. I would not give him the satisfaction. I pressed my lips together firmly and tensed against the pain. I could do this. He kept up for five more lashes before there was finally a reprieve. I didn't move, scared he would start again if I revealed the girl below me. The room was silent besides her jagged breath and his hectic breathing.

"Get out of my class," he snarled.

I kept my eyes on the teacher and the whip in his hand. He stared back. Even though my head went fuzzy from the eye contact, I didn't look away. I collected the girl's shirt and bra. I helped her up from where she'd collapsed. I heard the swish of the whip in time to shelter her again. The tails sliced through my battered skin.

"And that's for insolence. Get cleaned up. I expect to see you both back in here tomorrow."

Cal followed as I rushed her from the room. She wasn't supporting her own weight and leaned heavily on me. I wasn't convinced she was conscious. Her bare skin pressed against my own. My glow longed to move from my chest to where our skin touched, but I couldn't let it. The pain of denying it coupled with my back was excruciating.

"Let's go to your new room. There should be supplies there," Cal suggested.

I allowed him to lead the way. I struggled under her weight, not ready to admit defeat. *Come on.* What were all my muscles for if I couldn't support someone in need? When we finally arrived at the room, I was relieved. I set her down on my bed, and I pushed her raven hair out of her eyes. She moved around slowly, like she was barely awake. I looked to Cal for guidance.

"She's in shock. She'll come out soon. You should her with antibiotics before that."

I rifled through the drawers below my bed. There were all kinds of ointments and salves. The third drawer down had syringes. Haphazardly, I ripped into the first pack labeled antibiotics. I flicked it to remove air bubbles before sticking her. I put a bandage over the injection spot on her thigh. Cal raised an eyebrow.

"I know how silly it looks. Quit judging me and help me take care of her."

"No need," the girl replied, stretching.

Had the prick woken her up? Her eyes were hazy. I turned my attention to her back and started blotting at the wounds. One closed right beneath my fingertips. I gasped. Her back glowed softly. I looked nervously up at the clock by the door. Was this room like mine? Or was it camera free like Nash's? No one barged in either way.

"Thanks for grabbing my stuff. That's pretty nice of you. Mind handing it over now?" The girl asked.

I handed her the clothing I had clutched in my hand and looked away to give her some privacy. She'd had enough eyes on her; she'd been through a lot today.

"You can look back now. I'm as dressed as you are," she teased. "You're lucky your bra held up. It does look like it's seen better days. This is your room, right. Maybe change before we leave."

"I don't know if I have anything else. I was moved to this room today," I admitted, blushing.

I dug through the dresser to find a drawer full of undergarments. They had all of this and only gave us one set when we arrived? I kept digging. A shirt drawer! I held the two items in my hands, not the least bit excited to pull them on over my injuries. The girl jumped up, examining my back. She clucked her tongue as she surveyed the damage.

"You really took a beating, didn't you? And all for little old me. Here." Her hand was on my skin before I could stop her.

She coughed, her hand moving to clutch her stomach. I wrestled my glow back by my heart. It could be curious about what was going on later. Right now, I needed it to settle down. There were more important things than being safe from another's touch.

"Are you okay? I'm sorry about that. I wasn't expecting you to touch me," I apologized.

"It's cool. I should have said something. These things have minds of their own. May I? You look like a hot mess. No offense." She chuckled.

"None taken. Please," I encouraged.

I held still as she touched the torn flesh on my back. I hummed softly to myself as she worked. The feeling of my skin knitting itself back together was far from a pleasant one. Still, I endured it. I was lucky she was willing to heal me. Many wouldn't have risked glowing in front of a soldier. When she was done, she turned her focus to Cal. He stood by the far wall. His sandy hair blended in with the background. She pressed her tongue to her teeth and sucked in air. Was that normal? I tried to replicate it. Oh, gross. The feeling of the air against my tongue was far from pleasant. I readjusted it in my mouth, displeased. This girl was odd.

"So what's your deal? You follow us on teacher's orders? You gonna rat me out?" she spat at him.

"He's assigned to me. He's cool," I assured her.

She looked between the two of us, the gears turning in her mind before her eyes lit up devilishly.

"Oh, you should have said that from the start."

What was with the weird intonation? She'd practically sung the words. She looked back and forth between us a few more times. Cal's face was red. Wait, she didn't think—oh no. I flushed bright red. That was ridiculous. We were— We were accomplices if anything. I waved my hands wildly as I tried to wipe the thought from her head.

"I think you have the wrong idea," I suggested.

"Then what? Spill. I showed you mine, now you tell me what's going on."

"He's nice. He helps me out when I get stuck. It's nothing physical," I assured her.

"I'll take that for now. I'm Sasha by the way. Thanks for your help back there. He gets under my skin. The information he gives is only ever half right. I have all the books in my room. I'm not even sure he's read them all fully. He talks out his ass. I act out. He retaliates and goes hard on me because of my ability. I heal myself, and we repeat. It's an endless cycle." She shook her head.

Her eyebrows twitched with irritation. I gestured for her to take a deep breath. She rolled her eyes.

"I'm Simerra. Maybe be more careful next time?"

"Being careful won't fix that. He's always looking for an excuse to hurt someone. Besides, this is a great test," she said, examining her nails.

"What do you mean by that?" I fiddled with the hem of my shirt. Had I missed something?

"For seeing who's who. You're the second one to help me out. The first one was a girl who moved up to the big leagues. I think it was already too late for her when I got to her. I hope it's not too late for you. See you around."

She swayed as she stood, collected herself, and flounced from the room. I sat, slack-jawed. Maybe Sasha was an acquired taste, like my great aunt we used to visit. She pinched my cheeks and called me her defective darling. Mother always said she did it out of love. What did Sasha act out of?

"We should get you to lunch," Cal suggested.

"I'm going to change first if that's okay?" I asked.

"No problem. I'll wait outside."

I pulled off the old bra, wincing. My new skin was tender to the touch. I was grateful it was sealed, make no mistake. I rocked as I got dressed. The swaying helped me remain focused on something other than the pain. Once fully dressed, I looked down to inspect the green shirt. It looked odd with the blue pants. I checked the last drawer to reveal green pants. I changed into them. It felt weird to have a full set of clothes on. The tag in the shirt felt like a needle on my spine. I pulled it off and searched the room for a way to be rid of it. I happened to notice a pair of scissors on my roommate's desk. I snatched them up and dug all the little pieces of it out of the collar. I set her scissors back where I'd found them and donned my shirt. That was better. I sucked in a deep breath. *Here we go.*

CHAPTER TWENTY-EIGHT

A NEW ROUTINE

C W: INDOCTRINATION, ASSAULT MENTIONS

I walked into the lunchroom and the whispers immediately picked up. So the change in colors was something people cared about. I held my head high. No turning back now. After getting my food, I wove through the tables. There were a few others in green scattered through the room. New hopeful soldiers. Did they fully understand what they'd have to do in that role to secure small comforts for themselves? Did they care? I wound up at the high-level table next to Trish.

"When'd you get the new digs?" she asked.

"You mean my clothes, right? I've only heard that word used a handful of times, and my clothes are the only thing that's changed so—"

Great to know I was still brilliant at word vomit.

"You worry too much. Yes, your clothes. When did you get the upgrade?"

"Today. They think I'm moving on with my training. I'm on the soldier track now."

There was no reason to lie to her, not when I wanted her on my side. With any luck, all the high levels would join me. Then I wouldn't have to fight them. They'd been nice to me. The idea of hurting them felt wrong.

"What's with the frown?" Rachel asked between bites of her apple.

She was covered in a purple bruising that spread from her wrists up her arms and across her face. It reminded me of my own. I self-consciously glanced at my own wrists. Shock blossomed in my stomach. The marks were gone. It must have been Sasha's glow. Well, good. I didn't want to carry that bastard's marks any longer than necessary. Right, I needed to reply.

"It's nothing. I'm thinking," I clarified.

Rachel tapped the table in front of me. My head jerked up. I hadn't been expecting that. She kept her palms down to the earth and smiled.

"I wanted to thank you. I don't know what you did. I probably don't want to know either. I owe you one."

"It was nothing." I shrugged.

"I'm not thanking you because I feel bad for you. You're a big girl and can make your own decisions. I want you to know that whatever your reasons were, I appreciate it," Rachel said.

"You can have anything you want in this place if you're willing to pay the price tag," Jack snarked from the corner.

He was picking apart a roll, only eating the middle bits. Pieces of crust littered his tray. He slid closer to the rest of us. The apple on his tray rolled into my arm. He grabbed it, taking a huge bite.

"It's a damn shame too. There's plenty I'd like to do, but there's also plenty I'm not willing to risk for it. What are you willing to risk?" he asked, gesturing with his apple.

"Really smooth, jackass," Trish grumbled.

"It's just Jack," he retorted, taking another bite.

"I think Rachel's right. You don't want to know," I mumbled.

No one replied. All of them were suddenly busy with their own plates. I sighed. Well, so much for that conversation. I poked at my pasta. Better eat instead of being hungry and sad. I felt marginally better when I finished my food. The others were about finished too. Rachel caught me looking and smiled. I returned one. She held a finger to her lips. I nodded, confused. Be quiet for what? She raised her other arm and pulled the sleeve up to reveal finger marks. She smiled sadly this time, her eyes full of forbidden tears. Water jumped unbidden to my own. I brushed it away. This was not the place to cry. Rachel slipped her sleeve back down. The other two were too focused on themselves to notice us, but we noticed us. Even as the world had looked away from the learning center's crimes, we were seen. Survivors of a vast, confounding nightmare.

Trish and Jack led the way after lunch. Rachel and I hung back. Neither of us spoke. Both of us were comfortable in the silence. It was enough to know the other understood. I hadn't realized how isolated I felt from everyone. It was like I was an entire reality away from them. A reality in which monsters were real. Rachel knew about monsters. She'd been with them for weeks. Of course my doctor wasn't the only one. It made sense. The adults that claimed to be keeping us from chaos were the only monsters many of us would ever encounter. There was some sort of poetic disaster in all of this. One day, when I looked back, I would be able to appreciate it. Currently, it solidified the need to destroy this place and places like it.

Once outside, we chatted and sat in the sun. We kept the conversation light. No one wanted to delve into the darkness of this place. Not while the sun warmed our skin and the breeze kissed our faces. All too soon, it was time to return inside. We hung towards the back, barely going fast enough to not get yelled at. Trish set the pace. We walked with her up the ramp and back into the building. I waved goodbye before searching for who I was supposed to follow. Seeing Cal, I hurried over to him. He spun on his heel and walked off down the hallway. His boots clacked against the floor. The empty hall amplified the sound. The quiet smack of my newly acquired sneakers sounded even smaller next to his steps. One day, I'd learn to move with that kind of authority. I observed his stride and tried to mimic it. He almost glided forward. Even with my best efforts, I was unsuccessful. I'd have to ask him to coach me after all this was over.

I entered the enrichment room. People trickled in from the other doors around the hall. At least I wasn't late to this one. They started stretching at their own pace. I joined in. Zane and I used to stretch before training with Mother. Since being here, I'd only done it a handful of times. My muscles protested even the most basic movements.

"Hey, hey," Devin called, stopping before me.

"It's good to see you."

"You too. Who do you normally have enrichment with?" He swung his arms through a big sweeping stretch.

"Zane, I guess. I barely know my schedule. It's been him a handful of times."

"I think that's how they like it. Come on, it's time to go in circles till somebody drops." He held out a hand before pulling it back to rub his neck. "Sorry, it's been a while."

"No problem. Let's get moving," I encouraged.

We walked in silence. I was comforted by it. Devin was not. He tapped his hands as we walked. His eyes never settled anywhere for long. I waited for him to speak. I knew how hard it could be to find words. When he was ready, I'd be here.

"Speaking of Zane. You two are wearing the same color now. What's that about? Does it mean something? He keeps blathering on about a higher calling and securing our future. He's already told them about our relationship. Did you know that? It's ridiculous, right? And I'm not saying I don't love him anymore. That's not what I'm saying at all. I love him with my whole being. I'm worried about him. He seems kinda frantic. It's not like him to be so submissive. We snuck off to *ya know* and he was different. I-I like different. Different can be good. It was— I was— I'm worried." His avalanche of concerns washed over me in a hushed voice, barely audible over the stomping feet of everyone enduring enrichment.

"Zane is an idiot." I sighed.

"That I agree with wholeheartedly. Care to elaborate on how this specific instance makes him an idiot for posterity's sake?" Devin asked.

"He's agreed to a new training program that speeds up his path to becoming a soldier. He's going to have a new two-person room and special classes. It's the same program Nash was in."

He deserved to have the whole picture. He stopped in his tracks. Other students wove around us. He covered his mouth with his hands in horror. I grimaced. It was a shit situation. A soldier took interest in our still figures. I nudged him to keep walking. He'd have to process on the go. He took lilting steps, almost as if his body were moving on its own. I kept him from running into things as he came back to himself.

"Why would he do that? He knows— He knows," Devin lamented.

"I know. This place is convincing. You saw Nash."

He swallowed.

"I'm no happier about it than you are. There's an assessment that's coming up. I'll keep an eye on him. It's going to be okay."

"What about the plan?"

"It's still intact," I said.

"What if we can't get through to him?" Devin worried.

"Then I knock him on his ass and drag him," I insisted.

Devin laughed: a nervous titter that drew a few looks from the other students as they passed us. He made a heart with his fingers and held it up to me. I made one back. At least I could still make him laugh.

"You never cease to amaze me. I was telling Zane the same thing before we ended up here," he complimented.

"You were talking about me?"

"Nothing bad. It was more about our hopeful future. As a family, you know?" he clarified.

I nodded. I'd often heard Devin painting us the perfect future where we all lived together, able to be openly ourselves. He'd shown us in shadow pictures over many bonfires. Daisy loved the story, as did I. What I would give to be sitting around one of those bonfires now.

"I'm rooting for you."

"I'm sorry, what?" I asked, perplexed.

"Your plan. Your girlfriend. I'm here for all of it," Devin said.

I blushed. He pushed my shoulder lightly, his expression filled with mirth.

"Thank you. Nash has a lot to make up for but—"

"But she's worth it. I get the feeling," Devin finished for me. "It'll work out. We'll straighten those knuckleheads out. They'd lose their heads if it wasn't for us."

"Are you trying to pretend they haven't already lost them?" I joked.

"I give. You're right. Silly me." Devin chuckled.

We bantered back and forth for the duration of enrichment, never doing more than a brisk walk. We kept the conversation light, relying on prior knowledge to fill in gaps on sensitive topics. We couldn't risk someone figuring it out. It was nice to have this time with him. From the start, he was never afraid of Zane or me. People used to call him crazy. They probably still did. At the end of the period, I trudged towards Cal. Where were we headed now? We climbed three flights of stairs and entered the room across from them.

The chairs were arranged in a circle. In the center, there was a large, raised platform marked with a grid. Around the edges, there were labeled bins with different kinds of pieces including weapons, soldiers, undercover, tactical vehicle, tank, target, and support K-9. Was this class a giant strategy game? I sat on the back left side where I could survey the full room. No one even paid me any attention. Their eyes swept slowly over the seats before choosing one. My green clothes felt much less out of place in this group. Everyone matched here, and half of them wore the same boots Cal had. I must have missed those in the room. Someone clapped behind me. I nearly jumped out of my seat. I twisted around to see what was going on. The youngest teacher I'd ever seen stood behind me.

"You have to be ready for anything at any time. If you aren't, the chaos will kill you, and I won't cry at your funeral." He smirked.

The class snickered. I sank in my chair. This was the second time in a single day I was being made fun of. Did I have a sign on my back or something?

"Everyone is prepared for class, correct? Everyone in this course has high ambitions. You want to be the best. I didn't sign up to baby a bunch of prissy high levels. If you're here, then you're here to work hard. That's how I earned my position, and it will help you earn yours."

My eyes widened. Was I ready for this class? Crap, was I supposed to have a notebook or something? I didn't have anything on me at all. Cal set a notebook on my desk with a wink. He'd even brought me a pen. I shot him a grateful smile. I flipped to a blank page, ready to take notes.

"Now that we all look ready, let's begin. What's the best way to strike some idiot high level?" the instructor barked.

"Hard and fast before they can get their bearings," everyone shouted.

Guessed he asked that a lot. This class was going to be a trip and a half. I could already feel it.

"New girl. Did you wander in here by mistake, or are you here to be the best?" he interrogated.

He was barely two inches from my face. I could feel the warmth of his breath on my cheek. I had a strong urge to take him by the throat and throw him across the room. Thankfully, I knew that was a fool's idea. I glared back up at him. He didn't move. There was something about him that reminded me of the adults from Mother's group.

"I'm meant to be here," I snarled.

"Now everyone, take note. New girl didn't back down. Unlike some of you, she has a spine." He turned back to the rest of the class.

I was still fuming. How was I going to endure his arrogant ass for two weeks? My glow thrashed within my chest. At least I wasn't the only one that was irritated. The class passed as I worked to calm myself down. Anytime I was close, the instructor would look back over at me and the urge to fight rose within me. When we left the room, I stalked down the hallway, still livid. I kept half a step behind Cal. I didn't know my way around this floor. We rounded the corner at the end of the hall to reveal another long, boring hall. The art here was different. The faces in the paintings were younger. "In memory of the lost," a placard read mid-hall. At the end, there were empty spaces with blank nameplates. There were so many empty spaces. Did they think we were all going to die? A sense of dread filled me. I hunched my shoulders against it, still investigating the wall. It had only been six years, even less since this building was built, and so many had been lost. I froze.

Echo Chaven. It was scrawled neatly in the small placard. I looked up to see the picture memorializing him. In typical Echo fashion, he was laughing. My hand hovered over the picture. I wanted to snatch it off the wall. He may have died for this place, but he deserved to be remembered by those who cared about him, not this cold, unthinking, unfeeling wall. I rushed to catch up to Cal. Echo's picture was still on my mind.

Chapter Twenty-Nine

KAREN

Here we went again. Would I ever be done walking into strange rooms? The little placard with Karen's name on it didn't go unnoticed. I hid my groan with a cough. She was the last person I wanted to piss off. The office smelled sickly sweet. There were flowers on the desk, but that wasn't it. There was something else, something stronger. It attacked my senses and my head ached horribly. The room was a soft rose color. There were pieces of stylized gold silverware on the wall and picture boxes with bits of moss and butterflies in them. As if I didn't already have enough questions about Karen.

"Take a seat," she encouraged. She pulled a tin off her tidy desk, offering it to me. "Cookie?" she asked innocently.

I reached out to grab one. She pulled it back sharply with a look.

"Manners," she reminded me, a small, venomous smile on her lips.

I could hear the venom behind her words. Mark used to use the same tone.

"I'm sorry. Yes, please," I corrected.

She offered the tin again. I grabbed a little one from the edge. She shut it and sighed dramatically. I nibbled the edge of the cookie, unsure of what she wanted.

"You know, my daughter is very bright. She's one of the rising stars of this institute," Karen explained.

"I'm sure you're very proud," I replied.

Was this another test?

"I am, dear. It wasn't always easy. She struggled, as many have, to rise to the call and fulfill her duty. As a mother, I coached her the best I could. I set her on the path of the righteous."

Karen moved to the window. She set a hand on the glass. The light danced off her ring.

"Do you like it? My husband got it for me before this whole mess. He didn't survive the disease, but this ring did. It reminds me how important our daughter is. Am I making sense, Simerra? Surely, you get it. I understand you have a brother in our center?" she asked.

"Yes, ma'am."

What the fuck did Zane do now? I swore, that boy was going to be the end of me.

"He informed us of many things. Including a fanciful idea of escape. Is he correct?"

Don't freeze. Don't freeze. Don't freeze. Act confused. Come on, drop your jaw and scrunch your eyebrows. Even as I worked to hide my fear, I felt like I'd been punched in the gut. What the fuck had he been thinking? This could get us killed.

"He said your group of misfits was going to make a break for it. He wants to protect you all from the chaos, so he came forward. It was rather noble of him, don't you think?" Karen's venomous smile widened.

Lie. Lie through your fucking teeth. Too big of a pause wouldn't look good. I needed to answer her now. I forced a small smile to my lips.

"It would only be noble if it was true," I replied.

Karen came around the desk and smacked me across the face. My head jerked to the side from the force. My glow reared up in my chest, ready to hurt her. I shoved it back down. I needed to stay calm. Hurting her would make everything worse and prove her suspicions.

"Don't lie to me. Your brother told us everything," she screeched.

"Everything? We may have once thought breaking out was right, but those days have passed. I'm not wearing green for nothing," I reasoned.

"Don't you patronize me, little girl. Only the chaotic question authority," Karen hissed.

She slapped me again. My neck cracked painfully. *Deflect. Do something. Lie better. Don't mess this up. What to say? What to say? Zane doesn't know everything? Yeah, that could work.*

"Zane doesn't know anything about me. I've only seen him a handful of times during enrichment. I want to serve my country. I want to keep it safe from chaos."

"You are a liar and you know it," she accused.

She dug her hands into my curls and pulled my face up to hers. There was hatred burning in her eyes. I wanted to spit in her face and tell her all the ways she could shove her opinions somewhere unpleasant. I held my tongue. My focus was better spent controlling my glow. She threw me back down into my chair.

"If you aren't a liar, then why would your brother be so concerned?" Karen interrogated.

She straightened her own clothes before sitting behind the desk once more. Her legs crossed before her. Were we getting somewhere?

"My brother is easily concerned. He's been that way as long as I can remember. He worries about me constantly. He's a worrier."

"Right, you're defective. At least the others have the good sense to be useful in their defect. You're not even a high level. You're contained to merely touch."

I stiffened in my chair. Had she really said that? I had to be imagining things. This was a joke, surely. I inspected her face, but it gave away nothing. If it were a joke, it was in extremely poor taste. The whole thing put a sour taste in my mouth. How did one say fuck you politely?

"I'm not defective," I argued.

"You aren't defective? Well, I suppose they all say that." She moved suddenly, shoving a stack of books to clatter to the floor. I held my hands to my ears and rocked slightly. She smirked.

"Pick up the books," she ordered.

That venom sweet tone was back in her voice. I kept rocking as I picked up the stack of books and set them on her desk. I sat tall in my chair. I wouldn't give her the satisfaction of having more to critique.

"I'm impressed. I expected more of a show from you," she complimented.

Like it would have made me any less of a person. I couldn't help the scowl that clung to my face. She was testing my patience in ways I wasn't prepared for.

"Autistics aren't defective. We're just different from you," I argued.

My mouth was getting away from me. Karen glared, but I wasn't going to take it back.

"Listen here, you little shit. If I say you're defective, then you're defective. Say it," she ordered.

I knew I was looking at her like she was ridiculous, but I couldn't help it. She stood and raised her hand in preparation to hit me again. I winced. Her grin widened. She barely looked human.

"Say. It," she growled.

"I'm defective," I said dejectedly.

"I can't hear you."

"I'm defective," I repeated louder. My hands twisted around each other in my lap.

"One last time, dear."

One day, I'm going to watch this place crumble and you along with it, you wretched woman.

"I'm defective."

"Right, and defective children should stay away from my daughter, shouldn't they?"

What fresh, cyclical trap had I fallen into? Why were we back to her family? I didn't even know who her daughter was. How was I supposed to avoid someone I didn't even know? She ripped at my hair again. I gasped in pain. She jerked me forwards into the desk. That was going to leave a bruise. *I literally just got healed but sure, make new marks. White people love marking things that aren't theirs.*

"I worked too hard for you to ruin all of my progress, you defective little shit. My daughter will not fall in with the likes of you. It was one thing when you were a target, now you're just a pain in my ass. You will stay away from my daughter and you will like it. Do you understand me?"

"I don't even know who your daughter is," I hissed back.

Karen shoved me towards the chair, and I toppled over. My elbow slammed into the floor, breaking my fall. Wasn't this a hot mess? I righted the chair and sat again. I didn't need any more of her misguided anger pointed at me.

"I don't know who your daughter is," she mocked. "Does this clear it up for you?"

She flipped the frame on her desk around to reveal a picture of Nash. She was younger in the photo. Her hair hung a tad below the chin. A large bow was set atop her head. She was wearing a dress. In any other circumstance, the picture would have been a hilarious peek back at who she used to be. In the hands of Karen, this was anything but funny. How had Nash come from this woman? Nash never mentioned her own mother. If my mother were this cruel, I wouldn't have mentioned her either.

"Now then, you will stay away from chaos and hold the course towards becoming a soldier and protecting our bright country. You will also stay away from my daughter. She has had enough of your distractions. It took me days to get her back to her true self after your tampering. I will not have you interfering again. She will pass this program in full with such stellar colors that she will give me grandchildren that are free of chaos one day, and you will not ruin it with your conniving ways. Am I understood?"

"I will avoid chaos and remain focused on the program."

She clucked her tongue and wagged her finger at me like I was a toddler who acted up.

"You will stay away from my daughter. Say it," she pressed.

"You can't keep us apart. As long as we're both following the program, there's no harm. I'm not trying to lead anyone towards chaos," I lied.

"I heard about the incident in your class earlier. You caused a scene. You blocked a chaos-ridden child from receiving corrective actions," she accused.

We weren't children. Anger made it hard to think of a reply.

"I—"

"I will not go easy on you because my daughter has a soft spot for you for some unknown reason. I will bring the full weight of this center down upon anyone who breaks the rules, including Nash. Do I make myself clear?" she threatened.

"Crystal."

"If I have to hurt my child because of your influence, I will make sure you feel it. I will be within my rights as an official of this program to do so," she assured me. "Now, I'm assigning you two hours of reeducation with your doctor. Perhaps after that, you will understand that you can't interact with Nash any longer. You may even like it."

My heart started to race. She didn't mean—she couldn't. I slung an arm across my chest, not ready to accept this as reality. She smirked. What sort of horrid woman enjoyed tormenting people like this?

"Hurry along. If you go now, you may even have time for dinner afterwards," she said slyly, holding out a piece of paper.

Nausea crashed into me as I rose from my seat. I took the paper she handed me and walked out of the room, shutting the door. The click rang with a finality I wasn't prepared for. My breathing hitched in my throat. What was I going to do? I fell to the ground, tears already falling. I couldn't do this again. I couldn't.

"What is it? What happened?" Cal knelt beside me.

I shook my head. I didn't have the words. My breathing was erratic. I was getting lightheaded. Shallow breaths were all I could manage, and each one came more rapidly than the last. I scratched at my sides, trying to become smaller. Was I rocking? I couldn't tell. Everything was kaleidoscope-fuzzy through the tears.

"It's going to be okay. Whatever it is. Try to breathe. You're going to make yourself pass out. You have to breathe," Cal encouraged.

I took a long, jagged breath and then several shallow ones.

"That's it. Keep trying. You can do it." He rested his hand on my shoulder, and my breathing picked up even faster. "I'm sorry."

He removed his hand, but I could still feel it. If this was how I reacted to him, I was screwed. I careened back and forth, searching for something that would make me feel better. I was overstimulated, right? Right? Then why was nothing helping? These were the strongest tricks I knew. Was I supposed to stay like this: crumpled in the hallway, unable to move? I wasn't sure I could handle much more of this. The world spun violently. Cal was right. I needed to calm down.

What was that sound? Someone was whimpering. I glanced around, looking for the whimpering person. My hand fluttered to my chest. I felt the vibrations, and they corresponded with the sound. Great, so that was me too. Karen's door was still firmly shut. She knew I was out here. She could probably hear me. Was she really that heartless? All because I cared about Nash? Fuck this place. Fuck her. Fuck everything. My glow hummed through my body. I did not have time for this, but Cal didn't gasp. There was no need to pull it in tighter. The hum gradually slowed, and I found my head clearing. I kept my breathing in time with the low, pulsating hum of my glow. Eventually, I was able to breathe at a slow, measured pace. My glow settled fully, purring. Had it just actively helped me on its own? I looked to Cal, shocked.

"It's okay. I believe in you," he assured me, misunderstanding my expression.

I didn't bother to correct him. I rose to my feet. The cool cement of the wall helped me to stay grounded as I thought of the ordeal awaiting me. I could do this. I had to do this. My stomach rolled at the thought.

"I have two hours of reeducation with my doctor." The words weighed heavily on my tongue.

Cal stared at me, his expression blank. For that, I was grateful. The last thing I needed was pity. I was already scared enough. After a silent exchange of compassion, he led the way down the hall and to Dr. McCarthy.

SURVIVAL OF THE "FITTEST"

I exited the examination room, head still fuzzy. In a way, I was grateful for the blackness that enveloped me throughout the details of the exchange. I wasn't able to run over them on repeat. They were all a blur. A small piece of me longed to know, as if having specifics of the harm would make it easier to move past. I ached, but I had fewer marks than last time. A small blessing born of the destruction. Cal followed me as I dragged myself to dinner. He did not try to talk to me. Instead, he allowed a soft silence to exist between us. He always knew what I needed. Before I could enter the room, he offered me a small cloth for my face. I wiped the mess of tears and floor grime away. I returned his cloth and held out my hand.

"Please?" I whispered.

He took my hand in his own. I could feel my glow against his, but it stayed within my skin and swirled with his. The false calm allowed me to stop the tears that had waterfalled from my eyes these last two hours. He released my hand and swung the door open with one fluid movement. I sat at my usual table, even though no one else was there. It was good to be alone. I was not ready to chat.

Fuck, I was in a new room and I hadn't told anyone but Devin. He would have to tell Joey and have him relay the message. There was nothing I could do now. I ate three plates of food, hoping something would fill the cracks I felt inside the way cement could even out a sidewalk. Food always managed to make me feel a little better. Mother used to make cookies before the sickness. I'd often snuck off with the whole plate to gobble them down with Zane's pilfered glass of milk. I smiled at the memory. *Oh, Zane.* I'd have to warn the others he'd mentioned our plan to Karen. She seemed to believe we were past that, but I couldn't be certain. She'd been too hung up on me spending time with Nash. With a mother like that, it was no wonder she was so messed up by this place. Cal approached my table, cutting off my train of thought. The room had emptied while I was thinking. I trudged upstairs behind Cal.

"Your room." He pointed to the door on the right. "And the bathroom is down the hall. I'll escort you if you need it."

"So you're still my guard?"

"Until you pass your assessment and join our ranks," he asserted.

"Night."

He gestured for me to get going. I shuffled into my room, unsure of what to expect. It was weird not seeing Daisy playing on our shared bed or Kate braiding Nessa's hair. My bed still had dried blood splattered on the comforter. Oh well. I'd slept in worse. My roommate sat on her bed, a book in her lap. Her brown hair was pulled back in a bun and square-framed glasses sat on her face. She was shorter than me, but average height. Muscles, if she had any, didn't show while she was resting. So she was another one newer to the program. Perhaps I could save her too.

"Hello."

She glanced up at me before returning to her book. She gave a weak wave. Huh, not a talker? I shuffled through my drawers, looking for a salve to rub on my injuries. She sighed, snapping her book shut.

"Do you have to be so loud?" She pinched the bridge of her nose between her forefingers.

"I'll be quiet in a minute. I need to find something."

"What could you possibly need to find?" She groaned.

"I'm injured so lay off."

"Oh great, my roommate breaks rules. That's perfect. You better stay out of my way or else," she threatened.

I couldn't have gotten someone nice. It had to be someone that liked this place. I put my hand on my hip and cocked my head to the side the way Mother used to.

"Or you'll what? We aren't supposed to hurt each other. I'm here to succeed as much as you are, so why don't you give it a rest and let me do what I need to do?" I insisted.

She pushed off her bed and approached me, scowling. I held my ground with my jaw set and shoulders back. I could look intimidating too. I'd been playing this game for years. I was not about to lose now. She faltered for a second but recovered, her eyes hardening.

"The only way out of this place is up. I will not hesitate to crush you along the way. Don't try to be my friend. Don't try to talk to me. Don't even think about putting my name in your mouth. Do you understand?"

"My name's Simerra. It's so nice to meet you," I said with as much pep as I could muster.

She crinkled her nose in disgust but nonetheless, she returned to her bed to sulk. A victory was a victory. I found the ointment and sat on the corner of my bed. I could feel her eyes on me as I removed my shirt. I didn't bother looking over. I had nothing to say. There was bruising all along my rib cage. The bites along my stomach were particularly nasty. I spread a thin layer of the antiseptic over all of it. I pressed my tongue to my teeth, not wanting to whine. It stung. Thankfully, that meant it was working. I crawled under the covers of my new bed, reveling in how comfortable it was. It wasn't long before I fell into a restless sleep.

I awoke in the middle of the night, drenched in sweat. My roommate's light was on and she was staring at me. What the fuck was she doing? I thought she didn't want to associate with me? *Can I help you?* I squinted at her through the half-light, waiting for an explanation.

"You were screaming. Is this going to be a regular thing?" she complained.

"Yeah, probably," I replied.

I wiped my face on my shirt. I was so sticky. I'd have to wash these sheets later. My roommate stared her bed, her expression unreadable. I rolled over to face the wall. The hair on my arms stood up. *For the love of fuck, leave me alone and go to bed.*

"I can feel you staring."

Her chair creaked as she readjusted. Maybe now, she'd leave me alone. I dozed off again, this time without dreams.

It felt like minutes had passed when I was smacked awake with a pillow. I groaned and searched for the cause. Of course my roommate was right there, pillow in hand. Was this girl for real? I pressed my tongue to my cheek as I worked to find the right words.

"It's time to get up. Don't you hear the alarm?" she asked, gesturing towards the clock.

Come to think of it, there was a low, consistent beeping. I must have really been out of it. She threw a stack of clothes at me before turning back to her own bed. I watched her shut off the alarm and make her bed before getting dressed. I stretched my sore muscles and changed my own clothes. What was I supposed to do with the old ones? She threw hers in a hamper. I went to copy her, and she pointed to a basket on my side of the room. I grabbed my comforter and put that in there as well. Hopefully, whoever actually did laundry around here would get to it later or I would be granted time to do it myself.

"Come on. We're going to breakfast, and then I'll show you around."

I followed her through the breakfast line all the way to her friends. She sat, gesturing to the empty seat. So much for updating people on what I knew. I could feel their eyes on me even as my own were directed at my plate. Didn't they ever get tired of wandering around, shocked? Whenever I looked up, their eyes darted away as if I'd burned them.

"So, this is your roommate. She seems plain enough. To think you were worried, Heather," her friend teased.

"She's kind of banged up though. She's a troublemaker," Heather said.

Heather adjusted her bun. I blinked slowly. I couldn't make this stuff up if I tried. At least they weren't trying to hurt me.

"I think I'm going to check in with my own friends." I stood to leave.

"Yeah no. You're my problem now. You aren't leaving my sight." She grabbed my wrist.

Oh, you sweet summer child. I didn't block my glow as it rushed through the connection. She gasped. Her face went pale. She released me, taking large gulps of air. Her friends looked on, confused.

"I'll be back when breakfast ends. Oh, and next time, don't touch me," I ordered, a hard edge to my voice.

I slumped into a chair at the high-level table, still irritated. She was going to be a bur in my side these two weeks. The others looked concerned, but I shrugged it off. I really couldn't catch a break.

"Not liking your roommate?" Trish asked.

"Not liking is too tame. She's worried I'm too prone to trouble," I complained.

"The girl planning a breakout is prone to chaos. Who would have thought?" she deadpanned.

"I don't appreciate the lack of support," I whined, chucking a piece of potato at her.

"Listen, I'm here for it. Did you make any progress?"

"I still need to find someone to power the chairs, but we have a more immediate issue with the batteries and other tweaks the chairs need," I speculated.

"I'm concerned about the logistics of all this. I had training in an all-terrain room the other day. It was far from a smooth ride. I got stuck a few times. My arms still ache." Trish sighed.

"I'm hoping that the modifications will help with all that. We need a tech. Do you know anyone?"

"Not a soul. High levels aren't known for our extracurriculars," she mused. "Extra meds and medical supplies are going to be a problem too. I've only seen them wheel out actual medication if you end up in isolation. Once a day or so, they come by to patch you up so they can keep you going without guilt."

"Motherfucker." I groaned and smacked my head against the table. Oddly enough, it helped. Trish waited for me to compose myself again.

"It makes sense. You have to be severely hurt for the people here to give half a turd about you," I said, annoyed.

"Half a turd?" she asked, amused.

"I'm sorry. Do you have a problem with how I speak?"

I leaned on my elbow to keep a better eye on her. She shook her head in disbelief or amazement. They looked the same to me. I really needed to brush up on my emotion reading. Had I always struggled this hard? I probably had. Everything seemed more life or death here. I would either get it right and navigate further into this place or fail and have to restart. If they let me live. I could almost feel the flames from the first time I'd laid eyes on this place.

"No, no it's fine. You do you, hun," she assured me.

"I feel like you're saying that to placate me."

"Maybe a little," Trish bantered. "Don't think you can change the subject. What are you planning? I've seen that look before on Rachel."

"It's usually right before I do something stupid," Rachel agreed.

"I'm not going to do it right away," I said.

I shrugged, batting my eyelashes at them the way I'd learned from Devin. It was true. I needed to pick the right time to execute this plan. It had to be done in a way that didn't hurt anyone else. Right now would cause too much upset, and as much as I didn't like her already, I wasn't trying to actually injure my roommate. I doubted she would extend the same courtesy. So was life. Neither of them spoke. What were they going to do: out wait me?

"If someone has to be in isolation to figure out where the supplies are—" I explained.

"You have to be joking. She's joking. That's white people shit. Look me in my face and tell me you're playin'?" Trish ordered.

"I know it's a bad idea. I also know it's the only one we have, Trish."

"Or you could leave us behind. Everyone else ignores us. Why are you so determined?" Trish grilled.

"I'm not in the business of leaving people behind."

"We aren't easy to bring along," Rachel persisted.

She raised her cane as if that would remind me that they were disabled and somehow less important.

"Survival of the fittest," I stated.

"That's what we're saying," Trish agreed.

"People use the phrase wrong all the time. Mother used to bring it up when people asked her why she kept my brother and me. It doesn't mean that only the strong will survive. It means that the group can only survive if they work cooperatively and utilize their shared skills for the betterment of all. Including those who can't contribute directly," I explained.

"That kind of makes more sense than the way I heard it back in middle school," Rachel agreed.

"That's the definition I go with, and I'm sticking by it. You're coming with us."

Trish beamed. It was good to see her in high spirits. We chatted about everyday stuff, like who else was wearing green or who broke up with who, for the rest of breakfast. Then it was time for her to go off to the high-level training program and my job to spend the morning with Heather. Her nose was so crinkled upon itself, it practically disappeared.

"Something stuck in your nose, or is that the stick in your ass?" I asked, false concern in my voice.

"Har, har. You must be a delight at parties. Come on," Heather chirped.

She took us back up to the fourth floor and all the way down the hall to the last room on the left. There were games on the tables, art supplies tucked away in the corner, a sand table, and a foosball table. There was a TV in the middle of the room with a bunch of game stations hooked up and a DDR pad. The only soldier there was

Cal. There were big kids, little kids, and adults all sharing the space. Heather slumped in a beanbag chair, waiting for me to catch up as I stood, eyes full of wonder.

"Nice, right? This room is where you get to relax when you don't have courses," she explained.

"There's a time when we don't have courses?"

"I mean, yeah, everyone has at least one free period, and there's the hour before lights out. Are you saying that you don't have free periods?" She seemed as confused as I was.

"I have never had one. My only breaks are mealtimes," I elaborated.

Heather's jaw practically hit the floor. Was it something I said? I looked around for the cause of her shock. Everyone else was minding their own business. Huh, must have been me.

"You have a full schedule? Do you know how rare that is? No wonder you have a permanent guard. You have the same assignments as a high level."

"Could you keep it down? People are starting to stare," I urged.

"What did you do to get it? I've been here for months and I barely got the offer to move up. I do everything they ask of me. What makes you so special? Are the rules somehow meant to be broken? Do I have to show them I can stay clear of the chaos even without their guidance? That must be it." She continued muttering to herself.

I had to stand there and listen to it. I waved at anyone who looked. It made them uncomfortable enough to look away, which was nice. Cal hung towards the door, emotionless. Apparently, he'd be no help with this. Well, if she wanted to question me, then she'd have to follow me. I backtracked out of the room and down the hall. She followed me back into our room. I shut the door and searched for a lock. Of course there wasn't one. I muttered a low oath. Nothing was easy here. I'd have to block her way till she calmed down anyway.

"I didn't do anything special. I'm new, and I have catching up to do. There's a lot of information, and I have less time to learn it. I'm not special or extraordinary. I'm Simerra," I explained slowly.

"Shut up! Shut up, okay? You don't even realize how special you are. You could probably get away with murder," she accused, a frenzied look in her eyes.

"Only in training," I quipped.

"This isn't a joke! I want to get out of here! I practice my technical skills all day, every day. I've never made anything that's proved useful to this facility. I'm never going to get anywhere, while you are going to be eating off of a golden spoon in no time."

"I think the term is silver spoon," I corrected.

"That's not the point and you know that," she said scathingly.

She collapsed to the floor. Her legs made a "W" around her. She threw her head in her hands and cried. I shifted my weight back and forth. Why did anyone even want to thrive here? I finally finished processing everything she had said. Technical skills, huh? Of all the people in this place, it had to be here. Luck was funny like that.

"What kind of technical skills?"

"I'm no engineer, but I do weapon upgrades and mechanize silly things like doors and windows. I want to take on a project this place would be proud of. I haven't had a good idea since my last one blew up in the director's face. He said it had promise and passed me through to the program but still. It was so embarrassing. He's the most important person around, and I got soot on his tie!" she lamented.

I needed to convince her she stood to gain from helping me. She wanted to be more like me anyway, right? This could be like a crash course on how to break the rules. What should I say? Join me? No, too formal. I needed to appeal to her wants and desires. *Think, Simerra. How can you make it sound like it's everything she needs and not like*

you're using her? It could be seen as a helpful gadget for this place. What
were a few white lies to escape?

"I have an idea for a project you could work on to show the director. He's due here in two-ish weeks, right? Plenty of time for you to
complete a project," I encouraged.

"It's plenty of time if I actually had an idea. Everything I've tried has
gone up in smoke. I'm waiting for inspiration or a stroke of genius. I
haven't had one," she admitted.

"Well, there are high levels in wheelchairs. Their current chairs
aren't suited for missions. There's a need for a way to modify existing
chairs to allow them autonomy in the field. The easier they can keep
up, the better, right?"

"I mean, yeah. I've seen a few models. They at least have the low
back to self-propel, but they don't have the right wheels and aren't
designed to be equipped with the mech necessary to move with any
kind of speed. It would take a major design overhaul to be ready for
modifications."

She pulled a notebook off her desk, flipping through in search of
a blank page. She scribbled a rough sketch. It looked similar enough
to Trish's chair. I clasped my hands together behind my back to keep
myself from flapping. I was way too excited. She moved the notebook
to her bed. She scribbled frantically, talking to herself in a low mumble
this time. She drew a new chair, this one with bulkier side wheels and
a slicker frame. How fast was she planning to make this thing?

"Wait, I'm supposed to show you around right now," she said,
setting down her pen.

"Why don't you work on this and I'll show myself around?" I
suggested.

"That's a good idea. You'll stay out of trouble, right? I need to get to
work on drafting so I can use my free period to seek out materials. This

is going to be a monster of a project. Please just stay out of trouble," Heather asked.

"Yeah, it's no problem. I'll peek around our floor. Maybe spend some time in that room at the end of the hall. You can come find me when it's time to go to a class, or I'm sure Cal will take me wherever I'm needed."

Relief filled her eyes; she turned back to her notebook. Well, it looked like I'd found my mechanic. I gave myself a mental high five and let myself out of the room. Cal had a small smile on his face. I'd been wondering if he could hear what happened through a shut door. Good. I raised an eyebrow. He shrugged, smirking. I didn't want to have to fight him at the end of this, and it was shaping up like I wouldn't have to.

There were several doors on this hall with name plaques beside them. All of them seemed to be double rooms like mine. The only shared rooms were at the ends of the hall. The rooms in the middle appeared to be laundry rooms. Cool, so we did do our own laundry. Maybe I would get to do laundry tonight during the hour of free time. How long could it really take to wash clothes? I hadn't seen machines like these since before. It would be nice to not have to hand scrub everything, and the dryer, if it worked, was a game changer. Not having to hang everything on a line and hope it dried before the weather changed was exciting. I would almost miss the surprise spiders, *almost*.

I already knew the game type room and the bathroom were on the far end of the hall, so I turned around to investigate the close end. On the side of the hall where my room was located, there was a workout room with weights, a giant mirror, and a variety of machines. Cal helped me figure out how to work them. There was one with a fast-moving belt, apparently to take the place of running outside. The other machines had similarly strange purposes. The government thought up the weirdest things to keep us busy. Across the hall, there was a room with padded walls and a squishy floor.

"It's for training," he informed me. "Hand to hand, things like that."

"So it's useless to me," I snarked.

"Not if you're still out of control," he sassed back.

"You know what, I'll let you have that one."

Chapter Thirty-One

PLANNING

The game room was emptier than it'd been when we'd first explored it. There was a guy playing on the far side of the sandbox. I settled down on my side. The teen looked up at me, smiling, and I returned it. The two of us played in the box parallel to each other. The feeling of the cool sand as it slid through my fingers and into one of the toys was one I relished. There were different colors of the stickier kinetic sand as well. You could build tall castles with it like an old school beach trip. Memories of the salty water along with the crescendo of waves played in my mind. I could almost taste the salt and sunblock mixture that lived on my lips during those trips. It was like the other kid was another beachgoer, the two of us building near each other, enjoying the competition of it all. It was easy during times like these to forget where we were. The danger and the sense of urgency drained away, revealing the simple joys of being a kid again for a moment, regardless of how brief our actual childhoods had been. At least I had had more of a childhood than Daisy. I would have to take her to a beach sometime when all this was over. It could be part of our victory trip.

I hadn't realized the other kid had moved on to something else while I was playing. I took apart the towering castle before me color by color. It was important to leave things neater than I'd found them. Mother had managed to instill a few manners in me. The irony of acting politely in a place that wanted nothing more than to politely destroy and remold me was not lost on me as I reduced my castle to nothing. I returned the lid to the sandbox and moved on to peer at the art supplies. There were stacks of markers, paints, pens, pencils, erasers, and all other manner of provisions. Was a room like this where Nash grabbed her supplies to create masterpieces? I grabbed a few pens, a new notebook, a set of colorful pens, and a few other things. Maybe I could try my hand at art over the next few days.

"I wonder what the assessment will be this time," a girl sitting behind me speculated.

"I heard last time, it got out of control, but no one will tell me any specifics. Upperclassmen are so freaking aloof," another student complained.

So much for learning more. I fiddled with the craft stack. The longer they didn't notice me, the better my chances of getting something useful out of their exchange. There were so many different types of supplies here. Maybe I should reconsider my selections.

"I know. They already passed. What do they have to lose by helping us?" the girl argued.

"We become their competition if we succeed," one speculated.

"Bullshit, we're all supposed to work together to keep out the chaos." She threw her marker down to the table with a huff.

"You really buy all that?"

"You don't? Haven't you seen how beat up all the new ones are when they come in? There's some bad stuff going on out there."

I couldn't help but roll my eyes. It wasn't *that* bad. We'd survived fine before being brought here. Sure, we were a little dirty, but so what? The people glaring at us as we saved their children popped into my head. Maybe everyone wasn't as lucky as we were. There had to be some kind of middle ground where people like us were safe.

"Does it even matter what they come in like? They rock the test scores from the minute they get here," the first girl bemoaned.

"Relax, we're catching up now. All of us who grew up here will get an edge. We've had more time to train. When it comes down to it, we will destroy them and make our mark on this dump." Two of them fist-bumped.

"Then it's smooth sailing all the way out of here."

The group broke into laughter, and high fives could be heard between the lot of them. So much for trying to make friends with any of them. It made me wonder if they knew I could hear them, or did they really think I was taking this long to pick out supplies? I got set up at a table with the things I had grabbed. I spread them over the surface, taking in the different hues. The colors intimidated me. I grabbed a simple pencil and began crafting the line art for the piece I was imagining. The landscape came to mind easily. I left a space for the figure I wished to include. I was scared I wouldn't do it justice. I tried implementing all the tricks Nash had shown me. My heart swelled from thinking of her. I could work on the figure now. I worked to get her form. Her strong legs and thick core flew from my pencil to the page. Her hair caused an issue. I strove to picture the flowing curls I'd seen recently. They looked flat no matter what I tried. I pulled her hair back into a tight bun. I added grime to her clothes and shoes. No need to show a pristine version of her.

Now it was time for her face. There was a twinkle of mischief that lived eternal in her eyes and something else I couldn't put my finger on. I worked diligently, drawing, erasing, and drawing again. There was so much I wanted to cram into her expression. Nash's picture of the girl surrounded by fireflies was so lively, and I dreamed of evoking the same life from this piece. Every version fell short. Finally, I settled on an expression that held Nash's kind determination on display. A small lift lived at the corner of her lips as she plotted. This was the Nash I knew best. My heart felt like it might burst as I looked down at the picture, not at its perfection but in that it held the one I loved. I would have to find a way to convey the half-light of dusk later. I was done with this for now. I grabbed a fresh piece of paper and worked to immortalize our little group. When I finished, there was still room on either side. I added the friends I'd made here. Trish, Rachel, and Cal came first. Their likenesses easily took shape. I moved on to include Sasha, Karley, and Heather. They were prickly but still friends. I wondered if the others had anyone they would want included in our new group.

"There you are. Come on, we're going to be late. You saw everything, right? We've got to go," Heather urged.

So much for working on art. We grabbed our notebooks and booked it. Heather held a finger to her lips before she led us in. I followed her, taking care to lighten my steps. The teacher's back was to us, so I hoped we would emerge from this one unpunished. The door clacked shut, and he spun to stare at us.

"Is my class not important enough for you?" he asked.

He didn't bellow it the way others would. There was a quiet fury that scared me more than screaming ever had. Heather sunk lower in her seat. He awaited our responses. I stood up, hunching my shoulders in anticipation of his reaction. It couldn't hurt to act apologetic. This place loved manners.

"I'm sorry we're late. Heather was showing me around since I'm new to this part of the center. Any punishment should land on me for our tardiness. It won't happen again," I assured him.

"There's no need for that. Don't make it a habit." He waved me off.

I sat down, smiling. That had been far easier than I'd expected. Heather looked on in shock. I waggled my eyebrows at her conspiratorially. She jerked her head back towards the front. I knew better than to expect any kind of thank you from her. It was enough she was working on the adjustments. The class passed without much excitement. It was a simple "history of our nation" course. The teacher droned on about how political systems in our country were inclined towards chaos previous to the sickness, and how those systems had been adapted to make our country the utopia of peace we now strove towards. Blah, blah blah, everything would be better if we all stayed focused on our goals, blah, blah, blah. I doodled in my notebook to appear like I cared, but I was a lifetime away. Our freedom was so close, I could taste it. There was nothing I wanted more than the kiss of earth beneath my feet, and I meant for longer than some short break on the asphalt, baking in the sun while the grass called to me, barely out of reach. When the lesson was over, I followed Heather to lunch. She didn't try to stop me this time when we parted ways. Each of us headed off towards our friends. I had to hand it to her, as nosy as she was, I expected her to put up a fight or at least for her to follow me.

"She has arrived," Devin celebrated.

Kate elbowed him in the ribs. Her eyes trained on the soldiers around the outskirts of the room. Devin ducked his head.

"Any updates?" Devin asked, fiddling with an apple.

I bit my lip. Was there a right way to say this?

"That's an outstanding yes. Lay it on us," Kate said, gesturing for me to continue.

"Zane betrayed us."

"He wouldn't. I know he's not himself right now. I get it, but he wouldn't do anything to put us directly in danger," Devin argued.

"Well, if it happened, then he clearly would," Kate reasoned.

Devin glared at her. When they both looked back to me, I told them what had happened. I skated over my punishment, but I told them about Zane's piece of the interaction. It felt wrong to tell them about Nash's. It wasn't relevant. Nash was nothing like her mother. I would continue to protect her privacy. Besides, it would only serve to make them trust her less. I needed everyone on the same team when we broke out of here. They couldn't have any doubts that they could trust each other. Devin stared at the table. His shoulders slumped in defeat. I wanted to comfort him. My hand twitched towards his before I pulled it back. *Damn it, Zane.* Couldn't he see all the pain he was going to cause? Kate was out of witty words. She rubbed Devin's back. At least one of us could comfort him. He took a deep breath, a sad smile on his lips.

"We'll have to drag him out of here and back to his senses. I won't talk to him about our plan anymore. I'll do my best to keep him distracted," Devin decided.

"I wouldn't ask you to lie to him if it wasn't pertinent. I don't want to hurt him either," I assured him.

Tears shone in Devin's eyes. He looked up towards the light, trying to wish them away. I waited for him to compose himself again. Lunch was long enough; we could wait.

"I know. Let's keep him safe." He tapped the table with his fist a few times. "We should run through the plan."

"Well, the director should be here at the end of next week. If we time it right, everyone will be focused on the assessments. The director is meant to watch them all to decide who is fit for an advanced program. Zane and I both have them."

"While the director's busy with you, we'll be able to move around more freely."

"If you can get away from your soldiers," I corrected.

"What do you mean?" Devin asked, eyebrows furrowed.

"Wait, do you not have someone always on your ass, following you around?"

They both shook their heads. *Well fuck me, I guess.*

"That's weird. I've had one since day one," I informed them.

"I mean, Zane has one too. It has to be something to do with how you're doing in training. From what he's said, Zane is leagues ahead of what I'm doing. He's using a giant room and doing targeted training instead of general stuff. It feels more like they're getting him ready to get out of here," Devin filled us in.

"The better he'll be at helping us get out of here," I suggested.

"How's it going?" Heather asked from my right.

I plastered a smile on my face. *Play nice. You can't afford for her to go digging into your life.*

"It's good. Devin, Kate, this is Heather. We're roommates," I informed them.

"It's wonderful to meet someone else who's taking their training so seriously." His voice always did this raspy thing that people ate up. Heather's eyes fluttered as if on cue and her hand rose to her chest.

"Th-the pleasure's all mine," she said.

"Enjoy the rest of your lunch." He looked down before smoldering up through his eyelashes as his hand ruffled his locs.

"You too," she said breathily.

She turned and strode back over to her friends. I couldn't help but laugh. Kate shoved him playfully.

"Knock it off, dude. We have planning to do." Kate shoved him again.

"She's right. Lunch is nearly over, and I have to go into isolation soon."

They exchanged looks.

"Isn't isolation the opposite of a good idea?" Devin asked.

"It's not my best idea, but I need to see where they keep the medication."

"For the powerful glows." Kate caught a glimpse of pain as it flashed across my face. "I'm not saying it in a bad way. This is something that we mostly need because you want to bring them with us. It would be easier to leave them behind."

"You know Zane and Simerra have powerful glows, right?" Devin pointed out.

"They're part of our group. It's different. We know them," Kate argued.

"And people say I'm shallow," Devin mumbled.

"I know them," I added softly. "Even if I didn't, someone's glow shouldn't determine their worth."

"You picked people based on how they can help us." Kate crossed her arms. Her chest puffed out.

"Yes, because we need specific things to be able to get away, but anyone and everyone who wants to can come with us. I don't care. What I care about is ensuring those that choose to follow us are able to. What would you do if Joey were in the high-level group?" I shot back, quirking an eyebrow.

"I'd make sure he was coming with us, but I still know him." She rolled her eyes.

"Every person should be as important to us as those we love. That's what separates us from the people here. People matter outside their inherent usefulness. People matter because they exist. If we can't remember that, we don't deserve to be free from this place." I locked eyes with her, refusing to look away until she did. If this is what it took to get through to her, then I would do it. I was not sacrificing my morals to get out. I was not going to be like our keepers.

"Get off the soap box, I get it," Kate relented.

"Good. While I'm in isolation, keep an eye out for Karen. She's going to be on your asses to see if any of you are going to act out too. Once I'm back, I'll make a plan to get down to the medical equipment during the morning while everyone's at breakfast. After that, we wait for the assessments. I'll make a scene and you grab anyone you can and get by the main door. I'll be relying on you, Kate, to get everyone together."

She sighed, fiddling with her tray before nodding. She was the fastest person in our group. Hopefully, it would keep her safe.

"Do we need to find her?" Devin asked, a thumb pointing towards my roommate.

"She also has an assessment, so she'll be closer to me than you. Focus on the others," I suggested.

Perfect timing. Everyone was dumping their trays and moving towards the door to the blacktop. I led our little group out into the bright light and squinted against the sun. The smell of freshly cut grass filled my nose. The blades were now cut short. It was a shame. The long, flowing strands would have provided some needed cover. That was probably why they cut it to begin with. A flashing light caught my eye. On the far left of the blacktop, Jack was playing with a mirror.

"I'm going to talk to Jack. I'll catch you both later, okay?"

They peeled away without a word. It was still strange to be listened to. It would be nicer if they liked me. I rolled my eyes at myself. *Of*

course they like me. Why else would they stick with me through all of
this?

CHAPTER THIRTY-TWO

CHAOS INCLINED

C

"I thought I was the only one that liked watching the colors dance," I speculated.

The rainbows the cracked mirror cast danced on the back of my hand. I couldn't stop a soft coo at their beauty. I grabbed at my arm, embarrassed.

"How are you holding up?" Jack set his mirror down, a smile breaking over his face.

"Been better, been worse." I shrugged.

"I suppose I'm the same. Want a turn?" he asked, holding up the mirror.

I snatched it from his hand gleefully. Such a pretty piece of glass.

"I'll take that as a yes."

"Sorry," I sing-songed.

I played with the little mirror, casting rainbows all around. I twirled in a circle. The rainbows sashayed with me. I turned the mirror back towards Jack. The rainbows played across his face and chest. He smiled, both of us enjoying the moment. I cooed softly over the mirror, still playing with it. The pretty lights distracted me from any intent I'd had before.

"I wish I could be as carefree as you. You're so open about everything," Jack observed in awe.

I frowned. What was he going on about? I crossed my legs over each other and folded down onto the pavement. The warmth of the ground seeped through my pants. I fiddled with the mirror in my hands so I'd be able to listen.

"I don't know what you mean," I informed him.

"You don't care who knows what's wrong with you. You leave it out in the open for anyone to see. It's like you're always shouting, 'Here I am!'" he marveled.

"And you wish you could be like that?" I clarified.

I caught his nod out of the corner of my eye. I leaned forward, setting my head on an upturned palm, my other hand still casting rainbows.

"First off, there's nothing bad about having something wrong with you or with being different. Could you imagine a world with only the sun and no moon? Or a world with light and no darkness?" I pressed.

He made no reply. The crickets filled the air between us. I allowed it to stretch too long. He began shifting around. Right then.

"It's not that I'm brave or whatever you're implying. I'm autistic all the time. It's not something I can turn off. This is who I am."

"See, that's what I mean. You're just declaring it. Aren't you worried about what people are going to say or do?" he asked.

"Of course I am. That is not going to be the reason I stop being me. Even if they don't know I'm autistic, they are still going to know I'm different. Who I am changes how I interact with everything and everyone. Yes, I act more or less open at times. It depends on how comfortable I am, but I am still always interacting with the world as an autistic person. People pick up on that," I explained.

"What do you do when they hurt you because of it?" He stared off into the grass.

"I remember that not everyone is kind, and I move on. It's not my job to fix them or forgive them. It's my job to endure them until I can get away. It's scary and painful at times, especially when people you thought understood treat you like you're lesser, but you have to understand that already. You're a high level. People treat you differently all the time."

"They treat me like I'm *dangerous*. That's different," he rebuffed.

"How is it different? They're treating you like your difference has to be controlled for your input to be valuable, right? I get that every day. I'm too autistic to understand things or be in charge or even trustworthy. It must mean I'm unstable. It must mean I can't control myself. I've been beaten while here because I'm different. Whether it's my glow or being autistic, the result is the same. People respond with fear to what they don't understand. The only way to win is to stand tall," I reasoned.

"That's terrifying." He leaned back, staring off at the grass. I danced a rainbow up over his face until he looked over at me.

"If they're going to be cruel either way, I might as well be comfortable with myself. My mother let me be openly autistic. I was always able to be myself. In that way, I was lucky. My glow was always a source of contention as something dangerous, but you're not afraid of me, right?"

"Of course I'm not!" he said without hesitation.

"See, that's new to me. You barely know what I can do and you're here chatting with me. To me, that's brave. To you, it's average. Maybe we can help each other," I suggested.

He offered his hand. I bit my lip. Was my glow under control enough for that?

"We'll work at it together," he coaxed.

I took his hand gingerly in mine. I felt his own glow barely contained under his skin. My own jumped up to greet it. The two of them tapped lightly against each other. It reminded me of how my cat used to rub on me. I looked down at my palm, expecting to see them, but there was nothing visual there. I marveled at our hands.

"You've never done this before? All the high levels do it. It helps us to know who's safe." He shrugged.

"It's so cool."

The soft exchange of energy continued between us. Jack squeezed my hand lightly. I squeezed back. My glow never tried to hurt him. Instead, it thrummed happily. I pulled my hand back, and a comfortable tiredness set over my limbs.

"That was amazing. You'll have to tell me more about it when we get out of here," I urged.

"I wondered when you would fill me in on that. It's soon, isn't it?"

"Yeah." I rubbed the back of my neck, abashed.

"If I were going to tell, I already would have. I think I've made it pretty clear where my depressed ass's allegiance lies," he reminded me.

I giggled, leaning back on my hands. None of the soldiers were keeping a particularly close watch on us except Cal. He caught my eye and winked before scanning the crowd once more. Always looking out for me, it seemed.

"Ask Trish about details. She's coordinating the high levels she thinks will want to come. Be careful so you don't get caught," I advised.

"I'll be careful. Care to give me back the mirror? It's time to head in." He dusted himself off.

I jumped to my feet, the comfort from the energy exchange still present in my mind. Not seeing my doctor, I continued down the hall where my classes usually took place. With only minor corrections from Cal, I found my way to the level one class. Karley sat ahead of me, doodling in her notebook. It took a lot of finger-tapping to stop myself from launching straight into a stream of questions.

"You're early," she mused.

"I do my best," I replied, trying to channel the aloofness Mother always held so close.

"I see you met Sasha."

I glanced back to the raven-haired girl. She wiggled her fingers back in a weak wave.

"I guess I did," I agreed.

Was that the right thing to say? I never knew how these things were supposed to go. If I messed this up, everything else was going to be all the more difficult. *Come on, tell her why you need her. You can do this.*

"I could use a glow like yours and hers, if I'm being honest," I said.

"You still call them glows even here? You've got spunk. I like it," she complimented.

"Thank you?" My voice rose awkwardly through the words.

"What are you planning?" She leaned over the back of her chair lazily while she waited for my reply.

That was abrupt. Allistics were never that direct with me. There was a low hum of voices as everyone waited for the class to begin. *Please let the din of conversation be enough to cover this.*

"I'm getting out of here, and I'm taking as many people with me as I can. I need your help."

Her eyes widened. What, had she expected me to hesitate? Time was of the essence, and to be honest, if she moved to tell someone, I was fully prepared to kill her where she sat. I needed to end up in isolation anyway, right? The ease I felt around killing unsettled me, but not enough to deter me from my plan.

"Why do you need us?"

"I have modified wheelchairs that need powering, and it's never a bad idea to have a healer around. Will you come with me?" I pressed.

"Not so fast. If you want us to come with you, you have to prove yourself," Karley informed me.

I groaned. Was now really the time for games? There were lives on the line. Karley sat stoically. *Have it your way then.*

"What do I need to do?" I asked, resigned.

"Don't sound so sad. I mean, this won't be fun for you by a long shot, but think of the alliance you can forge." Her eyes sparkled with mischief.

"Not helping. Come on. Stop beating around the bush."

"Get yourself landed in isolation. When you get out of it, we're all yours," she said.

The corners of my lips twitched. Did she think this was going to be difficult? I already had to do that anyway. So much for a challenge. I coughed to cover my smile. The teacher entered the room, already grumpy.

"Do we have a deal or not?" Karley hissed.

"So we'll talk about the specifics of your glow after I get out, and you'll come with us?" I clarified.

"Well, yeah. That's like, the whole point."

"Cool, I'll go now."

"What do you mean you'll—"

I flipped the desk and laughed. I put my whole body into it as I rocked back on my heels. That should look good and chaotic. Everyone's eyes whipped to me. Karley looked like she was about to faint. She's the one who told me to go to isolation. Why was she surprised? It was her demand.

"I fucking hate this pointless ass class."

"I will take the whip to you," the instructor berated.

"I'm terrified. Can't you tell?" I snarked, shoving things off his desk.

"Restrain her!"

Cal moved towards me. I could sense his hesitation. That wasn't safe. I needed to force him to act. I threw a stapler at him.

I hid a nod in the movement. He had to do this or they would hurt him too. He rushed forward in earnest, his gun raised. That was more like it. *Come and get me, Cal.*

"Your country needs you. Don't make me shoot," Cal barked.

The hard edge had returned to his eye. Good. He would be safe at the end of all this. I lowered my palms. His body crashed into mine as he shoved me to the ground. I kept my breaths even and my glow close. I didn't want to hurt him. He slid my hands into gloves and tied them behind my back. I was grateful for the ability to release my glow slightly. It twisted around in my palms. I writhed underneath Cal, trying to be as big a pain as possible. I needed to be in more trouble than just a whipping.

"Do you want to whip her?" Cal asked, pulling me upright.

Bad idea, Cal. I spat at him, still wriggling around. *Oooh, look at me. I'm so chaotic.*

"I think I'll pass. Send her to isolation. Maybe there she will learn to fight her own chaotic nature. Would anyone else like to join Simerra in isolation?"

No one moved. Karley and Sasha were in shock. I made sure to keep my gaze moving so no one would think I'd had an accomplice. It was easy enough with how much I despised eye contact. Cal jerked me out of the room and into the hallway. No one followed us. Apparently, they thought he had it under control. We made it into the stairwell before Cal flipped me around to face him. His face was haggard from worry.

"Make it believable. I'll be okay. There's a lot at stake here, Cal. Just stay safe and trust me. I've seen you look away when I talk to others. You clearly care. Please," I implored.

He gave me a weary smile before he gripped my arms tightly. Thank goodness for the protection my sleeves offered. I didn't have the control for much more skin-to-skin contact. I allowed him to rip me down several flights of stairs. The air grew cold against my nose. We exited onto the bottom floor and proceeded halfway down the hall. The clank of boots sounded more ominous down here.

Cal rifled around for a key. Upon finding it, he unlocked the door and shoved me through. I fell to the floor. The room was dark but unmistakable. It was a viewing room. The large one-way glass sat positioned in the wall before me. Cal ripped me up and marched me through the doorway into the holding room.

"Take off your shoes," he ordered after freeing my hands.

I did as I was told, throwing them over to him when finished. He picked them up and left the room without another word. The half-light from the dull bulbs above was just enough to notice the spiders crawling on the cinder-block walls. The dirt beneath my toes felt comforting, even in this harsh environment. I knew there were bad things coming, but this part? This part wasn't so bad. *Welcome to isolation, Simerra.* All there was to do now was sit and wait, so I did.

Chapter Thirty-Three

ISOLATION

Hunger tore at my stomach. I swallowed my spit, pretending it was a full meal. I could imagine the sounds of the meal room if I closed my eyes. I'd been hungrier than this. Time between hunting trips had taught me to be patient. I wasn't going to starve, but I was going to hurt. The hairs on my arms were already on edge. The cool dirt beneath my feet zapped any warmth my body produced. My hair was down but despite its length, the tight curls barely reached halfway down my neck. I shivered. I tucked my hands into the sleeves of my shirt, bunching the fabric at the ends to help hold the heat in. I was already tired. A bowl slid into the room through a flap. I went over to it hopefully, but it was only water. Better than nothing. I grabbed the ice-cold bowl and retreated to my corner. I took a small sip, the cold water splashing down into my empty stomach. I had grown too accustomed to three big meals a day. I set the bowl down. It could warm up overnight. At least if it was the same temperature as the room, it wouldn't be so bad. I mounded up some dirt to make a pillow and hummed myself to sleep.

The next morning, the bowl was gone. So they were watching me already. I flipped off the mirror. Call me crude, but it made me feel better. Might as well make the most of this. I did my usual morning stretches with my back to the door. Once done, I sat and tried meditation. I could feel my glow nestled against my heart. I left it alone. The last thing I needed was to make them any angrier. I played with the dirt, doodling pictures. Time stretched on around me. The only indication it was passing was my steadily increasing hunger. Were they going to deny me food till I behaved? I turned back to the mirrored glass. What did they want? I fell back against the dirt. I had severely underestimated how boring this was going to be. I mean, I knew it was going to be acutely painful eventually, but the waiting really was getting to me. My ideas about what they would or wouldn't do to me were out of control. It felt like an eternity when, finally, the door opened and in walked Karen.

Her heels sunk slightly into the soft ground. I wasn't sure if it was the half-light or her face in general, but she was intimidating. Our last conversation replayed in my mind. I knew better than to speak out of turn after last time. She leered at me. I repositioned and suddenly, she was approaching. I tensed against the impact I knew was coming, but she stopped just short of me. Was she toying with me? Primal rage filled her face, but it was joy that twinkled in her eye. Yeah, I was screwed.

"I warned you I wasn't going to go easy on you, and the next day you're causing a scene in your courses. I'd like to think I'm fair. My program plans are well laid out. My methods are peer reviewed. And yet you refuse to see sense," she raved.

I held perfectly still. My only focus was on not using my glow, even as my fear mounted. I had to take it. Anything else risked my entire plan. She hurled herself at me, claws up. Her nails dug at my skin before they found purchase in my hair. She was surprisingly strong for how tiny she was. She twisted my head back, exposing my neck.

"I fed you a cookie from my tin. My warning was thorough. Brats like you should start out in isolation. You learn nothing by being allowed to mingle."

She threw me to the ground. She kicked me in the side. My back spasmed against the force. The skin was still tender from my last run-in with authority. She kicked me again and again. I gritted my teeth against the pain even as I saw stars. I had to hold it together.

"You think you're so special with your fucking abilities. You defective little shit. You aren't special. People like you shouldn't even exist. That wasn't even the point of the fucking disease."

She punctuated each sentence with a kick. My mind reeled. What was she on about? I didn't have long to think about it before she lifted me off the ground by my hair only to slam my face into the earth. Dirt filled my nose and mouth, clogging them. I couldn't breathe. She pressed my face into the earth harder, and I couldn't help but squirm under her grip. I needed air. Was she going to kill me? All I could see, all I could feel was the cool, moist soil. She released me. I gasped and spluttered, trying to get air to my lungs. Air tasted different after you'd been denied it, a cross between delicious and relieving.

"So why did you do it? Answer me." Her voice reverberated in the room.

"There isn't a reason." I gasped.

"There had to be a reason. You little shits always have a reason, even if it's stupid. Come on." She dragged me back over by the glass. "Look at yourself. You're a worthless mess. You know all that. So who put you up to it? I need to root out the chaos, and you are going to help me."

"Go fuck yourself," I spat out.

I couldn't help myself. She was so self-righteous and self-assured. It enraged me like few things could. It was still a terrible idea. She rammed my face into the glass with a dull thunk. I couldn't see stars, but I felt my brain slam into my skull. The world spun around me. She rammed my head into the glass again before letting me fall to the ground.

"You did this to spite me, didn't you? Your defective, little brain twisted my words and took them as a challenge," she accused.

I lay there. The world was still a fast-moving haze. I couldn't tell which way was up. I may have underestimated how angry ending up in isolation would make her.

"Answer me!" she screeched.

I put my hands over my ears. She was so loud. It felt like my head was exploding. I'd almost forgotten my breathing. *Come on, Simerra, pull it together. You can't kill anyone right now. You have to stay calm. You can do this. Think of the payoff. Come on, answer her before she hurts you again.*

"Yes, I was angry and not thinking." The words tumbled over each other in my efforts to placate her.

"Of course you did. Well, thank you. We can now proceed with your reeducation."

"Thank you," I mumbled.

"Don't thank me yet. We still have to get the chaos out of you. It's obviously pretty deep in there for you to act out in such a way." Karen cackled.

Wait, that wasn't all of it? Dread turned my stomach as nausea washed over me. I searched her face, hoping to see she was lying. All I found was feral vindication. She smiled down at my curled-up form. She seemed more monster than person. I'd never feared someone as much as I feared her at that moment. She turned to face the glass.

"Cal, get in here," she barked.

Why Cal? What had he done? I held my tongue. Anything I said would only make things worse for him. My brain was still fuzzy. I would have to trust my gut on this one. I watched as Cal entered the room. I faked a wince to hide my relief. He was still wearing his normal clothes and appeared unharmed. I hadn't gotten him in trouble. Cal stood straight-backed and cold-eyed as he stared down at me.

"You called for me, ma'am," he stated.

"You're responsible for her. Make her regret it. Only then will she be freed from the chaos that's taken root. Unless you've gone soft?"

"No, ma'am."

"That's what I like to hear. Come on. She has a big day coming up. She needs to get back to the program asap. Feel free to use severe methods. For the good of our country." She sauntered out of the room, her dress swishing behind her.

I shut my eyes, trying to ready myself for what was to come. Nothing prepared me for Cal's boot connecting with my face. That time, I saw stars. I moved back several feet from the force alone. I was going to feel that later. The vision in my right eye was already blurring. Oh yeah, that was going to swell shut. He came at me again. I held my hands up to block, and he kicked me square in the palm. My wrist cracked against the blow, and I screamed. Something was wrong with my wrist. I cradled it to myself, rocking. I tried to count back from ten. I needed to do something to maintain control. His boot connected with my ribs one, two, three times. I screamed each time, the pain echoing throughout the rest of my body. I scrunched my eyes shut against the onslaught. My glow writhed within me: down to my toes, and up to my head, and back again as it begged to fight for us. I held it tight, refusing to let it leave. We would not hurt Cal. I had to trust him. He wouldn't kill us. I had to hang in there. He stomped on my leg with both of his feet. My toes curled against the pain, and I let loose another echoing scream. My body was on fire. I was on fire. I clung to my glow with everything I had, even as the world faded to nothing more than ever heightening agony.

• • • • • • • • • •

Waking up was like slowly being set on fire. Every breath was agony. The only way I could describe it was the subtlety of a sleeping limb. Sure, first, everything was fine, but as the blood returned, the entire area exploded in tiny pinpricks, and moving on said limb did nothing but worsen the experience. The key difference being that the pain was everywhere and, unfortunately, it would not just wear off eventually. I was stuck like this. I wiggled my toes and fingers to ensure they were all still there. On the bright side, I wasn't hungry anymore. I smiled at my own humor. So maybe that wasn't the brightest idea I'd had. My head throbbed against my skull. The pain of existence itself tore at my body. Was I still clothed? Yes, I could still feel the material against my limbs. Oh, the pains of being hyperaware.

I tried to open my eyes, emphasis on tried. They were practically glued shut with mucus and blood. I was going to have to move, really move, if I wanted to be able to see anything. I sat there, trying to decide which arm hurt less. A strong throb from my right wrist reminded me of its personal ordeal, so that arm was out. *Come on, left side, don't let me down.* I twitched my left arm to assess the damage. It protested but no more than the rest of me. I raised it slowly to my face. I was a mess of crusted on gunk and dirt, so it took a few minutes to clear my eyes. My eyelids were puffy, but I was able to open them. No one was in the room with me. To the far side, I could make out the water bowl from before. I groaned internally. Was I going to be able to make it over there? I had to at least try. My throat was so dry, and what if it was actually food? I braced with my left arm and sat up slowly. My rib cage protested the movement, but otherwise I felt no worse for wear. Now to get up. I was really close to the wall. I dug the fingers of my left hand in between the cinder blocks above my head and pulled with everything I had. I positioned my good leg beneath me and leaned against the wall, still desperately grasping at the cinder blocks. My bad leg twisted wrong, and I crashed back to the ground in pain. I drifted back into unconsciousness.

• • • • ●• • ● • • •

My glow pinballed around inside me. Had it woken me up? I shook the absurd thought from my mind. There were more important worries, like how the hell I had ended up back in the same spot. My left leg sat out to the side, twisted off at a funny angle. Traitor. The bowl was still there. Slowly, I repeated last time's process with more care. The slick surface of the glass wall wasn't going to grant much support for balancing. The only thing to do was try, right? I teetered precariously, always one wrong step away from crumbling back in a heap. Sweat beaded across my brow. Once close, I flung myself off the wall towards the bowl, but I fell into it, dumping the contents into the dirt. I reached for it unthinkingly with my bad wrist. I howled in pain as the last of the water slipped through my fingers. My body protested the deep sobs that racked though me, but I couldn't stop. Anguished slumber dragged me back under.

• • • • ●• ● • • • •

I didn't try to move from my spot again. Every time, I woke up to the same symphony of pain. No one came in while I was awake, and I didn't leave. The days blurred together. I was doing everything I could by breathing and hanging firm in my knowledge that this would pass once they decided the "chaos" had left me. They would let me out like they had Rachel.

Around the tenth time I woke up, something was different. Why didn't breathing hurt? I opened my eyes to see Sasha healing me. Confusion scrawled across my face. How had she gotten here? Behind her, I could see a tall cart. That had to be the medicine cart. My heart leapt for joy. I'd outlasted Karen. I happy wiggled. Sasha pressed her hand against my chest.

"Be still. This is easier if you don't move," she urged.

She was soaked with sweat. It must have been the exertion of having to heal so much in one fell swoop. She was a trooper. She didn't stop until all I had left was bruising. I could have kissed her. She sat back on her heels, panting. I waited for her to get a handle on herself. She had done me such a kindness. I could be patient a little longer before getting answers.

"You need to take an antibiotic," Sasha insisted. She rose to her feet, swaying. I wanted to help her, but I didn't trust my own legs either. She grabbed a small bottle off the cart, returning to my side.

"Here, take one of these every day until they're gone." She handed me the bottle.

I took one, not wanting to get in trouble for missing directions. *Gross, I mean, this was how they got you, wasn't it?* Sasha stood, returning to the cart. This was my chance.

"Where are you going?"

"Someone has to get this cart back to the supplies corridor. Cal will escort you shortly. I'm glad you've recovered from the chaos."

Sasha and the cart were devoured by the doorway, and then I was alone again. I wiggled my fingers and toes. This time, it didn't hurt. Relief coursed through my body as I reveled in my working joints. My wrist and leg felt great aside from some general stiffness. I glanced at the mirrored glass. Was Karen on the other side, plotting how to hurt me best? I rolled my shoulders in an effort to release the tension. She was there or she wasn't. Either way, it wasn't doing me any good to dwell on it. The handle on the door moved, and I tensed. Cal stepped into view, and I worked to hold on to the tension. I couldn't give him away now. They had to think I was scared of him.

"Come on." He spun on his heel, retreating from the room.

I scrambled to my feet, rushing to catch up. We were going too fast for me to speculate on Karen's vindictive smile as I'd rushed past. There simply wasn't time. I blinked against the bright lights of the hallway. Where were we going? I was covered in dirt and blood, hardly ready to be seen by people. We ascended the stairs, climbing higher and higher. It felt like my legs were going to give out. We exited onto my floor, sweeping past the training rooms to my own. He gestured for me to hurry up into the room. He didn't have to tell me twice.

Once inside, I pulled off the crusty clothes and slipped into fresh ones. I didn't know how much time we had in this room, and I didn't want to waste any of it. Cal tapped my shoulder softly, so I spun to face him. He held his arms out, waiting for permission. I returned the gesture. Half a second later, I was enveloped in an all-encompassing hug. I hugged back enthusiastically. I needed to know he was safe, that I was safe. We held each other tightly; neither of us worried about the slight skin-to-skin contact. He needed to see I wouldn't hurt him as much as I needed to know he wouldn't hurt me. It was like getting a hug from Zane before he lost his damn mind, comforting and strong. He pulled back to look me over, taking in all the bruises. His hand hovered over my black and blue cheek. I pulled his hand to my face, leaning into the touch. His hands were coarse but gentle. He cleared his throat, pulling back. I flushed crimson, glancing at the ground. I looked up to see even the tips of his ears were red.

"We should get you to your training session," he decided, still looking anywhere but at me.

"Yeah, let's go."

Chapter Thirty-Four

FIRE AND EMPTY PROMISES

C W: ASSAULT (OFF PAGE)

"We have so little time now! We have to proceed as if you hadn't missed days. We have to stay on target for your assessment this week. We have three days left. Come on, get out into the training room," Dr. McCarthy ordered.

I hesitated. What target were we trying to reach? On a normal day, training was exhausting. Was I really supposed to make it through a training session without eating? The doctor raised an eyebrow, daring me to challenge him. So much for appealing to his humanity. His hand brushed against my hair as I passed. I shuddered and quickened my pace. I didn't stop until I was in the dead center of the training room. It still wasn't far enough for my liking, but it would have to do.

"Okay, we're going to start with the usual."

He put a few larger fires around the room. I lurched to put them out. My sore body protested, but I was able to do it. The fires rose back up. I started to put them out before I noticed more and more fires cropping up around the edges of the room. Was he trying to kill me? Fires continued to crop up and as their numbers soared, so did the temperature.

"What are you doing?" I yelled as more fire appeared.

"I told you we have a schedule to keep," he insisted.

"I can't put all of these out!" I screeched.

"Fight the chaos in your mind and withstand it or stop it. Get with the program, girly. We don't have all day. Here's some more motivation."

What was he going on about? A fire jumped from a grate directly below me. I yelped as it licked at my skin. I reached for my glow, and it responded in an instant, enveloping me. My hair whipped around my head, but I couldn't find it in me to care. He couldn't see all of this clearly enough to work out more details about my glow. The flames didn't drop. The doctor watched me from the safety of the viewing room as my glow held the flames just off of my body. I felt it pulsing through my body stronger than it ever had before. Sweat beaded on my forehead. The heat and fatigue started to wear on me. Could I really hold this for the rest of the session? Dr. McCarthy didn't seem intent on stopping any time soon. My body shook from the force of my glow. It circled up and down inside me as it pulsed to ensure our safety. I gave it my determination and my strength while standing in the flames, untouched. I sat down between two intense fires to conserve energy. Knowing the good doctor, the fire was likely to last a while. I didn't dare play with the minimal amount of protection needed. Whatever felt right was what we were going with today. Experimentation was for smaller blazes, where I felt like I could breath. The smoke was so thick in the room that I would have suffocated if my glow wasn't as strong as it was. Thankfully, I didn't have to worry about air quality. What if I had been honest about my glow? I would be dead right now. It was a sobering thought.

As the flames persevered, I contemplated my mortality. There was a chance, and that chance grew stronger by the minute, that I would not make it out of here. I looked up at the viewing window. Dr. McCarthy stood there, grinning. Beside him stood Cal, his muscles tense as he watched me sit, engulfed in flames. I wanted to assure him we would come out the other side of this training. Cal was just one of the people relying on me. I couldn't give up now. We had to get out of here together. We had to save Zane and Nash and everyone else we could out of this wretched place. I pulled my glow close to my core. It fought me, but I forced it into a smaller ball. It pulsed strong and true. *Don't forget to breathe. One, two, three!* I allowed it to explode forth from me unrestrained. It crashed into each bath of flames with an audible clap. The fires were out. I fell to my knees, weak from the effort. I smiled up at Cal, and it could have been the smoke, but I could have sworn I saw him wink.

"You may return to the observation room." Dr. McCarthy sounded defeated.

So the bastard was trying to kill me. I wiped the ash from my clothes and staggered back in. I shook the soot from my hair as the doctor looked on in disdain. Oh, so he didn't like it when unpleasant things happened on his nice clean floor.

"You can leave now. Go on." He waved me off towards the door, and I was gone without another look back.

"It's lunch next," Cal whispered.

Thank goodness. I made my way slowly down the corridor. Inch by inch, all I could think about was the food that would be awaiting me in the meal room. I was too focused on food to look for anyone. The meal helped with the deep tiredness that had set into my bones. Some of the fogginess left my brain, and I was able to notice the stares from the table's other occupants. Okay then, lunch was over for me. I dumped my tray and walked out the door past Cal, still dragging my feet.

"Come on. You need a break," Cal suggested.

Anywhere he was leading, I would follow. We returned to the soundproof room. I looked at him, confused.

"Forty minutes and then you have enrichment. I know it's not much, but you look exhausted," he apologized, rubbing the back of his neck.

I didn't think. I just wrapped my arms around him, pressing his chest into mine. He hesitated for a moment before reciprocating. I drew back, and we exchanged small smiles before I settled on to the ground of the small room. I was out in an instant, dreaming of more moments like this one.

Cal nudged me gently. I arose, groggy but aware of the time constraints. I followed Cal to the enrichment room and shook the tiredness from my body. Time to wander in circles. I joined the group of glow wielders, and Cal joined the soldiers. I scanned the room for Devin hopefully.

"Erra!"

I knew that voice too well. A pit of dread wormed its way into my stomach. Since when did my brother's voice bring me more concern than some of the instructors? I flattened my affect as his sloppy steps approached. He jogged around me in a circle, pretending to punch at things that weren't there to get a rise out of me. I forced a laugh, not wanting him to see how concerned I was.

"You bit the bullet too? I can't believe it. We're going to get to move up at the same time. That's awesome!" He pumped a fist into the air.

"Yeah, our assessments are coming up," I reminded him.

"Yup, two more days and then BAM! We're on the up and up. It feels so fucking good to be noticed by somebody!" His eyes shone with excitement.

Oh, Zane, what have they done to you? I hid my concern behind another smile. Zane studied me. Had he figured it out? He frowned. Well, shit. What was I going to do now?

"I know: you're worried about your assessment. You're going to do great! You have the skills." He finished his encouragement in a whisper.

At least he had the courtesy to give me that. I still couldn't tell him a damn thing. Any information he gained for me would be used against us. I really was going to have to drag him out of here kicking and screaming. Where was my fierce protector? Did I even still need one?

"I hope so," I played along.

"Believe me. I've talked with them. It'll be different than when we were with Mother. This place cares about us, and we can shape the country. I can keep Devin safe. You can see Nash." He wiggled his eyebrows.

If only it were that simple.

"You know Devin's worried about you?"

"What are you talking about? I talked to him yesterday. He seemed fine," Zane assured me. "Why would he be worried?"

"I don't know. He feels like you're different somehow," I alluded.

Zane switched to walking backwards to study me further. *Come on, bro, take off the rose-colored glasses and smell the giant wedge in your relationship.* He shrugged, still perplexed, and spun to face the right way.

"I'll talk to him if you think I should. You've always given the best advice, Erra."

Where was the hopeless romantic that would jump from a really high branch into a shallow pool just to see Devin smile? *Was my brother even still in there?* No, it was worse than that. He was still in there. He used my nickname from when we were kids and joked with me, but all our ideals and all our ambitions were gone, replaced with regurgitated bullshit about chaos and the government. I had broken through to Nash, and I would break through to him. Not now, that was too risky, but when we got out of here. *I'll get you back, Zane. Whatever it takes.* Wait, was he still waiting for me to reply?

"I think it'll blow over," I assured him.

"I'll keep you safe, Erra. You wait and see. We're going to have it made," he boasted.

He continued to brag and speak highly of the government for the rest of enrichment. I wished it had been Devin instead. That way, I wouldn't have felt like crying right now. I laughed at his jokes and pretended they were tears of joy. Zane left enrichment cup full to bursting with the contents of our conversation, whereas I felt drained and empty and nearly hopeless. Fuck this place. Fuck this place so hard. It couldn't have Zane. I wouldn't allow it. Rage fresh on my mind, I stalked off to my level two strategy class.

Some of the faces around the room were familiar now. Were they on the same floor as I was? As I was pondering this, the instructor strode in. Maybe he hadn't realized I'd been missing for a week. I was wrong.

He scanned the room, and his eyes landed on me. A tired bemusement settled on his lips.

"So you decided to join us again," he speculated.

"It seemed worthwhile," I shot back, not missing a beat.

"How kind of you to grace us with your presence. Care to share your strategy for a mass breakout?" he inquired.

Whispers broke out across the class as others sought to devise a strategy before it was their turn to answer. Too bad, teacher man. You gave me something I know about.

"Before or after?" I questioned innocently.

"Touché. Now class, Simerra raises an excellent point. Are we planning to be proactive or reactive? You. Come on." He snapped his fingers for them to hurry.

"Proactive with a reactive backup if things don't go to plan," the student replied.

"Fantastic. Now, what would we look for with a proactive approach?"

"Chaos?" a bulky guy answered.

The teacher laughed, a raucous sound that carried through the room. Some of the students joined in, hoping to gain brownie points. He stopped, suddenly going serious.

"I didn't ask you for the official answer. I'm asking you for the details. One day, you are going to stare chaos in the face and have to tell it not today. Now, what do you look for in these kids?"

"A student that is dissatisfied. Perhaps someone who is not being challenged to their fullest. Someone who seems to know everyone," I said, hand raised in the air.

So what if I outed myself a little. There was no better way to blend in than right under this man's nose. If anyone was going to catch us, it was going to be him.

"Good. Now, you wouldn't happen to be someone like that would you?" he asked.

The question was meant to sound innocent, but I'd learned allistics were fickle creatures that rarely said what they meant. He was fishing for information. I was almost sure of it.

"I couldn't name two people in this room besides myself if you ordered it. I don't think I qualify as popular." I rolled my eyes and slumped slightly.

This was how they conveyed irritation. I'd seen Joey do it many times before. The teacher moved on to bother other students, and I was able to breathe easy. He didn't turn his focus back to me for the rest of the class. Sometimes, they made it too easy.

CHAPTER THIRTY-FIVE

CAL AND NASH

C W: BEATING MENTIONS, BRAINWASHING mentions

I went to the laundry room and loaded my things into the washer. Hopefully, it was a simple push to start the machine. I found the button, and I went to start it when I realized Cal was holding something up. I set a hand on my hip, turning to face him.

"It won't come very clean without soap," he teased, shaking the container.

"Give it here then," I said with grabby hands.

He handed it off, a smile playing at his lips. My eyes lingered a tad too long before I turned back to my laundry. I started the machine and slid to the floor. The cool tile felt lovely through the fabric of my uniform. The machine clanked and rocked behind me. Maybe this was a bad idea. I mean, I had already started it. I probably had to wait it out. Cal slid down the wall beside me, hand outstretched. I took it, grateful. There must not have been cameras in this room. From this spot, we could see anyone as they walked in well before they would see our hands.

"I want to show you something another high level showed me," I murmured.

I floated my palm above his. Our fingertips barely touched. I coaxed my glow down my arm to meet his. He went to pull his hand back.

"Trust your glow. Trust me," I whispered.

He left his palm below mine. My glow danced back down my arm to play at my fingertips. His came up to meet it. The two didn't just tap. They twisted around each other. I could feel his as intimately as I felt my own, and I knew he felt the same. A small gasp escaped my lips, but I didn't move my hand. I shifted so my head was resting on his chest, our glows still intertwined. His heartbeat matched the movements of his glow so perfectly. He tucked his chin on top of my head, and I allowed my eyes to close.

This safety felt different than the one I experienced with Nash. With her, my soul was laid bare as she held the most delicate pieces of my autistic self. With Cal, it was like my glow didn't have to hide anymore, and it was silly it had ever had to. Both brought me more joy and comfort than I would have ever thought possible. There would be more time to contemplate later. Now was the time to enjoy the moment as I sat tucked under Cal's chin.

We didn't move again until the washer buzzed. Reluctantly, I pulled away. I moved my clothes to the dryer and pressed the start before I hurried back over to his side. We sat in comfortable silence for a while, enjoying the company. The sound of the dryer punctuated our silence with its kerthunking.

"That was . . . ," he started.

"Intense?" I offered.

"That's one word for it." He chuckled. "I didn't think you'd want me any kind of close after everything that happened."

"None of that was your fault," I insisted.

I jerked to face him. He couldn't think like that. None of what happened was his fault. I had a plan that I had to execute. He had to understand that.

"You're scared of me," he asserted.

"No, I'm not."

He raised his hand sharply, and I winced. I could see the pain in his eyes. He dropped it back to his side. No, no, no, it didn't mean what he thought it meant! I took his hand in both of mine and positioned it around my throat. I waited for him to hold it there before I dropped my own hands. I raised my eyebrows for emphasis.

"You are not what scares me. This place scares me. The way it chews people up and spits out husks scares me. You did what you had to, and I do not blame you for that. Yes, I flinched, but it's because of this place. It's because they made you hurt me. I am not scared of you."

He was slack-jawed, and he did not argue again. I wove my fingers between his, wanting to be closer. I knew I wouldn't hurt him.

"If you need to talk about how you feel or any of the guilt you're harboring, I'm here for you, okay?"

He broke down crying. I wrapped my arms around his form. He was tall, but I was determined. His green eyes shone with all the pain he needed to let go of. I didn't stop him or tell him it was okay. I knew what it was like for people to say the wrong words. I held him, standing testament to his pain. Occasionally, I reminded him that I was there for him. He clutched me tighter with each rendition. I sat with him, waiting for the tears to pass.

Soon enough, quiet hours were upon us. I grabbed my laundry slowly to allow him time to collect himself. When he was ready, I strode back into my room and straight into an upset Heather.

"I've been working on these adjustments, and you're the only one that knows the people who are going to have to test them. I see what you're playing at," Heather accused.

"You were bound to find out eventually," I conceded, flopping back against my bed.

"Exactly, you're trying to sabotage me so I only have a half-baked idea for the director to judge again. I'd lose my spot," she accused.

"I mean, it wasn't that well thought out but some variant of that, yes," I lied.

"Well, I beat you at your own game. I've already finished the modifications. All I have to do is equip my changes, and I'm ready to go," she boasted.

I felt lighter. The chairs were going to be ready in time. This was fantastic news.

"You could equip them tomorrow during our free hour. I'll ask my friends where their room is," I offered.

"Fine," she agreed.

• • • • • • • • • •

I made my way to my level one course early. Karley was there, like always. Sasha hadn't arrived yet. Karley eyed me curiously. Was she genuinely concerned or merely worried I'd changed my mind? I plopped down in my seat and tugged lightly on her hair.

"I believe you owe me some information."

"You really don't fuck around. What do you want to know?" Karley asked, perplexed.

"Can you charge batteries?"

She looked insulted, a hand raising to her chest. She would have clutched at pearls if she had any. Dramatics must be an age bracket thing. I suffered from it too sometimes.

"Of course I can charge things. I can also do a load of other cool things. Why would you care about that?"

"I need chair batteries powered up when they get low. I know you'll contribute in other ways, but this is something we need," I clarified.

"You're taking high levels with you." She raised her hands to her mouth. Silent tears slipped down her face. I-I miscalculated somewhere. Why was she upset? Had I offended her?

"One of the girls I came in with is a high level. I've been worried about her this entire time. We were friends before they sorted and separated us," she informed me.

"What's her name?"

"Rachel," she breathed.

"She's coming. I've talked to her," I assured her.

"Sasha and I are in one hundred percent." She wiped away her tears and determination took their place.

"I'm glad. On assessment day, wait for the chaos. Then run for the woods past the asphalt. There's an old road that winds by a river there. Hide under the first bridge you come to. If you take that path, I will find you," I ordered.

The rest of the class began to fill the room, and we fell silent. Both of us turned back to our own desks. I doodled in my notebook through the entire lecture, only pausing to jot down the few pertinent pieces of information that left his mouth. Thanks, asshole.

Next was enrichment. Thankfully, I didn't know anyone today. I was able to think as I walked around. There was a lot going on, and I hadn't been able to see Nash. Having Cal near helped, but I needed both of them to feel fully safe. Was Karen hurting her? Was she keeping her away from me on purpose? Was she brainwashed again? Maybe it wasn't so good to have enrichment alone. When we were released, I walked to lunch, still thinking about it. It wasn't until Trish tapped me on the forehead with a spoon that I snapped out of it.

"There she is. She lives!" Trish cheered.

She wiggled the fingers of her right hand at me, not dropping Rachel's hand as she did. So Cal and I weren't the only ones holding hands. Wait, did they feel how we felt? Worth a shot.

"Congratulations," I offered in a small voice.

They beamed at the recognition, so I was right.

"It's thanks to you really. We don't have to worry about them tearing us apart anymore." Trish kissed the back of Rachel's hand while the guards looked elsewhere.

"I'm happy for you guys. Tonight, we're coming to fit some of the adaptations to your chairs. Heather still doesn't know what's really going on. She thinks you're helping with her assessment project. I'm hoping I can tell her soon and have her wait with you in your rooms, since she'll have a later assessment slot than those of us testing for the first time. We've got this," I whispered.

"We're down near the med wing on the second floor, room six. We'll see you later tonight. It looks like that girl wants you." She gestured to the far door.

I squinted. Who was trying to pull me out of lunch? I leapt to my feet when I realized it was Nash. I tried my hardest to keep my steps even as I made my way past her and out the door. I knew this game. Once the door had shut, she grabbed my hand and we raced up to a supply closet. Cal came in with us.

"Do you need to be here?" she interrogated.

"He does. He's important too," I said, setting a hand on either of their chests.

"Fine. What's going on? I haven't heard anything from you. Are you okay? You look like you took another beating." Concern poured out of her mouth.

"I'm okay now. I had to find out where the supplies were located. There's a lot of people coming. I also met your mother," I informed her.

That was not what I should have led with. Her face filled with shame and fear. I would never let that woman hurt Nash once we were free. I gave her the overview of everything that had happened. I didn't even leave out Cal's and my connection. It wouldn't have been right. Her nostrils flared when she heard that part, Her face went blank. Was she mad at me?

"I guess guys are more interesting," Nash deadpanned.

Was that the only comment she had for me? I bit my lip, upset but unsure of how to fix this. It wasn't like I was choosing. I was trying to be open. I wanted us to talk through this as a group. I wanted her to be a part of this conversation. She clearly didn't see it that way.

"Can't you see you're hurting her?" Cal complained.

"You're one to talk about hurting her," she shot back.

Cal flinched. I squeezed both of their hands lightly. Cal struggled to compose himself. Shit, what was I supposed to say?

"You landed me here," I reminded her.

It was Nash's turn to flinch. I squeezed her hand again. We were already past both of these things, but it wasn't fair to look at one without the other. We'd all made mistakes that had brought us here, to this exact moment.

"Look, I'm still coming. We can work all this out later. I'm going to fight for you. You're worth more than I can even express."

She held my face by my chin before pressing our foreheads together. I sighed contently. She pulled back, smirking.

"I'm not looking for a fight," Cal said.

"She's the most beautiful person I've ever met, and I will fight for her," Nash asserted again.

"If you make this a competition, I will win," Cal warned.

"Look, you're both wonderful, and I know we have a lot to talk about, but now isn't the time. I have two days to finish pulling things together. Two. Days. Later," I said firmly. "We have to focus."

"I can handle that," Cal relented.

"Same," Nash agreed. "As long as he understands I'll destroy him if he hurts you.

"I would hope so. Same to you." Cal ran a hand through his hair, smirking.

"Maybe you aren't so bad," Nash teased, elbowing him in the side.

Cal's eyes softened ever so slightly. Thank fuck. Nash hugged my left side, and Cal hugged my right, both of them careful not to touch each other. This was going to be a long road. Worth it, but long.

• • • ● • ● • • •

I lounged on my bed, grateful for everything we'd achieved during the day. Heather sat on the edge of her bed facing me. Oh no, what was wrong?

"When were you going to tell me you're planning to leave?" She glared at me, hands balled into fists at her side. "Am I not smart enough for your group? You can't use me for my skills then ditch me here. Those chairs all have a major fault. They'll short out in three days if I don't repair them. You either bring me with you or your friends will end up stranded!" she hissed.

"Woah, no one said you were being left behind. It would be cruel, and we could use someone with tech knowledge on the team. You seemed really into this place, so I was going to tell you the day of and hope for the best," I said plainly.

Heather blinked slowly before me. Had I been too blunt? I forgot how little allistics liked that. I bit my lip while she chewed on my words. I allowed my fingers to tap against my side, making new patterns to help pass the time.

"So I'm coming?"

"Of course you are. Pack your bag," I encouraged, giving her a thumbs-up and a tired smile.

"I did that the second I figured out what you were doing. I mean, these mods were going on chairs that likely wouldn't see action for years. There's no other reason for them to need my mods any more than a random out of use chair. Don't worry, I submitted all the paperwork. They have faked schematics so they can't rebuild or dismantle my work, but they also won't stop your friends in the halls tomorrow for having new features. I'm sure you thought of that already."

"You give me too much credit. Sometimes, things just fall together." I laughed.

Chapter Thirty-Six

Assessment Day

With the extra patrolling, the soldiers were more on edge than I'd ever seen. That wasn't the part that had me nervous now. No, that would be the small animal that was raised into the training room. The bunny twitched its nose gently. I knew what he wanted to test. I sank to my knees before the small creature. It wasn't fair it had ended up in front of me, a sacrificial offering to something this place didn't understand. I took a deep, harrowing breath and set my hand on its fur. It was so soft. I stroked it gently for a moment. A tear trailed down my cheek as my glow pulsed down my arm and into this rabbit. It fell to its side, twitching. I pushed my glow harder, not wanting it to suffer. The rabbit fell still, my hand still stroking its fur. I hung my head heavy with the weight of my training. *Sorry, little guy.*

The worst part was they weren't even going to use this animal for mealtime. It would likely be thrown into the trash, a total loss. They could at least do it the dignity of serving a purpose in death, but no, this backwards place lived for the excess of it all. The sound of the raising mechanism took me from my thoughts. Of course they were going to have me kill again. I clenched my hands into fists and moved on to my next target. By the end of it, I'd killed ten animals. It was easier than fires, but I didn't want Dr. McCarthy to know that. I feigned weak knees when he called me back to the observation room.

"Excellent work today. You'll do great in your assessment," he praised.

"Thank you." I couldn't stop the flat tone that crept into my voice.

"Don't be a downer. This is an accomplishment. You want to help your country, don't you?" Dr. McCarthy asked.

Did we have to do this now? I bit back a snide remark before it could leave my lips. *Give the cruel man what he wants.*

"There's no greater honor." I forced a smile to my lips.

Think about how it'll feel to be out of here. Keep it together. Come on. Dr. McCarthy seemed pleased with my answer. My legs carried me out of that place and through the rest of my day. I couldn't shake the dread that senseless killing caused me. Even Cal's side comments weren't able to cheer me up. The day passed slowly, as if the time of this place knew what we were going to do and wanted to actively block me. I found myself counting down the minutes until my free hour. When it finally came, I sat on my bed, unsure of what to pack. Some part of me hadn't expected us to get this far.

· · · ● · ● · ● · ·

"Take this. You slept like shit," Heather said, like this was news to me.

I took the pills she offered. Hopefully, we were past a point where she'd try to kill me. Regardless, my head was killing me, and I was willing to try almost anything. Now to wait and see which one it was. I slapped my face, trying to wake myself up.

"We should go eat," Heather encouraged.

The hall was filled with a long table full of energy bars, snacks, and traditional breakfast food. Heather wasn't fazed at all. She filled up a plate with waffles and bacon. It all looked delicious. I scarfed down a muffin as I loaded my plate with protein bars and fruit. Heather looked on, confused. I shrugged. I wasn't going to explain out in the hall. We returned to our room with our food. I dumped the contents of the plate into my bag.

"That makes so much sense," Heather said, mouth full of food.

"It'll help with those who need to eat frequently, but we'll have to hunt almost immediately. I can't carry enough food for everyone," I said wistfully.

If only the bed would fit in my bag. I would miss sleeping on things so soft. A sharp knock on the door caused me to jump.

"It's time to report for assessment day," Cal called through the door, the cold edge back in his tone.

"Ready?" I asked.

She nodded, gripping her bag tightly. *Okay then. Here we go.* There was a steady flow of people towards the stairs. I followed the crowd. I could feel Cal just behind me. This was the only chance I'd get to fill him in.

"Cal. I know you can hear me. I need you to get a vehicle and get medical supplies. Empty the damn room if you can."

"What about you?" he breathed.

"I'll be okay. I have to get to Zane. Go. We only have one shot, and they'll all be watching us and guarding the director."

"I'm on it. Be safe." He gave my hand a quick squeeze, and then he was gone.

He slipped away from me, lost in the crowd. I readjusted my pack. Now to focus. We made our way down the stairs and over to the enrichment room. There was a tall platform I'd never noticed before in the middle. Soldiers were clustered around the bottom, guns drawn. I peered up, trying to catch a glimpse of the director. Was he hiding from us?

"Everyone, spread out. Come on. Let the director get a good look at all of you. I said spread out. Let's go." Doctors at the front of the room hurled directions at us.

Everyone shuffled around, trying to comply quickly, not wanting to endanger their chances. When we were properly spaced, the bubble of conversation died away. Karen walked into view quickly, followed by the director. A bird sat on his shoulder. It flapped its wings as it readjusted. The blue underwing was clear, even from this distance.

A jumbled mess of strong emotions rocked inside me. I tapped my fingers against each other with newfound ferocity. Long to short. Short to long.

"Welcome, students. Today is the first day of the rest of your lives," Karen began.

As opposed to what? Couldn't she say that every day? It made no difference. I could ask Zane about it later. Was he in here? I craned my neck, trying to catch a glimpse of him.

"Now, a word from the director before we begin." Karen passed the microphone to the director.

It was odd seeing him in person. After all, I was used to seeing him on the little TV in the observation room, but now he was here to ruin my life in person. Lucky me.

"Thank you, Karen. What a lovely group of students you've trained up here. A group of students who are determined to fight chaos in all its forms. Now, I think that is super cool. Give yourselves a round of applause."

I clapped and cheered with everyone around me. The energy in this room was ridiculous. Would I even be able to convince any of them to come with us? My only chance would be if I could get to that microphone.

"I know you're all excited to prove your skills. There is one tiny problem. There simply aren't enough spaces for everyone. More of you showed promise than we thought possible. We need you to prove that you will give anything for your country. Look to your left. Look to your right. These are the people that stand between you and your place in this program. Are you going to let them keep you from fulfilling your purpose?"

I glanced around to see others doing the same. Some hands were already glowing softly. This was going to be a bloodbath. They had to know that. I glanced up at the director. He stared down at us. His demeanor was cool and calculating. He didn't care about any of us. Was this the new burning ritual? We were going to do all of his dirty work for him. You had to be fucking kidding me.

"I will call time when appropriate. Those of you left standing will continue on your path to protect our country. Thank you for helping us secure the future. On Karen's command, you may begin." He handed over the microphone to a smiling Karen.

"Alright, students. This is an opportunity for you to show off your abilities. Think of this as a giant training exercise. I believe that each and every one of you is ready to embrace your potential and show us what you're working with!" She laughed at her own comment. "Now is not the time to hold back. Show us you deserve to be here. Show us how free of chaos you really are. Is everyone ready!"

The students cheered again, a loud roar of acceptance. I nudged at my own glow, waiting. At least my bag could protect my back.

"On my mark! Get set! Go! Your country thanks you for your service." The last sentence was said over the wave of screams that had already begun.

Chapter Thirty-Seven

FIGHTING FOR OUR LIVES

CW: graphic depictions of violence, gore, mass death

Someone grabbed at my neck. My glow lashed out at them, unfettered. I heard them gasp and splutter on the ground. I pulled it back towards myself. I didn't want to kill anyone. Was this what training had been working us all up to? A world of unrestricted chaos as we harmed each other? After everything they'd done to keep us contained and docile . . .

The girl before me crashed to the ground, taken out by some unseen force. Her screams ripped through my skull, curling my toes. What had hurt her? I looked around for the high level responsible, but it was impossible. We were a writhing mass of bodies. Like feral dogs, we lunged as if every hand had potential to hurt, and we weren't far off.

Someone used my bag to throw me. I collided with a group of fighting kids. A hot hand brushed past my face, leaving a burn where it touched. I swept my leg under his, dropping him to the ground. I turned to the man who had thrown me and raised my fists. He raised his palms in a wide stance. *Fucking try me.*

He dodged my swing. My fist instead connected with a different girl who slashed at me with her knife. That was not fair. Had someone warned her what this was about, or were other kids actually allowed weapons? She rushed me, knife flailing. I shoved her away with a wall of air. I turned back to face the first person, but he was already gone.

I needed to focus. He wasn't my target. I had enemies, and they were sitting in a tower, watching us tear into each other. A blockade of soldiers stood around the base of it, weapons raised. If I wanted to stop this, I was going to have to get through the mass of young adults trying to prove their worth and all those soldiers. No pressure.

A new scream broke over my ears. I was going to have to get there fast before everyone was dead. My glow pulsed strongly, wanting to help. Now wasn't the time. I had to save that for our exit. I started dodging through the tussling bodies, but a familiar scream stopped me in my tracks. Nash! I spun around. I had to get to her. Where was she? It was impossible to see her in the mess of people.

"Nash!" I screamed.

I twisted back and forth, trying desperately to find her in this mess. Someone cut my arm. I pulled back and punched him in the face. With the added force of my glow, he flew backwards, cracking his head against the floor. Blood pooled from the wound. The dark red mixed with the grime and corpses being smashed into the floor under the feet of the desperate.

"Simerra!" Nash called from the far side of the room.

I turned my back on the director, knowing where I needed to go. I dodged under a person who was suspended in the air by someone's glow only to run headlong into two people who had each other in headlocks.

"Sorry," I mumbled.

Did manners apply in the heat of battle? The two of them stopped harming each other and reached for me. I tried to pull back, but they grabbed my shirt. The smaller one shoved me to the ground, and they started kicking me. I covered my head, trying to stay safe. Their desperate need for survival was as strong as mine in this sick game of chance we were forced to contend with. When they gave up, I jumped to my feet. They both seemed shocked I was still awake. Did they even know how to kill anyone? I smashed their heads together before shoving them apart to continue my search. At least if they were stunned, they would hurt fewer people.

"Simerra!" Nash screamed.

I needed to hurry up. My glow bubbled softly over my skin the way it wanted to. The low hum of the energy soothed me even as I continued my way through the fighting. Someone jerked me near them then dropped to their knees a moment later, choking. I wrenched my arm free, and they fell back against the ground, sprawled out like roadkill.

A soft hand tapped on my shoulder. I spun, confused. My face was met with her fists again and again. She pummeled me.

"I'm sorry," she muttered, setting up to punch me again.

Oh great, this one felt guilty. I ducked away from the next punch. Her words had given me enough time to prepare. She looked at me. Her eyes filled with fear. I didn't have time for this. I punched her in the stomach as hard as I could. My thumb ached horribly. It seemed when things got rough, my form went to shit. I would have to have that looked at later. The girl turned and ran away. *Good luck out there.*

"Nash!" I yelled, shoving my way through yet more people.

"Simerra!" Her voice called from my left.

Was that her head? It had to be her. A girl squared up directly in my path. I groaned. I swore I was going to lose it. I raised my own hands, palms up. I had somewhere to be. She turned and attacked someone else. What was that about? Someone grabbed me from behind and squeezed tightly. Memories of what had happened in the observation room flashed through my head. I screamed, terrified. I didn't even have to reach for it. My glow jumped up, and I felt their grip slacken. They gasped for breath, clawing at their throat. I was still trapped, feeling the doctor's hands. No one was ever going to touch me like that again. I wouldn't let them. It wasn't until my assailant lay still that I was able to come back to myself. Their body was an odd purple color. I sank to my knees. I hadn't meant to do that. A person flew overhead. Right, middle of a battle, I could pity myself later.

I crawled away from the corpse through the legs of people who fought overhead. Nash finally came into view. She was surrounded by people trying to kill her. I wasn't surprised. People knew who she was, and I doubted I was the only one she had wronged during her long stay here. I pushed my way through to the center of the circle. People cheered, thinking I was going to attack her. Oh how wrong they were.

"Stay down," I yelled at her.

Nash dropped to the floor. I clapped my hands together before stretching them wide the way Zane did for an ice blast. The people around the circle were thrown back into other people's fights. My hair whipped around my face from the force. Nash grabbed my hand and pulled me up into her arms. I wrapped my arms around her neck, trying to help support some of my weight.

"Hang on," she urged.

She rushed us back into the fray. I tucked my head into her neck. Even in all this, a sense of calm spread over me. My glow purred. This felt right. You know, outside of the fact we were in the middle of a death match, but it wasn't until she set me down that I remembered that.

"Hands up, thumbs by your knuckles, stand tall," she reminded me.

I did as she said, readying myself for the next onslaught. A few people were taking notice of us. Couldn't they bother someone else? We were only halfway to the platform.

"We need to get to that microphone," I informed her.

"Why do you need that? We're not letting you through. We need those spots in the program," one of the girls hissed. Her own fists raised to fight.

"I don't want to fight you. I want to stop this," I pleaded.

"That sounds pretty chaotic, don't you think? I won't feel bad breaking your neck," a guy asserted, running his thumb across his neck.

So much for talking to them. Nash struck first, her fists connecting with the neck guy's torso. He barely moved as she strained against him. He was a tank of a man. He laughed. The girl who spoke earlier swiped at me with a cleaver. Where had she gotten that? She swung again, this time barely missing my nose. The transition between cleaver and arm was sudden. Was that her glow? Knife hands? She swung again, the force almost pulling her past me. She had so little control like this. The weight of the knives threw her off balance with each strike. I squared my feet, a vague plan forming in my mind. She rushed me again. I ducked, sliding my leg under her own. I'd have to thank Nash for teaching me that one. It had already saved me twice. The girl toppled over, and her knife sliced into her own leg. She screamed. Her hands took the place of the knives in a grotesque transition. Blood oozed out of the gash. I ripped the sleeve of my shirt and rushed over to her.

"Get away from me!" she screamed, holding her hands up to keep me at bay.

"I'm trying to help!" I shouted.

I pushed her hands away and covered the gash. I pressed down sharply, and she screamed again. She pounded on my back, trying to get me to stop. Her knives sliced into the delicate skin there. I uttered a low string of curses. This girl was lucky I had some control.

"If you touch me, I will hurt you. Knock it off. You need to keep the pressure on this till the bleeding slows."

I grabbed her sleeve and guided her hand to replace my own. She stared up at me, confused. Had I not said I didn't want to fight before all this? I didn't have time to explain. I squeezed her shoulder lightly and jumped back to my feet. Nash was still fighting the big one.

"Your friend is hurt. Go take care of her," I commanded.

He threw Nash to the ground, but he didn't move to check on her. Great, they were taking the whole no friends thing very seriously. Nash rolled onto her back and kicked upwards with all her strength. He gasped, knees shaking. Nash pulled back and kicked him in the back of the knees this time, using him to launch herself upright. He fell to the ground. We ran forward, taking advantage of the opening. I looked around. There were still a bunch of us, but blood droplets streaked across the ground and everyone was fighting and the smell of iron coated my nose and throat. Screaming was a constant as we all tore into each other.

We jumped over a corpse and into open space. Several guns were trained on us now.

"Get back in there. You aren't done," a soldier ordered.

"I really hope you have a more convincing argument than that," I shot back.

I took a step forward. A warning shot ricocheted off the ground near my feet. Nash raised her own gun. When had she gotten that? I swore everyone was more prepared for this than I was.

"You all know I'm a faster shot than you. Who's willing to die for their convictions?" she asked, smiling.

She was gorgeous when she smiled. Her powerful stance drew me in, the glint of cunning that filled her eyes as she challenged those in our way. Okay, wow. Now was not the best time to be pining after Nash. *Get it together, Simerra. We're literally in danger.* And yet I couldn't take my eyes off her. She gestured with her gun for them to drop theirs. A stray hair from her bun curled from the sweat and hung in front of her face. She was the picture of strength.

A gun clattered to the ground, but the rest opened fire. I shoved Nash to the ground. The screams behind us intensified as people behind us were struck by the onslaught. We didn't have time for this. I shoved my glow at the soldiers in one strong burst. They dropped to their knees, writhing. Now was our chance.

We had to stop this. The door at the bottom would surely be locked. I ran through the soldiers, still gathering speed. I rammed into the door with my body and my glow. The door crashed open from the force. Something I hadn't planned for was stopping. I slammed to the ground, narrowly avoiding hitting my head on the tile. Did they think that would stop me? It was a cute try. I'd give them that. I staggered into a wall as the kickback hit.

"You alright?" Nash yelled as she barricaded the door.

"Yeah, I'll be fine." My voice wavered, but I pushed off the wall regardless.

The tower wasn't any wider than a stairwell. So much for government luxury. Nash glanced over at me from the winding staircase, a smile on her face. She bowed, her hair falling into her face. Her ponytail had long since been mussed up.

"After you," she said conspiratorially.

"Thank you."

"Always so polite. I'll guard the stairwell. I don't know if I can—" The words caught in her throat.

"And I don't expect you to. I'll be back."

She nodded, still uncertain. I grabbed her hands and looked as close to her eyes as was comfortable.

"It's going to be okay. We're going get through this."

She took a shaky breath. I hugged her close, savoring the moment. She melted into me. If only we had more time, I'd hold her forever, but we didn't and I couldn't. Something slammed into the barricaded door, and I raced up the stairs. The door at the top wasn't even locked. The cocky bastards. My hatred for them grew. My glow jerked around in my chest, as agitated as I was with their arrogance.

I stalked in, still seething. Karen stared at me, horrified. Good. It was her turn to be afraid. The director frowned. With the lazy wave of his hand, the two soldiers present advanced.

I dodged the first soldier, but the second landed a blow on my jaw. My teeth slammed together, and I tasted blood. They didn't come to fuck around. I protected my face the way Nash taught me while he threw punch after punch. He was relentless. The second kicked the back of my knee and I careened to the floor. The first held a gun to my head.

"Give her five minutes in case she decides chaos isn't the way. Her skills could prove useful," he drawled. His eyes focused on the blood-bath below.

Think of something, Simerra You need to get it together. I tapped my fingers together. Long to short. Short to long. The soldiers' focus had shifted to the events outside the tower, and their guns pointed uselessly at the floor. I threw myself at the soldier closest to me, sending him flying into the wall. The second grabbed me. I pushed my glow at her with everything I had. Her life drained away while she tried to scream. The second soldier raised a hand to try to ward me off. Small sparks flew off his palms. I threw him into the wall again. He didn't get back up. I trained a discarded gun at the two of them.

"Sorry to interrupt but I need that mic," I said, holding out my hand.

The bird on his shoulder shrieked, flapping its wings. He soothed it before begrudgingly handing it over. Perfect.

"Hello."

My voice was still at a normal volume. I tapped at it, trying to discern what was wrong.

"Turn it on!" Nash yelled.

I blushed red as I flipped on the little button. The microphone screeched. A few heads turned, but most kept fighting. What was the best way to address this? Fuck if I knew. There was no time to prepare. Here went nothing.

"Everyone, stop."

More heads turned towards me. It was probably strange hearing someone who was neither Karen nor the director on the microphone. They stood there waiting for me to say something profound. I wished I had better words.

"They don't deserve your loyalty. How could someone see us killing each other and do nothing? You know each other. You have friends!"

"For the good of the government!" someone called out, their fist raised in the air.

"Fuck the government! Fuck this place! Don't you want to be your own person? Don't you want to walk around without the fear of reeducation? All of you won't make it if you stay here. This place doesn't care about you. The director doesn't care about you. If he did, why would he say there was no space in the program? We all have rooms and go to classes. He's making it up, and now we're doing his dirty work," I reasoned.

"Who the fuck are you?"

"Good question. I'm Simerra. I'm one of you, and I just want to see my friends again. I want us to all have a chance. We don't have that there. I've been outside. Yes, it's messy, and it's hard work, but it's home," I explained, looking over the conflicted crowd. They were bruised and bloody and scared and tired. *Please come with me.*

"You're lying! There's chaos out there," Zane shouted back. His chest puffed out with conviction.

My heart ached. Tears jumped to my eyes. My brother was set against me even now. *Come on, Zane. See sense.*

"Yeah, and what the fuck do you call this? A vacation? They watch our every movement and hurt anyone who sticks out," I shot back.

"The difference between here and out there is simple. Here, they feed us and we have somewhere to sleep. Out there, it's all hard ground and scavenging. Is that what you want?" Zane protested.

"It's working together to get through the hard times. It's working for the good of the group. It's having the ability to go where you want, when you want." Tears fell from my eyes. Was this when I lost him?

"It's also getting soaked in the rain and getting frostbite when it snows. It's being at the mercy of the elements. Don't lie to them, Simerra!"

"It's being safe to love who you want to without being called chaotic for caring. It's being treated like a person. It's hard, but it's doable, and I would give anything to be back out there. I know some of you agree with my brother. I know it can seem easier to go with the flow and stay here doing what the director tells you. But I'm here to tell you there's another way, and I'm taking it. Anyone who wants to come with me is welcome. Get your stuff and meet me outside. I'm leaving with or without you." I locked eyes with Zane.

He stood in the crowd of faces defiantly. *Oh, you're coming. I'll be back to drag you out of here soon enough.* People rushed around, but Zane continued to stare me down. I rolled my eyes. I had things to do. I flipped off Karen on my way past, chucking the mic at the wall where it smashed apart. I couldn't help but giggle. I bounded back into the bowels of the tower, tripping over one of the steps. Nash caught me effortlessly. The soldiers outside the entryway stared as we ran past.

"You're all welcome to come with us. Get your friends and hurry up," I yelled behind me.

"What now?" Nash asked, eyes full of hope.

"Now we make it loud."

A dark glint came into her eyes. She offered me her hand. I took it, and we ran together through the sea of people.

Chapter Thirty-Eight

ZANE

C I stared at the PA system gleefully. This was perfect. Nash stood by the door, ready to pull the fire alarm. It chirped to life.

"Hello, we interrupt your regularly scheduled programming to bring you an update live." I parroted the reporters from before.

That was a good way to start a broadcast, right? Whatever, everyone was listening. Time to make an announcement.

"Attention: this place is ridiculous and we all deserve better. I'm getting out of here, and I have one question. Do you want to sow some chaos?"

I cued Nash. She pulled the fire alarm and all the doors sprung open. We ran from the room, laughing. An explosion from the floor below shook the pictures on the wall to our left. Dead people's pictures crashed to the ground, and I fell into Nash's arms.

"We've got to keep moving," she urged.

"One second." I stepped away from her over to where the pictures lay scattered.

The glass crunched beneath my feet as I searched the pile. Where was it? I looked up at the wall. It was still hanging. Echo's picture. I slammed my elbow through the glass. It clattered to the floor, leaving behind the picture. I pulled it from the wall, folding it neatly. I tucked it away into Nash's pocket. Nash's eyebrows pulled together.

"Now I'm ready. Where's your bag?"

"I already gave it to Cal. I saw him earlier," she explained.

"Hey, you two! Stop!" a soldier yelled from the other end of the hall.

"We should go," she urged.

"We can take them. They shoot blanks to capture regular glow wielders, right?" I asked.

A bullet whipped past my ear, embedding itself in the wall.

"Nope. This is a full-blown rebellion. They use real bullets on everyone for those. Come on."

We ran back down the hall as bullets peppered the walls around us.

"Your distance shooting is shit!" Nash jeered as we reached the stairs.

"Don't encourage them!" I scowled as the door shut behind us.

She pouted. I couldn't help but laugh at her. Even at a time like this, Nash was up to her usual antics. We rushed down the stairs, back towards freedom. We exited onto the ground floor. It was utter anarchy. Students glowed all over the place, fighting soldiers and teachers. Others tipped cabinets and movable objects.

"Everyone, return to your classrooms at once," a soldier behind a shield ordered.

A book collided with his shield. Cheering came from all around the hall. Nash wiggled her eyebrows, laughing. Was this all because of me? A sense of pride burned within me at the prospect. We were really doing it. We ran into the thrall. Nash picked up a desk and hurled it at the soldiers. It smashed into one of their shields. The others retreated. She was so beautiful. *Come on, Simerra. You have to focus.*

"We have to get outside. Come on," I yelled to the group.

Students tumbled over each other as we stampeded towards the outdoors. I could feel the pressure of the bodies behind me. We ran out into the sunlight. On the other side of the cement stood every single soldier the facility had left. Their weapons were raised and ready.

"Stop!" I screeched.

No one listened to me until the first bullets collided with the fastest students. They crumpled to the asphalt in messy heaps, blood leaking out of them. People screamed, everyone pushing back into the building for protection. We stood there, facing down the soldier. No one on either side moved. Everyone was sizing up the competition. Karen moved to the front, a megaphone clutched in her bony hand.

"This is your last chance. Your government understands this is scary and that you are not ready to move on with your training, but this is not the way. We are here to guide you. With the government, you can be great. It would be a waste to destroy so many. We want to help you," Karen lied.

"Fuck you!" I yelled.

Others hurled their own insults. Good to see I wasn't the only one utterly sick of her shit.

"Why do you curse me? Is it because you feel the chaos within you? You can fight it. You can do the right thing." Her voice was full of that sickly sweet tone she loved so much.

I could hear people behind me deciding what to do. So many of them sounded scared of retribution, as the high of acting out wore off. I had to do something or this place was going to win.

"That's bullshit! You only care about turning us into soldiers. We aren't disposable. We aren't tools to help you further your schemes!" I turned to face the students behind me. "They are scared of us. That's why they want you to turn yourselves in. You're all incredibly powerful, right? You know that from your training. So what's stopping you from taking them on right now?"

"If we're so powerful, why don't you go first? They have guns!" someone shouted.

I smiled. Clearly, this person didn't know me. I took a deep breath and stepped out away from the others. I held my arms up, welcoming whatever came next. I stopped, restraining my glow. The temperature dropped immediately around me. The wind whipped everyone's hair around. I squared my shoulders and stood halfway between the soldiers and the students.

"I am leaving. We all are leaving," I snarled.

"Fire at will."

A hail of bullets whistled through the air, coming ever closer. I brought my arms together in front of me in a large sweeping motion, sending air rushing towards them in a solid wall. Some of the bullets changed course with it in turn, battering back against the soldiers. Half of them fell to the ground from the force. The last time I had done this, I could barely stand afterward, but now, after all my training, I didn't even break a sweat. I pushed forward again. Some of the soldiers scattered. I could hear the students behind me beginning to press forward as well, comforted by my win. I couldn't help the smirk that broke out across my face.

"Send in the good ones," Karen yelled.

Students in green and some of the soldiers rushed forward. I could feel the people behind me waiting for me to make a decision.

"The only way out of here is through them! Come on!" I yelled.

Our feet pounded against the concrete as we advanced. A soldier ahead of me raised her hands, the ground cracking beneath her feet. It would have been so much cooler if she wasn't trying to destroy me.

"You don't have to do this!" I raised my own hands.

"You can't convince me to embrace chaos!" she roared.

The ground beneath me cracked and buckled against itself. I fell to my knees. The hole was growing larger as it approached me. For real? I slid back as fast as I could, scrambling to get to my feet. The crack stopped spreading as a rock collided with her skull. I heard a scream. I twisted around, trying to find the cause. Trish sat, palms outreached towards the sky. A small cloud swirled over her head. She jerked her head and a bolt of lightning flashed out of the cloud, striking at soldiers. Now, that was impressive. Where was Nash? I swiveled around as panic mounted in my chest. I couldn't lose her.

"I'm here," she said from behind me.

She was covered in debris but looked otherwise okay. I gestured for her to follow me. We made our way through the fighting and back up towards the front of the group. We had to lead everyone away from here before the soldiers could get to their vehicles. As if on cue, a giant truck came bustling towards us. Were they going to stop? Was it gaining speed?

"Watch out!" I screamed.

I ran in front of it, getting ready to try and stop it. I'd never tried moving something so big before. I squared my feet, my hands coming up. It beeped at me. I squinted. Why would it do that? A hand waved out the window. Wait—it couldn't be. Cal stuck his head out the window, still laying on the horn. *Impeccable timing, that one.* He jumped out and opened the back of the truck. I could kiss him.

"If you're coming, get in!" I yelled to the group.

People started to peel off, running full force towards the truck. I kept my eyes peeled for those who were against us. I'd made that mistake once. I wasn't ready to make it again. Besides, I still had to find Zane.

"We're burning daylight here. Your friends are here. Let's go!" Cal called over.

There were still people locked in the fighting. Some of them were people I promised to take with me. I still hadn't seen Zane . . . . I knew what had to happen. I grabbed Nash's hand and ran her over to the truck. I gave Cal a pointed look. He nodded. *Please let this work.* Nash looked between us, confused.

"You need to stay safe."

"You too. Come on," she urged.

I cradled her cheek in the palm of my hand. Was it possible to burst from how much you cared about someone? Her soft eyes stared down into mine. She was as mesmerized as I was. I would have one shot at this. I crashed my lips into hers. She kissed me back immediately. Her lips were soft and tasted of something sweet. She gasped, allowing me to deepen the kiss. My hands slid back to tangle in her hair. Her own hands wandered my back before she pulled me closer by the hips. Could she tell how desperate I was? I pressed my lips to hers harder for a moment before I broke off the kiss. She opened her eyes, dazed and joyful. I shoved her back into Cal's waiting arms.

"Get her out of here. Check the first underpass. There are people there. Drive to the main road, take the second left. I'll meet you there. Keep them safe. I will find you."

"I hope you know what the hell you're doing," he quipped.

I nodded.

"I trust you. Stay safe."

"No, Simerra. What are you doing?! Simerra!" Nash begged.

Tears streamed down my face as I ran away from her screams and back into the fray. I had to hold all of this off if they were going to have any kind of chance of getting away. I repeated the move from earlier, sending another wall of wind over the battlefield. It blocked out the revving of the engine as Cal carried them away to safety.

"Erra!" Zane called over to me.

There he was! Time to get him and run. I rushed over to him, excited. I stopped short, noticing his expression. There was no kindness in his eyes, only a cold, hard hatred.

"Zane, come on. Devin's already gotten away. We need to get out of here."

I grabbed at his hand and immediately felt cool ice spreading over it. I pulled back, shocked. He never used his glow on me on purpose.

"Please don't do this," I begged.

"You did this, Simerra. You led all these people astray. They're all going to need reeducation because of you."

"Watch out, Simerra. I can take him!" Karley called. I could hear the electricity crackling from her hands.

"Stop. He's my brother," I begged.

I looked back to him pleadingly. I held up a shaking hand. *Come on, Zane. Take it. Come on.*

"Please take it, Zane. We can walk out of here together, the same way we came into this place. Remember? The plan was to get out all along," I reminded him.

Hot tears burned a path down my face, streaking in the dirt. I kept my arm up. He had to come to his senses. He was my brother. I couldn't lose him here after everything. He clasped his hands neatly in front of himself.

"I know better than to touch you," he spat.

My heart broke. He couldn't have meant it like that. It was just what they'd done to him. My brother would never talk to me like that. He wasn't that kind of person.

"Zane, please." I sobbed.

"All students who set themselves against chaos should return to the protection of the soldiers. Your government thanks you and urges you to be quick so that we may keep you safe," the director urged over the megaphone.

"Your condition is clearly clouding your judgment. Mother always said I would have to keep an eye on you. I can see why now. We need to go with them back into the center. Come on, Erra. They'll help you get your head on straight. Then we can be close again," Zane coaxed.

I flinched from his words. How could he say something like that? Had he always felt I was a burden?

"They'll never let me out of reeducation. We can't go back there. Think this through!"

"I have. They want to help. I'm going with them," he asserted.

I slung an arm across my chest, trying to hold myself together. There were people I had to protect. This was about more than just me. If Zane wasn't going to come with us, then there was nothing I could do. *I'm so sorry, Zane.*

"Then go," I said.

"Erra, see sense," Zane begged.

"Go! If you think they're so great, leave! But I can't go with you. They hate people like me, and if that's who you want to be, then you shouldn't come with us." My voice broke over the words.

I felt the pieces of my being shifting around. There was no glue left to hold them together. I was cracking. Zane's eyebrows rose sharply. He reached out, grabbing my arm—over the sleeve of course. He was scared to touch me like always. I ripped my arm away, pulling it back to my chest.

"Don't touch her!" Trish yelled.

"Have it your way. I'll bring you back one day. I'll bring you all back," he threatened.

Zane jogged back into the building and out of sight. I collapsed to the ground, unable to stand the pain. Our little family was fully shattered. I sat there. My tears scattered in the wind that wrapped itself around me. I found no comfort in it. I had failed, but I couldn't give up. I stood back up on shaking knees and wiped the tears away. This was far from the time. We needed to get out of here.

"Turn your chairs to electric. Let's move," I ordered the group.

No one argued with me. We marched away from the center. I waited for someone to jump out and follow us or for a trap to set off, but there was nothing. Maybe they needed time to regroup. Regardless, it was giving us the time we needed to get away. We proceeded in silence. I wasn't even sure who all was in this group. I hadn't bothered to check before I started walking. I knew Trish and Karley were there. I doubted Karley was here without Sasha or that Trish was here without Rachel. I peeked around curiously. The only other two people in the group I knew by name were Jack and Heather. At least they had all made it out. We were only short. My heart twinged at the thought of Zane.

"Where are we going?" Trish asked.

"We have to meet up with the others. They're about two miles away," I informed the group.

"What if they aren't there?" Heather speculated.

"They'll be there."

What would I do if they weren't? I shut down the idea. That had been the plan. Cal would keep them safe. The fear tickled at the back of my mind the rest of the walk. We pulled off the second left, peeking around for the truck. No one said anything as we walked down that road, looking for any sign of the truck or Cal or anyone. We stumbled across the truck, not even covered. I ran over to it, excited to see everyone and check in, but it was empty. There wasn't anyone around it either.

"I think it's time to face the facts," Heather speculated.

"They might have kept going if they thought they were in danger," I admitted.

"I think the center qualifies as danger," Trish added softly.

Tears stuck in my throat as I processed. They kept going without us. We could chase them for weeks on foot and never get any closer than we were right now. The sun was already sinking in the sky. I swallowed the lump in my throat. We needed to take action. We had to take the truck. It was the only way we stood a chance. I could process later.

"We have to take the truck," I informed the group. "It's where all the medical supplies are."

"Where are we going?" a gangly girl asked.

"We're going to get somewhere safe and figure out where the others are going, and then we're going to find them. We're stronger together," I asserted. "Now load up. We should get moving."

I helped everyone into the truck before I shut them in. I clambered into the front seat alone and tried to turn the keys in the ignition. They weren't there. I looked over at the seat. A single piece of paper sat there. I couldn't stop the wave of sadness that washed over me. It was the picture Nash had drawn of the girl in the clearing with the fireflies. The keys were set on top of it. I snatched it and the keys up into my arms, pressing it all close to my chest. I flipped the picture over, looking for a clue about where they were going. It said two words. *Stay Safe.*

A loud sob broke from my chest. I bent over, unable to best this pain. Of course they hadn't said anything else. They didn't know for sure that I would be the first one to make it here. I wiped my nose on my sleeve and tossed my bag onto the seat. I carefully slid the picture in between my notebooks. I would keep us safe, and I had to hope Cal and Nash were doing the same. I put the truck in drive and headed down the road.

About the Author

Moss Nightwing is perpetually on the go either taking care of animals, working on upcoming projects, or dodging the people that help make the hurt/comfort elements sing. Story-telling is a great way to address the hardships around us, work through trauma (stay in therapy kids), and to remember there are happy moments, glimpses of hope, even in the darkest of times. Those moments will get us through as long as we know to hold on to them.

Coming Soon:
The Glowstick Chronicles: Book 2

Follow Moss Nightwing:
Instagram: queerly_beloved_services
Tiktok: Mossnightwing
Patreon: queerlybelovedservices

www.ingramcontent.com/pod-product-compliance
Lightning Source LLC
Chambersburg PA
CBHW020236010826
48973CB00006B/1542